FOOTPRINTS
IN THE
ASH

A POMPEII MYSTERY

STANLEY
SALMONS

UKA PRESS PUBLISHING
LONDON

"There was this Bronze-Age eruption about 4,000 years ago, and then 2,000 years ago there was the AD 79 event. It seems that just about every 2,000 years, there's been a major eruption of this scale at Vesuvius. Using a standard statistical test, there is more than a 50 per cent chance that a violent eruption will happen at Vesuvius next year. With each year that goes by, the statistical probability increases."

– March 2006

Michael F. Sheridan, PhD,
UB Distinguished Professor in the Department of Geology,
State University of New York at Buffalo,
Director of the Center for Geohazards

UKA PRESS PUBLISHING
55 Elmsdale Road, Walthamstow, London, E17 6PN, UK
Olympiaweg 102-hs, 1076 XG, Amsterdam, Holland
St.A., 108, 2-5-22 Shida, Fujieda, Shizuoka 426-0071, Japan

2 4 6 8 10 9 7 5 3 1

First published in Great Britain in 2008 by UKA Press

A CIP catalogue record for this book is available from
the British Library

ISBN: 9781905796175 and 190579617X

Cover and interior design by Don Masters, St. A., UKA Press

Printed and Bound in Great Britain

ACKNOWLEDGEMENTS

When Vesuvius erupted in A.D. 79 it encapsulated, within the cities, towns, and villas it buried, a unique record of provincial Roman life in the first century. My first duty is to acknowledge those who have uncovered something of this lost world for us and who are trying to preserve it for future generations. I have tried not to offend their scholarship: the dig in this story is a plausible fiction, but in other respects I have stayed true to what we know of the relevant historical events and locations. Where there are minor departures from published accounts it is because I am not ready to suspend my critical judgment as a scientist. I am grateful to my colleague Bob Connolly, for allowing himself to be waylaid in the corridor on matters such as the recording of finds and the ways bodies burn. I have interpreted these conversations with a little licence, for which he is not responsible.

My wife, Paula, and our children, Graham, Daniel, and Debby, have been a constant source of encouragement and helpful feedback in the writing of this book and, like the rest of my life, it owes everything to their support. Finally my thanks go to fellow members of the Liverpool-based Wordsmiths (formerly Rose Lane) Writers' Group, particularly Kate, John, Rachel, and Linda, for their unfailing enthusiasm and valued comments. The finished product is a tribute to the editorial and graphical skills of the people at UKA Press, in particular the Editor in Chief, Don Masters.

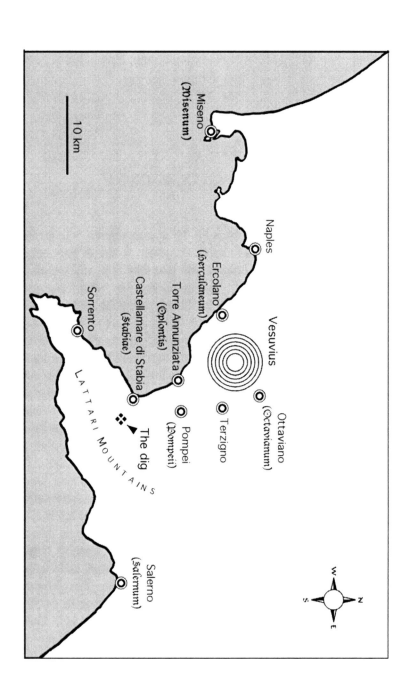

Miseno
(Misenum)

10 km

Naples

Ercolano
(Herculaneum)

Vesuvius

Torre Annunziata
(Oplontis)

Castellamare di Stabia
(Stabiae)

Sorrento

Ottaviano
(Octavianum)

Terzigno

Pompei
(Pompeii)

The dig

L A T T A R I   M O U N T A I N S

Salerno
(Salernum)

N
W   E
S

Glossary

atrium: Entrance hall and central court of a Roman house.

Basilica: Imposing public building which served as law court and meeting place.

biga: A chariot drawn by two horses.

caldarium: In the sequence of chambers that constituted the Roman bathhouse ritual, this was the hot bath and sauna room.

Capitolium: Temple dedicated to Jupiter, Juno, and Minerva, at the northern boundary of the Pompeiian Forum.

Forum: Large square, used as a market place and for conducting all public business.

gladius: The Roman shortsword, a weapon used for cutting and thrusting.

impluvium: Square basin in the floor of the atrium. It collected rainwater conveyed by a system of pipes and channels from the compluvium, an aperture in the roof directly over it that also let in light and air.

Macellum: Large market and commercial exchange in the northeastern corner of the Pompeiian Forum.

palaestra: Building and open area with facilities for training, athletics, and competitive activities such as wrestling.

peristyle: Internal courtyard in a Roman house, bordered on one or more sides by a colonnade, and looking out onto a garden.

pugio: Dagger, used by Roman soldiers as a utility knife and as an auxiliary sidearm in combat.

tablinum: Important room in a Roman house, lying between the atrium and the peristyle, used as an office, study, and business reception room.

Temple of Isis: Temple dedicated to the worship of the Egyptian goddess Isis, which was popular in the first century AD.

tepidarium: Warm room of a Roman bathhouse, used by patrons to acclimatize in preparation for the hot bath, and for massage with oils after it.

The House of Octavius Quartio: This beautiful villa and garden is usually referred to as the House of Loreius Tiburtinus, after election slogans found on neighbouring walls. It is more likely, however, that the owner at the time of the eruption was Octavius Quartio, whose bronze seal was excavated there.

triclinium: Dining room of a Roman house, named after the arrangement of couches, which formed three sides of a square.

vestibule: Entrance hallway, leading to the atrium.

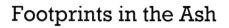

Footprints in the Ash

Prologue

"Julian! I'm off now."

Julian Lockhart glanced up to see the figure of his colleague silhouetted against the bright sky. He rose, stretching his back and his long limbs, a trowel dangling from one hand.

"Alex?" he shouted back. "Come and have a look at this before you go."

Alex Cothill walked down the slope into the excavation and picked his way between the younger members of the team, who were busily scraping the layers of soil down to the next level.

While he was waiting Julian took off his battered felt hat and used each rolled-up sleeve of his shirt in turn to wipe his forehead, leaving a dark patch on the khaki. At this time of the morning the air was cool on these mountain slopes but the sun was rising in the sky and its heat was already building.

He replaced the hat and pointed to the ground with the trowel. "I wanted you to see this before we photograph it and bag it up."

Alex looked down on a jumble of blackened, broken bones interspersed with rusty objects.

"No wonder it showed up on geophysics," he said. "What is it, armour?"

"Yes. The individual leaves would have been backed with leather, but that's all rotted away now. So are the crossed belts. But the buckles and scabbards are intact."

"No helmet."

"No, not so far. Still, there's no question about it. We have a soldier."

"A soldier and what else? That's not just one skeleton, is it?"

"Quite right, it's two: one male, one female. The male was tall, strongly built – you only have to look at the long bones."

Again he pointed with the trowel, more closely this time, tracing the outlines. "The female's an adult but she was small, even for those days. It's fair to assume the armour and the weapons were being carried by the male. And that, my friend, is where we are presented with a small mystery."

"Oh?"

"Yes. See, here's the pugio – the dagger – still in its sheath. Both of them pretty badly corroded – we certainly won't be able to separate them here. And here's the longer scabbard for the gladius. Nice piece of work. Bronze, intricately pierced. This wasn't standard issue."

"High ranking soldier?"

"Almost certainly."

"So?"

"So where's the gladius?"

Alex hesitated, then pointed back towards the sloping end of the dig. "Didn't Pippo uncover a gladius up there?" he said. "Bone handle, some decoration – just the sort of thing that would go with that scabbard. We haven't found any other weapons so that's probably it, isn't it?"

"Yes, it most probably is. So why is the gladius over there and the body over here?"

"See what you mean."

Nearby, a strongly built young woman had been listening to their conversation, her lively grey eyes moving from one to the other. She was kneeling where she'd been helping Julian to clear soil from the skeletons. Now she got up and dusted off her hands.

"The party was attacked by robbers, maybe," she said. "He is fighting them, and he is wounded and comes back here to die."

Julian shook his head. "It's a good try, Claudia, but I don't buy it," he said. "If he was fighting, why was the pugio still in its sheath? He should have been holding it in the other hand."

"Maybe it was a surprise attack," offered Alex. "He didn't have time to draw both weapons. The attackers killed him up there and the woman down here, and threw the two bodies together."

Julian shook his head again. "I don't think so. We haven't seen any cuts on the ribs or skulls or neck vertebrae, or defence wounds on the arms. And they weren't just thrown together. The legs are folded and they've both fallen on their right sides. He's on top, but we haven't got his right hand yet because it's partly under her scapula and upper arm."

"Has Professor Montalcini seen this yet?" asked Alex.

"Yes, he had a quick look earlier," Julian replied. "He's sitting on the fence, as usual. He agrees there isn't any obvious sign of violence but he won't venture an opinion until he's had a chance to put all the bones under his microscope. You know Montalcini."

"What do you think, then? You reckon they died in the eruption?"

"Yes, I'm pretty sure of it. I still can't work out which stage, though. It's the way they're lying. If I didn't know better I'd say he had his arm around her shoulders when they died. But that just doesn't seem to fit with people choking their life away on noxious gases. You're the geophysicist; what do you say?"

Alex shrugged. "It all depends on the particular combination of mephitic vapours sent ahead of the surge. An unreactive gas – carbon dioxide, for example – would cause death by anoxia; they wouldn't know what hit them. There are others that induce a kind of delirium. They didn't have to die in agony."

"Mmm. In that case it could have been the sixth surge."

They both gazed at the horizon, where a wisp of cloud obscured a ragged conical peak. Vesuvius was just eight kilometres away to the north, and it dominated the landscape. At its feet lay Pompeii, Herculaneum, Oplontis, Boscoreale and Terzigno. Unlike the present site, all had been the subjects of excavation and study for many years.

Claudia got back on her knees and resumed work on the skeletons.

Julian rested a hand on Alex's shoulder and took him to one side. "When is it you're actually flying home?" he asked.

"Tuesday. But I've got people to see in Naples before then, so I won't be around much for the next few days. I'll look in before I go. I take it you'll be staying to the end, to tie everything up."

"I don't know about 'tie everything up'. Each time I think I've got a handle on what happened here, something new crops up. If only there was time, I'd enlarge the trench."

"It's already pretty big, Julian."

"Not big enough. I'd make it twice this wide and ten times as long."

"The farmer would go mad."

"I know."

"Professor!"

Claudia was pointing down at something. Julian reached her in a couple of long strides and dropped into a crouch. He saw that she'd lifted the scapula of the female skeleton and uncovered the right hand of the soldier. On the fourth digit of the hand was a gold ring.

Claudia held back the scapula while Julian scratched away at the soil and then carefully slid the ring off the bony digit. He and Claudia stood up together and Julian held it out in his palm for all three of them to look at. He poked it around with one finger.

"It's an intaglio," said Julian. "I think the stone's carnelian. Fantastic workmanship, isn't it, to engrave it with a detailed little head like that? All done without a magnifying glass, too."

"Is it a portrait of the man?" Claudia asked breathlessly.

Julian took the ring and passed his thumb lightly over it to remove some soil.

"Could be. They often used these things for seals. But it could be a God or an Emperor – it looks a bit like Vespasian, actually. We'll be able to tell when we've cleaned it up properly. Well done, Claudia! Listen, when the team bags this lot up make sure the bones and the scabbards and the ring are recorded separately. I want to take a look at this later."

"Okay."

"Hang on, there's an inscription on the inside."

The other members of the team had wandered over, crowding around to see the new find. They looked on as he wiped some more soil away and rotated it carefully. "IMP. C. FRATELLUS", he read.

"He was an emperor!" cried Claudia.

"No. 'IMP.' is short for *Imperatur*. It's Latin for General."

He looked thoughtfully at the group, but his gaze seemed to go beyond them. "So, our high-ranking soldier was a General," he said. "What the hell was he doing up here?"

"Julian," Alex said slowly. "The name – Fratellus – it's not that common. Does it ring any bells with you?"

"Fratellus, Fratellus... of course – Salernum! The villa with the great library and scrolls and tablets. We visited it together."

"It was quite a dynasty, as I remember: advocates, praetors, generals... Later than this, though."

"Not by much. Beginning of the second century, wasn't it? That was only twenty or thirty years after all this. But the historians told us there wasn't any sign of the family in Salernum before that."

"Maybe this is why. Maybe the family came out of Pompeii."

Julian looked at Alex and blinked rapidly. "You're right. The team's probably still excavating there. We should tell them."

He turned back to the skeletons, and the broken skull of the soldier.

"You didn't make it, old boy," he said softly, "but somebody did, didn't they? Who was it?"

PART 1

Campania, Italy

Chapter 1

August 14, A.D. 79

Claudius Fratellus strode down the Street of Abundance, savouring the special atmosphere of this busiest of thoroughfares.

During the night, donkey-drawn carts had delivered sacks of grain to the bakeries, and amphorae of wine, garum and oil to the shops and restaurants. In spite of the careful sluicing of the street, the animal smells lingered; they mingled with the acrid odours from the laundries and the more wholesome ones of baking bread, pastries, spices, stewed meat and fish.

The street teemed with people buying, selling, bartering, eating, drinking, gossiping, or simply parading. Some gathered under awnings, stopping there to discuss business or politics. Snatches of conversation drifted Claudius's way, in his native Latin, in Greek, in Arabic, and in tongues he did not recognize. He walked briskly. Pigeons leaped out of his path and strutted erratically in the roadway.

The slap of bare feet on the large cobbles made him look up.

An elaborate litter came past, borne by four tall African slaves, and from inside it the corpulent Trebius Valens waved cheerily at him. No doubt Trebius was on his way to the Forum.

He was running for magistrate, and the litter would be a way of demonstrating his wealth as much as an escape from the burden of walking. Claudius afforded him a patrician nod, no more nor less of an acknowledgement than he gave to the many others who greeted him as he passed.

Ahead, an intersecting stream of humanity marked the Holconius crossroads. A group of children were playing on the corner, laughing and flicking water at one another from the brimming fountain. A few drops landed at Claudius's feet and he sensed a sudden hush of alarm, but ignored it.

The ragged procession trudging up from the Stabian gate paused respectfully as he approached, allowing him to cross.

Without slackening his pace he passed through the great arch and ascended the steep final section of the street. This terminated in three vertical slabs of stone, a reminder that conveyances were not permitted in the Forum. Trebius's litter was here, empty now. The four Africans were nearby, talking to the driver of a carriage and two horses, the biga of the chief magistrate.

The buzz of conversation swelled as Claudius entered the great square. He narrowed his eyes against the searing whiteness of the sunlight reflected from the travertine paving, felt its heat through his thin sandals. He turned left to walk in the shade of the colonnade, scanning the knots of people.

The air was suddenly full of the clatter of wings as all the pigeons rose off the square. In the same instant the ground heaved. He staggered and put out a hand to steady himself against a smooth marble column. He felt it vibrating beneath his fingers and with the growing vibration came a sound: a low rumbling, like distant thunder.

The ground trembled harder, and the sound grew louder. The trembling and the sound died away.

A deathly silence blanketed the square. Conversations remained suspended in mid-sentence. Peddlers stood frozen, trays of drinks, sausages, or hot food in their outstretched hands, their cries caught in their throats. An old beggar sat, a motionless bowl raised in his bony fingers. A black cat paused in mid-stride, one forepaw raised. The Forum had become a tableau, of which the equestrian statues on their pedestals formed part.

Dust rose off the square and hung like a dawn mist over a lake. Small currents of air caught the dust, sending waves rippling through it, the solid surface of the square converted into an undulating veil. The dust thinned, a dog barked, and the cat scuttled behind a vending booth. The pigeons circled low, dispersed to new landing places and resumed their strutting. The familiar noises of the Forum crept back, but they were subdued.

Claudius walked up to a group of prominent citizens at their habitual meeting place, in the colonnade outside the Basilica. They broke off their conversations to greet him.

"What make you of this latest earthquake, Claudius?" asked the rotund young Julius Polybius. "We ate with Gnaeus last night, and I could have sworn it was his feast had disagreed with me."

Claudius ignored the jest. Julius was a self-assured young man, newly wealthy. Claudius thought him lacking in good manners. He addressed the whole group.

"The tremors get longer and more frequent every day," he said. "I fear our lives are in serious danger."

Fabius Rufus sniffed. "Come now, we have had tremors like this many times before. They always go away after a while. We're not afraid. Don't be a woman, Claudius."

Someone sucked in his breath. Claudius was known for the sharpness of his tongue, and he did not suffer fools gladly.

"Why, Fabius," he said, his voice even, "it surprises me to hear such a remark from you, whose appetites are so similar to those of your esteemed wife."

It was a triple barb, alluding not only to Fabius's predilection for young boys, but also his wife's well known indulgences with young men, and the unsatisfactory state of their marriage. Fabius changed colour up to his gills.

The tension was relieved by Vesonius Primus.

"If it's appetites we speak of, then Trebius here has enough for the both of you, and the rest of us combined."

Trebius joined good-naturedly in the laughter, his shoulders shaking and his large stomach swagging back and forth inside his toga. The remark pleased him. Everyone knew that a man was fat because he could put a great deal of food on his table, and if he could do that, then he was rich, and if rich, ergo a man of good sense and judgment, and one favoured by the Gods, certainly more so than those who were not rich. His election prospects depended on quips like these, which he accepted as a compliment.

"When was the last time you saw your prong, Trebius?" Julius asked.

Trebius's face became suddenly serious and thoughtful. "Let me see," he said, fingering one of the numerous folds through which his chin descended to his chest. "When was I married? It was the third day before the Kalends of Augustus and the year was 798. You know, I distinctly remember seeing it then."

They were silenced by Aulus Clodius Flaccus, the white-haired chief magistrate.

"Come now, gentlemen," he said. "This is no light matter that Claudius puts before us. Your memories are indeed short if you have forgotten the damage wrought by the last great earthquake. The Basilica, the Capitolium, the Temple of Isis, your residences and countless others… why," he paused, pointing over his shoulder and raising his voice over the sound of hammering, "it is seventeen years since, yet the restoration of the Basilica continues there behind us even as we speak."

"There are those," said Numerius Propidius darkly, "who have no reason to regret that event."

Claudius understood the innuendo. His neighbour, the formidable Julia Felix, had profited handsomely from the disaster by renting property to people whose homes and shops it had destroyed. In denouncing her, Numerius was drawing attention to his own nobility in having borne personally the expense of rebuilding the Temple of Isis. Claudius had little time for such point-scoring. Numerius was not charitable by nature. His gesture – made, it was widely suggested, at the urging of his new young wife – had secured the political future and social standing of their six-year-old son. Julia, on the other hand, sought neither high office nor civic favours and had nothing to gain by dispensing largesse. She'd merely been as astute in this respect as she was in all her business dealings.

"You speak only of money and property," he said. "Don't forget the great loss of life that resulted from that disaster. Such a thing should not be permitted to happen again."

Aulus frowned. "What are you suggesting, Claudius?"

"In my view the only wise course would be to evacuate the whole population to the open countryside until the danger passes."

Fabius Rufus had regained countenance sufficiently to rejoin the debate.

"I think Claudius makes too much of it. The worst is now over. These shakings of the ground will soon go as mysteriously as they came."

"What is the reason for them?" asked Numerius. "That is what I should like to know."

"The Gods are angry," said Trebius. "We will make sacrifices and appease them."

Vesonius said, "I have heard that we are witnessing the passage of a giant worm who makes his way beneath Pompeii. When the worm has passed, the tremors will cease. What say you to that, Claudius?"

"It matters little what is the cause. What is real is the danger. The tremors come by night as well as by day. If we stay here we could be entombed in our own houses, even as we sleep."

"But if we leave, our houses will be looted of all our possessions. Does this not concern you, Claudius?"

"Of what use are possessions, Numerius, if we do not have our lives with which to enjoy them?"

"We could quarter legionaries in the houses to guard them while we are away," offered Trebius.

"No. I have commanded these men in the field of battle and I would not expose them to any danger that I would not face myself."

Fabius said, "You speak nobly, Claudius, but from what I know of soldiers they would leave even less than the looters."

"Well, well," said Numerius. "You may go if you wish, Claudius, but I for one am staying here. I will not desert Pompeii."

"Nor I."

"Nor I."

"Nor I."

Aulus regarded Claudius uncomfortably. "We share your concern, Claudius," he said diplomatically, "but perhaps the time is not yet ripe for such drastic measures."

"As you wish. I can but offer my counsel to you. For myself, I will act as I think fit. I wish you good day."

He walked briskly away. Normally he would have completed the circuit of the Forum, perhaps taking time to wander among the richly varied market stalls of the Macellum. It was different today. The encounter – or perhaps it was the earthquake – had left him feeling strangely agitated, and instead he retraced his steps. At the end of the square he paused to gaze along its length, over the Capitolium and beyond to Vesuvius, which rose majestically above the city. The tall, slender cone was green, the curiously fertile soil on its slopes clad in vines and trees. In turbulent times such as these their mountain was a comforting sight: solid, permanent, reassuring.

He strode on.

A white cloud obscured the peak of Vesuvius. It was the only cloud in the sky. Tendrils of vapour curled quietly from the upper slopes of the mountain.

Chapter 2

Steam rose thickly in the caldarium of the Forum Baths.

Figures, dimly visible through the mist, sat on wooden benches, getting up from time to time to splash their faces and necks in cool water from the large marble basin. This was usually accompanied by a heavy sigh.

Claudius Fratellus and Octavius Quartio came in from the palaestra and seated themselves away from the others.

Claudius told his friend what had taken place in the Forum earlier that afternoon.

"I'm sorry I couldn't be there, Claudius. A large shipment arrived in the port and I had to supervise the unloading. If you don't watch them, these people will spirit away whole crates and then swear it was never in the cargo in the first place."

Claudius flicked a hand dismissively.

"It would have made little difference; their minds are closed. Aulus, perhaps, shares my sense of foreboding but still he sees his place as here, with the others. I won't try to advise them again. I must act alone."

"Not alone, Claudius. We have ever been friends and I think your counsel is wise. If you decide to leave, I and my household will accompany you. We will be safer as a group. There are bandits in the countryside and if they hear of our departure they'll know we are taking our most valuable possessions."

"That's true. Even if it were not, I'd be glad of your company." He sighed. "Perhaps it is well that the others do not perceive the danger. It would, I fear, be beyond their talents to organize an orderly evacuation of the whole city."

"What do you suggest, then?"

"A small party, one that can be mobilized quickly. Our two

households will form the nucleus. We could include others, but they would need to be equally committed."

"Did you have anyone in mind?"

"Octavius, if there is going to be a large earthquake, and if it turns out to be as disastrous as the one seventeen years ago, it will lay waste to much of Pompeii. We should take with us people who can help with the reconstruction. I've been impressed with the young architect Oppius Gratus. He has a wife, Quartilla, but their house is modest and I don't think they have more than one or two slaves. They would not add greatly to our numbers."

"What about an engineer? He could be useful to us, as well as in the rebuilding of the city."

"Is there one you can commend?"

"The man who's been supervising repairs in the Castellum Aquae seems very capable. His name is Fulvius Tiro. He comes from Sicily. I believe he lives on his own, in lodgings on the north side of the city. But Claudius, none of them will feel easy about leaving their homes and occupations. They'll need to be convinced that it's the only sensible way."

"You're right, of course. I must learn more about the likely nature of the earthquake and when it might occur. I thought I'd go to Misenum and consult with Gaius Plinius Secundus."

"Pliny? Well, there is surely no one better versed in matters of natural history. But I understand that he guards his time jealously. He may not welcome an interruption to his studies."

"I'll send word to his nephew, who lives with him. He's only seventeen – the same age as my own son Cornelius – but he has wisdom beyond his years. I'm sure he'll advise us of a suitable time. And I'll take a gift of wine that should please the old man. When I return, the two of us should meet with the principals so that we can determine our strategy."

"Invite them to a small feast, perhaps? It would be a conventional courtesy; you could have the discussion afterwards."

"That is an excellent idea."

"I'd be happy to offer my own villa for the purpose, Claudius. I know entertaining of this kind is not in your nature."

"That's very kind of you, but I feel that I ought to be the host on this occasion. Perhaps, though, I could ask a favour?"

"Of course. Anything."

"As you say, Cottia and I entertain on a modest scale and only for good friends like Calpurnia and yourself. In consequence the slaves in my household have little experience of preparing a table in the proper manner. I don't want to be failing in my duties as a host. Could you lend me the use of Lutulla and perhaps one or two other slaves of her choice, to supervise the preparations?"

"Gladly. When is the feast to be?"

"Early next week. That should give me ample time to visit Misenum. Good, that's settled. Are you ready for the tepidarium?"

"I am."

The two men got up and left the chamber.

After a pause, a new voice came softly out of the mist.

"Marcus, have you heard this conversation?"

"I have, Helivius. But I think it no concern of ours."

"You think not? Listen well, Marcus. If these two leave with their households and others too, there will be a flood of citizens after them."

"But you heard what took place in the Forum. Aulus and Numerius and the others are opposed. They will advise against it."

"And do you think the populace will pay any heed to them? Oh, they're content enough to leave the routine management of civic affairs to such men, but when it comes to life-and-death decisions they'll respect the judgment of a General who never lost a battle, not the advice of comfortable politicians."

"Are you sure?"

"There's no question about it. These are substantial men, Marcus. They have as much to lose by leaving Pompeii as anyone and perhaps more than most. Their departure would cause a panic. The city would be emptied of its population. Do you have any idea what would happen to trade in Pompeii? We would be ruined!"

"But surely there's nothing you and I can do about it?"

The voice descended to an almost inaudible murmur.

"Oh, I think there is, Marcus, I think there is. Send a message to Claudius Fratellus. Say you have learned of his intention to escape the danger of an earthquake in Pompeii. Don't mention the baths; rather suggest it has been told to you by someone in the Forum. Say you would like to accompany him, and that you have many useful contacts in other cities. He is sure then to invite you to his feast. Mark well what is discussed there, and bring it back to me. We'll decide then what is to be done."

"But this is spying, Helivius! I am not sure I approve of it."

There was a moment's silence. When the voice came again, it was barely louder than the hiss of steam into the caldarium.

"Marcus, you know you have my support for your candidature in the coming election and with it the support of the society of traders. It would, of course, be hard for me to justify such a stance if I thought you were lacking in resolve."

"No, no, Helivius, I assure you," came the hasty reply. "I will send a message as you suggest."

"That is good, Marcus. That is a wise decision."

The noise of conversation faltered briefly as the expensively attired merchant entered the tavern. He stood by the door, scanning the room. Then he saw the man he was looking for, crossed the room, and stood over him.

The man looked up insolently, with flat, bloodshot eyes. He opened one hand to indicate the vacant bench opposite him.

The merchant, however, remained standing and jerked his head towards the back of the room. The man shrugged, picked up his beaker of wine and followed. As they passed the barman the merchant pushed some coins across the counter to him and their eyes met. The barman nodded almost imperceptibly.

The noise of the tavern fell behind them as they entered a dim, sparsely furnished room off a corridor at the back of the tavern.

They sat down facing each other across a small table.

The merchant's eyes flickered over the soiled tunic and the unkempt beard and hair, and his nostrils twitched at the odour drifting from the man's body. He moved his chair back a little.

"We have done business before, Licinius," he said.

"What is it this time? Murder, kidnap, extortion?"

Helivius thought for a moment. "Let us call it abduction. Yes,

I think that is the right word. Suppose I ask you to abduct someone?"

"What do you mean, 'suppose'? Are you asking me to abduct someone?"

"I *may* ask you to abduct someone. Could it be done?"

The man sniffed. "Abduction, kidnap – it's the same. I don't like the risk. Once they return to society they can identify me. And," he eyed Helivius, "a trail that leads to me can lead to you."

The high colour in the merchant's cheeks faded.

"No, no. There must be no question of a return."

"So it is murder, after all?"

"Not exactly. If I wanted you to murder someone you could knife them in the street after dark or strangle them in their beds. No, no, I have something different in mind. You must leave behind no sign of what has happened. People disappear all the time – do they not? – kidnapped or sold into slavery. That is what it has to look like."

"It won't look like a kidnap if there's no demand for ransom."

"It matters little. I want this person taken somewhere and disposed of where there is not the remotest chance of them being heard or the body discovered. Do you know of such a place?"

The man smiled unpleasantly, baring his blackened and broken teeth.

"Well?"

"You want me to tell you where?"

"Certainly. You know from our previous dealings that I don't act on impulse. Plans must be made and scrutinized in advance. I must be sure that all the arrangements are suitable."

"Very well, if you insist, I'll tell you. The great earthquake that did for much of Pompeii opened up some large rents in the ground. I know of one on the upper slopes of Vesuvius. It's like the deepest of dungeons. A person put in there has no way of getting out. You could keep them there as long as you like, if you throw down food and water. And if you don't..." He shrugged.

"On Vesuvius, you say? What about the men tending the vineyards and the shepherds herding the sheep?"

"This is higher up: a barren, rocky region beyond the trees. There is no planting there, and the pasture is poor. No one would come upon it by chance."

The merchant nodded thoughtfully.

"I can't fix a price," Licinius added, "without knowing more. It makes a difference how much of a risk I'll be taking and how many men I'll need."

"The risk is not high, and you probably need only one other."

"I can use Myro, then. Is it a male or a female?"

"I haven't decided yet."

"A female would be cheaper."

Helivius glanced at the man's lascivious expression, and understood why.

"I said I haven't decided yet."

"When do you want it done?"

"Probably towards the end of next week. I'll meet you here again. By then I'll be able to give you all the details and we can come to some arrangement."

The merchant got up, opened the door to leave, then turned.

"If you breathe a word of this to anyone, Licinius..."

The man exposed his teeth again, and lifted his beaker in a mock toast.

Chapter 3

August 16, A.D. 79

The villa at Misenum occupied a promontory overlooking the Gulf of Naples. Slaves took charge of the horses and the unloading of the amphorae, and a servant bowed and invited Claudius to follow him.

The back of the villa faced the sea and was furnished along its entire length with a balcony. Here Claudius paused to admire the magnificent view of the bay and the Campanian coast. Almost directly below them was the harbour, where the light Liburnian galleys and the heavier quadriremes of the Roman fleet rocked gently at anchor, their sails furled. All of them were under the command of his host, who was prefect of this naval base. The servant waited politely, then led Claudius off the balcony, out of the brilliant sunshine and into a windowless room. He strained to see in the dim light.

A strong voice emanated from the gloom.

"You may put that away now, nephew, we have an honoured guest. General Claudius Fratellus! Enter, enter, we welcome you."

As his eyes adjusted Claudius realized they were in a small private bathhouse.

Pliny was sitting naked on a stool, being dried and rubbed down by a slave. His nephew, who had risen to his feet, had evidently been reading to him by the light of a candle. The man had a reputation for never losing a minute that could be given over to study and Claudius saw that it was well earned.

"I apologize for this intrusion, Gaius Plinius," he said. "It is good of you to receive me so cordially."

"Not at all. We have much in common, you know, Claudius. First and foremost I am a scholar, but when I was younger I saw military service in Germany. You are a General who has commanded victorious armies in campaigns abroad. We are both servants of Rome, each in our own way."

Claudius inclined his head graciously.

"There, sir, I fear the similarity ends. For you continue in many official capacities whereas my public services are slight."

"You are too modest, General. I – eh, what's that?"

The servant who had conducted Claudius here, whispered in his host's ear.

"Ah, capital! I understand you have brought me a quantity of wine from Pompeii."

"A humble Vesuviana, unworthy I am sure of a man of your refined palate, but acceptable I hope as a token of my esteem."

"Most acceptable, I assure you, General. I regard the wines from that region as of the finest. But you've had a long journey and it's time, too, for our own refreshment. We eat simply here, but enough, I hope, to revive your spirits."

The slave who had been drying the old man now offered up a robe, which Pliny wrapped around his huge torso. He led the way to a small triclinium, where the men reclined on heavily upholstered couches arranged around three sides of a table. Pliny took the couch opposite the empty side of the table and Claudius accepted the place of honour on his right.

For a few moments the only sound in the room was the heavy wheezing of Pliny.

Then a procession of slaves entered and they were served an assortment of fare: lettuce, cheese, barley-cake, olives, beetroots, gherkins, onions – and piping hot cabbage.

"You really must try the cabbage, Claudius," Pliny said. "It is grown for me in the marsh by the mouth of the Sarno and I maintain that it's unmatched for tenderness by any elsewhere. Not that wine, idiot!" he said, turning suddenly on a slave. "Get the Holconia for our guest."

The cabbage was hot enough to burn his fingers and Claudius was obliged to plunge them into the bowl of perfumed water between each mouthful. It was, however, as tender as his host had promised.

A few minutes later two slaves returned, one to each handle of a heavy terra cotta amphora, which they hoisted onto a stand. One of them unsealed it. He dipped a silver ladle into the vessel and poured a little wine into a goblet, which he handed to Pliny.

Pliny passed it under his nose and nodded to the slave, who then prepared the wine in a bowl, adding herbs, melted honey, and water, and cooling it with snow before pouring and serving three goblets.

The main course was bass and lamprey, which was set on a cucumber and watercress salad buried under sliced eggs. It was accompanied by pheasant stuffed with apricots.

The meal was completed with a dish of apples, pears, grapes, figs and nuts.

Claudius was impatient to raise the purpose of his visit but he knew better than to do so while this hospitality was being extended.

At last Pliny gave the signal for them to retire to his study, the tablinum, and Claudius saw that the opportunity had arrived.

"Earthquakes?" Pliny said, in response to the question. "I have written much on the subject, have I not, nephew?"

"Indeed you have, uncle. Both of the wonders themselves and of the signs of their approach."

"You have observed, Claudius, the sound made by these earthquakes? It is like thunder, is it not?"

"It does resemble thunder..."

Pliny stabbed a finger towards him.

"You see! That is the key to the matter! The Babylonians knew this. They deduced that earthquakes are governed by Saturn, Jupiter and Mars, the stars responsible for thunder. Ancient times, my friend, ancient times, but they were clever people, the Babylonians." His manner became conspiratorial. "There is more. Have you observed that the earth never trembles but when the sea is calm and the air so still that birds cannot hover? And have you wondered why this is?"

"I had not..."

The old man sat back in triumph, his voice strong, every phrase punctuated by grandiloquent gestures, as if he were addressing a huge audience rather than a single guest.

"It is because the spirit and wind has been withdrawn. And where has it gone to? Why into the concealed fissures and hollow caves of the earth, where it stirs and strives to get free! At some times it troubles us with tremulous motion; at other times it tears the very earth open in its struggle to escape."

"And what of the sea? I have heard sailors say that even at sea their vessels can be suddenly shaken."

"That is true! The masts creak and the birds that settle on them cry with alarm. And this motion likewise is not raised by any wind."

"So how may one predict such an earthquake?"

"Aristotle has said that when a shock is near at hand a thin line of cloud may be seen stretched out in a clear sky."

"And have you observed this?"

He waved a hand. "It needs me not to observe it if Aristotle has said it. There are other signs, which we will return to in a moment. But let us not forget that just as these forewarn of an earthquake, so the earthquake itself is an ill omen. The city of Rome never suffered an earthquake that was not followed by some great calamity."

The younger man added, "And you have written too, uncle, of the manner in which buildings should be constructed to avoid their destruction in earthquakes."

"Ah yes. This is a most interesting topic..."

The monologue continued in this vein for some time, with occasional promptings from the nephew. Claudius was not sorry when the topic switched to campaigns, which Pliny recalled in remarkable detail. At one point he said to Claudius:

"What interests me, General, is that you never sought the high public office to which your leadership skills and achievements would entitle you. Pray, why is that?"

"It is because I am a coward, Gaius."

There was a shocked silence, broken by wheezy laughter from the older man. "You will have to do better than that, my friend!"

"Let me elaborate, then. I was a leader of soldiers, not of men, Gaius. There is a great difference. When you lead soldiers into battle they know there will be casualties. If you make good decisions, the losses may be light; if you make bad decisions, the losses will be heavy. But you cannot always make good decisions. Sometimes there are no good decisions to be made: only ones that are bad and ones that are worse. The soldier understands that; the civilian does not. The same people who follow you with enthusiasm as you embark will turn on you when things are not as they expected; those who first praised you will just as quickly denounce you and load you heavily with blame and guilt. That is not a burden I ever wanted to bear."

"An honest answer, by Jupiter."

Soon after this, Pliny decided it was time to resume his studies. "The sun is getting low. You will, of course, stay the night? It would not be safe to return to Pompeii after dark."

"Thank you."

"My nephew will introduce you to his mother and she will see to your accommodation. Plinia has lived under my protection since she lost her husband. Her situation is regrettable, but the arrangement has much to commend it to me, as I have no wife to manage the household."

The nephew appeared totally at ease as he conducted Claudius through the villa. Claudius saw no hint of the shyness he found in his own son, Cornelius. He suspected that Cornelius was reserved by nature. He himself had suffered from crippling shyness at that age; it had gradually receded as he gained confidence in his growing knowledge of military history and strategy and in his physical abilities in wrestling and the handling of weapons. The self-assurance he now saw in Pliny's young nephew must have been honed by a training in rhetoric, as well as frequent contact with the high-ranking visitors who came to see his uncle.

"My uncle is a great man, General," the young man said.

"I never doubted it," Claudius replied, "but that you affirm it does you credit."

"He has been like a father to me. There is little enough I can do in return, but in two years' time I will begin to practise law and I hope I can bring honour to his name. Ah, here is my mother."

"You are most welcome here, General." Plinia inclined her head deeply to him.

Her accent and manner were those of a well-born matron. She was a little shorter than her brother, but no smaller in girth, a fact that the copious folds of her stola could do little to conceal. He observed with approval that her hair was conservatively styled. He found quite outrageous the vogues indulged by the fashionable women of Rome, who looked down on their provincial cousins and, for that good reason, were disliked most heartily in return.

After an exchange of formal pleasantries, Plinia assigned a slave to show him to his quarters.

"I have, of course, made the necessary arrangements for your driver and your horses."

"Thank you, madam. You are most kind."

"Good night, General. I hope you rest well."

He rose with the rest of the household at daybreak, took a light breakfast with his hosts, and departed. There was no more talk of earthquakes.

Chapter 4

August 18, A.D. 79

Claudius responded good-naturedly to his wife's curiosity about his visit to Gaius Plinius. Cottia was interested mainly in the domestic arrangements: the villa, the furnishings, and especially the feast. Food had never been an important topic with Claudius. In the field, he made a point of being served the same fare as everyone else, so that he could assure himself that it was sustaining but not sitting too heavily with his soldiers. Nevertheless, he described the meal as best as he could, and in terms sufficiently approving to convince her that the feast they themselves were about to host should be similar in construction, though not identical in content.

Cottia conveyed these instructions to Lutulla, the senior slave and supervisor of Octavius's household, who was on loan for the occasion. Lutulla's dismay at the absence of the numerous rich and rare dishes that would be considered the norm in Pompeii was met with stubborn resolve on the part of the diminutive Cottia, who was as determined to please her husband as she was her guests.

And so the preparations were made, overseen by the capable Lutulla, and never far from the scrutiny of Cottia's watchful blue eyes.

The slaves cleared the last of the main dishes from the table and replaced them with trays laden with fruit, figs and nuts. It was a good moment to withdraw. Claudius laid a hand on his son's shoulder and spoke quietly to him.

"Accompany our guests to the tablinum, Cornelius. I'll join you there shortly." Then he murmured instructions discreetly to his wife. "My love, I believe everyone has enjoyed the feast. Could you tell the slaves I'm satisfied with what they've done? Once everything's been cleared away they can take any food that's left over to their quarters."

She smiled and nodded. He left the ladies at the table, where they continued to pick contentedly at the fruit and, out of the earshot of the men, indulged in friendly gossip.

Six were in the tablinum: Claudius, Octavius and Cornelius had been joined by the architect, Oppius Gratus, the engineer, Fulvius Tiro, and a merchant, Marcus Holonius Priscus. Octavius was anxious to know what Claudius had found out during his visit to Pliny.

"Without question he is a man of great learning, and yet..."

"And yet what?"

"And yet much of what he said he had gathered from other sources, like Cicero and Aristotle."

"Well, what is wrong with that?"

"Look, Octavius, if you were leading an army up a hill and a bystander said to you that the enemy encampment was on the other side, what would you do?"

"Why, I would send a scout to see if it were true."

"Precisely. You would not put all your trust in the word of another. In the same way I would feel more secure about the information Gaius Plinius gave me if he had seen at least some of it with his own eyes."

"Are you saying you discovered nothing of value?"

"I discovered much. As to its value, I cannot say with confidence."

"What about signs of an impending earthquake?"

"Well he did report a prediction by Pherecydes, who foresaw an earthquake by taking a draught of water from a well. Pliny assures me it is general knowledge that when a shock is near at hand the water in wells is more turbid than usual and gives off a foul odour."

"I have heard that, too," said Oppius.

Fulvius spoke up. "Well if it's true, one must surely be at hand, for I've observed those signs myself."

The others all looked at him in surprise.

"When?"

"Why, in recent weeks, during my travels between here and Salernum. I always check the springs and rivers on my route. Close to the Sarno there are several that have dried up, and some smell like rotting eggs."

Octavius frowned. "I thought I caught such an odour when I was at the lagoon, supervising the unloading of cargo. There's always such a variety of smells there that I didn't attach any significance to it at the time. But I did notice some dead fish on the bank. That was unusual."

"Those springs drain into the Sarno. That could account for it."

"Isn't the drying up of a spring supposed to be a sign of the Gods' displeasure?" asked Cornelius.

"Well, I'm not a God, but it certainly displeases me," said Fulvius, laughing.

"Claudius, did Pliny make any mention of Vesuvius Mons?" asked Oppius.

"No. Why do you ask?"

"Because it is a volcano."

Lutulla presided over the meal in the slave's quarters with the same authority she had exercised over the feast they'd served earlier. She ensured that the table was properly set out and that the inferior wine allotted to the slaves was adequately watered. It was well known that she would tolerate high spirits but no drunkenness. No one questioned her right to be at the head of the table. She sat straight-backed, her braided hair making her appear taller than she was, her broad cheeks flushed with the pleasure of a job well accomplished. Claudius's steward, Junius, proudly took the place of honour on her right, his great black head shining in the candle light.

Junius raised a beaker. "A toast to Lutulla for mounting an excellent feast – and for ensuring that there was enough left over for us!"

Beakers were raised and Lutulla coloured more deeply to hear her name repeated around the table.

"You are a rare woman, Lutulla," Junius said. "When I've purchased my freedom, I'm going to marry you."

"Oh yes?" she retorted. "And do I have any say in the matter?"

The hapless expression on the big man's face provoked a good deal of laughter.

She became aware of someone standing next to her and looked round.

"Yes, Fannia?" she asked.

Lutulla had found Fannia in the street, some five years before, destitute and cuddling a young baby. After speaking briefly to the girl she had prevailed upon Octavius to take her into the household as a kitchen help. Lutulla had started by getting two of the female slaves to bathe Fannia and comb the lice out of her hair. When they took off her clothes they discovered she was wearing a solid gold bangle on her upper arm. There it had escaped the attention of thieves. She would not take it off, she said. She was not expecting to live long and it was all she had to leave her son.

Lutulla asked her about the initials G. L. T. on the bangle. She wouldn't reveal the name, but it transpired that they were the initials of her previous master, who had exercised his rights of ownership on the pretty fifteen-year-old, impregnated her in the process, and had given the bangle to her out of guilt when his wife ejected her from the house. Ever since joining the household she had worked hard. She was devoted to Lutulla.

"Please, ma'am, I wondered if little Victor could join us. It is late, I know, but..."

Lutulla thought for a moment, then said briskly, "Yes, all right. But you must sit separately. Take the small table over there – and be sure that he doesn't make a noise."

Later Lutulla passed by Fannia and her child, saw that they were eating only modest scraps, and slipped onto the table a plate with a whole roast pigeon that she had hidden behind a fold of her ample tunic. She turned back before the girl could stutter her thanks.

When she returned to the main table, Junius was still

37

enthusing about the banquet.

"You know, Lutulla," he said, "the General's tastes are plain and normally he eats very frugally, but tonight he seemed to be eating everything you put in front of him."

"He would do that out of politeness to his guests," Lutulla replied. "But yes, the feast worked quite well. Even so, I think we should have had oysters. Oysters from Brittania – they are the best."

"The General doesn't care for them. He says they're greatly overrated."

"Perhaps that's why he has but the one child," she mused.

"You will not find me wanting in that regard, Lutulla," declared Junius emphatically.

She raised her eyebrows. "You are quite right, Junius," she said tartly. "One seldom finds what one has no intention of looking for."

The others laughed and again Junius subsided in confusion, but she patted him affectionately on the hand just the same.

After the food and wine disappeared, the room became quieter. The long day's work and the unaccustomed richness of the fare were taking their toll.

As soon as everything was cleared away, Lutulla sent the kitchen staff and one or two others off to their bunks. She and Junius would wait in case anything further was required, together with the slaves who would be needed to prepare their ladies for bed.

And Lutulla found herself thinking fondly about the slow-witted but good-hearted Junius, and wondering how long it would be before he could buy his freedom.

"A volcano? Vesuvius?"

"Yes," replied Oppius. "Did you not know? I ask only because Pliny writes much of volcanoes, and I find it odd that he never mentions Vesuvius. It has been quiet for many years, of course."

"When did it last show fire?" asked Octavius.

"Who can say? There's no record of it. It is a volcano, though,

38

without question. You can tell from the shape and from the appearance of the rocks at the summit. I thought everyone knew."

"I did," said the engineer, "but then I have lived near one that was less tranquil. As you may know, I grew up in Sicily and worked there for some years. There's a mountain in the east part of the island called Aetna. You can see its fire at night."

"Pliny writes that lightning, as well as thunder, are captured into the earth along with the wind and spirits of air and sea. He says the fire of Aetna and similar mountains is the lightning breaking out again."

"It didn't look much like lightning to me, Oppius," said Fulvius.

"Perhaps it's transformed during the time it spends in the earth."

"That is possible. I have a reason for mentioning Aetna, though," Fulvius said. "There are numerous earthquakes in that area, as there are here. On several occasions I observed that after an especially violent shock, the fire would be visible by day as well as by night."

"That sounds much like a campfire," said Claudius. "When you stoke it, the flames grow higher."

"Come now, gentlemen, I think you are going too far," Marcus said. "Many of us were here in Pompeii at the time of the last great earthquake. There is no dispute, I imagine, about the size of that shock, yet flames did not leap from the top of Vesuvius. Why do you suggest it's going to happen now?"

"I am not suggesting it," said the engineer. "But perhaps it is not unconnected. There may be more of these crevices and cavities in that mountain than elsewhere, so it stores up the wind and spirits and brings about the tremors whenever they struggle to escape."

The others nodded at the logic of this argument.

Claudius returned them to the subject.

"The immediate question," he said, "is what are we going to do about it?"

"I wasn't here at the time of the last earthquake," said Oppius. "I came because I'd heard there was a lot of rebuilding to be done.

When I arrived and saw the damage with my own eyes I was appalled. I wouldn't want to be in the city if it happened again."

"My feelings, entirely," said Fulvius.

"Tremors are not uncommon in this region," said Marcus. "I don't understand why we should interpret them now as evidence of something more."

"Tremors are not uncommon, Marcus, but these are becoming longer and more severe," Claudius replied. "We also have the sign reported to us by Fulvius: the drying up of springs and the foul-smelling water. Do we need more evidence than that?"

"I say we do not," said Octavius. "I have many business commitments here in Pompeii but all the same I would not expose my wife and daughter – or myself – to a risk as great as that." He went on quickly, "I'm only thankful that my sons are both in Rome. I've sent letters instructing them that on no account should they return to Pompeii."

"We go then. Is it agreed?" asked Claudius.

All but one nodded. Marcus alone looked on passively.

"But where should we go to?" asked Cornelius.

"Nuceria, perhaps?" suggested the engineer.

"Nuceria suffered badly in the last earthquake," said Oppius. "Fortunately there were no fatalities, but there was a great deal of damage. What about Stabiae? They felt the shock there, but I believe it was not as severe as elsewhere."

"Stabiae would be a good choice," said Octavius.

The others murmured their agreement.

"Very well, Stabiae it is." Claudius paused, then added, "But we should not leave Pompeii by the Stabian gate; we don't wish to parade through the city. I suggest we assemble at the Palaestra and leave via the Nucerian Gate. How soon can we be ready?"

"It is for you to decide, Claudius," Oppius said. "Your household and Octavius's are much larger than ours."

"Then let us be prepared to leave one week from now."

"General?" said Oppius. "Would you consider inviting Diomedes to accompany us? I've been employed on some repairs at his villa. He has a large household but it's well equipped and there's a great diversity of skills among his staff."

Claudius nodded. "A good suggestion, Oppius. I'll write him a message immediately."

"If you would entrust it to me, General, I would be happy to deliver it for you tomorrow."

"Thank you, Marcus."

"Well, Marcus?"

"It's decided. They leave in one week. Three complete households and the engineer. And now they've invited Diomedes too – Claudius gave me this message for him."

Helivius held out a hand for the wooden tablets. He scanned them, then picked up a straight-edged blade and drew it across the waxed coating on each in turn, erasing the message.

Marcus licked his lips anxiously. "I thought only to show it to you before I delivered it."

"Well, now I have saved you the labour of delivering it." His voice hardened. "Marcus, these people must be stopped."

"They are too many, Helivius. You can't stop all of them."

"Ah, but we can. You see, if Claudius does not go, then none of them will go."

"What are you saying?"

Helivius gave him a sly smile. "Just suppose, Marcus, that someone went missing. Someone like Cornelius, his pretty son, upon whom the family name and all his hopes for the future are pinned? Do you think Claudius would leave then?"

"You could manage such a thing?"

"You are going to see, Marcus, you are going to see."

Chapter 5

They faced one other across the courtyard: the youth and the man with a scar. In the right hand of each was a gladius. They circled, then closed, and the courtyard rang as the short swords clashed again and again.

Cut, block high; cut, block low; cut, cut, disengage. Cut, block; thrust, parry; turn. Cut, cut, block; hold, slide, swing away.

Sweat beaded the young man's forehead, and his arm ached. His adversary showed no sign of fatigue; he smiled, the effect made sinister by a crease that ran from his eye down his cheek. His deltoids shone and rippled as he lifted into the attack. The blades met high, locked near the hilt. The man pressed; the youth resisted. Their arms quivered with the effort. Then suddenly the man turned and the youth gasped at the pain in his side. He fell back, doubled over, the tip of his gladius dragging on the ground.

The man laughed. He sheathed his gladius, stepped forward and gripped the youth's shoulder. "Not bad, not bad, young Cornelius, we'll make a warrior of you yet."

The youth straightened up slowly.

"What did I do wrong, Gavius?"

"You were too focused on the swords. Extend your awareness to the whole of your opponent's body. Be ready to pick up the slightest hint of a change in tactic. That could have been my pugio in your ribs, instead of my fingers."

The youth removed the leather practice helmet and shook out his curly blond hair. He wiped his forehead with the back of one hand, and squinted up at the bright square of blue sky above the courtyard.

"Yes, the sun is getting high," Gavius said. "Come, that is enough for today. Courage, Cornelius, you are doing well. Will you take some wine before you go?"

"Thank you."

Cornelius slid his sword into its scabbard and followed his instructor out of the courtyard and through the small doorway into the rear of the modest house. The stone-flagged kitchen was dark and cool. He placed the helmet on a wooden bench, unstrapped from his forearms the iron-studded leather guards, and laid them alongside it. Then he lifted the scabbard, looped the diagonal strap over his head, and added it to the pile before flopping down wearily.

Gavius brought out two pottery mugs, poured a little wine into each and filled them the rest of the way with water. He pushed one across the table to Cornelius, and raised the other.

"Just a Pompeiana. Not the spiced falernum you're used to, I'm afraid."

"I prefer this," said the youth, taking a deep draught. He sighed. "I'll never be able to fight as well as you, Gavius."

Gavius laughed. "Just like your father: you set your standards high. Remember, I was in the legions for many years and I saw many battles. Had I not fought well, I wouldn't be here now."

"Father tells me you were a valiant soldier. I am fortunate to have you to instruct me."

"The real honour is mine."

"What makes you say that?"

"I fought under many commanders, Cornelius. Of them all, Claudius Fratellus was by far the best. To have served him was an honour. To be entrusted with the instruction of his son is an even greater honour."

"My father never speaks of the wars."

"He's a modest man. Unlike some, he took no pleasure in the spilling of blood – ours or theirs. But he did his duty and he served Rome well."

"I know him so little. What made him such a good commander?"

Gavius leaned back, his eyes gazing beyond the smoke-blackened ceiling. "Sound judgment, based on the best intelligence. A superb strategist, always looking beyond the present position to the next. A willingness to share the same food, the same privations, the same dangers as his men." He broke off and looked at Cornelius. "You can describe the parts, yet somehow you do not have the whole. I believe some men are born leaders. Men respect them, they are drawn to them, and follow them without question. Your father is such a man. That's why in all of Pompeii they still refer to him as 'The General'. I've heard it said he was highly regarded by Vespasian himself."

"That's true. He wears a ring that was the gift of Vespasian. It carries the Emperor's image."

"There you are! Of course the Emperor may have had other motives too, such as reminding a General in the midst of his triumph where his allegiance should lie. Unnecessary in this case: your father's loyalty was never in question and he had no ambitions in Rome. In that, I suspect, he showed his usual good judgment. He's a man of simple tastes. The fashions and intrigues of Rome would not have appealed to him at all."

"I should like to be worthy of him."

"You should aspire to nothing less, for it will bring happiness to you both. Where do you go now?"

"A short rest, then to the house of Callimedes, for more lessons in philosophy and logic."

"Your father plans your education well. No doubt a mastery of logic will be of great value – except, perhaps, when you are in the company of Octavius's beautiful daughter."

Cornelius flushed. "How do you know about Anteia?"

"The birds know everything."

"That's true, but they seldom confide it, as they do to you."

The old soldier laughed, scratching his short, grey-flecked beard. "These birds are special. They spend much time in taverns."

"And what do they say, these birds?"

"That she has eyes as black as ripe olives, and the glances you two cast at each other would set the Sarno itself on fire."

Cornelius flushed more deeply.

"Have no fear," Gavius said. "I repeat this to you alone. Such gossip is like the sea; it washes up on my shore and goes no further."

"I don't doubt it. You're a good man, Gavius. A friend and adviser to me, as well as an instructor."

"I have little enough wisdom to offer, other than a knowledge of the ways of men."

"I give much weight to that knowledge, for that my own experience is so light. Gavius..." The youth paused.

Gavius raised bushy eyebrows. "Yes? What is it, Cornelius?"

"My father wants me to take up the law. He says it is the best route to high office."

"And...?"

"I don't know, Gavius. I'm no orator. Sometimes I think I'd be quite content to spend my life running a farm or cultivating vines. But everyone seems to expect so much more of me."

"It's natural for them to have ambitions for you, Cornelius, but in the end it's your life, not theirs."

"But I can't say even whether they're right or wrong. I just don't know what I'm capable of."

Gavius shook his head and smiled.

"This is a problem only you can face. When I was your age I had very little choice. It's harder for you because you can probably do anything you put your mind to, and you have more opportunities than most. Don't worry. In the end you'll make a decision, whether by design or by accident. Some more wine?"

"Thank you, no. I must go." Cornelius stood, and gathered up his leather purse.

"Do you have your stilus?"

"Yes, and a wax tablet. Would you like me to write something for you, Gavius?"

"No, I wanted only to remind you that your stilus is a useful weapon, and not just with words. There are thieves and bandits everywhere. You can not carry a sword in the city but be sure you can lay a hand easily on the stilus."

"I'll remember. Thank you Gavius. Until the next time."

They clasped hands.

"Go safely, my young friend."

Cornelius followed Anteia into her father's garden. Behind them, maintaining a discreet distance, was Lutulla; decorum required Anteia to be escorted if she was in the company of a young man, even one as familiar to this household as Cornelius. Lutulla was tactful enough not to make her presence intrusive. In the garden she settled down on a bench in the shade of a tall cypress and busied herself sewing.

Anteia led the way along a pergola draped with vines. She was tall for her age, her height accentuated by her bearing. A stola, suspended by short straps from her shoulders, was draped over a sleeved tunic whose hem brushed lightly on the path. Her hair was pinned modestly in ropes, in the Campanian manner. As she walked she glanced at the fish swimming in the deep pools that ran the length of the pergola.

She paused, and half-turned. Cornelius smiled. She responded with the merest twitch of her lips and an arched eyebrow; then moved to a stone bench and sat demurely, her hands in her lap.

Cornelius perched next to her and followed her gaze, taking in the delights of the garden.

The sun was still high, its heat bringing up the scents of clipped yew, and of the herbs in their raised beds. Ivy wreathed the bases of the statues. Roses, acanthus and amaranth were in flower, eagerly attended by bees. In front of them a fountain glittered like diamonds in the sunlight and cascaded down miniature steps into the pool.

"Father loves it here," she said. "Especially when he's been working at the port all day. As soon as he has bathed he goes into the garden."

"I can understand that. By comparison to the port, this is a paradise."

"I've never been there, Cornelius. Is it as bad as people say?"

"You wouldn't like it. It's full of people – traders, sailors, porters – and wherever you go, you're in somebody's way. The air is almost too thick to breathe. And if the wind is in the wrong direction it carries salt in, from the salt works of Hercules. That stings your nose, and gets into your clothes and hair. No wonder Octavius likes to return here."

"He never wanted my brothers to follow him into the business. It has given us a comfortable life but he told them they should set their sights higher. 'Each generation should advance beyond the one that went before' – that's what he says. So now they're both studying in Rome. Have you decided yet what you are going to do, Cornelius?"

"Not really. But I'll be eighteen next year. It's the right age to start service as a soldier."

She spun towards him, eyes wide. "You're not going to join the legions!"

"Why not? The legions travel to every part of the Empire. I've never set foot outside this area. I have no experience of life, Anteia. Somehow I have to find myself."

"You'll find yourself killed – that's what you'll find."

He stiffened.

"I think there would be little chance of that. But if I did see action, I hope I would acquit myself with honour."

"Honour! You men are always speaking of honour. What's the use of honour, if you're dead?"

"So you'd rather be the wife of a coward than the widow of a hero?"

She drew herself up. "Happily I don't have to make such an idiotic choice because we're not betrothed. And there is not the slightest chance that we will be, if you persist in this folly."

He swallowed hard. "Anteia, please. We have so little time together. Let's not spoil it by quarrelling."

She took a deep breath and expelled it slowly. "I wonder at you sometimes, Cornelius. You speak of the blissful life we have ahead of us, and then you come out with, with... an insane idea like this. Do you really think I want to be the wife of a soldier?"

"But it's a noble profession! My father was a soldier!"

"And does he want you to join the legions?"

"Well, no." He grimaced. "He'd like me to practise the law."

"That sounds like excellent advice to me. Perhaps you should take heed of it."

She glared at him, but he was devastated to see that her beautiful dark eyes had filled with tears.

"Anteia..."

She bit her lip, then got up abruptly.

"Go away," she said, her voice cracking.

He rose to his feet, opening his hands to her, aware that Lutulla had heard their raised voices and was coming uncertainly towards them.

"Anteia, please don't be angry..."

"Go away."

He paused. Then his hands dropped limply to his sides.

"All right."

Cornelius left Octavius's villa with his eyes downcast.

In the narrow street that separated the villas of Octavius and Claudius two men were waiting.

He was an easy target.

Chapter 6

8.30 p.m. August 23, A.D. 79

Claudius stepped carefully around the packing cases and entered his private quarters. Only his steward was allowed in here.

"It's late, Junius, and there's only one day left. Will we be ready on time?"

"I believe so, General. The kitchen is all packed now. Bread, cheese and olives for everyone tomorrow, I'm afraid."

"Others survive on that; so can we. The furniture?"

"Just a few chairs, and the pillows from the triclinium, as you instructed."

Cottia entered the chamber, looking around. "I thought Cornelius might be with you," she said to her husband.

"I haven't seen him. Isn't he in his chamber?"

"No, I just looked there."

"He said earlier he was going to Octavius's villa."

"He can't be there still, Claudius! The light is already fading."

Claudius frowned. "I'll go to Octavius and see if he's still there. Junius, you'd better come with me."

Fifteen minutes later they hurried back – without Cornelius. Cottia began to breathe quickly.

"According to Lutulla, he left hours ago," Claudius said. "Junius, get the slaves to stop what they're doing. As soon as Octavius and his household are here we'll organize everyone into search parties."

When Cornelius recovered consciousness the first thing he became aware of was a pounding in his head. The second thing was the pressure of a cold stone floor against his cheek. He tried to move but he was tied hand and foot. His mouth was stopped with a foul rag.

The door opened, and he heard voices.

"They're looking everywhere for him, Licinius. How are we going to get him out of here?"

"That's why I do the thinking, Myro. We lie low for the night and go out soon after daybreak."

"But they'll still be looking! And there are the sentries."

"Myro, what comes into the city during the night?"

There was a pause. "You mean the wagons? We're going to send him out on a wagon?"

"No, idiot, they'll be searching the wagons. But wagons are drawn by donkeys, or mules or oxen, aren't they? And their mess has to be cleared up, doesn't it? What happens to it?"

"That's the worst job in Pompeii, shovelling shit and barrowing it away to the farms. You get next to nothing for it."

"That's exactly right, Myro. And tomorrow morning, I'll be doing the worst job in Pompeii. But underneath the shit will be a sack, with this," he kicked Cornelius, "inside it. Once we're clear of the city he can start walking."

"That's very clever, Licinius."

"That, Myro, is why I do the thinking."

It was deep into the night when Claudius returned to the villa. He was grey with fatigue, but he went straight to Cottia. He could hear her anguished cries echoing down the hallway long before he entered the chamber.

"Corne – lius! I want my son! Oh, where is my son? Give him back to me!"

Cottia's slave, Istacidia, was standing behind her, her pale hands resting lightly on the woman's shoulders. When the General came in, she gave him a helpless look, and stepped away.

"Cottia..." he began, then frowned. His wife continued to rock back and forth; she seemed to have isolated herself in a world that contained only her own grief.

Gently he cupped her chin and raised her swollen face to him. Her hair was wild, her eyes inflamed, her cheeks glistening with tears. His expression softened and he put his arms around her.

"Cottia – Cottia, listen to me. Try to keep a grip on yourself. We are doing everything we can. Octavius and Junius and I have called on all our friends and we've quartered the entire city a dozen times. The commander of the garrison has given instructions to the sentries at the gates. Octavius has spoken to the people at the port. Gavius is making inquiries in every tavern. We will find Cornelius if it is humanly possible to do so."

Cottia's sobs, muffled against him, continued unabated.

Claudius was out again at daybreak, riding his horse through the streets of Pompeii. There was little traffic at this early hour, but he was aware of the activity behind the shuttered shop fronts, the stoking of ovens, the stacking of shelves, the baking of fresh bread, and the preparation of food for a new day. He knew there was little enough point in searching in this fashion, yet it made him feel he was doing something, and it gave him time to think.

No one had found any sign of Cornelius, and he'd disappeared during daylight hours. That didn't fit the pattern of robbery or assault. The most likely explanation was that he'd been kidnapped. He hoped desperately that his son wouldn't be badly treated. If he was still in the city they'd find him, he felt sure; everyone was on the look-out. Whoever had taken him couldn't get out of the city either; every gate was being watched. The main worry was that those responsible had got him out before the alarm was raised. In that case his son could be almost anywhere, and all he could do was wait for them to deliver a ransom demand.

He began by traversing the city, starting at the Stabian Gate, his attention focused on the houses and shops on each side of the street. Instinctively he kept his horse away from the ruts that the passage of countless wheels had carved into the basalt roadway and stepped the animal carefully over the slabs which had been set at intervals to enable pedestrians to cross. He passed the Street of Abundance and progressed slowly up towards the Vesuvian Gate. Ahead of him, a man shovelled up some dung and tossed it into a handbarrow. He guided the horse around him and continued on his way. The man looked up at the receding horse and rider.

His lips peeled back in a smile, exposing broken, blackened teeth.

At the Vesuvian Gate the sentry stepped smartly out from the recess in the wall and snapped to attention. The early morning light gleamed on his polished helmet and shoulder armour.

"How long have you been on duty, soldier?"

"I took over about an hour ago, General."

"Have you seen anything?"

"No, sir. And I'm told it has been quiet all night."

He sighed. "All right. Keep your eyes open, won't you?"

"Sir."

The slow clop of the horse's hooves faded into silence. The sentry stepped out again to challenge a man wheeling a barrow.

"What have you got there?"

The man grinned impudently. "What does it smell like?"

The soldier glared at him, taking in the soiled clothes, uncombed hair and bad teeth. He lifted his lance, preparing to stab it into the contents of the barrow.

"Go ahead," said the man. "It's not me who'll have to stand there all day long with a shitty lance."

The soldier hesitated, then jerked his head for the man to proceed.

"Shit-shoveller," he muttered as the man passed.

As Octavius led Claudius into the garden, a child's laughter rang along the vine-covered pergola. A young woman chased him out.

"Quickly, Victor, quickly. The master is here." She bowed and muttered an apology to Octavius as they passed.

With the child and its mother gone the only sounds to be heard were those of bird song and the soft playing of the fountain as it splashed into the pool.

Claudius sank onto a bench, oblivious to the soothing delights of the garden. "I don't know what else to do, Octavius," he said. "I haven't slept all night. Cottia is hysterical."

Octavius sighed, placing a hand on his friend's sagging shoulders. He had never seen him in such a dejected state.

"I know. Anteia is the same. She thinks she's responsible. She says she was horrid to him when they met yesterday. The poor girl is crazed with guilt and grief."

Claudius looked round, eyebrows raised. "Anteia?"

Octavius smiled sadly.

"Have you not seen how they look at each other, my friend?"

Realization dawned on the General's face.

"I must be blind, Octavius! They've been companions since they were children. I hadn't noticed the change..." He gripped Octavius's forearm. "It would be my dearest wish to see them united..." Then he buried his face in his hands. "Oh, if only this nightmare would cease."

Cornelius stumbled up the sloping ground, aware of the malign presence of Licinius close behind him, a dagger in his hand. The man called Myro, a big brute of a fellow, had joined them some distance outside the gate. Licinius had then tipped the barrow over and, with an oath and a warning, cut his bonds. He still ached in every joint from being tied up and crammed into the sack, and the smell of the dung clung to his clothes.

They'd marched him some distance up the mountain. The sun shone down mercilessly and radiated back from the rocks, increasing the pounding in his head and making it hard for him to think. He knew his mother and father would be frantic about his disappearance. How would Anteia react? His chest still ached when he thought about the way they'd argued. He felt very badly about it. He hadn't given any thought to her feelings at all. If he had he would have seen the problems it would pose for her – for them – if he embarked on a military career.

No good dwelling on it now, he thought. *I need to do something. Otherwise I won't have any sort of career, military or otherwise.*

He could guess what they were up to, these two. They'd taken his purse, but that didn't mean anything. If robbery was all they had in mind they would have killed him right there, outside Octavius's villa, or at least left him in the street. That probably meant they were planning to extort a ransom. But kidnappers didn't always take the risk of returning their captives alive. He had to act on the assumption that they intended to murder him. If they did it high enough up the mountain they could keep people guessing a long time about whether or not he was still alive.

Earlier in the day there'd been another tremor, and he'd heard one or two explosions, which seemed to come from the direction of the mountain. There was nothing to see, except perhaps a low line of grey cloud rolling over the ground away from the summit, but the muttering the sounds had elicited from the two behind him had given him the germ of an idea. He'd rounded on them slowly, raising a finger in solemn admonition.

"Do you hear the Gods?" he said, doing his best to adopt the impressive tones of a priest he'd once heard during a ceremony at the Temple of Isis. "Do you hear their displeasure at what you do? Be warned, Licinius and Myro, be warned. The Gods are angry with you."

Myro had looked distinctly uncomfortable, but Licinius had simply snarled and told him to shut up and walk on.

All the same, Cornelius was pleased with the result. Perhaps, he thought, he'd underestimated his abilities as an orator. These men were ignorant; he might still be able to work on their gullibility.

Of course he'd hoped for another tremor, and perhaps some more explosions that he could pass off as thunderbolts. Unfortunately, everything had remained almost preternaturally still in the three hours or so that had passed since then. Even the birds seemed to have stopped singing.

"Halt!" Licinius commanded. Cornelius turned warily.

Licinius stood wiping perspiration from his face. Sweat was soaking through the man's grubby tunic.

"We're nearly there," he said to Myro. "There's a spring over here. I need a drink of water. Keep an eye on him."

Cornelius sensed Myro moving up close beside him as Licinius sheathed the pugio and descended into a fold in the ground that held a long pool of water.

The man scooped some water into his mouth, swallowed, then spat. "Pah!" he exclaimed. "Why does it taste so brackish today?"

He splashed his face and scooped water over the back of his neck. Eyes closed, he scooped more water and his fingers passed through air. He scooped deeper, and again his fingers met nothing. He dabbed his eyes hastily with his tunic, opened them, and froze. The water that had been there a moment before had gone. Even as he watched, the last of it drained away, leaving behind a moist layer of mud.

It was the chance Cornelius had been waiting for.

Pretending not to have noticed what had happened, he lifted his eyes to the sky. He raised one hand, and pointed the other accusingly at Licinius.

"Show them a sign, ye Gods," he intoned sonorously. "Show them your displeasure."

Myro whimpered. Licinius turned, his face black with hatred.

Cornelius raised his voice. "Jupiter, best of Gods!" he proclaimed. "Vent your anger on the wicked ones!"

Slowly Licinius drew the pugio and began up the slope, the dagger held level at his hip.

Cornelius felt terror constrict his throat. Could he control his voice enough to try once more? He tried to draw breath. Suddenly the ground began to tremble and a noise like thunder rose from the entire landscape. It went on and on, the sound growing and the ground shaking so violently that Cornelius had difficulty holding his balance. Licinius stopped, nonplussed. Myro let out a high-pitched wail and ran.

Licinius shouted, "Myro, you fool! Come back here!" He turned back to Cornelius, his eyes narrowed to venomous slits. "You pampered little mother's brat. I'll show you..." He stepped forward and Cornelius braced himself for the dagger thrust.

A colossal explosion rent the air.

Cornelius was knocked off his feet by something like a huge gust of wind. It sent him tumbling down the mountainside, arms and legs flailing; then, with a jarring impact that knocked all the breath out of his body, his fall was arrested by a large boulder. He lay there, winded, his head swimming. His hearing was dulled, as if someone had boxed him about the ears. He thought he should try to get up, but his limbs rebelled. In the recesses of his clouded mind he pictured Licinius covering the ground between them, standing over him, grinning triumphantly as he raised the pugio.

He managed to lift his head, then fell back, eyes closed, waiting for the death blow.

It didn't come.

He made another attempt to rise. This time he succeeded in rolling over. Slowly he raised himself to his knees. He took deep breaths and his vision began to clear. He focused on his hands, the fingers spread on the ground in front of him, then peered cautiously to either side. There was no sign of Licinius.

As his hearing returned, he became aware of a roaring noise that was getting louder and louder. He felt the ground shaking under him like a blanket.

He lifted his gaze and his mouth dropped open.

A wide column of smoke and flame was jetting for miles into the sky. All around, great boulders were thudding into the ground, or bouncing down the slopes, each one leaving behind it a long, curved trail of vapour.

The clear danger energized his limbs and the mist in his head evaporated abruptly. He got up and ran.

Chapter 7

1.00 p.m. August 24, A.D. 79

Myro crouched behind a tall rock, panting as much with terror as from exertion. A shadow loomed over him and he cried out in fright, then realized it was Licinius, who'd followed him down.

"Fool! Idiot! What did you run for?" Licinius shouted.

Words jumbled through the big man's trembling lips. "The Gods... thunderbolts..."

A stinging blow from the flat of Licinius's hand made him blink. A dangerous look flashed in his eyes, then faded.

"We've been duped, you fool."

"But the mountain... the Gods..."

Licinius tried to slap him again but this time Myro caught his wrist and glared with fierce resentment into Licinius's eyes. For a moment they stayed locked, then the moment passed and Licinius withdrew his hand.

"The top has blown off the mountain," Licinius said, raising his voice only enough to make himself heard over the rumbling.

"But why...?"

"I don't know why, it just has. It's got nothing to do with the Gods."

"So if it's got nothing to do with the Gods why were you running?"

"I wasn't running," Licinius snarled. Then he added, almost to himself, "I was looking for shelter, that's all."

"And what about the thunderbolts?"

"They're not thunderbolts, they're just rocks. The top blew off the mountain and the pieces came down. See? It's finished now."

Myro looked around. Although the rain of rocks hadn't

finished, it was certainly dying out. But the ground was still trembling. He pointed to the great black cloud spreading into the sky above them.

"What about that?" he demanded.

"Well, it's on fire now, isn't it? It's like a great big bonfire and that's the smoke from it. You weren't ever hurt by the smoke from a bonfire, were you?"

Myro blinked, still unsure.

"Come on, we're going back for him."

"What?" Myro's voice rose to a shriek.

"I said, we're going back for him. If he gets back to Pompeii they'll know who snatched him. They'll scour the country for us and when they find us we'll be fed to the lions in the amphitheatre. Is that what you want?"

"But..."

"Come on, get up. We're wasting time."

A smoking boulder flew through the air, struck the ground and careened over Cornelius just as he threw himself under an overhang. He lay there for a moment, chest heaving and heart pounding. Slowly he drew himself up and sat, listening to the roaring and the rocks whistling through the air and crashing into the trees further below. After a while it dawned on him that the terrifying bombardment was easing off. He tried to gather his wits, forcing himself to recall the conversation in the tablinum.

Fulvius said Vesuvius is a volcano, like Aetna. How can that be? Aetna burns all the time, at least at night. Perhaps Vesuvius burns too, but the fires are hidden deep inside. What else did Fulvius say – that an earthquake made the flames of Aetna higher? Father had said it was like stoking a campfire. Is that what happened? The tremor made the flames rise higher inside Vesuvius – so high that the top of the mountain could no longer contain them. Then the top blew off the mountain and the pieces fell out of the sky. Surely that means the immediate danger is over?

He emerged tentatively from his place of shelter. The ground continued to shake and the air was still full of noise. High above him the column disappeared into a roiling mushroom of smoke that was growing all the time and spreading to the south-east. He bit his lip. It was enormous.

His instinct was to get back to Pompeii, to his family and Anteia, as soon as he could. But what about Licinius and his accomplice? Maybe they'd also decided there was no longer a threat from the sky. If so, they'd surely come back for him and this time they wouldn't hesitate. Fearful as the phenomenon overhead was, he couldn't help thinking that those two were the more present danger.

They'd expect him to take the shortest route back to Pompeii and they'd probably be waiting somewhere below, ready to intercept him. He could evade them if he descended on the opposite side of the mountain. He'd come out somewhere to the south of Herculaneum and then he could follow the coast road and approach Pompeii from the seaward side. There was only one drawback: it was a very long way round. The direct route would be much quicker.

He balanced the options, made his decision and set off.

At first Claudius thought it was just another tremor. Then the whole villa shuddered under an explosion of sound fuller and louder than any clap of thunder. The shock continued in a succession of diminishing waves, as if some giant bird were flapping its wings. Stepping into the atrium, Claudius saw a small blizzard of dust sweeping along the street outside. Some of it was deflected at the entrance to the villa and fanned across the mosaic floor of the vestibulum. He hurried to the threshold and looked out. Along the length of the street people were running outside, looking around them wildly, some with their hands still clamped over their ears.

Octavius appeared, frowning, and Claudius walked over to him. They said nothing but stood together, trying to make sense of what was happening. The slaves had followed them out of the villas and they gathered around their masters, waiting to be told what to do. Then, audible even above the continued rumbling, came a collective gasp as a huge black cloud came into view and rose higher and higher into the sky. The villas opposite blocked the horizon but there was no doubting where the cloud had come from. Claudius watched it in awe.

"Fulvius was right," he breathed.

"It reaches to the very heavens," Octavius gasped.

The entire street was now filled with a gabble of fearful voices. The cloud spread as it climbed and fingers of smoke began to point towards them.

"It seems to be coming this way," said Octavius. He glanced at his friend and saw there an expression that alarmed him. "What is it?"

Claudius was viewing the spectacle through narrowed eyes. Below the cloud there was something else: a faint curtain that it seemed to be drawing with it. He took a deep breath.

"Inside!" he shouted. "Get everyone inside. Immediately!"

He remained to the last, directing both their households into Octavius's villa, which was the nearest. With a final glance around him he mounted the steps. As he did so he heard a sound like an arrow in flight and a stone the size of a large beach pebble struck the street and skittered along the paving. Another bounced off a wall. Yet another clattered onto the roof. And another. And another.

The two households assembled in the atrium. The slaves gathered in groups around the impluvium, the central pool above which a square aperture in the roof had been constructed to flood the spacious room with light. But now a shadow moved across that square of sky and the room darkened. Stones dropped with increasing frequency into the pool, splashing the water out over the tiled floor. The slaves shrank back against the walls. Some began to cough, for with the stones came a fine choking ash that hung in the air. Perceiving the problem, Octavius ushered them into the chambers that led off both sides of the atrium. He rejoined Claudius, who was pacing in the peristyle.

Above the rattling of stones on the roof and the splashing in the pool, both men heard the more regular rhythm of footsteps on the vestibule. They looked up and recognized the figure striding towards them.

"Fulvius!"

"Forgive the intrusion, gentlemen," he said, shaking hands with each in turn. "When I saw that thing go up I thought I'd better come straight here, in case you wanted to rethink the plan." He turned to Claudius. "Any news of your son, General?"

Claudius shook his head.

"I'm sorry. In that case I should not have come."

"No, it is well that you've come. I had hoped that Oppius Gratus, too, would join us here. How did you escape the stones?"

The engineer raised his leather bag and placed it on his head in mute demonstration.

"There were few when I started out," he said. "It's a good deal worse now."

"Have you ever seen anything like this in Sicily, Fulvius?" Octavius asked.

"No. I've seen Aetna angry, but it doesn't bear comparison to this mountain's fury. It's..."

He halted, looking at the impluvium. Some of the white stones were lying on top of each other, but others were floating in the pool. One had bounced out onto the floor. He picked it up, turned it over in his hands, and hefted it.

"You know, I've seen sponge-stones just like this on the slopes of Aetna. For their size they're remarkably light."

He handed it to Claudius, who was surprised to find that it was warm as well as light. He examined it thoughtfully, then looked up at Fulvius.

"When I was in the army I once saw a curtain in the sky over the German plains. It was just before a storm of giant hailstones," he said. "That's what I thought was approaching."

"This is no hailstone. It came from the mountain, not from the heavens."

"How is that possible? The largest siege engines in the Roman army could not throw a stone this size such a distance."

There was a commotion at the entrance and Oppius Gratus came in. His clothes were dusty and he was bleeding from a cut on his forearm. Claudius stepped forward.

"Oppius," he said. "Are you badly hurt?"

"No, I'm all right."

"I'm very glad you've come. Did you bring your household with you?"

"Yes – I trust I have not presumed too much..."

"Not at all. As you see, Fulvius is here. Now we can move as soon as the time is ripe."

"Your son, Claudius...?"

"Not yet," he replied briskly. "Ah, here is your retinue."

"You have met my wife, Quartilla," said Oppius.

Claudius inclined his head.

"I am happy to see you are safe, Quartilla. How have you managed to come through this deluge of stones?"

"We started to load a wagon, General, but you cannot drive animals in these conditions. We saw two horses bolting, dragging an overturned carriage behind them. They were terrified – I could see the whites of their eyes. We could not take the risk."

"We left the wagon," said Oppius. "We put a few bags with the most important things onto a table, lifted it by the legs and walked under it through the streets. A table makes a fine shelter," he added.

"We had to leave a lot behind, though," said Quartilla, her voice tight. Then with a great sob she threw herself on Oppius's chest. He exchanged glances with them and led her quietly away, talking gently all the time.

Octavius wandered to the entrance and looked out. The rain of stones had now thickened into a lethal downpour. He beckoned to two slaves and instructed them to close the great wooden bronze-studded doors.

"Don't fasten them," he added. "We must keep out the worst of the stones, but we should not deny access to anyone who seeks shelter here."

Claudius strode restlessly to and fro in the atrium, listening to the irregular percussion on the adjacent roofs. The noise had changed. At first the impacts had been short and sharp; now they had become dull thuds. The pebbles were beginning to pile up, layer upon layer.

Cornelius made his way down through thick woodland. By the time he emerged below the trees the daylight had gone. He looked around him in surprise. It had not taken him that long, surely? Or was there a storm brewing? Then he looked up and realized what had happened. The cloud from Vesuvius had continued to grow and it was now blotting out most of the sky. Soon the darkness was so complete that it seemed to press in on him. He could no longer run, or even walk quickly, for fear that he would collide with a tree or rock or fall into a crevice. He proceeded warily, one hand extended in front of his face.

Many hours later, he reached the road. With a sigh of relief, he turned towards Pompeii. He thought it must be past the middle of the night, although the constant darkness made it difficult to judge the passage of time. He had little idea how much further he had to go, but he'd be able to make faster progress now. He broke into a steady run.

There were no other travellers on the road, apart from occasional carriages, most of which came from the direction of Pompeii and sped by without stopping. Lightning flickered through the cloud above, lending a fitful illumination to the scene below. Now and again a flare rose from the top of Vesuvius and the underside of the cloud glowed briefly before swallowing it up.

Then the ground shook violently, making him stagger. As he recovered he heard a new sound, a great roaring. He stopped, and looking behind him he saw a glow travelling low through the sky. Whatever it was, it seemed to be heading towards the coast, somewhere in the region of Herculaneum. He watched it disappear, his mind blank with incomprehension. Then he turned and continued on his way. One thing alone was driving him now: he had to get back to Pompeii.

His feet pounded on the road in an unending rhythm and the black sails of darkness unfurled constantly in front of his eyes.

Chapter 8

2.30 a.m. August 25, A.D. 79

A haze of ash hung in the atrium, revealed by the faint illumination leaking from the chambers on each side, where candle lanterns had been lit in an attempt to hold back the oppressive darkness. The feeble light also fell on a large heap of stones which now dominated the centre of the atrium, reaching more than halfway to the ceiling and almost to the walls. Somewhere underneath it lay the impluvium. The only sound was an occasional sob from one of the women. The clattering on the roof had ceased.

Octavius took a flaming torch, walked slowly to the back of the villa, and held it out over what had once been his green and pleasant garden. Now it was as still and grey as a necropolis. The pebbles had completely buried the roses and clipped yews, and reached to the chins of the statues. Ragged remnants of his carefully tended vines clung to the shattered stumps of the pergola. Even the cypress trees seemed petrified beneath their layer of ash. He swallowed hard and returned to the atrium.

Claudius had been pacing for much of the night. He had fought many battles at daybreak, and the hours ticked off in his mind just as surely in this constant darkness. Now and again he paused, listening carefully for any sign of a resumption in the hail of stones, but there was none. It was time for action.

A creaking at the entrance and the sound of running footsteps made him look round.

A skinny boy scrambled over the edge of the pile of stones and arrived breathlessly at his feet. Octavius hurried up, raising the torch to reveal the boy's pale, dirty face.

"Message for General Fratellus, sir."

"I am Claudius Fratellus."

"From my master, sir." The boy held out a set of waxed tablets. Claudius took them, frowning.

"What do we have here?" asked Octavius.

"It's a message from Marcus."

"The merchant? What does it say?"

The tablets were scrawled in a hasty hand. Claudius read the message out, turning each tablet on its leather hinges.

"MY DEAR GENERAL

I HAVE HEARD OF THE DISAPPEARANCE OF YOUR SON. THE NEWS GRIEVES ME. IT GRIEVES ME TOO THAT I FAILED TO TAKE YOUR WARNINGS MORE SERIOUSLY.

THE SLAVE WHO BEARS THIS MESSAGE IS A SHIP'S BOY WHOM I ACQUIRED FROM THE CAPTAIN IN PART PAYMENT OF A DEBT. I LEAVE HIM TO YOU AS A GIFT. MORE VALUABLE THAN THIS GIFT IS THE INTELLIGENCE HE CARRIES. AS A SUPREME STRATEGIST YOU WILL KNOW WHAT USE TO MAKE OF IT.

I WISH YOU FAREWELL AND MAY THE GODS BE WITH YOU.

MARCUS HOLONIUS PRISCUS."

Claudius looked from the tablets to the boy.

"You may stand," he said gently, and the boy got to his feet. "What is your name?"

"My master calls me Simius, sir."

"Simius?"

"Yes, sir, because he says when it comes to running up masts or ropes I'm quicker than a monkey."

Claudius squatted in front of him. "Simius, do you know anything of my son, Cornelius Fratellus?"

"No, sir."

The General's face fell, but he recovered quickly. "Where did you bear this message from?"

"From the port, sir. My master was there on business when

the mountain exploded. He always takes me with him when a shipment is being unloaded. I cover the ship quickly for him, and I know all the places where merchandise can be concealed."

"What is the intelligence that your master refers to in this message, Simius?"

"He said I should tell you how things lie down there, sir."

"And how do they lie?"

"There's no freedom of movement on the road to Stabiae, sir. He said you should know this." Claudius raised his eyebrows, and Simius went on quickly, his voice rising, his hands outstretched: "It's one great stream of people, sir, mothers with babies, men, women and children, carrying what they can in their arms and on their heads. Some had wagons with them, but they left them behind when the rain of stones began. And there is much thievery – in their desperation, some people have lost all restraint. I myself saw a carriage with two horses trying to drive through. They overturned it, sir, and took the horses. My master had thought to go that way, but when he saw the crowds he took one horse and rode across country towards Nuceria. He could not take me with him, so he gave me the message to bring to you. Sir."

"Is there no escape by sea?"

"There is not, sir." Simius shook his head. "Even if you could see it for yourself, sir, you would think your eyes deceived you. The sea has gone –I could not see the edge of it. Ships are lying on their side in the port and fish are flapping in the sand. There is no escape that way."–

"The river, then?"

"The river is not navigable, sir. The sponge-stones are floating on every part of it. Those who would have escaped by ship simply swell the numbers on the roads."

"What of the road north, to Oplontis and Herculaneum?"

"This I do not know, sir, but if it were me I would not go towards that mountain for all the gold in Rome."

Claudius nodded.

"General, sir?"

"Yes, Simius?"

"May I stay here with you now?"

"Yes, Simius. You have done well. You have earned your place with us. Octavius, would you bring Oppius and Fulvius here? We must prepare to leave."

The candle lantern on the table lit the faces of the four men in the tablinum and cast their shadows over the richly decorated walls. From time to time the flame quivered with the tremors that had continued, with greater or lesser force, ever since the explosion the previous day.

"That, gentlemen, is the situation," said Claudius. "The road to Stabiae is in chaos. We have to change our plans."

"Perhaps we should take the Nuceria road after all," said Oppius.

"In all likelihood that will be equally bad. Either way, we'll be bottled up and in the pressure of a crowd we could lose one another. If I have learned one thing, it's the need for mobility. Marcus rode across country to Nuceria. I'd favour this option if we were on our own, but we have others to think of."

"We could go south, to the coast and thence to Salernum." The suggestion had come from Fulvius. The others stared at him.

Claudius pursed his lips thoughtfully.

"I had heard that there is a way through that wall of mountains," he said, "but I have never used it myself. You say it is possible?"

"Possible, yes. There is a pass. It is steep, and the going is rough, but it could be done. I doubt that others would try to go that way."

Oppius said, "But how would we cross the Sarno?"

"No doubt at the mouth of the river the situation is as the young boy says. But I know a place where the river can be forded when the water is low. If these stones have fallen in equal measure on the Sarno, it should be possible to cross there."

"We will have to be lightly loaded," said Claudius, "for both the crossing and the ascent. We will take just one wagon. Everything else we must carry by hand or leave behind."

"What animals should we use?" asked Octavius. "Oxen?"

"They're strong, but slow, and suited to level ground. Horses

67

would be better through the mountains, and more useful when the journey's ended. We'll yoke up Ulixes with Sylvian. They should pull well together and both were trained for war, so neither thunder nor earthquake will unsettle them." He looked around the table. "Are we agreed, then? Let's tell the others and commence the loading."

"What – now, Claudius?"

"Yes, now, Octavius."

"But what about Cornelius...?"

The hollows of Claudius's eyes deepened in the lantern light and a muscle moved in his jaw. "Octavius, the deluge of stones has stopped, but we don't know for how long. If we do not leave now, we may not get a second opportunity. The lives of many are in our hands. I cannot jeopardize them all for the sake of one life, precious though that life is to me."

"Should we not at least wait until daybreak?"

"That would delay us by three hours or so, to no advantage. The black cloud covers the sky; you are not going to see the sun rise, and we will travel in darkness no matter what time we leave. But this much is clear: unless we leave now, none of us will ever see the sun rise again."

Claudius strode at the side of the wagon. He had donned his helmet and body armour, and wore the gladius and pugio on crossed belts. If there were mobs abroad, as Simius had indicated, it would be a worthwhile deterrent.

Simius was proving his worth. He ran ahead, scuttling over the piles of stones and guiding them through at the best places. Claudius saw how well he deserved the nickname Marcus had given him.

Cottia, Quartilla, Calpurnia and Anteia rode on the wagon. In case the fall of stones resumed, Oppius had improvised a shelter by strapping the table in place over their heads. Cottia had stopped crying. She stared with wide, vacant eyes back into the darkness, shivering slightly.

Anteia, enfolded in Calpurnia's arms, was more vocal. "Make him stop, mother," she sobbed. "Don't let him leave without Cornelius."

"Hush, child." Calpurnia stroked her daughter's hair, her own eyes full of tears. "Do you think the General does not feel the pain of leaving his beloved son behind? He does it for the good of us all. Cornelius is a resourceful young man. If the Gods smile upon us, we may yet see him again."

Fulvius gave a signal and they halted. The four men went forward.

Octavius lit a torch and held it out in front of them. It revealed a flat expanse of pebbles, bounded on each side by a shallow bank, but they could see no water.

"Are you sure this is the Sarno, Fulvius?"

"Yes, I'm sure."

"And this is the fording place?"

"Of that, I'm less sure. I've been here a few times but always in daylight. It looks very different at night – I mean, in darkness."

Claudius frowned. "If there is any thickness of water under those pebbles they'll slip as soon as there's some weight on them. The wagon will overturn in an instant. The horses could be injured, too."

A small head popped up between them. "Let me go out there, sir," said Simius. "I'll try it for you."

"It could be treacherous, Simius..."

"I'll be all right. Watch me."

He stepped down the bank and gingerly out onto the pebbles, feeling his way forward with each foot and testing the ground. Soon he was in the middle.

"It's good here," he said, bouncing up and down.

He moved a few yards to one side and did the same thing. The pebbles shifted, and he lost his footing and fell. He scrambled up with a sheepish grin, despite the cuts on his knees.

"Not so good there," he said.

"Right," said Claudius. "Junius!" he shouted. The big man put down his bundle and hurried forward. "Find a couple of big tree branches and lay them down here to guide us in."

"Yes, General. Could I borrow the torch?"

"Here," said Octavius. "You'll need both hands. I'll go with you."

Minutes later they heard the sound of splintering wood. The torch came weaving back out of the darkness, casting its reddish light on Junius, who was carrying, without apparent effort, two heavy branches. Simius was still prancing up and down in the middle of the river, and by pointing the branches to each side of him they defined the path. Oppius walked across, in case his greater weight made a difference, and returned with a nod of approval.

Claudius went back to the wagon, and the women soon appeared at the side of the river on foot. He had told them he wanted to lighten the load as much as possible.

Junius untied the two goats that had been tethered to the wagon and another slave came forward to hold them. Then he and Claudius started to lead the horses, with Octavius walking in front, doing his best to light the way.

The wagon creaked and rocked as it went. One of the horses gave a snort of alarm as it put a hoof through the pebbles; it staggered but managed to recover. Fortunately its shank had been protected by the leather gaiters they'd tied to the horses' legs.

Three-quarters of the way across, the wheels of the wagon sank slightly and jammed.

Octavius ran back. Junius called out to some of the other slaves and they came forward, ready to push.

"Ready..." called Junius, putting his shoulder to the wagon. "Now!"

The horses strained and the slaves grunted with the effort and the wagon slowly rose and then suddenly rolled forward and kept rolling.

Claudius ran with the horses, the wagon rocked and bounced up the shallow bank and shuddered to a halt on the other side.

They had crossed the river.

Chapter 9

4.00 a.m. August 25, A.D. 79

Again Cornelius tripped, but managed to catch his balance. It was happening more frequently. It wasn't fatigue – although he knew his legs were tiring – it was the pebbles that littered the road. At first there had only been one or two, but now there was barely any space between them. Also, it was getting increasingly hard to breathe; the air seemed to be full of some sort of choking ash which pricked his eyes and grated between his teeth. He assumed it came from the fire on the mountain and had been blown in this direction by the wind. That much he could understand, but there was so much more that he could not.

Where had all these pebbles come from? What was that strange glow that he'd seen descending on Herculaneum?

Lightning forked through the cloud overhead and illuminated a silver ribbon on the hillside not far from the road. He climbed wearily up to the stream and tried the water. It tasted sweet. He cupped his hands and drank deeply. His tunic was soaking in sweat so he stripped it off, plunged it into the stream and used it to mop over his head, neck and chest. Before putting it back on, he tore a strip of cloth off the wet tunic and tied it around his mouth and nose as a protection from the ash. Thus equipped and somewhat refreshed, he returned to the road. He began to run again but the pebbles were getting thicker now and moved dangerously under his feet, so he slowed to a fast walk.

After a while he stopped and looked about him in confusion.

He could no longer make out where the road was. The pebbles lay in every direction, glowing eerily in the flashes of lightning. The sea was not far to his right – that much he knew – and normally he'd be able to hear its comforting rhythms, but all this was now masked by the rumbling of the volcano and the hiss of his breath through the cloth over his mouth and nose.

He thought it must be close to dawn, but there was no way of telling that either. And then, to his great relief, he saw lights ahead and he hurried forward.

He'd reached the city walls. The double doors to each passageway of the Marine Gate had been thrown wide open. People were pouring through, hurrying down the steep slope or descending the steps on the pedestrian side, the two streams coalescing outside. Some carried candle lanterns and he was shocked to see their ragged, dust-covered appearance. Men and women, some carrying children, were shouting each other's names, trying to stay together in the heaving crowd. An old man passed close to him wailing, "Too late, too late!" Some people drove mules loaded with packs, and were cursed by others who struggled around them. Over the entire sea of bobbing heads hung that pall of choking dust. The air was filled with shouting and coughing, the swish of sandaled feet, the rattle of shifting pebbles, and the constant thunder of the volcano. Several times he tried to stop someone, to ask them what had happened or where they were going, but they would not pause in their headlong rush. He tried to push across the moving mass of people and found himself swept along with them. He fought and clawed his way through and finally emerged, dizzy and out of breath, and left the crowd behind him.

He scrambled round to the eastern side of the city, following the base of the wall. Its top was outlined from time to time by lightning, and by the diffuse light of lanterns moving through the streets inside. The familiar profile seemed strangely low to him now, as if he were wearing stilts. He began to appreciate how thickly the pebbles lay on the ground.

At the Stabian Gate he encountered another surging mass of people, flooding out through the open doors. A wagon drawn by two oxen jammed at the side of the gate and people flowed around it like waves around a rock. He saw his chance. He leaped up onto the wagon, ignoring the shouts of the people huddled on it, ran over the top of the crates and bundles, and jumped down just inside the wall.

He wanted to get to the villa as quickly as possible, but he thought the Street of Abundance would be as crowded as the Gates, so he hurried up the back streets. Now the full extent of the fall of stones was apparent: he was stumbling along at the same level as the upper stories of the houses. He found it easier to travel close to the walls, as the stones shifted less under his feet. In this way he suddenly came face to face with an elderly man who was holding a lantern and looking out of his second floor window.

Cornelius paused, nonplussed. "Why do you not flee?"

"I have a better question," the old man replied. "Why do you not stay? All this panic for nothing. Can't you see it's over now? A young man like you should be helping to clear this lot up."

He withdrew with a contemptuous sniff and Cornelius continued on his way, chasing along the stony embankments that had once been the streets of Pompeii.

Ahead of him lay a long line of houses that had fallen in. He guessed the flat roofs had collapsed under the weight of the stones. People could still be trapped inside, he thought, but it would take half the Roman army to get them out. Then he saw an arm waving.

He hurried up. A pale face, covered with ash and dirt, looked out at him. "Help me," the man pleaded.

Cornelius stepped uncertainly over the rubble and felt around. A good deal of masonry had fallen, but what seemed to be pinning the man down were a couple of heavy beams. He clasped his hands under the end of one; it moved and he slid it slowly to one side. Then he did the same with the other.

"There," he said. "Can you get up now?"

The man reached for him, but as Cornelius offered a hand he grabbed him. "Take me with you," he hissed.

Cornelius tried to pull himself free but the fingers closed around his arm like talons. The man's voice rose. "Take me with you."

Again Cornelius tried to tear himself away. Then lightning forked through the cloud overhead and he saw that the man's leg was covered in blood and ash. It ended short, in a white stump. There was no foot.

Cornelius used his other hand to prise the grasping fingers off his arm, staggered back and ran, slipping and sliding, falling and picking himself up, until the feelings of panic subsided. Then he slowed to a walk, took a deep breath and gathered his senses.

He was a little ashamed of his reaction. At the same time, he was beginning to realize how narrowly he'd escaped death or serious injury himself. If he'd decided to come down Vesuvius by the quicker route to the south-east, he too would have been caught under this deluge of stones. Had Licinius and Myro come back to wait for him? Even if they had managed to survive the journey it seemed unlikely they were still here. Just the same, he was watchful as he approached Octavius's villa and the spot where the two men had ambushed him. When was that? It seemed like weeks ago.

The villa was in total darkness. He moved carefully through the atrium, feeling his way along the wall. His foot contacted something light that slid and clattered away across the mosaic floor. Then the interior of the room was illuminated brilliantly by a flash of lightning and he was astonished to see that it was dominated by a great pile of stones. He fell back, seeking the solid reassurance of the wall. His fingers contacted the entrance to a chamber and he peered in. Lightning flickered again. It was enough to afford him a brief glimpse of a chaotic jumble of discarded candle lanterns, blankets, pieces of bread, packing cases, a bag of clothes spilling out over the floor – all the signs of a rapid departure.

He mounted the stairs. The rooms in the upper level were similarly deserted. He threw caution to the winds and shouted, his voice unnaturally loud in the darkness, his heart beating fast.

"Anteia! Octavius! Calpurnia!"

The only sound was the rumbling of the volcano.

"Anteia," he moaned. He tried to fight down the emotions that were rising into his throat.

Another tremor shook the villa and he staggered. Whatever that old man had said, the danger was not over yet.

He worked his way back to the entrance and ran swiftly over to his father's villa. It was in the same condition.

"Father! Mother! Junius!"

No reply. His spirits drained away. Until now he'd managed to stay focused on the one goal: he had to get back to Anteia, back to his family, back to the villa. He'd done it; he'd achieved his goal. And they had gone, all of them.

He wandered through the empty villa, ending up in his own chamber. So far as he could tell, it was as he'd left it. He plucked at his torn and soiled tunic, on which the smell of dung lingered, then quickly stripped it off and slipped on a clean one from a stack in the corner. Then he knelt by the low bed and reached underneath until his fingers contacted his spare leather purse. He put the purse on and felt around inside it. The contents seemed to be intact: some coins – he'd left a few hundred sesterces there – a set of waxed tablets and a stilus. He straightened up. He was ready to join the others – if only he knew where they'd gone.

He put his hands to his temples, trying to think. The plan had been to take the road to Stabiae, but that was before the mountain had exploded. It would be impossible now; every road was awash with a river of humanity. Where were they? Who would know? There was no one left to ask, no one who could help him. Wait...

...there was someone!

Chapter 10

"Gavius!"

Cornelius stood on the pebbles at an upper window of the small house and rapped on the shutter with his knuckles.

"Gavius!" he called again.

He stepped back and tried to remember whether the alley to the right led to the courtyard at the rear of the house. As he stood there he glimpsed a light moving in the upper levels of the inn next door. His hopes rose. Then he heard unfamiliar voices and laughter.

A window opened and two men climbed out carrying a large amphora. One stood there, swaying slightly, while the other went back inside. The light shifted and he glimpsed leather armour.

Gladiators! And they were looting!

The man looked up and saw him.

Cornelius felt a surge of revulsion.

"And you a gladiator!" he said. "Have you no shame?"

The man stiffened and began to approach menacingly.

"Who is it who talks to me of shame?" he said.

"I am Cornelius, son of General Claudius Fratellus!"

"Well, son of a General, meet Frucius!"

The fist came out of the darkness, catching him in the stomach. He doubled over and fell back against the wall of Gavius's house, pain and nausea flooding through his body.

Lightning caught the flash of a blade. There was a brief pause, then out of the ensuing darkness came a cry and a prolonged gurgling sound.

A candle lantern appeared at the window.

"Frucius? Where are you?"

The lantern came out further and moved to one side, then the other, then stopped abruptly.

"Frucius!"

The gladiator was lying on the stones, eyes rolled up, blood still spurting from the wound in his throat. The light swung round to catch Cornelius leaning against the wall, breathing hard, a bloody stilus still in his hand.

The man set the lantern down.

"You little..."

Cornelius heard the ring of metal as the gladiator drew his sword. The gladius lifted and Cornelius prepared to receive the fatal blow.

There was another sound and the gladius remained in the air. Beneath it, blocking the blow, was a second sword.

"Gavius!"

"Run, Cornelius. I'll look after this one."

Cornelius heard the sliding of the blades as the man stepped back. Then he attacked. The light from the lantern cast giant shadows on the walls of the houses as the blades met again. Cornelius watched, frozen in terror. Gavius was an experienced soldier but he was a much older man. This young gladiator was a professional fighter, practising his art for hours a day. He knew that the life of his friend and tutor hung by a thread.

It seemed to go on for ever, the blades clashing in semi-darkness, lit from time to time by a flicker of lightning. They met low, then high, close to the hilts, and the gladiator pressed down. There was a sudden movement, a grunt, a long gasp, and the sound of someone falling. Then silence. Cornelius strained to see. A figure stepped out of the darkness.

"The old pugio trick," came the voice. "Works every time."

"Gavius! The Gods be praised!"

He ran forward and embraced the old soldier, then recoiled, his hand sticky with blood.

"You're wounded!"

"Not too badly, I think. The light was very tricky. He caught me up here."

Cornelius went to get the lantern and lifted it to see blood pouring from a deep gash in Gavius's left upper arm.

"We need to bind that," he said, putting the lantern down and preparing to remove his tunic.

"No need to use yours," said Gavius. "Take his, he won't be needing it."

Cornelius looked at him and then at the fallen gladiator. Suppressing his distaste, he took the razor-sharp pugio from Gavius and cut a long strip from the hem of the man's tunic. Gavius offered his arm and he wound the strip round several times, cut the end lengthways to make two tails, and tied it over the wound.

"That's the best I can do. Is it too tight?"

"No, it's fine." He picked up the lantern with his other hand. "Take his gladius, too, my friend," he said. "You might need it."

As Cornelius went about removing the belt and scabbard from the dead gladiator Gavius held the lantern over the other one.

"Stilus?" he asked.

"Yes. I had it in my hand when I came up. He didn't see it in the darkness."

"Why did you go for the throat?"

"I couldn't be sure of the body. He was wearing leather armour."

"Quite right. Well, you caught him perfectly. I've taught you well."

"And thus you have saved my life – twice."

"Where did you go, Cornelius? We were looking everywhere for you."

"I was kidnapped, but I managed to get away. When I got back both the villas were deserted, ours and Octavius's. The households must have left together. I was hoping I'd find you here."

"Well I wouldn't still be here if I had a horse – you can be very sure of that; I'd be galloping through the open countryside. But I haven't got a horse so I thought I'd try some friends down at the port. It's hopeless. The lagoon has drained; it's total confusion down there, like everywhere else. So I came back here – and who should I find but my young apprentice, taking on two gladiators."

Cornelius smiled ruefully. "I had not intended to. I was looking for you. I was hoping you might know where the two families had gone."

"I'm sorry, Cornelius. No one said anything to me."

The youth's shoulders drooped.

"I'm adrift, Gavius. My family's gone; Anteia has gone. You were the last hope I had of finding them."

"Don't despair, my young friend." He put his good arm around Cornelius's shoulders. "Listen, I served for many years with your father and I know a little about the way his mind works. Like I said, nobody's getting away by sea. I'm sure the General would avoid the roads too; they're jammed with people and he's always been a great believer in mobility. No, he'd travel cross-country just as I would, given the choice. The question is: where to? He wouldn't go north, towards that fearful mountain. He could go east, to Nuceria. Or south into the hills. The question is, which?"

"Well, in either case they would have to ford the Sarno."

"You have it! We'll follow the bank of the Sarno inland until we see their crossing place. It won't be hard to find – not with a group that size – and there we'll pick up the trail."

"You will come with me?"

"Well of course I'm coming with you. You don't think I'd let you go on your own, do you? Come back inside the house. We'll pick up some bread and water, and a few more candles for this lantern, and some torches."

As they emerged from the house, he said, "You know, I'd wager they've made for the hills. Your father once said to me, 'Gavius, always retreat to high ground. Then if the enemy catches up, you have at least one strategic advantage: height.' Habits like that die hard."

"But they must have left hours ago."

"A couple of hours, not much more – they wouldn't have left while the stones were still falling. And I expect they're heavily loaded so they won't be moving fast, especially uphill. One way and another they can't have got very far. Come on, my friend, cheer up! As we go you can tell me how you escaped. I want the full story."

Chapter 11

The party toiled slowly up towards the pass. No one spoke. The only sounds were the creaking of the wagon, the snorting of the horses, and the ever-present thunder of Vesuvius. Lightning flickered through the blackness overhead, and from time to time the landscape was illuminated redly by a flame from the mountain before it vanished into the thick smoke that still poured into the sky from the shattered peak.

Junius led the horses. In the wagon, the women huddled under the improvised shelter of the table. Although they were packed around with bags and crates they were thrown from side to side as the wheels climbed and fell over the uneven ground. They made no complaint. The slaves, all carrying bundles, were beginning to fall back in a line that straggled down the hill.

Claudius was still armed and armoured. With Octavius, Oppius and Fulvius he patrolled the group constantly, trying to keep them together; one of them would even shoulder a load himself for a while, to enable a woman to catch up with the rest.

The slopes were littered with pebbles. Claudius stooped to pick one up, weighed it in his hand, and turned it over, frowning. Sponge-stones had fallen; even at this great distance.

As he straightened up he noticed a light that was bobbing about, a short distance below. He stared, trying to make sense of it; something down there seemed to be burning. Then the light moved – it was a torch! He heard a shout. With a low cry he hurried towards the sound.

Cornelius put down the torch and ran into his father's open arms. Claudius held him close. He was blinking back tears of relief, and for once he was glad of the darkness that concealed it from his son.

"Cornelius!" he gasped. "I did not dare to hope you were still alive!"

"I owe my life to Gavius."

Claudius released him, and gave Gavius his hand.

"Your son is as modest as he is valiant, General," Gavius said. "He escaped two would-be murderers and killed a gladiator with a stilus before I took a hand."

Claudius laughed, unable to put into words his relief, wonder and pride. Then he exclaimed: "What am I thinking of? Cornelius, go quickly, join the others. Your mother has been distracted ever since your disappearance. To say nothing of Anteia."

With new-found energy, Cornelius bounded up the hill.

Claudius watched him go. Then he picked up the torch and looked round, but Gavius had sunk to his knees. Claudius glimpsed a gleaming red arm below a blood-soaked bandage.

"Gavius! Old soldier, you're wounded. Let me help you."

He hooked Gavius's right arm around his neck, gripping the wrist and taking the man's weight. The torch, held aloft in his other hand, illuminated their way up the hill, where they came upon an emotional reunion. Cornelius and Anteia were holding one another tightly. Octavius looked on happily, his arms around the shoulders of Calpurnia and Cottia.

"Oh, Calpurnia." Cottia said, wiping her eyes. "I thought I had no more tears to shed, and yet I find more for this moment."

Claudius lifted Gavius onto the wagon. He waved away the man's protests. "You've done quite enough, my friend. The time has come for us to look after you."

He approached the others. There was a low conversation and then he fetched Cornelius and Anteia to join the group. "Listen carefully, Cornelius. Ahead, there's a pass through the mountains. That way lies safety. But we're a large party and it will take time for us to reach it. We want you and Anteia to ride ahead."

"But father, surely my place is with you..."

"My son, even valiant young soldiers must learn to take orders."

"But we are safe now, aren't we?"

"Who can say? Our lovely mountain has proved to be a

sleeping monster. It casts a long shadow and we could yet find ourselves within its embrace. You must hurry. Take Sylvian. He's a strong horse with a great heart. Ride him over the pass and do not rest until you reach the sea. Then head east for Salernum and there seek out Lucanus Maximus. He's a kinsman of your mother's and he'll take good care of you both. Junius? Untie Sylvian from the yoke. Simius?"

"Sir?"

"You are light of foot and we achieve nothing by keeping you here with us. I give you your freedom. Run up and over the pass and may Mercury lend you speed."

"The Gods preserve you, master. Freedman or not, if ever I find your house again I'd be proud to serve you."

With these words the boy turned and scampered up the hill, disappearing instantly into the darkness.

Cornelius's arrival had lightened their spirits, but once he'd left with Anteia the weight descended again. In the wagon Gavius rocked silently from side to side with the three women. Ulixes was drawing alone now and, willing and muscular as the big dappled grey was, the load was clearly taxing him. After half an hour he stopped abruptly. Junius lifted a whip, but Claudius hurried up.

"Stay your hand, Junius. These animals sometimes sense things we do not."

All stood still: the horse's ears swivelled, the men remained alert, the slaves stopped, or sank to the ground with a sigh, glad of the respite. Then they heard it.

To start with, it was no more than a faint rumble that grew out of the noise of the eruption, but it became louder and louder. They stared down the hill, trying to penetrate the darkness. Glimmers of red light winked and disappeared all across the landscape, like lanterns held by a line abreast of chariots, a long line that was approaching at unconscionable speed. Then a vivid flash of lightning illuminated a cloud many miles wide and hundreds of feet high rushing over the ground towards Pompeii.

"What is it?" whispered Octavius.

Claudius shook his head. "I've seen cavalry charging on a dusty plain, but the greatest army in the world does not raise a cloud like this, nor travel at one tenth of its speed."

In a few seconds the roar died.

They waited and watched, hoping another flash of lightning would reveal more to them. When it came, all they could see was a high cloud billowing and folding over the very edge of the city.

"It seems to be stopped by the northern wall," Claudius said.

"A terrible sight! I fear for the people who live in the villas outside the Herculaneum Gate."

"The villa of Diomedes is one of them. I wish he had responded to my invitation. Perhaps they escaped or found refuge."

"Ahh!"

"Octavius? What is it?"

"Something stung my face. Ahh, there it is again!"

Claudius's voice rang out. "Everyone, move forward! Turn your backs on Pompeii. The air is full of ash from the fire of Vesuvius. Carry your bundles on your heads. Cover your faces."

The slaves murmured and grumbled, the wagon wheels started to creak again and the group began to move. All around them the hot ash was floating down, blanketing the slopes. Claudius circulated with redoubled energy, slipping and sliding on the treacherous surface but urging everyone to hurry. He heard a child's cries and came across Fannia. Her little son was at her side, hopping from one foot to the other.

"What's the matter with him?" demanded Claudius.

"Sir, his feet are yet tender and the ash is burning them. I'd carry him but I cannot manage him as well as this bundle."

"Give him to me. I'll find a place for him on the wagon. What is his name?"

"Victor, sir."

"Come, Victor. I will not see a small child suffer like this."

"The Gods reward your kindness, sir."

The ash began to fall less thickly. The slaves shifted their bundles and settled into a steady climb. Then gradually, the eerie grey landscape reddened. Glancing over his shoulder, Claudius saw flames shooting again from the fiery torch of the mountain. Within minutes huge shards of glowing rock were arcing through the sky and falling among them. A goat squealed in agony as it was crushed by a red-hot boulder. Gavius and the women shrank back under the flimsy shelter afforded by the table.

Someone shouted, "Lutulla has fallen!"

Junius relinquished the halter, called for another slave to take his place, and ran to her.

She was on her back, eyes open, her bundle near outstretched fingers. To her other side a great stony mass sat smoking in the grass. Junius bent to raise her gently, his hand cupped around the back of her head. Then his fingers slipped unobstructed through her hair and into something soft. He slowly withdrew the blood-stained fingers, turned his face to the blackened heavens and let out an animal howl that chilled every spine.

Claudius and Octavius hurried back to him. The General laid a hand on the big man's shoulder, feeling it quake.

"Come, Junius," he said gently, trying to control his voice. Familiar as he was with battlefield casualties, the sight of that burnished black face streaming with tears was as much as he could bear. "Junius, there is nothing you can do for her now."

"Please, sir, leave me with her," Junius sobbed. "As I have been your faithful servant, in peace as in war, now leave me behind to be with her."

"Very well," Claudius answered softly. "I am truly sorry, Junius. Farewell, old friend."

In the red twilight cast by Vesuvius, the slaves stood as silent as statues, watching Junius rocking back and forth, the lifeless body of Lutulla in his arms. Octavius and Claudius climbed slowly past them, heads bowed.

The mountain air was no longer sweet, and Claudius felt strangely light-headed and short of breath. He saw Octavius falter and put a hand to his head and knew that he was experiencing the same odd sensations.

The light cast by the mountain faded and the deadly rain of rock ceased. They moved forward again, but it seemed to call for an even greater effort.

Then they heard that sound again, a distant thunder that came ever closer, grew, and died. Within minutes another came, longer and louder than before. They knew in their hearts that this time the deadly cloud had overwhelmed the whole city of Pompeii.

The wagon halted as one wheel became wedged between two rocks. Claudius, Octavius and Oppius helped their wives down, and Fulvius assisted Gavius. Suddenly alone, little Victor looked about him and his lower lip began to tremble, but Fannia stepped up, lifted him off the wagon, and crouched down a short distance away, hugging him tightly to her.

A great lethargy seemed to have settled on everyone. They stood or sat on the ground, gasping. It was as if those racing clouds of ash had robbed them of the very air they breathed.

Claudius stood motionless, looking at the wagon. Strength was leaking from his own limbs. He could not command the slaves to do what he no longer had the will to accomplish himself. He turned away from the wagon.

He felt an overwhelming sense of loss. Something huge, something too terrible to grasp, had befallen his beloved Pompeii. Step by step their world – possibly the entire world – was being extinguished, and their stricken souls would be crying into emptiness for centuries to come.

He surveyed the scene. In the feeble light, he could see only pathetic white heaps scattered down the hillside. It resembled the aftermath of a battle, the exhausted lying in their own sweat, waiting for life to return, and the wounded in their own blood, waiting for life to ebb away. Claudius tossed his helmet aside. It bounced and rolled down the hill. He sank to one knee and cradled Cottia in his arms. Her breathing was fast, her small body straining with the effort.

She turned her face up to him. "It is over."

"Yes. I have failed."

"No, you have prevailed. Cornelius lives, and your good name lives in him."

"May the Gods protect them both."

Strange colours swam across his vision. His mind drifted and it took a great effort to bring it back into focus.

"My dear Cottia, I have one thing left to do. Ulixes never failed me, even in the midst of battle, and I will not fail him now."

He rose with difficulty and walked slowly and unevenly back to the wagon and to his beloved horse. The harness jingled as the animal tossed its head. He drew his gladius and stood, swaying for a moment. The horse snorted and looked round at him. He lifted the gladius.

He cut through the halter and the saddle harness and brushed them aside. The horse stood free and faced Claudius, ears turned towards him, waiting for a command. He filled his aching lungs, slapped the horse on the rump, and shouted "Go! Go, old friend. Now."

The horse snorted, walked a few paces, paused, and with one last look at its master began to canter towards the pass.

The gladius, too heavy now for Claudius's weakening fingers, slipped from his grasp and clattered to the ground. He returned to Cottia and took her in his arms. She placed her slender fingers on his jaw and kissed him.

"Noblest of men," she whispered. "Short though my life has been, I would not have shared it with any other."

And now the sound came again, a deep-throated roar that grew and grew without limit so that it dwarfed anything that had gone before. The ground trembled at its approach and the sound swelled until it filled the entire landscape and the earth and the air vibrated as one and there was nothing now but the sound.

The sound faded, but they heard no more.

Lightning laced the black clouds. A dappled grey horse stood outlined on a ridge. He lifted his great head and fanned his nostrils, scenting the air for the subtle coloration left behind by his stablemate and the young master. Then he stepped forward and began the long descent to the sea.

PART 2

Oxford, England

Chapter 12

The house was set well back from the road. Nick opened the front gate and started down the path, his practised eye taking in the details. Georgian, faced with limestone. It probably had five or six bedrooms and two or three high-ceilinged reception rooms. The garden was large, well-tended. No way did he buy this on an Oxford professor's salary. The money must be from her.

"Go carefully, Roberts," Detective Chief Superintendent Allison had said, over a desktop totally unencumbered by paperwork – a constant source of wonder to Nick, whose own desk was always piled high. "I'm telling you this woman is well connected." Allison placed his thumbs against the edge of the desk and tapped briskly with his fingers. "She's been an art critic for the Times, she's editor of some glossy art magazine, and she's on the boards of several galleries and museums. She's also on a committee that advises the Minister for Culture, Media and Sports. She knows just the right buttons to press and by God she's pressing all of them right now. The Home Office is doing what it can, but it wants us out there, working with the Italian police. The Chief Constable's passed it down to me. I want you to take it on. I've picked you because you can show a modicum of tact – when you put your mind to it. Between the Italian police and this lady you're going to need it."

What was she like, then, this woman? Small and overbearing, he'd decided. Waspish tongue. One of those irritating people who talks over you, won't let you get a word in edgeways.

He approached the front door, rang the bell, and glanced at his watch. Right on time. That, at least, was a good start.

The door opened. He blinked.

"Mrs Lockhart?"

"Yes."

He showed her his badge. "Detective Inspector Nick Roberts. I believe you're expecting me."

She gave the badge a glance, then appraised him with eyes that were an astonishing colour, green rimmed with hazel. He met her scrutiny unflinchingly, mainly because he was conducting an appraisal of his own.

His preconceptions had gone out the window. She was tall and elegant. She wore a suit made of some silky plum-coloured material: matching trousers, sweater, and a draped jacket that finished at mid-thigh. Her left hand rested lightly on the door and the sleeve had fallen back to reveal a narrow gold watch strap. She wore no other jewellery. Not beauty in the conventional sense, he thought, but the sort of handsome features that got better and better with time. He guessed she was in her mid-forties.

She stepped aside.

"Come in, Inspector." The voice was low and well modulated.

He followed her through an oak-panelled hall. She moved with smooth grace, and for some reason it made him feel large and clumsy. She opened double doors and they entered a spacious sitting room. He gazed around in wonderment. The place was full of artifacts, seemingly from all over the world. Without thinking he began to wander down one side of the room, looking at vessels made of pottery, some glazed and richly decorated, others clearly pieced together from fragments; goblets made of silver and glass; a metal ladle; brooches and buckles, covered with verdigris; a case containing coins; glass vials, presumably for oils or perfume; some primitive statuettes; a small collection of flint arrowheads and bone fish-hooks; a bracelet exquisitely fashioned from gold wire and tiny brick-orange and pale blue beads... He suddenly became conscious of what he was doing and turned back to her.

"Sorry," he said. "I didn't mean to be nosy. It's just that I never expected to see a collection like this outside of a museum. Superbly displayed, too."

"Thank you, Inspector, I'm glad you like it. Shall we sit down?"

Two large soft sofas were arranged on either side of a low table in front of the fireplace. She indicated one and took a seat on the other, facing him across the table. She crossed her legs elegantly and waited for him to start the conversation. So much for getting a word in edgeways.

He cleared his throat. "The Chief Super briefed me about the conversation you had with the CC – the Chief Constable. I know it's tedious, but it'd be helpful if you could go over the same ground with me, just in case he left things out. Also it'd give me a chance to ask you questions. Is that all right with you?"

She shrugged. "There's not a lot to tell," she said. "When Julian's away he normally phones me every day or every other day, just to make sure everything's all right. I hadn't heard from him for two days. Then Alex came to see me – Alex Cothill. He's a colleague of Julian's, a geophysicist. He went out there to help, but he couldn't stay for the whole dig; he had to come back to supervise some research here. The morning he left he was aiming to have a word with Julian, to see if there was anything he wanted him to do back in Oxford, or anything he needed to have sent out. But Julian wasn't around. None of the vehicles had gone so he thought Julian must be sick but he wasn't in his quarters and he couldn't find him anywhere else. Alex spoke to Enrico Montalcini – he's the joint expedition leader. He didn't seem too bothered but he said if Julian didn't turn up soon he would contact the police. Alex was quite worried. He didn't want to alarm me but he thought I ought to know because he wasn't convinced Montalcini was going to do much about it. He was wondering if I could pull a few strings and get the police to check it out."

"You have influence in Italy?"

"I have a few contacts, yes. And I speak good Italian, which helps."

"And...?"

"It was infuriating. I spoke to the local Commissario. He was unbelievably condescending. In these cases, he said, nine times out of ten the missing person reappears after a few days, maybe a few weeks. He made some innuendoes of the 'boys will be boys' variety."

"Which you discounted?"

She looked across at him sharply. "Of course."

He waited, expecting more. She clearly sensed it. "Look, Inspector, I know what you're thinking. There are nubile, impressionable young girls on the dig. Maybe he's having a fling."

"I didn't say..."

"Well let me tell you. Julian's totally professional when it comes to students. We have a stable marriage and two lovely daughters and he's very attached to them. We've had our ups and downs, like anyone else..."

"Arguments?"

"Yes, of course."

"What about?"

"What about? Who knows? It always seems important at the time. Afterwards you can't even remember what you got so worked up about."

"Did you have an argument just before he went away?"

"Look, it's my private life we're talking about. Is this line of questioning really necessary?"

"Necessary? No. Helpful? Yes. If I'm to do my job properly I need to get inside the minds of the people involved, understand how they'd react in a given situation. Any situation. You can help me to do that. Is he contented, or frustrated? Is he happy with his lot, or ambitious for more? If someone tried to mug him would he hand over his wallet or have a go?"

"I can tell you that. He'd have a go. Once when we were in Florence a young man tried to steal my handbag. Julian was livid.

90

He punched him out. If I hadn't restrained him I think he would have killed the poor chap."

"What happened then?"

"The man picked himself up off the pavement and ran away. It would surprise me if his jaw wasn't broken, though. Julian fetched him a humdinger."

"So Julian was violent?"

"Violent?" She laughed. "No, very gentle, normally, but you wouldn't want to get him worked up, that's all."

"Was he ever violent with you?"

She looked at him patiently. "I see. Husband beats wife, abuses daughters. Wife arranges to have him killed hundreds of miles away and calls in the police to make herself look innocent."

He smiled ruefully. This woman was as sharp as a razor. No wonder the Chief Super had warned him.

"Okay, forget that," he said. "So what were things like between you before he left?"

She shrugged. "All right. We had a bit of a row over Sophie. Sophie's my youngest daughter. Kendra's at the University of Bristol, but Sophie's just started A-levels. She likes her local school but she hasn't been doing all that well there. I thought there were too many distractions. I made arrangements to have her moved to another school. When Julian's away I have to make these domestic decisions on my own. Sometimes when he gets back he doesn't agree with everything I've done. It's not easy. I have professional commitments too."

"So you had a row about it. Was it resolved?"

"Yes. Well, not at first but he phoned me after he'd been in Italy for a couple of days and we talked it through. We'll try the new school for a term or two and if she's not happy we'll reconsider it."

"Okay. And he's never gone missing before this."

"No. When he's on a dig he's totally focused. He's living two thousand years ago, visualizing how things were, fitting each piece into the picture. He can hardly bear to be away from it, let alone go missing."

"Have you considered the possibility that he's been kidnapped?"

"It crossed my mind, of course. But it's been three days now and there's been no ransom demand, not even a claim of responsibility." She swallowed and dropped her voice. "Something's happened to him. I'm convinced of it."

He was aware of the tension mounting inside her. It was as if she was walking towards a precipice. He needed to steer her away.

"It's early days yet, Mrs. Lockhart. Let's not assume the worst."

She nodded.

He watched her carefully. "If you feel up to it, do you think we could talk a bit about his job? I'm afraid I'm rather ignorant when it comes to archaeology. This collection, for instance. Is that what it's all about? Collecting treasures like this?"

"No, no, that's not what it's all about. Archaeology is... It's like unfolding a story, a story about a civilization. How they lived, how they dressed, what materials and skills they used, how their society was organized..."

She got up and he followed her over to a display.

"Artifacts like these give us a window into their world. It so happens that the things they valued are often preserved, and we value them too. That's no accident. If you bury a gold ring for a thousand years, it comes out as bright as new. Do the same thing with iron, and you find a heap of rust. Precious metals retain their lustre because they're so unreactive. That's why they're precious."

"So all these are things your husband brought back from his digs?"

"Not all of them, no. My husband's reputation is international. We entertain visitors from around the world and they often bring gifts. These arrowheads and fish-hooks, for example, came from a colleague at Harvard; they're early native American. This beautiful bracelet," she indicated the bracelet made of gold wire and orange and blue beads, "is from ancient Egypt. They presented that to him when he gave a lecture series in Cairo.

Julian acquired most of the Roman artifacts himself, though. That's his particular area of expertise."

"I would have thought museums would want stuff like that."

"Some of it, not all. You see, the real value of a find like this," she rested slim fingers on a large pottery jar, "is that it helps them to identify the date of the site and what it was used for. Also it might say something about the wealth of the occupants or the extent to which they used to import goods from other places. This amphora, for instance, had contained oil, so it may have been found in a shop, or the kitchen of a tavern or large house. This one here probably contained wine. They're fairly commonplace, but you find other items and together they start to build up a picture. Once you've finished, the items themselves can be a bit of an embarrassment. They've got to be stored somewhere but not everyone wants them."

"What about gold and silver items? I mean, they'd be worth something for their scrap value alone."

"The exceptional ones are extremely valuable, of course: hundreds of thousands of pounds. There are normally constraints on a dig that make it clear how items like that are to be disposed of. But the museums will only take so much. Most of them have enough Roman coins and amphorae; they don't want any more. Julian represents the interests of the Ashmolean if the terms of the grant allow it, and they purchase some of the better items on his recommendation. And some he purchases himself, for me."

"What's this?" he asked. "It looks like a soup ladle."

"No, not a soup ladle! It's a simpulum, a silver ladle used for serving wine. Of course they never drank the wine straight – it would have been lacking in refinement. Look, this is what they did."

She picked up a silver bowl and handed it to him. He accepted it nervously. He'd seen objects like this in museums but he'd never expected to handle one. Shouldn't he be wearing white gloves? She held out the simpulum and he took that from her too. Then she placed a silver goblet on the shelf in front of him, next to an amphora.

"Now, Inspector, you have to imagine that you are a slave in a grand household two thousand years ago. Your job is to mix the wine. You unseal the amphora, dip your simpulum into the wine, pour a little into a goblet, and hand it to your master – or in this case, your mistress." She paused. "Go on, then, do it."

He looked at her uncertainly and back at the objects in his hands. Then he went through the motions of dipping the ladle into the jar and filling the goblet. He handed the goblet to her. She passed it under her nose and pretended to take a sip. She nodded once and gestured to the room.

"The wine is good. The master gives you the signal to serve his guests. Now you pour wine into the krater... " she waited for him to mime the action with the bowl, "and then you mix it with water, and sweeten it with melted honey, and cool it with snow... "

He stopped, confused. She laughed and, to his relief, put the objects back onto the display shelves.

"Now you know what Julian does. He projects himself into the past, recreates the moment, puts it together." She sighed. "I often wish I'd done archaeology myself. Having a husband doing it is the next best thing."

Her expression suddenly hardened and she turned away, a small muscle twitching in her jaw. He had a strong urge to reach out to her, but suddenly she was facing him again, her expression open, her voice pleasant.

"Would you like some coffee?"

"Oh. That's very kind. Thanks."

She indicated the room with a delicate turning gesture of one hand. "I won't be long. Please make yourself comfortable."

Alone in the room, he tried to recover some sort of equilibrium.

He walked along the displays again, examining the artifacts, trying to conjure up the sensations she'd been talking about. It was hopeless: all he could see was a bunch of museum specimens. To him, the past was an impenetrable barrier; the people who lived in those times – the ones who made or used these objects – might as well not have existed.

He'd never thought of himself as being unimaginative, so it must be a void in his education. It left him with a distinct feeling of inadequacy.

He reached the end windows, paused, and looked out onto the garden. Then he turned back to the room.

A burglar alarm fixture winked red and green at him from the far corner of the ceiling. That, at least, was something he knew about.

Movement and heat sensor, he thought. *Fair enough, the place has to be secure with this sort of stuff around.* The display was worthy of a superb museum and yet integrated into a comfortable living area, with the usual books, paintings, soft furnishings, photographs...

He went over to the photographs. Two teenaged girls, presumably their daughters, tall and slender like their mother. In the next frame a young man squatting on his heels, trowel in one hand, on a sandy landscape pitted with holes. It seemed as if he'd looked up at the camera at the last moment, his face partly shaded by a wide-brimmed felt hat...

"Jericho," a voice said.

Chapter 13

She was standing behind him, holding a silver tray. She carried it past him and set it down on the low table in front of the fireplace.

"Jericho," she continued, "is a good example of what I was telling you about. There were a lot of very old skeletons, far too many to examine in detail. The museums didn't want them. We've got one in the house, actually, but I keep it in the attic. I don't like to display things like that. To some people it's just an interesting collection of bones. Not to me. I can't forget that it was a person once."

"And this is your husband in the photograph, presumably."

"Yes, that's Julian. Taken during his first dig. Before I met him."

"Do you have any more recent pictures?"

"I thought you'd ask me that. You can have these."

She took a large manila envelope from the table and handed it to him. He withdrew some photographs and leafed through them quickly. The portraits showed a clean-shaven, weathered face, a heavily cleft chin, crow's feet around the eyes, probably from squinting too much into the sun. There were some group pictures. Julian wasn't hard to spot; he towered over the others. He had the build of an athlete, perhaps a distance runner.

"If it's all right with you I'd like to have these copied. Then I'll return them to you."

"As you wish."

She took her seat on the sofa again and he hastened to take his place opposite her. The silver tray was lined with a lacy white cloth. She pushed the plunger on the cafetière and poured coffee for both of them. As she handed him the bone china cup and saucer they seemed large in her hands yet small in his. He'd seldom felt so clumsy and ill at ease.

"Help yourself to cream and sugar, Inspector."

"I'll take it black, thanks," he said. "Look, you don't have to call me Inspector. Actually I'd feel a lot more comfortable if you called me Nick."

She inclined her head. He was trying to build a relationship with this woman, but he knew she could see through that.

"Did Julian – I mean Professor Lockhart – know the other people on the dig?"

"I think he must have met Enrico Montalcini at conferences, but he hadn't worked with him before."

"How did they he get on?"

"Not terribly well, actually. To start with he didn't say much about it when he phoned, but I gathered they were arguing quite a bit. Then there was a problem about a gold ring they'd turned up during the dig. A ring with an intaglio."

"Sorry, I ought to remember what that is, but I don't."

"It's a semiprecious stone, engraved with a design: a portrait, or animal or something like that. This one was a carnelian, and from the inscription on the ring they knew it had belonged to a Roman General. It was a really important clue to the identity of the people they'd found in the dig. But when he went to take another look at it, Montalcini denied it had ever existed. Julian was incensed. They had a major row about it. A day or so later he disappeared."

Nick nodded, making a mental note.

"Who else was there?"

"Well, Julian and Alex went out together. Montalcini had someone with him too, I think. From what I gather the rest of the team was mostly made up of summer students. Something to do with the terms of the grant. Designed to give young people opportunities, that sort of thing."

"You've mentioned the terms of the grant several times. It sounds like something I ought to check out." It was always worth following a money trail.

"I don't know the details. But the University administers all these grants. You could contact the Research Support Office. They'd have a copy of the conditions."

"Good. I'll do that."

"All right, and what are you going to do after that, Nick? Time's getting on."

"Well, the Chief Super's had discussions with the police in Naples. He's normally reluctant to call for a joint operation. These things can be pretty sensitive, you know – if we tread too heavily on the Italians' toes it could be counterproductive. But they have agreed to us sending two people out there to assist in their enquiries."

"You and...?"

"Well, I wouldn't necessarily be going myself..."

She gave a short laugh. Then she fixed him with those strange green eyes.

"Let's be practical, shall we?" she said. "I know the Chief Superintendent has made you Senior Investigating Officer on the case. And you know as well as I do that you won't be able to run things from here. So you'll have to be there yourself, won't you?"

He swallowed. He was picturing the pile of work on his desk.

"I'll ask the Chief."

"You do that. But don't let it delay you making your travel arrangements."

He was constantly off balance with this woman. One moment he'd be worrying about her vulnerability and the next moment a steel hand would emerge from the velvet glove. She knew how to apply pressure all right but she was clever; she only did it when she felt it was necessary. Then suddenly a soft touch:

"Don't feel badly about it, Nick. You came here to establish some sort of rapport with me. Well, you've succeeded. I have confidence in you. That's why I want it to be you out there, looking for him." Her voice caught. "If he is dead I'll have to learn to live with it. God knows it won't be easy."

He frowned. "Mrs. Lockhart..."

"Dawn," she supplied, unexpectedly.

"Dawn, he's only been missing three days. The way I see it, there's still a good possibility he's alive."

Her lips set.

"And if he's not?"

"If he's not? Well, I'm afraid all I can do then is try to bring the perpetrators to justice."

"Justice." For a moment she fell silent. "Is that what I want? I'm not even sure it is. What I need is some sort of resolution. It's not knowing one way or the other – that's what makes it so unbearable."

He nodded. "I understand that. I'll do my best."

"That's all I'm asking for. I'm not expecting miracles."

He got up to go. She led the way to the front door.

"Obviously if there's any progress I'll let you know," he said, then hesitated. "This may be a trying time for you, Dawn. Is there anyone you can call on for support...?"

"That's very thoughtful of you, Nick. My daughters and I are very close. We'll support each other. I'll do what I can to smooth the way for you. Call me if you think I can do anything else. There are still a few arms out there I haven't twisted yet."

"Thanks, I will. Goodbye."

Chapter 14

The Research Support Office was an open-plan affair, with a dozen or so secretaries sitting in front of computer monitors.

The Director showed Nick into his private office.

"I'm sorry I couldn't give you a bit more notice, Mr. Matthison," Nick said. "I'd greatly appreciate it if you could spare a few moments of your time, though."

"Yes, yes, of course. This is most disturbing news, Inspector. Do you have any idea at all what's happened to him?"

"Not yet. We may be able to tell more when we get there. But I need some background from you. I take it you're acquainted with Professor Lockhart?"

"Oh yes. We sometimes work together on his applications. Full Economic Costing's a bit of a minefield, I'm afraid, and the staff aren't used to it yet."

"So you know about the funding he has for this dig in Italy."

"Of course. We had to scrutinize it very carefully."

"Oh? Why was that?"

"Well, to be perfectly frank, Inspector, archaeology isn't the biggest source of grant revenue in the University. Professor Lockhart has done better than most, but it isn't easy to find support – substantial support, I mean. He's had a few grants from the British Council and they've been straightforward to administer, although I know he had to work very hard to get them. This one was new to him and new to us. And I gather it more or less fell in his lap."

"So where did it come from?"

"The Pliny Institute," Matthison said. "It's a charity registered in Italy. Only Italian citizens can apply. It seems this Professor Montalcini had made some sort of fortunate discovery in the Naples area and he wanted to conduct a full-blown investigation.

The Institute was an ideal source of support, but they needed a high profile collaborator, preferably one who could bring geophysics expertise with him. So they contacted Professor Lockhart. The grant was substantial. He couldn't believe his luck."

"Anything special about the conditions?"

"Yes, a number of things. I have it here – I got the folder out after you phoned." He opened a yellow pocket folder and withdrew a sheaf of papers. "Here's the Mission Statement. 'To support the rediscovery of any period of Italy's rich past and to provide interesting and motivating employment for young people'. Now, Conditions of Award... "

Nick noticed that a number of passages had been marked with a highlighter pen.

"Much of this stuff's routine. 'First refusal on material of cultural or historical value will be given to the J. Paul Getty Foundation.' I gather that's a quid pro quo – the Institute gets a substantial donation from them. 'Personnel: the Institute will underwrite the costs of travel and subsistence for up to four permanent members of staff of a university, museum or research institute, and up to ten young people, not in permanent employment.'"

Matthison ran his finger down the pages, reading out selected passages. "All temporary posts are to be advertised... applicants to be not more than thirty years of age... do not necessarily have to be in full-time education, although preference will be given to postgraduates, or undergraduates in their final year of studies.... The Institute will have a representative on the selection panel, with a view to ensuring that the composition of the group complies with equal opportunities legislation... This one's interesting: they supply an Apple laptop computer and a Canon digital SLR camera for each investigation, and the cost of these don't have to be included in the application."

"That's unusual?"

"Yes. Normally you'd have to include things like that in the equipment component of the grant. They say, let's see, where is it...? Yes, here it is. 'The Institute is committed to the most modern methods of archaeological investigation. All finds are to be recorded digitally on site, and the information is to be stored on a single database, which will be relayed at regular intervals to the Institute's central computer facility to ensure security. To this end, a laptop computer will be provided, equipped with a satellite link, together with custom-designed software that accepts both text entry and digital photographs. A member of the team is to be designated to make the record at the time of discovery. This task may be rotated through different members of the group by local agreement. No informal records of any other nature are to be kept. In this way, the Institute can be assured of a comprehensive record of the progress of the investigation and the members of the team can be spared the necessity of preparing lengthy catalogs at its termination.'"

Nick nodded.

"Seems sensible to me. Would make some of our scene-of-crime paperwork a lot simpler if we did the same. Was Professor Lockhart happy about working that way?"

"Yes, on the whole. The only comment I remember him making was, 'Why did they have to make it an Apple computer?' Apparently other members of his Department use them, but he's more comfortable with PCs."

"I'm the same. I guess it's what you're used to. Anything else?"

"No, not really." He pulled out another sheet with a lot of figures on it. "This was the final award. Professor Lockhart got about forty per cent of the total."

Nick looked it over and whistled softly. Then he flicked back and forth a few pages and looked up at Matthison.

"I can't see anything about the number of investigators in the team," he said.

"It's in there somewhere. They asked for six young investigators. There were travel and living expenses for four permanent staff. Well, there were two from Oxford – the Professor and Dr. Cothill – and Professor Montalcini was the Principal Investigator so there must have been one other member of staff from the University of Naples. That makes ten in all."

"Thank you, Mr. Mathison. I think that's all I need at the moment. Would it be possible for me to have a copy of those Conditions and the final award?"

"Certainly. I'll get one of the girls to make one for you now."

They shook hands.

"Good luck, Inspector. I do hope he's all right."

The unsettled feelings engendered by Nick's interview with the Professor's wife had begun to recede, and he was regaining his customary buoyancy.

"She wants me to go out there myself, Chief. I think she has confidence in me. I must say she's an excellent judge of character, sir."

"That's enough of that, Roberts," the Chief Superintendent growled. "What about the chap who's just come back from there – the one who told Mrs. Lockhart her husband was missing?"

"Alex Cothill."

"Cothill, that's right. Have you spoken to him yet?"

"Yes. He couldn't add a lot to what Mrs. Lockhart told me. There was one thing, though. Mrs. Lockhart said her husband was pretty steamed up about a ring that had gone missing, a gold ring with an intaglio."

"What the hell's an intaglio?"

An amiable smile crossed Nick's features. "Oh, sorry, sir, I thought you knew. It's a semiprecious stone with an image engraved on it."

The Chief Superintendent grunted. "All right, all right, go on."

"I asked Dr. Cothill if he'd seen the ring. He had – in fact he was very excited about it. He'd been in touch with a team of archaeologists working in Salerno. They're excavating a great library, early second century, and they'd identified the owner as a senator and prominent local citizen, one Cornelius Fratellus. Apparently the surname is the same as one inscribed on the ring. He and his descendants were very influential over the next couple of hundred years, but he just appeared on the scene and the team had no idea where he came from. When Cothill told them about the ring they were over the moon because it established some sort of link with Pompeii. He didn't know the ring had gone missing, though. He was cross about that; he said its archaeological value was far greater than its monetary value. He reckoned it was a lucky thing he happened to be around when they found it; otherwise they wouldn't even have that much information."

The Chief wagged his head impatiently.

"Well, a missing ring may or may not be relevant to this investigation. The important thing is, did he see or hear anything the night Lockhart disappeared?"

"No. He said he'd been working hard to finish everything he had to do before he left and he was absolutely knackered. So were the people who'd been working in the dig. I gather it'd been a really hot day and there was quite a lot of wine with the evening meal, so he slept soundly and the chances are the others did too. He had the cabin next to Lockhart's but nothing woke him. The following day Lockhart wasn't around. They looked in all the likely places. His bed had been slept in, so presumably he went missing during the early hours. I don't think we're going to learn any more until I get out there."

"I don't see why you have to go yourself. I thought we could send a Deputy over. You could manage things from here, couldn't you?"

"I get the impression Mrs. Lockhart isn't the sort who'll take 'No' for an answer, sir."

Detective Chief Superintendent Allison grimaced. "Oh well, I suppose we can spare you. No problem, is there, Roberts? You're a free agent, no wife to worry about."

"No, except I was working on the Snowshill armed robbery."

"We'll get someone else onto that."

"I'm going to need some help with this one."

"The Italians did agree to two people. Who do you want to take?"

"Detective Sergeant Fabri could be useful. She's fluent in Italian."

"All right. See if she's free."

"Thank you, sir."

As he opened the door to leave, the Chief Superintendent's voice followed him.

"We want results out there, Roberts. It's not a holiday for two."

He didn't see the expression on Nick's face as he called over his shoulder, "Of course not, sir."

"Hi, Lucy."

Lucia Fabri looked up from her desk.

"What do you want, Nick?"

"I'm on a special assignment. Need your language skills."

"I don't speak Urdu."

"You have a sharp wit, Lucy. I'm talking about Italian. Fancy a little job in the south of Italy?"

"What are you on about?"

He leaned against her desk, adopting an expression of casual innocence, and ruffling his fingers through curly brown hair.

"I just came from the Chief Super's office. He wants me out there. I told him I could use some help and he said it was okay to take you. 'Course, that's if you'd like to come."

"I'm on the Beniston murder case."

"You can get someone else on that. We've got a missing Brit out there. Archaeologist. We'll probably have to visit Pompeii and Herculaneum. Important background, don'tcha know? Sorrento's nice at this time of year, too. Come on, Lucy, how many chances do you get for a paid-up trip like that?"

She looked at him through narrowed eyes. "Are you on the level?"

"Never more."

"When?"

"ASAP. I'm going to try to book a flight for tomorrow morning."

"All right. Give me a bit of time to hand over, then I'll go and pack."

"Don't forget your swimming cossie."

She fixed him with a look of exasperated patience and held it on him as he grinned and walked away.

PART 3

Campania, Italy

Chapter 15

Lucia Fabri awoke, stretched, opened her eyes, remembered she was in Italy, and smiled. She got up, went over to the window of the small cabin, carefully drew back a corner of the gauzy little curtain and looked outside. The cabins were set in a level area of grassland punctuated with large grey rocks. To one side there was a stand of trees, mainly holm oak and chestnut, and further off she could see the occasional lone beech, pine or cedar. Within a few yards of the cabins the ground dipped gently away, then rose again into a low ridge, beyond which lay the excavation. The ridge obscured her view of the interlocking slopes below, with the scattered houses, olive groves, carob trees and vineyards she had passed on her way here the day before. But she was looking over that, out to the horizon and the Gulf of Naples. *Il Golfo di Napoli.* Bright blue and scintillating in the early morning sunshine.

They'd landed at Naples–Capodichino Airport and taken a taxi to a hotel in Castellamare di Stabia. That was where Nick was staying for the moment; he had to liaise with the Italian police before they made any sort of move. But there was no reason, they'd decided, why she shouldn't go straight to the dig; she could have a look around and let him know something about the set-up. As arranged, Professor Montalcini's research assistant had arrived at the hotel and driven her up here. It was a bumpy ride, she'd told Nick last night, using her mobile phone over the satellite link. The assistant, a taciturn young man called Antonino Torretta, had been friendly enough but his English was non-existent and her attempts to engage him in Italian had met with limited success. Professor Montalcini hadn't been around when she arrived – he was due back the next day – but Torretta did go as far as introducing the rest of the group and showing her to her cabin.

She began to dress. When she had her underwear on she took another peek out of the small window.

She didn't know this area at all; she was born much further north, in Brescia. She felt she should have seen more of Italy, but she was, after all, only four years old when they moved. Her father always said that the posting to the U.K. office was a temporary thing, that he'd only accepted it so that the children could learn English. But there always seemed to be a reason for not moving back: the children's schooling, his promotion, the work they'd done on the house and garden. Twenty-two years later, and they were still living there.

Every year they returned to Italy for several weeks to see the extended family they'd left behind. Those visits were among her fondest memories. For a small child it was like having an endless supply of doting mothers. Like any big Italian family, they loved children, and the women would smother her with kisses and cluck over her thick chestnut hair, her dark eyes, her dimples. Even now, if she made a trip back they would make such a fuss of her that she felt like a little girl all over again. There were never any communication problems, of course. Whether here in Italy or back in England, they always spoke Italian at home. She was so bilingual she worried in both languages.

She took a last look at the clear blue sky and dropped the curtain. It would be hot again today, but the heat didn't bother her – in fact she loved it. What should she wear?

"Civvies," Nick had said. "Pack civvies. The idea is not to look like we're going in like the U.S. Cavalry. In any case, you're young enough to be on a wavelength with some of those students.

It'll probably make the interviewing smoother if you dress a bit like them."

She put on a white T-shirt and pulled on her jeans, cinching the belt and smoothing the taut denim over her hips. The cabin was sparsely furnished, and she'd stood her empty suitcase on end and propped up a travel-mirror to provide a makeshift dressing table. She brushed her hair, then gathered it in the open fingers of both hands and tossed it back over her shoulders. As she did so she noticed how tight the T-shirt was. Nick would be around later today and she knew the effect it would have on him. She wasn't sure how she felt about that. Not that she found him unattractive. He was lean and full of energy. She liked his lively brown eyes with the long lashes and the way his cheeks folded into ridges when he grinned. But he was always so flippant around her. She'd worked with him on a case and she'd seen how sensitive he could be when he was dealing with witnesses and victims, so she supposed it was some sort of defence. Even so, she had no intention of being trifled with; she would be keeping him firmly at arm's length.

She checked that she had the key to the cabin in her pocket. It was a simple Yale lock, not even equipped with a deadlock, but there was nothing of real value in here. Then she took her toiletries bag and went outside, closing the door behind her.

It was early, and the washroom was unoccupied. These primitive facilities were the main drawback of living up here. She brushed her teeth and had a quick wash. Then she looked in the mirror, smoothing her fingertips over her face, thinking about make-up. Some of the girls here wore it; others didn't. She didn't really need to: her complexion was clear, and her lips and cheeks had the healthy blush that came from regular exercise.

The sun had already climbed well into the sky when she emerged from the washroom. The air was scented with pine, and heat was coming off the walls of the cabins and rising from the ground. As she returned to her little cabin, she imagined Nick sleeping late at his hotel in the comfort of a large, air-conditioned room.

Nick Roberts was standing in a hot train, rocking with the motion and sweating profusely.

He was on his way to see the Commissario di Polizei. It was protocol: they had to clear their presence with the Commissario before they could do anything. At the same time, he'd be testing the water to see how much cooperation they were likely to get. Then he wanted to talk to Professor Montalcini. If all went well, Lucy could start to interview the students after that.

He'd wondered what to wear for this morning's meeting. Not uniform, obviously, but it wouldn't do to be too casual, either. You couldn't go wrong with a suit and tie.

Half an hour ago, he'd left his hotel to walk to the station. An illuminated sign above a jewellery store in the Piazza Principe Umberto alternated between the time and the temperature, already 36 degrees Celsius. Now he was standing, swaying with the other passengers, in a crowded Circumvesuviana train going to Naples. He lifted his chin and ran a finger around the collar of his shirt, which had stuck to the short moist hair on the back of his neck. He'd kept his jacket and tie on, though – it was a matter of British pride. In any case he didn't have the room to do anything else.

It was, he thought, a bit like riding the underground in Central London during rush hour in high summer: the same suffocating air, the same irritating invasion of your body space. There were differences, of course. In the underground people were generally buried in newspapers or books, trying hard to avoid eye contact. Here, there was a constant buzz of animated conversation, accompanied by extravagant hand gestures. They really liked talking, these people. What impressed him even more was the graffiti. It covered the sides of most of the carriages and it was all over the stations. There was the usual ignorant spray-can vandalism, but some of the more creative work was worthy of the Tate Gallery. The closer they got to Naples, the more graffiti there seemed to be. It smothered every available surface. It even obscured the blue signs that were supposed to tell you which station it was. From Nick's point of view that wasn't clever. He'd know when they'd got to Naples, though; it was the end of the line.

The passengers' voices rose to drown the rising whines and whistles of the electric motors and the rumble of wheels on the track as the train accelerated out of each station. Windows were open all along the length of the carriage, but the breeze that came through was too warm to provide any relief. His mind strayed.

It was always hard to know what a case had in store. On the face of it, this was a simple missing person inquiry. But Dawn Lockhart seemed convinced it was something more: a kidnap or a murder. Was it just a feeling she had, or did she know more than she'd told him? What if it turned out to be dangerous? For all he knew, he could be holding his future in the cup of his hand. There were moments in life like that, weren't there? Would this turn out to be one of them? In a contrary sort of way, he hoped it would. He'd never been exposed to real danger, and he had no idea how he'd respond. Firearms and unarmed combat had all been part of his training but he'd never had much use for them. He'd had to deal with people resisting arrest, of course – most of them drunk, and some pretty violent – but nobody had ever taken a shot at him and he'd never lost a colleague on an assignment. It had been a good career but to some extent he still felt the need to be tested, to prove himself.

He took a deep breath of hot, humid air and blew it out, protruding his bottom lip in an unsuccessful attempt to direct it over his face. Probably this job would turn out to be pure routine. Still, it was an interesting part of the world and he might learn something – a bit of history, a bit of Italian. And there was always Sergeant Lucia Fabri...

He'd asked Lucy to keep her eyes open, and from their phone conversation last night she'd been doing that all right. It wasn't a total surprise. He knew she was capable – he hadn't asked her to come with him simply because she was a great looker. Well, not entirely.

They stopped at Pompei Scavi–Villa dei Misteri. Some other time he'd get off there and explore the ruins of Pompeii. It would be a nice thing to do with Lucy.

To pass the time, he began to study the warning notices under the windows.

"NON GETTATE ALCUN OGGETTO DAL FINESTRO." He repeated it to himself. It sounded like "DON'T JETTISON OBJECTS FROM THE WINDOW". Fair enough. What did it say underneath? *"E PERICULOSO SPORGERSI." "PERICULOSO?"* Sounded like "PERILOUS". It was dangerous to do something or other. Lean out, probably. In England it would be a polite request: "Please do not lean out of the window". Here, they'd just like you to know it's dangerous. After that, it's up to you.

Another three stops went by. He found a little more space for himself. The tie was in his pocket now, the jacket over his arm, and he'd unbuttoned his shirt as far as he thought was decent.

He continued on his way to Naples, rocking and sweating in the hot train.

Lucia wrote down the names of the summer students, well spaced, on her notepad. Yesterday she'd been introduced to all six in quick succession and had to concentrate hard on connecting names to faces. This morning she'd joined them again for breakfast and pieced together a little more information. Now she jotted down what she could recall about each one, added her impressions, and surveyed the list.

Angela Johnston
English. Third-year student. Reading Human Biology at Liverpool.
No make-up, round glasses with thin metal frames, frizzy black hair worn in two short plaits. Studious but friendly.
Justine Drexler
South African. Early twenties, probably not at university.
Very short hair, dyed an alarming mahogany red, brown eyes, poor complexion. Wore low-cut tank top with no bra. No eye contact.
Orkut Mansur
Turkish. Twenty-something. Reading Science and Arts at Gazi University, Ankara.

Dark hair, dark eyes, dark complexion. Stocky build. Stubble and acne. Struggles with English.

Francesca Infantino

Italian. Reading Fine Arts at Padua. Very pretty. Black hair, very dark eyes, long lashes. Slim figure. Seems to speak good English.

Claudia Schenk

Austrian. Graduated in Mechanical Engineering from Vienna. Currently unemployed, considering career change. Brown hair, grey eyes. Tall, well-built. Rough hands (working without gloves?). Good English.

Pippo Pellerano

Italian. Student? Slightly built young man. Shiny black hair. Never takes sun-glasses off. Listens in to conversations in English but speaks only in Italian.

She tossed the notebook on the bed, looked at the door, had second thoughts, and locked it in her suitcase.

Then she stood in the cabin wondering what to do with herself. It was getting stuffy, so she wasn't going to stay inside. Professor Montalcini wasn't due back until the early afternoon. She couldn't start interviewing the students until they had the Commissario's permission – and the Professor's.

She decided to scout the area around the site to see if she could pick up anything useful. She'd have lunch with the others and then wait in her cabin until Nick arrived.

Chapter 16

The train reached Napoli Centrale, and emptied. Carrying his jacket in one hand and his document folder in the other, Nick followed the signs to Piazza Garibaldi. He climbed the stairs to the mainline station, where tall trains stood waiting to depart for Milan, Rome, Trieste, Sorrento. The concourse was full of people trailing small suitcases. It echoed to the clack of the women's high heels. Everyone seemed to be in a hurry.

When he emerged into the Piazza he stood there, blinking in the strong sunlight.

Directly in front of him was a double line of white taxis. This was easier than he'd expected. He boarded one, gave his destination as *"La Questura"* – the police headquarters building – and was soon cruising out of the square. He settled back comfortably in his seat. A moment later he was sitting bolt upright, catapulted into traffic more chaotic than he'd seen in his entire life.

It seemed everything was going too fast, like a speeded-up film. Cars were coming from every direction, merging with the flow at undiminished speed. An endless succession of scooters, motorbikes and mopeds rode alongside the cars or wound in and out between them. A thin, blue haze of dust and exhaust fumes hung over the streets; it accompanied the warm air blowing in through the open windows and stung his nose and eyes. His head was filled with sound: the constant stabbing of horns, the rumble of tyres on the rough paving, the squealing of brakes. Even this level of noise was drowned from time to time by the siren of a passing police car or ambulance or the roar and whistle of an airliner passing low over the city.

The taxi made uneven progress, accelerating hard, braking even harder, then turning abruptly to go at speed along a fan-cobbled alley, clearing by inches the lines of cars and scooters parked on either side.

By craning his neck, Nick could catch glimpses of blue sky between tall buildings that were streaked and patched in faded pastel shades of ochre, terra cotta, yellow, buff, and grey. Every façade was punctuated with wooden shutters and the iron railings of balconies. Some of the balconies were furnished with plants – oleander, cacti, even palms; almost every one was festooned with washing.

Whenever they encountered a street of any size they had to negotiate the same surging press of traffic. He would wince as a car appeared out of nowhere and stopped just short of ramming them side-on. Neither driver seemed in the least perturbed by these near-misses. It began to dawn on Nick that the horns were not being used aggressively but as a genuine warning of impending disaster, best avoided. All the same he wondered what the accident rate was. Pretty high, to judge by the dents and scrapes on nearly every vehicle.

Eventually the taxi came to an abrupt halt, double-parked alongside a row of blue-and-white Fiat 5-doors with "POLIZIA" in large letters along the sides. A couple of dozen policemen were standing around between the cars and on the pavement, chatting in small groups.

The driver put his hand out of the window and pointed.

"Ecco, la Questura."

Nick got out, paid the driver and turned to look up at a tall grey-white monolith. The wide entrance was occupied with casual boredom by three policemen. A stone plaque adjacent to the entrance read:

QUESTVRA

INGRESSO VFFICI

Reluctantly he buttoned up the collar of his shirt, and put on the jacket and tie.

Lucia joined the excavation team in a simple lunch of panini with cheese, tomatoes, and olives accompanied by a salad of lettuce, rocket and peppers. It disappeared quickly; the students were ravenous after the morning's work.

She was friendly without being pushy. Clearly they weren't sure of her, which wasn't surprising; she was a cop, after all. Just the same, she was learning all the time, just by observing them. She noticed, for example, how careful Orkut Mansur was to pass things to Francesca Infantino. She'd mesmerized a few boys in her time and she knew the signs.

She took a fresh orange from the bowl on the table, put it to her nose and drew in the fragrance. It still had leaves attached. *The poor folk back in England don't know what an orange is,* she thought. She peeled it skilfully, divided it into segments, and ate it with relish.

After the table had been cleared she stopped by the washroom to rinse the sweet, sticky juice off her hands and face. Then she went back to her cabin.

The Commissario's welcome was more cordial than Nick had expected.

"Ispettore! This is a great pleasure! I hope you have had a good journey?"

"Thank you, fine. You know why I'm here, of course."

"Of course. I have spoke to your Sopraintendente Allisone and also again with Signora Lockharter. She is very strong lady, that Signora Lockharter."

"Yes, she is." Nick smiled. That explained the cordial welcome; Dawn Lockhart had been doing her stuff. "Look, I don't want to get in the way, Commissario. But chiefs like yourself are always short of staff and I hope Sergeant Fabri and I can help out."

The Commissario beamed. 'Chiefs' had been the right word to use, Nick thought.

"But of course. It is most unfortunate that the Professore Lockharter is missing. We will do everything possible to find him. The investigation is in the hands of Capitano Umberto Gardi. I think it is best if you speak to him direct."

He reached for the telephone.

It looked like the Commissario wouldn't be taking any further part in the discussions, so Nick decided to push his luck.

"Er, Commissario, before I talk to the Capitano, could I ask you something?"

The Commissario's hand stopped in mid-air and his eyebrows lifted.

"The way I see it, Professor Lockhart has either left the site or he's been murdered. Now I understand there are two vehicles up there, both four-wheel drives: a small Japanese one and a larger people carrier. They're still there, so if he left, he left on foot. He's very distinctive. Someone must have seen a tall Englishman, with light brown hair and a pronounced cleft in his chin. I've duplicated a good picture for you..."

Nick dipped into his document case and brought out a small stack of pictures, copied from one of the photographs Dawn Lockhart had lent him. "I'd like to circulate this photo to all the local villages and farms, to see if anyone has seen him."

The Commissario hesitated for a moment, then he said, "This we can do. Ask the Capitano."

"Excellent. Now if, on the other hand, Professor Lockhart was murdered, the question arises: what has happened to the body? We should have a thorough search of the area, paying particular attention to any disturbed ground. And I understand there's a small wood behind the cabins up there. That will need to be searched very carefully, by people who know what they're doing. Of course I would be taking part myself."

The Commissario's mouth slackened. "Such a thing will require many people. You know, there is much crime in Napoli. We need our policemen here."

"You have volunteers, though? People who help in searches for small children, that sort of thing?"

The Commissario swallowed hard. He was obviously thinking about his conversations with Dawn Lockhart.

Finally he said, "Maybe we can arrange. Ask the Capitano."

"But it's all right with you if we do that, is it?"

"Yes, if he can arrange, it's all right."

"Fine. Well, thank you very much for your cooperation,

Commissario. I'm sure you're very busy, so I can perhaps see to the details with Capitano Gardi."

The Commissario smiled, a little less warmly than before, and picked up the telephone.

Nick was well satisfied. If the Commissario had okayed it, the Capitano would have to go along with it, whether he was disposed to help or not.

At two o'clock Lucia heard a vehicle climbing the hill. She drew aside the curtain and peeked out. She caught a glimpse of two people in the front seats. Neither one was Nick. Presumably it was the Professor, with someone else. The vehicle disappeared beyond the line of cabins. A few minutes later it reversed out in an arc and then went off down the hill. The sound of the engine faded.

"The Commissario said it was all right?"

Capitano Umberto Gardi's soulful dark eyes were wide and his thick black moustache drooped with anxiety. His uniform fitted very badly and its appearance was not improved by the tight belt, which accentuated, rather than concealed, the convexity of his stomach.

He's a friendly enough guy, Nick thought, *but has he been sitting behind a desk for too long? At least his English seems good – better than the Commissario's. Maybe that's why he was chosen.*

"Yes, Capitano," he replied. "In fact, he is depending upon you to arrange things."

The moustache slowly lifted at the corners. The Capitano clasped his hands together, then rotated them back and forth, like someone warming his hands in front of a fire. He separated his hands to point at Nick.

"You must be one powerful man, Ispettore! Normally the Commissario... well, I must not say more. You have a photograph of Professore Lockhart?"

Nick opened his document case and offered him the sheaf of photographs, but the Capitano reached out and, with a delicacy unexpected from such plump fingers, plucked out a single sheet.

"I need only one, Signor. My Appuntato will fax this to the police stations in every local village, with instructions to make copies and post them in the windows of local shops, banks and supermarkets – in fact, everywhere. This will be the most efficient."

Nick smiled. It looked like this was someone who could make things happen, when he was given a little freedom to act. "Excellent," he said. "Now the search...?"

"It's a big area. If we are looking for disturbed ground then it is best to look from the air. I ask for the traffic helicopter and a pilot and you can go up with him."

"You can get me a helicopter?"

He shrugged. "Normally, no. But the Commissario said it's okay, so it must be okay, no?" He giggled and rubbed his hands together again. "It's all right tomorrow morning, if I can arrange?"

"Yes, tomorrow morning would be great. I'll contact you to find out what time and where to meet."

"Okay. I give you my cell phone number," he said.

"Good idea. I'll give you mine, too."

They scribbled the numbers down, then exchanged the pieces of paper. Nick said:

"By the way, I understand there is a small area of woodland, near the excavation. We won't be able to survey that from the air."

"No, you are right, Ispettore. This we must search by hand. Maresciallo Valentinuzzi will arrange. Maybe for tomorrow afternoon. I ask him."

"Lovely. I'll leave you to it." Nick extended a hand. "By the way, since we'll be working together I'm happy for you to call me Nick."

The moustache lifted in delight as he took Nick's hand.

"And I am Umberto. At your service, Nick."

Chapter 17

She heard the 4 X 4 long before she saw it, the engine note rising and falling as it negotiated the uneven terrain. Then it came into view, pursued by a plume of dust.

Nick drew up, giving her a wave out of his open window, and she pointed to the space where the Japanese 4 X 4 and the people carrier were. He parked alongside them, switched off the engine and got out. He looked comfortable in a short-sleeved shirt and cotton trousers.

"Hi, Nick."

"Hiya, Lucy."

"Where'd you get the wheels?"

"Rented it in Naples. I couldn't face the bloody train again and this way I can come and go. Bit hairy getting out of Naples, though."

"Traffic bad?"

"You wouldn't believe it. You sort of get used to it, though, driving on your reflexes all the time. The autostrada was quite civilized by comparison. So, how's it going?"

"Fine. Professor Montalcini's here. He arrived about an hour ago. Someone brought him. Whoever it was didn't stay." She glanced at her watch. "It's half-two now. There's a little time yet. Shall I give you a conducted tour?"

"Good idea."

He followed her down the line of cabins, with the hill sloping away to their left.

"How did things go with the Commissario?" she asked.

"Very good. Dawn Lockhart must have leaned on him. He gave me the go-ahead and I made the arrangements with the Captain. Capitano Umberto Gardi. Great guy, you're going to love him. He's faxing the picture of Lockhart to all the local towns and villages, and he's laying on a helicopter for me to survey the district from the air. He's going to try for tomorrow morning."

"Are you sure, Nick? You know the culture's different here. People tell you what they think you want to hear."

"Sure, I know, but I think this guy is on the level. I get the impression he's having to work half the time with his hands tied behind his back. The Commissario's given him carte blanche and he's in clover. I think he'll do what he said."

"So you'll be going back to Castellamare later on?"

"Yeah. I'll find out where the helicopter pad is and go straight there in the morning. We should be able to spot any disturbed ground."

"What about the woodland?"

"It was good you warned me about that. He says he'll get a search party together, probably for the afternoon. I can't do much till then, so once we've got things going up here I'll leave you to it."

They came to the end cabin and she pointed.

"That cabin's reserved for visitors. I think Alex Cothill used it when he was here. I'm in there at the moment."

"Show me, then."

She darted him a dubious look, but he seemed intent on going in. She fished the key out of her pocket and opened the door. Nick stepped inside. Somewhat to her surprise, he was all business.

"Single entrance and exit," he said. "No view to the rear. It's funny they only put in this small window in the front. Doesn't it get stuffy in here?"

"A bit. There's a vent high up on the back wall, there, so you do get some circulation."

He stooped to look out of the window and pointed in the direction of the ridge.

"I saw people down there when I was driving up. That where the dig is?"

"Yes."

"Right. Well, you can't see anything of it from here. Okay. We're done."

As they came out he paused and checked the lock carefully.

"You keeping anything of value in here?"

"No."

"Good. Because this lock's a cinch. Who's next door?"

"Well it was Lockhart's cabin. So far as I know it hasn't been disturbed – beyond checking that he wasn't in there."

Nick shook his head. "Dozy lot," he said. "Forensic should have been in there right away – and taped the door up after them. Oh well, so long as they haven't, we might as well give it a once-over."

Lucia raised her eyebrows. He leaned towards her with a reassuring smile.

"It's already compromised," he said. "We don't know who's been in there or what they've done. Don't worry, we won't muck anything up. I'll get Umberto's people to go over it properly later."

He produced a credit card, stepped up to the door, looked up and down the line of cabins, and slipped it behind the lock. The door opened. He went inside, beckoned to Lucia and closed the door carefully behind her. Then he took his shoes off and indicated that she should do the same. As they put them down he noticed two other pairs, close to the threshold. He put his fingers into the first pair and picked them up. They were lightweight lace-up deck shoes, an English size nine, dusty but otherwise clean. He replaced them and examined the second pair. These were strong shoes – like boots but without the high ankle support. They were very scuffed and dirty, and all the maker's marks had worn off, but they looked to be similar in size to the lighter pair. He straightened up.

For a few moments he surveyed the inside of the cabin. It was similar in layout to Lucia's, except for a small chest of drawers, at the side of which a well-worn suitcase had been stood on its end. There was a chair by the bed with a small pile of rumpled clothes on it. A padded, weatherproof jacket hung from a nail on the back of the door. Lucia stayed by the door as Nick walked slowly around the room, looking carefully at the bedding.

"Bed's been slept in, not made," he commented. "No sign of pyjamas. Maybe he didn't wear them."

His gaze swept again around the furnishings, the floor and the wall.

"No obvious bloodstains anywhere."

He sifted through the clothes on the chair: a pair of jeans, a short-sleeved shirt, a pair of underpants, a handkerchief, a pair of thick socks. He felt in the pockets of the jeans but they were empty.

He replaced the clothes and glanced in her direction. "Anything in that jacket over there?"

Again she looked at him, then reluctantly went through the pockets of the padded jacket.

"Nothing," she said, turning to him, but he was already going through the chest of drawers, using a couple of pens from his pocket to open the drawers in turn. He felt the clothes inside each one before closing it.

"Clean shirts, underwear, socks and hankies," he said. "About enough to last a week. Now, what do we have up here?"

On the top of the chest was a small pile of papers and next to it various other items. He looked quickly through the papers: articles from academic journals, a clean A4 notepad, some envelopes. He replaced them. There was a zipped waterproof bag, sitting on a folded towel. He had a quick look inside but it only contained the usual toiletries. He poked the other items around: some fibrepoint pens, a few euros, a comb, a multi-tool penknife and a leather key case. He opened the key case. There were some Yale-type keys, a mortise key and two smaller keys.

"He drove the small 4 X 4 but there are no car keys," he remarked.

"They leave them in the ignition. I suppose they think it's safe enough to do that up here. What about the penknife?"

"I know, but I'll have to leave that – they could get prints off it." He carried the keys over to the door, opened it slightly and tried the Yale patterns. The second one fitted the lock and turned back the bolt. He gave her a significant look and closed the door. "These other two could be keys to his house and his office. We can check them later with Dawn Lockhart. This small one looks like it belongs to a filing cabinet. And this one..."

He selected the key and approached the suitcase.

"Nick..."

"Take it easy, Lucy."

The key fitted. He turned the suitcase onto its base and opened it carefully. Inside he found a clean pair of jeans and a thick woolly sweater that presumably hadn't been needed. There was a grip-seal poly bag with some sterling coins in it, a travel insurance policy, and a passport. Nick opened the passport at the photograph and showed it to Lucia. It was Lockhart.

He replaced everything, relocked the case and stood it where he'd found it.

Lucia was feeling very ill at ease. "Nick, can we go now?"

He looked at her thoughtfully.

"Yeah."

They put their shoes on again. He opened the door, looked outside, then said, "Okay, after you."

Lucia watched him close the door.

"What now?" she asked.

"We continue the tour," he said brightly.

They stopped outside the next cabin.

She did her best to collect herself. "This one belongs to Professor Montalcini," she said. "I think all the cabins are the same as mine. There certainly aren't any windows to the rear on any of them."

He nodded, then looked further up.

"There seem to be two more."

"No, they're not cabins. The first one's the washroom. Very basic. No showers – you have to wash yourself down."

"Loos?"

"Not in there. Two chemical toilets at the rear."

"And the second one?"

"That's the office. They do all the record-keeping and administration in there. It's mainly used by the Professor and his assistant – the young guy who met us in Castellamare."

"Torretta?"

"That's right."

They walked to the end of the line of cabins and turned left to stand outside a cabin that had been added at right-angles to the rest, making the whole complex L-shaped.

She swept a hand around. "This is the kitchen and dining area. In theory, we could eat under cover but in this weather most of the cooking and eating's done outside."

"Who does the cooking?" he asked.

"A lady drives up once a day from a local village. I met her yesterday evening. Motherly sort. Cooked the evening meal and left us more than enough for breakfast and lunch. And big bottles of water. Everyone here drinks gallons of water."

"So how was the meal?"

"Lovely! Pasta, home-baked bread, fresh salad, fresh fruit, carafes of the local wine. Just the sort of thing I love."

His smile froze. "What's that noise?"

"The droning? A generator. It's in the corner behind the office and the kitchen."

He wrinkled his nose.

"Shame. I mean, up here the air's lovely and clean and you're too far from the autostrada to hear the traffic. It'd be really sweet if it weren't for that thing."

"I agree with you, but it seems they have to have it. Quite apart from lighting there's a big fridge in the kitchen and there's the computer and all the other communications gear in the office."

They rounded the kitchen and walked behind the cabins. She pointed out the generator, the antenna dish for the satellite link, and rows of fuel tanks.

"The fuel isn't just for the generator," she said, adding, "Did you see the earthmover?"

"Got a glimpse. Big yellow tractor with a bulldozer blade at one end and a bucket attachment at the other?"

"That's right. They use it to remove the top soil and I expect they'll fill in the excavation with it when this is all over. The fuel's for that, too."

They returned to the kitchen and turned to face an open area of ground dominated by an old cedar. Beyond the tree, four colourful tents had been pitched.

Lucia said, "The summer students sleep in the tents – in same-sex pairs, in case you're interested."

He didn't rise to the comment.

"There are six students, and four tents," he observed.

"Yes. Torretta has his own tent. The orange one there."

"Right." He turned to her. "Quite a little community, isn't it? Bit of an expense to set up and maintain. Why do it this way, do you think?"

"Apparently they only have so much time to complete the dig. This way they can put in many more hours than if they had to be bussed in and out every morning and evening and they don't run the risk of souvenir hunters raiding the site when they're not here. The students do have the weekends to themselves, though. The people carrier takes them down to Castellamare. They tell me there's a well-equipped hostel there. It's got washing machines and showers and they can sleep in proper beds and see a bit more of the region if they want to: Pompeii, Herculaneum, Paestum, the Amalfi coast – God knows there's enough in this area to keep them occupied."

She glanced at her watch.

"Time's getting on. I'll show you the actual dig later. Listen, Nick, once we've met the Professor you don't need me to stick around while you talk to him, do you?"

"Not really. Why?"

"Well, I just think it'd be better if you spoke to him on your own. And I'd like to get started with the students – if he doesn't mind."

"Good thinking. And we can compare notes later."

"Okay, let's seek him out. He'll be in the office."

Chapter 18

Nick knocked on the door of the office and they went in. The air inside was warm and humid and had a faintly earthy smell. Enrico Montalcini was seated at a desk, examining some charred objects with a magnifying glass. He rose when he saw them.

"Inspector," he said.

Montalcini was taller than Nick had anticipated. He looked to be in his early fifties, with wavy black hair that was greying at the temples. He was clean-shaven but had a heavy five o'clock shadow that stopped abruptly at thin, finely shaped lips. He wore a khaki shirt and shorts. To Nick's eyes he was strongly built, if a little thick around the waist.

Nick took the hand extended to him and said, in his best Italian, *"Sono molto lieto di fare la sua cognoscenta."*

The Professor responded, "And it is a pleasure to meet you too, Inspector."

"Not bad, Nick," breathed Lucia behind him. Then she stepped forward and shook the Professor's hand in her turn.

"Piace," she said.

He responded, *"Piace, Sergente."*

Lucia caught Nick's eye, suppressing a smile.

The Professor continued, still speaking to Lucia. "I understand you arrived yesterday, Sergente. I must apologize I was not here to greet you. You know, I have to divide my time between the excavation here and my Department in Naples. In many ways it is better when I have field work in Greece or Egypt – then they know they have to manage without me."

He smiled, pulled over a swivel chair and an ordinary chair and, with a courtly gesture, invited them to sit.

Nick said, "Thank you, Professor, but I think there's no need for both of us to stay. My colleague would very much like to talk to the students. Do you have any objection?"

"Me? Not at all. But, Sergente, I would ask you please try not to upset them. We are a team and the success of the project depends very much on people helping one another. I would not like to spoil the atmosphere."

"I can understand that, Professor," Lucia responded. "Please don't worry. I'll be as tactful as I can."

"Thank you."

"I'll see you later, then," Lucia said to Nick on her way out. "*Arrividerci, Professore.*"

Montalcini smiled in return. Then he sat down at the desk with Nick.

"Inspector, I am glad you have come," he began. "This is an extraordinary place, you know. It is perhaps the most exciting investigation of my career. Each day brings with it a new discovery. Everyone's spirits are high. And then my colleague, my valued colleague, Professor Lockhart, disappears. It has cast a shadow over the whole enterprise. And I hardly need to say that we miss his expert contribution."

Nick said, "His family are very distressed, of course."

"But of course."

"They said they'd feel more comfortable if we were around to assist in the investigation. The Commissario has been very accommodating about it."

"Naturally we will do everything possible here to assist you."

"Thank you." Nick drew a ballpoint and a small notebook from his shirt pocket and held them up. "You don't mind if I make a few notes while we're speaking?"

Montalcini waved a hand. "Not at all."

"So tell me, were you acquainted with Professor Lockhart before you embarked on this project?"

"Yes, we met at conferences. But I did not know him well. I was, of course, familiar with his publications."

"May I ask why you asked him to join you in this excavation, Professor? Wasn't there a danger that he'd get all the recognition for whatever you achieved here?"

The Professor frowned. "It was not a thought that occurred to me. Our expertise was complementary. I am an expert in human remains. He is an expert on Roman artifacts. It was the ideal partnership for a project such as this."

"And how did Professor Lockhart seem, the last time you saw him?"

"He was behaving strangely. He seemed agitated, I would say."

"But you don't know what about?"

"No."

"And up to then the dig was going well?"

"Extremely well. We are obliged to work very fast, of course. The farmer who owns this land wants to develop it. We have only a few months; after that anything that is left behind will be lost forever. But we are making good progress. We have already uncovered eleven skeletons."

"What about other finds? Gold, jewellery, that sort of thing."

"Ah, everyone wants to know about treasure!"

"Well, is that surprising? I mean, some of the objects must be very valuable."

"Yes. According to the terms of our grant, the J. Paul Getty Museum has first refusal on the more valuable items, but they only take the most outstanding ones. We offer the rest to the National Museum in Naples. The Museum doesn't like this arrangement, of course, but the Soprintendenza Archeologica was not in a position to fund the project, so they must live with it. Things were different twenty years ago, of course. At that time they would have supported a project such as this, at least in part."

Nick wrote something in his notebook.

"Forgive me, Professor, I'm not very familiar with your type of work. What happens if you do come across something valuable? Can you give me an idea of the procedure?"

"You mean after it has been lifted out of the ground?"

"Yes. Could you take me through it?"

Montalcini leaned back, pursing his fine lips, apparently gathering his thoughts. It was, Nick thought, typical of the academics he'd met. They wouldn't fire from the hip; they'd think first about what they were going to say. And this chap had to do it in another language.

"Well, it's no different to any other object we archive. The position and depth is recorded carefully, possibly photographed. Then the find is cleaned up a little, placed in a bag, given a number and recorded. If we take a photograph, that is added to the record. All this is done digitally, on site. It's a good system. The Pliny Institute insists upon it."

"And then?"

"The object is stored here." The Professor pointed to a cabinet fitted with drawers. Each drawer had small brass holder with a label, on which a range of numbers had been hand-written. Nick scanned down the first few. The intervals were not uniform: "0260 – 0270", "0271 – 0278", "0279 – 0281". He guessed that the larger samples, like skeletons, would take up more drawer space, so there would be fewer serial numbers on those drawers. There didn't seem to be a lock.

"Is that secure?" Nick asked.

"Well, you know, we have little need of security here. We do not publicize what we find. The Institute has a daily update when we upload the files, but they are the only ones to know. Even if someone did know what they were looking for, nearly everything is wrapped in tissue paper and stored by serial number, so it would take them a very long time to find it."

"They could use the computer, though, couldn't they?"

"They would have to be familiar with the software and it is not available on the open market. In any case they could not access the computer without the password."

Nick nodded thoughtfully. "So you'll be keeping all the finds here until the end of the dig?"

"Oh no. They are stored here only temporarily. Then we transfer them to Naples."

"How often do you do that?"

"It depends. If there are many finds we do it at the end of each week. There they are placed in the Department's vaults. The vaults are very secure."

"When was the last time that happened?"

Montalcini looked into the air, eyebrows raised, and scratched his cheek absently with a manicured fingernail.

"Let me see... It must have been just over a week ago."

"And the next time?"

"We should do it soon. Probably in the next few days."

Nick decided it was time to push a little harder. "So this was the first time you and Professor Lockhart had worked together. Were there disagreements?"

Montalcini looked at him in surprise.

"No, I wouldn't say so. We had different interpretations, and differences of opinion about strategy, but you would expect that from senior researchers. As I said before, our expertise was complementary. He could identify tools and weapons and pieces of pottery and say when and where they were made, and he had similar skills with the precious metal objects. My own interest is in the human remains. Out here we are recovering a lot of skeletons, some of them remarkably complete. Who were these people? What can their bones tell us about life in Pompeii more than two thousand years ago? What can we learn about their stature, their ailments? Did they have any deficiencies in minerals or vitamins? Did they suffer from arthritis, leprosy, tuberculosis? Is there any evidence of medical treatment? What does the pattern of tooth wear tell us about their diet? Above all, what can their bones tell us about the events that overtook them on their flight from Pompeii? These are the kinds of question that interest me. Not *baubles*."

He said the final word contemptuously, brushing it aside with a dismissive gesture of his hand.

Nick eyed him levelly.

"All the same, Professor," he said, "one of those *baubles* seems to have been the subject of a serious dispute between you and Julian Lockhart."

"What are you talking about?" he said brusquely.

"I'm talking, Professor, about a gold ring with an intaglio."

Chapter 19

The long lunch table had been judiciously placed where it could enjoy some shade from the wide green skirts of the big cedar. It was also far enough from the tents and from the office for conversations not to be overheard. Lucia found Angela Johnston, the English final-year undergraduate, at the dig and brought her over. Angela had struck her as being a sensible girl and she'd decided to start the interviews with her.

"What do I call you? Officer?" Angela asked, as they sat down at one end of the table.

"Lucia will do just fine."

"Well, Lucia, I've no idea why you want to talk to me. I don't know any more about this than anyone else." Her voice was tight and her movements were brisk as she brushed the soil roughly off her hands. Then she wiped above one eye, where her forehead was shining slightly with perspiration. It left a muddy streak.

"Don't worry about what you do and don't know, Angela. I just want to get some idea of how things work around here. Background stuff, really. Do you think you can help me with that?"

"I can try."

"Tell me, then, what did you hope to get out of your time here?"

Angela seemed to relax a little. "Well, you know, human biology's a pretty broad subject. At Uni we've covered human anatomy, comparative human biology, paleontology, archaeology – a whole load of things. I'm just not sure what I want to do after I graduate. I really wanted a career in forensics but it's pretty over-subscribed. And to do forensic pathology, I'd have to do Medicine. But I've been thinking seriously about forensic anthropology. Anyway, when I was trying to make up my mind and scanning possible jobs, this summer student thing came up. It looked interesting. I thought I'd see if I liked it."

"And do you?"

"Oh yes. It's been great. I'd love to do it as a career, but... Well, the thing is, I wouldn't want to do it unless I could be really good at it. And there's no way I could be as good as Julian."

"You've enjoyed working with him?"

"What's the word? Inspirational. When he looks at the dig it's like he's got X-ray vision. He's seeing under the ground and he's seeing back in time, and somehow he can make you see it, too. You know, what we're doing down there, it's pretty hard work. You spend hours on your hands and knees, scraping and stabbing away a bit at a time with a trowel. And it's hot, really hot. You sweat, you slow up – everyone does. And then he comes along and interprets what you're doing, and when he leaves you've forgotten you were ever tired, and you're digging away at three times the speed."

"Can you give me an example?"

Angela thought for a moment. "Yes, all right. There's a lot of stuff in this site, okay? Skeletons are coming up all over the place. In some places we even get them in twos; the bones are so mingled they have to be bagged up together and sorted out afterwards. Nearly everyone on the dig has found a skeleton, or at least one or two human bones. Everyone except me, that is – and I'm the human biologist, right? Great, just great. So I'm up near the sloping end, digging away, and I come across this bone. I get all excited, and then I take a look at it and I can see it's a humerus all right, but it's not a human humerus – it's probably sheep or goat. So I'm, like, really down. Here I am: the only one who hasn't found a human skeleton and I have to dig up a bloody sheep! So anyway Julian comes over and asks me what I've got, and I tell him. He looks at it. Then he says, 'You're right, Angela, it's sheep or goat, I'm not sure which. Well done, this could be very important.' So I say to him, 'How is it important? It's just a sheep or goat. It was probably just grazing up here and it got asphyxiated or hit by falling rocks and lava.' And he says, 'Think about it, Angela. Is that likely? A goat is wandering around on the hillside and a party of thirty or more people come along and probably wagons are trundling along with them. What's it going to do? It's not going to hang around, is it? Of course not. No, the chances are that the party took some livestock with them. This could be one of them. And to stop them running away they probably tethered them to a wagon. Now, if you can find the skull you should be closer to the wagon and you'll have an idea of where it's lying. Can you imagine the sort of stuff that they piled onto the wagon? This could be the most significant find yet, Angela. You're onto something!'" She laughed. "You see what I mean? I was that excited I worked without a break!"

"Why didn't you use a metal detector?"

"Julian doesn't go along with that approach. If you just pick up a metal object and dig for it you can miss a whole load of other things: bones, bits of pottery, things made of ivory, antlers, glass, semiprecious stones. So he gets us to work systematically. Then we get what he calls the *context* of the finds."

"And did it pay off?"

"Oh yes! He was right on the money! I found the mandible – they're pretty robust so there was always a good chance of finding that. Then I found a short strip of rusty metal, terribly fragile so I had to uncover it very carefully. Julian had a look, and agreed with me: it was part of the iron hoop that goes around the rim of a cartwheel."

"I didn't know the Romans had such things."

"Oh, you'd be amazed at their technology. Julian showed us a picture of a wagon that was probably something like the one we'd found. That one was more complete, though. All I found parts of the rim and a bearing for the axle."

"I suppose the wood had all rotted away."

"Yes. We wanted to know what kind of animals had pulled the wagon but we couldn't find any remains. Odd, that. Maybe they escaped. Pippo did find a few harness fittings, though; nice ones, silver on bronze. Julian said that suggested horses. Anyway, I was still scraping through the area and by that time Julian and several of the others were helping me. I found some more pieces of iron and they looked like the bindings of a chest. Then we started finding wonderful precious artifacts. They must have spilled out of the chest."

"When you say precious, you mean gold and silver?"

"Yeah, gold and silver, necklaces of gems and amber, stuff like that."

"They must be very valuable."

"I suppose so, but it's not just the value. They don't corrode so they come out of the ground in perfect condition. You can see the workmanship. It's fabulous."

"And were you the first member of the team to turn up those kind of artifacts?"

"Not the first, no. I think Orkut was first. He found the skeletons of a woman and a child, close together. She was only young – from the dentition Julian reckoned she was about twenty. That gave me a funny feeling – she was the same age as me when she died. Anyway, she was wearing this heavy bangle around the humerus, solid gold with the initials G.L.T. on it. That was pretty exciting, too."

Lucia nodded. "And who found the gold ring with the intaglio?"

She'd tried to drop the question in casually, but Angela looked up sharply. She was tense again.

"I knew you were going to ask me about that."

"Now be reasonable, Angela. From what I hear, Julian and Professor Montalcini had a major row about it."

"Among other things."

"What do you mean?"

"Julian was always rowing with the Professor."

"What about?"

"Oh, I don't know. We could hear their raised voices in the office. They were so different in style, you know – they just couldn't agree on priorities. It got pretty heated sometimes."

"Tell me about the ring."

Angela bit her lip. "Julian and Claudia found these two skeletons. We think one was the remains of a soldier. The ring was on his finger."

"What happened to it?"

"Oh, it got numbered and photographed and recorded like everything else. We had a longish break for lunch, because it gets a bit too hot to dig in the middle of the day, and we heard Julian and Montalcini having another shouting match. We couldn't hear what it was about. We just shrugged at each other. Then Julian came storming out and took the little 4 X 4 and drove off. That wasn't like him at all. He likes to be in there with us when we're digging. We carried on as usual. Later on Professor Montalcini came down and asked us about the ring."

"Who was 'us'? Were you all there?"

"I think so – most of us, anyway. We'd only got a quick look so we told him roughly what it was like. He just shrugged his shoulders and went back to the office."

"And that's what makes you think the row was about the ring?"

"Well, that and the way Julian acted afterwards. He wasn't digging with us at all. He just seemed to be charging back and forth in the 4 X 4 all the time. And then, of course, he went missing."

Lucia looked at Angela and asked her quietly: "What do you think's happened to Julian, Angela?"

"Maybe he's been kidnapped."

"There haven't been any claims of responsibility or ransom demands."

"All right, then, he's dead."

"What makes you so sure of that?"

"I don't know." There was a note of irritation in her voice. "I can only tell you how it looks to me. The man was really focused on the dig. He was there before us every morning. During the day he'd drive us all along, like I said before, explaining things and motivating us. At the end of the day he was always the last to leave. No way would he suddenly walk away from the dig. It was just totally out of character."

Lucia looked at her hands, nodding slowly.

A breath of breeze stirred the sun-baked branches of the cedar, scenting the air with the faint smell of cigar boxes. Angela fidgeted.

Lucia raised her head again and said gently: "Tell me, Angela. Did Julian ever behave unprofessionally towards you?"

"What do you mean by that?"

"Come on, you know what I'm talking about. A compliment here, a slightly risqué remark there, a suggestion that he could do things to advance your career, a hand brushing accidentally where it shouldn't... "

Angela was breathing fast now. "Look, I know what you're saying: he's gone off with some bird. Well, don't believe it."

"Angela, you haven't answered my question."

"All right. No. Nothing like that. Ever."

Lucia thought for a moment. "Okay, so he didn't do anything like that with you. What about with the other girls?"

"You'll have to ask them."

The reply had come too quickly.

A sudden firmness entered Lucia's voice. "I'm asking you."

Angela hesitated, then said sullenly, "I don't know."

Lucia looked at her. "Let's put it this way," she said. "If I were to start putting this question to the other girls, who do you think I should start with?"

Again Angela hesitated. Then she replied, "Well, you might start with Justine."

"Thank you, Angela."

Chapter 20

Montalcini's expression changed.

"I never saw it."

"You never saw a gold ring with an intaglio – one of the most significant finds to come out of the dig to date?"

Nick knew he'd have to push this man hard if he was going to provoke a reaction.

The Professor's voice was cold.

"I do not know that it was significant because I do not know it ever existed – other than in the imagination of Professor Lockhart."

"Ever existed...? But it must have been recorded! You said yourself everything was photographed and recorded digitally on site."

"See for yourself, Inspector." Montalcini held out an open hand. "The computer is here."

He got up, crossed the room, and returned with a laptop computer. He opened the lid and pressed the start button. The machine started to boot and moments later an Apple logo appeared on the screen. This was obviously the laptop mentioned in the grant regulations.

"I thought you kept the computer at the dig," Nick said.

"Normally, yes. It was recharging."

A dialog box appeared and the Professor typed in a password. Then he clicked on an icon and moments later the splash screen appeared, with the word "ARCHETYPE", followed by some rapidly changing text. The screen faded, leaving a display consisting of masses of figures, arranged in columns.

Montalcini pointed to the leftmost column. "This is the date column. We will scroll back a few days."

Figures ran off the screen in a blur, then slowed to a stop.

"This is the day in question, Inspector," he said. "But you are free to look wherever you want." He pointed to a column of numbers. "Here you see the serial numbers that are assigned to each and every find. Next to the serial number is a short description. Then the exact location and depth. And if there is a picture you see this symbol," he pointed to a camera icon in the right-hand column, but not in every row. "If you double-click on this symbol it brings up the picture. Now look carefully at the serial numbers."

He took a ballpoint from his shirt pocket and ran it slowly down the column of numbers. They were in sequence.

"Do you see any gaps in the sequence, Inspector?"

"No."

"No, because there are no gaps. You can scroll through the records for the entire dig, Inspector, and you will not find one gap – I know, I have tried. So there is not a single item missing." He straightened up. "You will also see that nowhere on the list is there a gold ring with an intaglio."

Justine Drexler was not unwilling to be taken away from the dig. She went to her tent first, returning with a lighter and a pack of cigarettes which she put on the table as she sat down. Then she selected a cigarette from the pack, lit it, leaned back and inhaled deeply. Lucia didn't like it, but she needed the girl's cooperation, so she let it go.

"What do you want to know, then?" Justine demanded, the words coming out with a stream of smoke from her mouth and nostrils.

"You're not at university, are you, Justine?"

"God, no!"

"So what brought you here, to this dig?"

"My Dad was keen. He went on a dig himself, when he was a teenager. He said I could do with the exercise and fresh air." She laughed, put the cigarette in her mouth, and scratched her left shoulder which, Lucia noticed, carried a tattoo. Then she took the cigarette out of her mouth and breathed more smoke out of her nostrils. She was waiting for the next question.

"Do you always do what your Dad says?"

"Oh, I went along with it. I thought it'd be a bit of a lark. I mean, I knew the digging would be pretty hard, but at least I thought we'd have a bit of fun in the evenings – you know, a few drinks, a few laughs." She snorted derisively. "Bad call. Look at it. I'm stuck up here with this lot all week."

"You can go down to Castellamare at the weekends."

"Oh yeah. I can tell you, the weekends don't come fast enough."

"Are you going to pack it in?"

She sniffed. "Nah. Dad would go ballistic. I'll stick it out."

"What do you think of Professor Lockhart?"

"Julian? Nice-looking guy. Full of himself. But fit – you know."

Lucia tried not to show how staggered she was with the girl's superficiality. Instead she pushed her in the direction she seemed to be going.

"Did he show any interest in you?"

"He had some thoughts about it. Caught him glancing at my boobs, that sort of thing. I had the feeling he was coming on to me at one point. Then *she* shows up and..." She made a little popping sound with her lips and flicked away the backs of her fingers.

"She...?"

Justine jerked her head. "Yeah, her."

Francesca Infantino was passing in front of the kitchen, on her way to the toilets at the rear.

Lucia blinked. "Are you saying Julian Lockhart had an affair with Francesca?"

She wrinkled her nose. "Well, all I know is, the whole team went to Pompeii and had a look round, and then he and Francesca took off on their own. So far as I know she didn't come back to the hostel that night. I'm only putting two and two together."

"I see. Do you have any idea where Professor Lockhart is now?"

She shook her head. "I don't know. Maybe he found a chick in town and took off with her."

"You don't think much of him, do you?"

"No, I don't. Bastard."

"What, because you think he seduced Francesca?"

"Christ, no! Because he didn't seduce me!" She laughed, but failed to hide the bitterness in her tone. "You all done with me now?"

They got up. Justine dropped the cigarette butt onto the grass and ground it with her foot. Lucia laid a hand on her shoulder.

"Thanks, Justine."

As Justine wandered back to the dig, Lucia pondered what she'd said about her father thinking she needed exercise. The deltoid under that tattoo was as hard as rock.

Nick's mind was in a whirl. Did these two really have a standup argument about a ring that never existed?

"Wait a minute," he said. "Somebody could have erased the record, couldn't they? And then the next record would get the next number, and the sequence would still be unbroken."

"No, Inspector, that's not possible. Look, I will show you. Please do it for yourself. Close this file and open a new one."

Nick had used Macs from time to time. He clicked in the red dot to close the file. Then he used the File menu to open a new one.

"All right. Now you can enter a record. It's under 'Record' on the menu bar, or you can click this icon, or you can use Command-N. Try all three."

Nick did so. Each time he opened a record a new line appeared on the screen, numbered in sequence, 0001, 0002, 0003, 0004, 0005, 0006.

"Now, Inspector, delete the last record. You'll find that is in the Record menu as well."

Nick selected "Delete Record" and a dialogue box came up. "Do you really want to delete this record? All associated data will be lost." There was a choice of buttons: "OK", "Cancel". He clicked "OK", and the last line was now numbered 0005.

"Now create a new record."

Nick did so. The new record was numbered 0007. He deleted some more records and added fresh ones. Each time it left a gap in the sequence. Finally he deleted all of them and started again. The first record was numbered 0012.

"You see, Inspector," Montalcini said. "This software is custom-designed, written specifically in a way that prevents fraud. That is why I am so confident that this ring never existed."

Nick thought for a moment. "Maybe the record was tampered with. Same serial number but the description's replaced."

"Try it."

Nick created a few records, writing a few arbitrary words in the description box of each. Then he went back to one, selected some text and tried to alter it. He couldn't. The backspace wouldn't work either. He searched the menus. There was no delete instruction except for Delete Record, which he'd already tried.

Montalcini smiled. "You see? It won't let you."

Nick pushed away the laptop. He still couldn't accept it.

"Professor, Julian Lockhart's a highly respected archaeologist. I find it really hard to believe he dreamed the whole thing up. A discovery like this would have caused some excitement at the time, surely? All the students would have crowded round to see it. What do they have to say about it?"

Montalcini seemed unperturbed. "Oh, they say they saw something all right. But what they saw I cannot tell. I only know I never saw it and there is no record of it."

"And that was what the argument was about?"

"Yes. Professor Lockhart was enraged. He said this object had been stolen. He wanted to search everyone's quarters – every student's, my assistant's, even mine."

"And you wouldn't allow it."

He shrugged. "Of course I could not prevent him. But I pointed out that we were the two senior investigators on the project and such a serious decision should be taken jointly. And I was strongly opposed to it. It would destroy completely the climate of trust and cooperation we had within our group."

"What did he say to that?"

"Nothing. He just stormed out of here. He took the small 4 X 4 and drove off."

"Do you know where he went?"

"I haven't the faintest idea. Usually he could not separate himself from the dig. The students were used to having him around; they were perplexed."

"Professor, earlier on you said you had no idea why he was agitated. Isn't it fair to assume that it had something to do with this missing ring?"

Montalcini opened his hands.

"First you would have to believe there was such a ring. To me his behaviour was quite irrational. Therefore I must repeat: I have no explanation for it."

"So did he return to the dig later?"

"No. But that was a Friday. We do not work here at the weekend; the students must have some time for themselves."

"Please go on."

Montalcini shrugged. "He returned on Monday but he did not go to the dig and he seemed to be avoiding me. After a while he drove off again. He came back that evening. I wanted to speak with him because I did not want this hostile atmosphere to continue, but he went straight to his cabin."

"And that was the last time you saw him?"

"Yes. The following morning Dr. Cothill was leaving and he could not find him. Then we all started to look, but he was gone."

"Neither of the vehicles was missing."

"No. They were both still here."

"Could someone have come in from outside?"

"No one heard the noise of a vehicle. Nothing can come or go up here without us hearing it."

"What, even over the noise of your generator?"

"That would not mask the noise of a vehicle."

Nick rubbed his lower lip.

"Well, you know what that means. If Professor Lockhart was murdered the killer would have to be one of you."

Chapter 21

Francesca reappeared from behind the kitchen and Lucia called out to her. She changed direction and came over. Her top stopped well short of her hipsters, which were low enough to reveal the blades of her pelvis. Between them her tanned satin-smooth skin was taut over the contours of her belly. A wide, studded leather belt hung at a slight angle from one hip; it did nothing to support her jeans, but accentuated her narrow waist. Lucia had seen similar outfits before, but never looking as good on someone as this. They sat down at the table and Francesca collected her dark hair together and fiddled with an elasticized band of wooden beads until it held most of it back. Lucia spoke to her in Italian, easing her in gently, talking about her course in Padua, her career aspirations, the progress of the dig. Then:

"Do you like Professor Lockhart?"

"Certainly."

"I mean do you like him personally?"

There was a moment's silence. Francesca batted her eyelashes.

"He's a clever man, a good archaeologist, and a good teacher – that's what I meant."

"Where do you think he is now?"

"I don't know. He seemed like a different person the last day or so we saw him. He was always working in the dig with us before that. Then suddenly he was coming and going all the time in the little 4 X 4. He didn't even look in at the dig, and he didn't speak to any of us. Usually he was so friendly. He was acting like something had possessed him."

"You don't know what."

"No, no idea."

"And you don't know where he was going?"

"No. I mean, I assume Castellamare di Stabia or Napoli, but it could have been anywhere."

"Francesca, it's been suggested that he's taken off with someone. From what you know of him, do you think that's a possibility?"

Francesca's eyes were wide. She swallowed. "No. No, I don't think so."

"You're sure?"

"Yes – I mean, I'm not sure, but I don't think so."

Lucia took a deep breath. She was getting nowhere. She didn't like to do this, but she was going to have to apply more pressure.

"Because," she said, "if he hasn't taken off, the only other possibility is that he's been killed."

Francesca's cheeks were flushed and she was breathing rapidly. She licked her lips.

"Oh no! Do you think so? Oh God."

"And if he's been killed, this isn't going to be a missing person enquiry any more: it'll be a murder investigation. You'll be called on to give evidence in court, on oath, and the prosecution will tie you in knots until everything comes out, one way or another. Look Francesca, I don't want that to happen and I'm sure you don't but I can only help you if you help me. If we can find out what happened to Julian, and we can find out who was responsible, all that can be avoided. I'm going to be perfectly direct: did Julian have an affair with you?"

Francesca looked at her with those liquid dark eyes. She seemed close to tears. Lucia laid a hand on her arm and spoke softly.

"You can tell me, Francesca. Come on, now, I need to know what happened."

Her eyes were swimming now. A tear welled up over those long lower lashes, dropped onto her cheek and coursed slowly down.

"It's Justine, isn't it? She told you!" she choked. "She's a slut! She hates me and she hates Julian because he wanted me, not her."

Another tear dropped.

"Let's take it from the trip to Pompeii."

Francesca wiped at her eyes with the back of one hand. She focused on the table, and when she started to speak her voice seemed to come from a great distance.

"We all went to see Pompeii. Well, all except Professore Montalcini. He was in Naples. And Antonino stayed at the dig – someone always has to stay at the dig, to keep an eye on things. We took the train from Castellamare and Julian met us at Pompei Scavi. We walked into the ruins of Pompeii and he showed us around. He was a wonderful guide. He could make us feel like we were there when it was a prosperous, bustling town.

"Anyway, we spent the whole morning with him and then we had a light lunch at the cafeteria behind the Forum. After that he surprised us a bit by suggesting that we explore the rest on our own. We could take the train back whenever we wanted to. Except for me. He said to me, 'Francesca, you come with me. There's something I want to show you.' Orkut heard him and he wanted to come with us but Julian told him to stay with the others. He wasn't very happy about it."

"Orkut seems to be rather taken with you."

"Yes. I don't know why. I haven't encouraged him."

Lucia recalled the gentle sway of that lissom figure as she'd strolled over to the table. How much encouragement did she think the boy needed?

"So where did you and Julian go?"

"We walked back to his little 4 X 4 and he drove to Oplontis – well, it was called Oplontis at the time of the eruption; it's called Torre Annunziata now. A huge villa has been found there; I think it belonged to Poppea, Nero's second wife. That's what most visitors get to see but Julian knows people so he took me to the Villa of Lucius Crassius Tertius. It was wonderful. People in the surrounding fields took refuge there from the eruption. Probably some came from Pompeii as well. They all died, of course, but they were probably asphyxiated so the skeletons were preserved.

"They found some wonderful artifacts, too. There was a big chest, decorated with iron leaves – it may have been something like the chest we found, except that ours had disintegrated and this one was intact because of the way the ash fell."

"Go on."

"Well, we spent a bit of time there and Julian explained some of the projects. And then he asked me if I'd been to Sorrento and I said I hadn't. So he said, 'It's not that far. Why don't we go there instead of Castellamare and we can look around and have a bite to eat.' It sounded like a great idea.

"It was a lovely warm evening and we strolled along the back streets. It was so pretty. Somehow I felt very safe, too. But then Julian is such a big guy you'd feel safe with him anywhere. After a while he pointed to a sign, 'Pizza al forno'. He said, 'This is a good place, let's have dinner here.' It was tucked away behind the via Fuoro, very quiet and private. On the way to the table we passed the traditional oven, which was just like the ones we'd seen in Pompeii earlier that day!

"We sat in the open air under a bower of vines. The waiter put a litre carafe of red wine on the table and a bowl of fat green olives – I love olives – and some bread, with the local olive oil to dip it in. We talked and ate olives, and dipped the bread, and drank wine and then the pizzas arrived, a little bit burnt around the edges – the best I've ever had. And after that we drank some more wine and talked some more… there just seemed so much to say…"

Her eyes had become even larger and darker. She turned them on Lucia.

"I don't suppose you can understand but try to picture yourself in my place. I'd had such a lovely, lovely day, and the evening was warm, and the food and wine was good, and it was all so, so romantic.

"It was getting late by then and he suggested we find a hotel in Sorrento rather than go back to Castellamare. Even the thought of that hostel made me shudder, especially after such a beautiful evening. So I said yes. When he checked us in he didn't ask for separate rooms. I didn't say anything. I mean, it seemed like the most natural thing in the world."

"So you went to bed and he made love to you."

"Yes." She looked down again, speaking in a low voice. "It wasn't at all like the boys I'd had before, all clumsy and in a hurry. He was slow and gentle..." Her voice tailed off. "Look, the sex wasn't that important. I was happy to have him all to myself. I just wanted it to go on for ever and ever.

"The following morning we had breakfast together and then we got into the 4 X 4, and before he started the engine he turned to me and said, 'Francesca, I want you to know that I'll always remember these moments we've had together. But much as I'd love to do it all over again, I can't. I have to be realistic. I'm married and I have two daughters. And if anyone found out I was having an affair with one of my students, my reputation would suffer – badly. I might even be thrown out of Oxford. You wouldn't want that to happen, would you?' "What could I say? I'd built myself a castle in the sky and now it was falling down around my ears.

"I think I cried a little. He put his arm around me and said if things were different and – oh, I don't know what he said. We drove back to Castellamare and he dropped me at the hostel. It was late morning, and the others weren't around. I can't remember what I did with the rest of the day. I think I cried a lot. Part of me was saying that it had been a wonderful day and a wonderful evening, and I shouldn't expect any more from him than that. And the other part was saying he took advantage of me. I suppose I only have myself to blame, really. I mean, I knew he was married; I went into it with my eyes open." She looked up at Lucia. "I've been very stupid, haven't I, Lucia?"

Lucia contemplated the lovely, sad creature in front of her.

"Not stupid, Francesca. A little naïve, maybe. A girl as pretty as you is going to have that effect on men. And you'll have to learn that not all of them want a permanent relationship."

"You're very beautiful, Lucia. Did this ever happen to you?"

"Oh, I've made mistakes, God knows. I'm busy trying not to repeat them." She hastily switched the conversation back. "Do you hate Julian for what happened?"

"No, I don't hate him. Perhaps he couldn't help himself. But he's older than me, more experienced. He should have known better."

"What about Orkut? Does he know?"

"I've never said a thing, of course, not to him or to anyone. But I think they all guessed what had happened when I didn't return to the hostel that night. I think Orkut is terribly jealous. And the girls aren't being very friendly now. I'll do what I have to but I'm already wishing it was over and I was on my way back to Padova."

She looked in the direction of the dig and then back at Lucia. "Lucia, do you have to tell anyone about this?"

"I'll have to say something to my boss – Detective Inspector Roberts. But I can't see why it has to go any further than that. No good would come of it: it would only hurt you, and it would hurt Julian's reputation and his family and all for no good reason. I just hope we can wrap things up here and then no one need ever know. Come on, I'll take you back to the dig."

Chapter 22

Montalcini looked not so much affronted as exasperated.

"Please, Inspector. You are not seriously suggesting he was killed, and by one of us?"

"I have to consider every possibility at this stage."

"Well now, Inspector, academics are well known for murdering each other but we do it with words not weapons. Perhaps there are other, more likely explanations."

"Such as?"

Montalcini took a breath and compressed his lips. He seemed uncomfortable. "I think there is no reason to suppose that Professor Lockhart is dead. He was quite an athlete in his younger days, you know. A middle distance runner, I believe. It is my understanding that he was still, ah, athletic in other respects. Perhaps that is a more likely hypothesis."

Nick looked surprised.

"He has a wife and two daughters..."

"So? It has been known."

"And none of your team is missing," he added.

"Ah no! He would be more discreet than that!"

"Well," Nick said. "He didn't take a vehicle so he'd have had to walk out of here. We've flooded every town and village in this area with photographs and a description. So far no one has reported seeing him."

"This means nothing. It was at night, remember. He could have walked to Castellamare. It is a good distance but he is a fit man. He could wait there and take the first train to Naples. He could be anywhere by now. The chances of someone noticing him would be very remote."

Nick grimaced. "We'll carry on looking, just the same."

"Of course."

Nick pushed the chair back. "Well, Professor, I don't think I have anything more to ask you at this stage. You've been very generous with your time. I appreciate that."

They stood and shook hands.

"By the way, my compliments on your English," Nick said. "It truly is excellent."

Montalcini gave him a slight bow. "Thank you, but it is of course a requirement of modern scholarship." Then he added, "Before you go, Inspector, may I invite you and the Sergente to my lecture tonight?"

Nick was interested. "You're giving a lecture tonight?"

"Yes. It is open to the public, although it is mainly academic colleagues and some visitors to the University who will be present. They have asked me to provide a progress report on the dig. The background may be useful to your investigation, or possibly just of interest. The students will come in the people carrier. There would be room for you. I would be pleased to see you. It is at eight o'clock in the Museum of Antiquities, in Naples."

"Thank you very much, Professor. We may well come along."

Nick was reaching for the door handle when he stiffened. He was aware of a distant rumbling and a vibration that came up through the soles of his shoes. The sound grew and the cabin started to shake with increasing violence. He put out a hand to steady himself. The Professor lunged for the laptop, which was in danger of sliding off the desk. The vibration and the rumbling died away.

Nick turned to the Professor, blinking rapidly.

"Good Christ," he said. "What in hell's name was that?"

"A small earthquake," Montalcini replied calmly. "That is not exceptional: this is a seismic area. But I must say the tremors have been more frequent of late. I heard a report that there has been a magma shift in the volcano. I suppose the activity could be associated with that."

"Jesus," said Nick. "Does that mean it's going to blow?"

The Professor smiled. "It could mean that, yes, but we have no idea when. Vesuvius's activity seems to follow a cycle of roughly two thousand years. In 1870 B.C. there was a very large eruption. Bronze Age settlements in the Naples area were completely destroyed. Next was the catastrophe of A.D. 79. If we project forward from that, it does point to the probability of another major explosive event some time this century. The volcanologists certainly think so. They are watching it even more closely than usual."

"I don't understand; it has been active since the Pompeii eruption, hasn't it?"

"Oh, yes. In recent times it has erupted at intervals of five to thirty years, and lava has flowed down its slopes. But really these are small events. In geological terms, this has been a period of relative dormancy. The last major eruption was in A.D. 1631 but even this was not on the same scale as the two-thousand-year events we are talking about. No, it could well be storing up something bigger."

As Nick opened the door, Montalcini called after him, "Don't be alarmed, Inspector. It may come to nothing."

Nick hurried from the cabin. "Lucy? Where are you? Lucy?"

"Over here." The voice came from the direction of the dig. "It's okay, we're all right."

As he appeared over the ridge he found the students all standing and looking in his direction.

"What the hell was that all about?" demanded Justine.

"Just a small earth tremor," Nick replied cheerfully, feigning a confidence he in no way felt. "This is a seismic area. Nothing to worry about. They get them here all the time."

The students looked at him dubiously, then slowly resumed what they were doing. Nick extended a hand to Lucia. They clasped each other's forearms and he helped her up the steep, sandy edge of the excavation pit. Her jeans and T-shirt were scuffed, as though she'd fallen over.

At the top, she turned to Torretta and pointed at the tractor.

"Antonino," she said in Italian. "I think you should move the tractor back a bit. It's too close to the edge. Another tremor like that, and it could fall in."

He shouted back, "No problem, I'll do it later."

She turned and followed Nick away from the dig. When they were out of earshot she put a hand on his arm, peered at his face, and giggled.

"Nick! I've never seen you like this! You're white as a sheet!"

"It's a small failing I have," he retorted crossly. "It's called an instinct for self-preservation."

She laughed. "Take it easy." She put a hand on his arm. "It's just like you said back there. They get them here all the time."

"You don't understand, Lucy. Something's going on. Montalcini says there's been a magma shift in the volcano."

Her face fell.

"Lucy, why didn't we hear about this before?"

"We haven't been following the news," she said thoughtfully, "and it may not have been reported in the U.K. You know, come to think of it, I heard a rumble earlier. I thought it was quarrying."

"I don't like it. I don't like it at all. I'm going to Naples. The police must be on top of this sort of thing. They'll have contingency plans for mass evacuation and they'll need to know when to activate them. Umberto Gardi may be able to clue me up. I'll have a word with him and talk to some of the experts if I can get hold of them. I want to find out if we're in any danger."

"Isn't Professor Montalcini concerned?"

"He's so laid back he's almost falling over. I'll see if I can find out something more definite. Look, the Professor's invited us to an open lecture he's giving tonight. In Naples. I think it'd be a good idea if we go along. The students are coming and there'll be room for you in the people carrier. Why don't you stay up here for the moment and I'll meet you at the lecture."

"Okay. That'll give me a chance to talk to some more of the students. It's getting kind of interesting."

"Good. We can compare notes later. See you at the lecture."

He backed out his rented 4 X 4. As he prepared to drive off he looked round and saw that she was waiting to see him go. They waved to each other.

Above her was an unbroken hemisphere of blue sky. And on the horizon behind her, Vesuvius sat in quiet majesty, its jagged top obscured by a lone white cloud.

Chapter 23

It was a large room, not a purpose-built lecture theatre. A few tubular steel and canvas chairs were stacked against one wall, and others had been set out on the wooden floor to accommodate the numbers expected for the evening. At the front there was a desk and a lectern with a small light. A projector had been placed on a stand in the central aisle separating the rows of chairs. It was humming quietly and projecting a title slide onto the white wall behind the lectern.

Nick took a seat a little more than half-way back and put his jacket over the vacant seat next to him to reserve it for Lucia. He sat back and read the title slide.

New discoveries dating from the Plinian eruption of A.D. 79

Enrico Montalcini, Professor of Roman Antiquities,

University of Naples

The Pliny Institute, The National Archeological Museum of Naples, and The Department of Antiquities, University of Naples

The room was already filling up when the students came in, followed by Lucia. The students immediately filed along the back row. Nick gave Lucia a wave and picked up his jacket and she shuffled along the row to him.

"All right?" Nick asked.

"Yep. I've seen four of the students. Two more to go."

"Good, we can talk about it after this is over."

"Did you find out anything more about the volcano?"

"Not really. There is something happening at the moment; they'll agree on that much. But it's just like Montalcini said: they can't say when it might blow or on what sort of scale. You could get a fissure opening and some lava creeping out. Or you could get a massive explosion with fallout and pyroclastic flows – the lot. The explosion's more likely because they tell me the conduit's closed at the moment and pressure could be building up. But no one can say exactly when. It could be any time; maybe tomorrow, maybe not for years."

She grimaced, then looked round to see if the students were settled – and froze. She faced the front again, then took another brief glance behind her.

"Nick..."

"Yes?"

"Those men who just came in, sitting on the left in the back row. Take a quick look if you can without being too obvious."

Nick got up, ostensibly to hang his jacket over the back of the chair, and let his eyes drift casually to the back row. The man was wearing a black suit, with a red tie and pocket handkerchief. He had black hair, slicked straight back, and he wore dark glasses. He sat bolt upright, motionless. The men on each side of him were much more active, scanning the room continuously. Nick sat down again.

"Who's the guy in the middle?" he asked.

"Carlo Rossi. Mafia."

"Jesus! How do you know?"

"Don't forget I spend weeks in Italy every year. I'm a cop; crime interests me. I read the papers. This guy's picture is quite often in them."

Nick frowned. "The mafia? We're in Naples. I thought it was the Camorra here."

"He's not from Naples. He's from Sicily. One of the Palermitani."

"Bit off base, isn't he? I wonder what the hell he's doing here."

"I was just wondering the same thing."

The buzz of conversation in the room died as Professor Montalcini came in and took a seat in the front row. The man who'd accompanied him continued to the lectern and addressed the audience, in Italian.

Lucia whispered a quick translation in Nick's ear.

154

"He's the Dean of the Faculty. He's just welcoming Montalcini... he's saying what a distinguished man he is... we're fortunate that he's given up his valuable time to talk to us."

The Director sat down in the front row and Montalcini took his place at the lectern.

"Good evening, ladies and gentlemen. First I would ask for your indulgence. I understand that there are a number of visitors here, and it would be a courtesy to them if I speak mainly in English. I think this will not be a problem for people from my Department and from the Museum, but from time to time I will summarize in Italian."

He began to speak rapidly in Italian. Nick glanced at Lucia.

"It's the same thing in Italian," she whispered.

The first slide went up: a map of Italy showing a line winding up from Sicily through the Naples area. Montalcini picked up a laser pointer and began to speak, without notes.

"Here in Campania we live on the boundary between two tectonic plates: the Eurasian plate and the African plate. Why? Why do we choose to live over two moving masses that are constantly at war with each other, causing earthquakes and volcanic eruptions all along their length? Of course there are many geographical factors that favour settlement here. Ironically one of them is the fertile volcanic soil of this area, which is ideal for farming and for the cultivation of wine grapes. It is so now, and it was so nearly two thousand years ago when Pompeii was a busy cosmopolitan city, its streets thronged with politicians, merchants, sailors, artists and craftsmen, builders and carpenters, philosophers and farmers, priests and prostitutes, slaves and freedmen.

"At midday on the 24th of August, A.D. 79, Vesuvius erupted. We now know that much of the population of Pompeii was extinguished by a pyroclastic surge that swept down the slopes of Vesuvius and through the city in a matter of minutes. But this did not take place immediately: the eruption had already been in progress for some nineteen hours. Those who had not been buried by the initial fall of ash and stones had started to flee the city. Some vainly tried to escape by sea. Others streamed along the roads to Nuceria or sought refuge in Oplontis and Moregine, carrying whatever personal possessions they could. Some stopped running and hid – in attics, in subterranean corridors – as you might hide from a human attacker. But this was no human attacker. There was no safe place for them to hide from the clouds of scorching ash and poisonous gases that then swept through the streets, the passages, the attics. In the countryside all around, cities and towns – and beautiful villas outside the towns – were buried, and their inhabitants with them. This is recorded as far away as Stabiae – now Castellamare di Stabia – where the fumes and falling rocks claimed the life of the elder Pliny. The ash rained from darkened skies as far north as Rome, and has even been recorded in Egypt and Syria."

All this time he was flashing up slides: colonnades, shops, statues, frescoes, plaster casts of bodies frozen in their last agony, grisly groups of skeletons. Now he paused the slides and spoke for a few moments in Italian. Nick couldn't help but admire the facility with which he switched in and out of the languages. He began to speak again in English.

"From the rediscovery of Pompeii in the 18th century, archaeologists and geologists and volcanologists have excavated much of Pompeii and Herculaneum and Oplontis and Stabia and other sites. They have assembled a good picture of Campanian life at that time and pieced together the sequence of events that destroyed it.

"So is the story now complete? Have we excavated the last remains of a Roman civilization of the first century? Archaeologists know better than to suggest such a thing. In Egypt, in the Valley of Kings, they told Carter that every tomb had already been discovered. He amazed the world by unearthing what must be the most spectacular tomb of all: that of the boy-king Tutankhamun – and there have been further discoveries since that time. So it is here at Pompeii. It has been my privilege to have the opportunity to uncover a brand new site, a site unaffected by the construction of roads, railways and buildings that now cover the whole coastline of the Gulf of Naples. How it came about is an interesting story in itself.

"In October last year the Ministry of Antiquities in Naples received a call from a farmer. He said he had found something curious on his land and he wanted to know if it had any value. Of course they asked him to describe it and when he did they asked him please not to disturb anything. They arranged for two people to meet him and investigate. One of those people was a geologist employed by the Museum. The other was me.

"It was not an easy drive. From Castellamare we ascended through the orchards, and vineyards and olive groves and now we were over 300 metres above sea level in a barren hilly area. And that was where we found him.

"It seemed this man owned a winery, which was doing well, and he wanted to plant vineyards higher up, on land his family had owned for generations but never cultivated. His idea was to develop the area for a different type of grape, one that is better suited to cooler slopes. He would clear the rocks, plant the vineyards, and then crush the rocks to make paths between the vines.

"They were using a truck equipped with a grab. The rocks were much lighter than they expected so they were able to lift them whole and they made rapid progress. They were about to break for lunch on the first day when they got a surprise. The rock they had just lifted had left behind a shallow cavity that was full of interesting marks. He showed it to us and I took a photograph. This is what we saw."

He showed a slide of a depression in the ground, lined with a greyish white material. Sunlight had thrown marks in the material into sharp relief. They were unmistakable.

The ground under the rock was covered with footprints.

Chapter 24

Montalcini smiled at the intake of breath the photograph had provoked from the audience.

"My geologist colleague examined everything very closely. The footprints had been made in a fine powdery deposit. To him, this looked identical to a late ashfall from the eruption of Vesuvius in A.D. 79 – he had seen it many times before in various excavations. It had probably absorbed water from the underlying soil, setting it like a very weak concrete and preserving the impressions with great accuracy.

"It was now many centuries later, of course, and little of this ash remained on the slopes of the mountainside, but under the rock it had been protected from the effects of wind and rain. The rock itself was light because it was pumice. As you know, this is a porous rock formed when molten lava, still bubbling with gases, is thrown out of a volcano and solidifies. From the colour and porosity of the pumice and the geographical location he felt sure that this had come from the same eruption. It had not bonded to the ash, and the two separated when the rock was lifted.

"We walked around the area and found other material, calcareous rocks that had landed here when the top third of the mountain was progressively torn off by the magma jet and flung into the air. All of this was consistent with the area receiving substantial fallout from the eruption of A.D. 79. Now let us look a little more closely at the footprints."

He used the laser to point.

"Here you see a mark left by bare feet. You can clearly make out the impressions left by the toes. There are more here and here. But this print and this one are different; the people who made those were wearing sandals. Do you see how deep this one is? It overlies some of the other prints, so this could have been a man or woman who was lagging behind the rest; perhaps they were overweight or carrying a heavy bundle. Here we have a straight line, a groove, travelling right through the deposit. What is it? The moment I saw it I was convinced that this was the rut left by a cartwheel.

"A picture started to form in my mind. It was a party – quite a large party to judge by the number of footprints – maybe consisting of several families, with their slaves. They had loaded their possessions, and perhaps the women and small children, onto wagons, and they were trying to escape across the mountains. The location was maybe eight kilometres south of Pompeii, and the terrain was not easy, yet the rocks had fallen after they passed.

"That meant the eruption was still in progress and they must have left Pompeii at an early stage or even before it had started. This area, too, would eventually have been blanketed with poisonous fumes, and the bombardment of rocks and red-hot lava would have continued for days. It was doubtful that they'd survived. But how far had they got?

"The geologist and I were thinking along the same lines. We looked up from the depression, following the direction of the rut. There were more of these rocky outcrops all over the hillside, some of them lying along the same route. We could lift those, look for more footprints, narrow things down. Then we could conduct a thorough geophysics survey and we would be ready to start digging."

"Of course, the farmer was not very pleased when he learned what we had in mind. It would delay his planned development. We agreed to seek funding, including compensation for the farmer, and we undertook to be finished in time for him to prepare the area for the following year."

Once again Montalcini paused to provide a summary in Italian. Then he continued:

"I am pleased to say that the Pliny Institute provided the funding we needed. We were able to identify the site where the party was finally overcome. We have been working very hard to uncover all that remains before we have to give the land back to the farmer. We have already uncovered the skeletons of a number of individuals."

He began to show slides of skeletons curled up in the excavation, photographed with black and white rules laid next to them, and he talked about their age, sex, stature, and the condition of their teeth and bones.

"Some of these skeletons are remarkably complete. That is a little surprising because bodies that lie above ground are often scavenged by wild animals and the bones then become scattered. This type of damage can usually be recognized from tooth marks on the bones. There is no evidence of that here.

"One possibility is that the animals had themselves been killed or had fled from the burning lava and by the time they returned everything was coated with ash. However, I think there is another explanation. You will notice that many of the bones I have shown you are blackened. I believe the flesh was consumed almost immediately by fire. It may be that these unfortunate people were set alight by a rain of incandescent lava. Or it may be that the grass and trees, in fact the whole countryside, was set on fire and their bodies burned where they had fallen."

By now Nick thought he'd seen enough grinning sooty skulls to last him for some considerable time, and it was a positive relief when Montalcini summarized the final part of his talk in Italian and thanked the audience for their kind attention.

There was a rattle of applause. The Dean stood up and said that Professor Montalcini would be pleased to answer a few questions.

A man in the second row raised his hand and the Dean pointed at him.

He asked, "Professor, you said the solidified ash was like concrete. How can you excavate skeletons from ground in that condition?"

"Thank you, I should have made that more clear. Although a thin layer of ash had fallen here it did not bury everything, as it did at Herculaneum, for example. In places the fall of ash was thick enough to take the footprints, as we saw, but it may be that the wind gusted or changed direction, because it did not accumulate uniformly. There was certainly ash where the party finally came to rest, but not enough to bind together to form a solid layer. We think the bodies were eventually buried by mud that was washed down the slopes by heavy rain. An eruption of that magnitude would have had a considerable influence on weather in the region. The accumulation of soil was especially deep just below the ridge, where we are excavating."

A hand went up on the other side and the Dean pointed again.

"You've spoken mainly about bones. Professor. What about valuable objects, like jewellery?"

"As you may know, it was not considered polite for men to wear jewellery at that time. A single ring was the limit of good taste."

"What about women, though? They wore jewellery. And if they were escaping isn't it likely that they'd be taking all their favourite pieces with them?"

"It's likely, yes, but you must remember, this was a large party with many slaves, and it may be that the bones we have looked at so far are those of slaves. You see, in order to assemble a complete picture we dig to one level all over the site. Only when everything has been excavated at that level do we take it down further. This is a slow process. We have only uncovered eleven skeletons so far. You have to be patient."

Another hand went up. The questioner spoke in Italian. Lucia was about to translate for Nick, but Montalcini did it for her.

"The question is about the phenomenon of spontaneous combustion. The gentleman knows of my expertise in burned or cremated human remains and wonders whether I have any explanation for these phenomena, in which an individual, often in his or her own home, catches fire and burns completely to ash.

"In answer, I have to say first that I have never investigated such an occurrence myself. It would of course be necessary to look at each case on its own merits, so I can't comment on how those people actually caught fire. I can, however, give you some relevant information about what happens after that.

"Fat is highly flammable – you only have to see a barbecue in progress to know this." (There was a murmur of subdued laughter.)

"If an individual has a lot of body fat and is in a confined space, the temperature could get high enough to reduce everything to ash, including bones. On the other hand, an individual who did not have a lot of body fat would burn less fiercely, particularly if he or she was in the open air. In this case the flesh would burn, leaving behind charred bones. I believe these were the conditions that gave rise to the skeletons we have been finding.

"Of course, this does not mean that the party fleeing Pompeii were all fit, athletic individuals. If there did happen to be a fat man amongst them he might have burned to ash, even in the open air. In that case, of course, we would not find his remains."

The Dean now intervened, again speaking in Italian, and it was clear that he was closing down the proceedings. There was another rattle of applause and people started to get up to leave.

Nick took his coat from the back of the chair.

He turned to Lucia. "Well, what do you think?"

"I think it was very good. He knows his stuff all right."

"Not a single mention of Lockhart. Does he intend to take all the credit now?"

"I'd be inclined to give him the benefit of the doubt. He was in a difficult position. I don't know if it's general knowledge that Lockhart's missing. If he'd mentioned Lockhart he might have opened himself up to questions about where he'd gone. But did you notice the way he dodged the question on valuable artifacts?"

"Yes, I thought he did that rather well. It's fair enough. He wouldn't want people to think there was anything of value up there – it might encourage the wrong sort of visitor. Let's go and say hallo."

They strolled to the front, where several people had stopped to talk to the Professor. They waited until the last had left, then stepped forward.

Nick said, "Thanks for the invitation, Professor. That was a fascinating talk. Congratulations."

"Thank you. Look, they've invited me to dinner so I can't really stop now, but we will see each other up at the excavation."

"Fine."

They were just leaving when Nick suddenly turned back.

"By the way, Professor, do you happen to know Carlo Rossi?"

Montalcini raised his eyebrows.

"Carlo Rossi? No, I don't believe I know anyone of that name."

"Really? A notorious mafioso, reported almost daily in the newspapers, and you haven't heard of him?"

"No. Current events do not interest me. The past is what interests me. I live for my work. I do not have time for these other things. But why do you ask me if I know him?"

"Oh, I was just wondering what he was doing at your lecture."

"He was here? How interesting! Il Signore Rossi must be cultivating an interest in our glorious past."

"Yeah, that's what I thought too. Enjoy your dinner, Professor."

Chapter 25

"This one?"

The narrow street terminated in a depressing line of buildings, the street lamps on their brackets throwing into relief the scales of faded cream paint peeling from the walls. An even narrower street branched away from it, but set into the corner; and sending a warm glow of light and colour into both streets, was a small trattoria. It had a comfortable, tavern-like, look to it. Nick and Lucia nodded to each other and went in.

Looking around, Nick took in an arched ceiling, painted terra cotta pink, which was diffusely illuminated by lights concealed in the tops of the walls. The pink continued down to meet vertical wood panelling at waist height. The chairs and tables, also of wood, were of a sturdy design. There were no tablecloths. In the centre of the room and purely, Nick guessed, for the ambience, was a fluted plaster column. The floor was tiled and the walls were hung, at intervals, with what appeared to be reproductions of Roman frescoes.

At the window to the left of the entrance, two tables had been pushed together for eight people, who were engaged in boisterous conversation. They weren't Italians but they weren't speaking English; Nick thought it was a Slavic language. He pointed Lucia to a table in one of the deep corners of the room. There were two other diners, but the noise from the party in the front would ensure that they weren't overheard.

A warm, appetizing aroma floated through an open doorway to one side, and a sudden clatter of utensils confirmed that beyond it lay the kitchen.

A waiter came over and gave them each a menu.

"Buonasera, signore e signora. Volete ordinare prima le bibite?"

Nick looked blankly at Lucia, who made a small drinking movement with one hand.

"Oh! *Una birra, per favore.*"

"*Piccolo? Grande?*"

"Oh *grande*, definitely."

Lucia caught his eye and suppressed a quick smile.

"Lucy, what would you like?"

"*Lo stesso,*" she said, half to the waiter, half to Nick.

"*Due birre. Sì, certo.*"

The waiter left.

Lucia looked at Nick. "I see you know how to ask for a beer," she observed dryly.

"Got to get your priorities right," he said with a grin.

"And that was quite a mouthful of Italian you used to greet the Professor this afternoon. Have you been holding out on me?"

"Not really. Umberto coached me. He told me there was a short form, but I said I'd do the full monty."

"Why?"

He shrugged sheepishly. "I wanted to impress you."

He looked up and found her eyes on him. Her voice was low.

"Say 'piace'."

"Pi-ah-chay."

"Now say 'Lucia'."

"Lu-chi-ya."

"Good. Now you've impressed me. From now on, no more of this Lucy business. Deal?"

"Deal. But it has to be sealed with a kiss."

"Really, Nick! I don't know, you're a serious danger to women. You shouldn't be allowed to roam the streets. You ought to be castrated."

"I think you just did that with the look you gave me."

"Serves you right."

"It's not a deal yet..." He leaned forward and puckered his mouth expectantly.

She raised one eyebrow, touched a finger to her own lips and then to his.

He sat back reluctantly. "Oh well, I suppose that'll have to do."

"It most certainly will," she said, picking up her menu with a clear sense of purpose.

Nick smiled, opened his own menu and, after a final glance at Lucia, studied it carefully.

It was in both Italian and English, although some of the translations were rather quaint.

The waiter returned with a tray and placed two empty glasses and two green bottles on the table. He removed the crown caps and, with a slight flourish, poured a little into each glass. *"Ecco"*, he said, with a small gesture towards the glasses, and withdrew. Nick turned the bottle of Peroni Nastro Azzurra, frosted with condensation, so that he could view the label, and noted with approval that the contents equated to just over a pint. He topped up both glasses, pouring the beer down the side of the glass so as not to add to the head of foam already generated by the waiter. Then they raised the glasses and drank. He sat back with a sigh.

"Have you decided what you're having, Lucia?"

"I fancy the spaghetti with the meat sauce."

Nick located the item on the menu. He liked the look of that too, but he felt a bit self-conscious about his ability to handle spaghetti so he said he'd go for the risotto with shrimps in white wine.

He took his jacket off and placed it on the empty chair next to him. Lucia cast a speculative glance around the room, which evidently helped her to decide that it was warm enough to take hers off, too. As she turned to hang the short leather jacket over the back of the chair Nick noticed how the movement stretched the thin wool of the sweater she was wearing. He hastily attended to the business of hanging his own jacket over the chair.

"Allora, cosa prende?"

Nick looked up at the waiter and indicated Lucia.

"Un piatto di spaghetti al ragù e un risotto con gamberetti in bianco, per piacere."

"Ci vorranno venti minuti, signora."

"Nick, they'll have to prepare your risotto from scratch. It'll take twenty minutes. Is that all right?"

"Yeah, that's okay."

"Va bene," she said to the waiter.

"Altro, signora?"

"Would you like a side salad with that, Nick?"

"Good idea."

"Allora, prendiamo una insalata di contorno."

The waiter checked the pad he'd been writing on. *"Un piatto di spaghetti al ragù e un risotto con gamberetti in bianco, e due insalate miste. Va bene."*

Lucia nodded and the waiter tucked the pad into a pocket on the front of his apron, topped up the glasses, and disappeared in the direction of the kitchen.

"How was the drive down?"

"All right. Pippo Pellerano drove."

"Not Antonino?"

"No, he had to stay behind to look after the camp. Pippo drove quite well. Slower than Antonino, but that's just as well with seven in the car. How did your interview with Montalcini go?"

"I didn't get a whole lot out of him. It's like interviewing a politician. He doesn't get riled and he only says what he wants to say."

"Does he have any idea what happened to Lockhart?"

"Not really. His best guess was that Julian had some sort of assignation. Walked down to Castellamare in the night and went off somewhere with a young lady in tow."

"Do you buy that?"

"Well, Dawn said her husband wasn't like that."

"I'm afraid Dawn has been deluding herself."

"Oh? How do you mean?"

"He had a one-night stand with Francesca. Sounds like he set the whole thing up. Afterwards he told her to keep quiet because they wouldn't be doing it again. She was very upset. The other students guessed what had happened, so one way and another things aren't going well for Francesca at the moment."

There was an outburst of raucous laughter from the front of the restaurant. Nick shot a deprecatory glance sideways at the party, then returned to Lucia.

167

"By the way, I told her I wouldn't mention it to anyone – other than you, that is."

"Okay, it's not the sort of thing we want to spread around unless we really have to. Has he bothered any of the others?"

"Justine was rather hoping he'd bother her. If he didn't, it wasn't for lack of encouragement. She thought he'd shown some interest but then he went off with Francesca. I spoke to Claudia this afternoon. He seems to have behaved very properly with her. And with Angela. No, it's just Francesca, poor kid. Perhaps it's the first time he's done something like this, but somehow I doubt it."

The waiter came back with a large bowl of crusty bread and a two small dishes of olive oil.

Lucia said *"Grazie"*, picked up a piece of bread and dipped it into one of the dishes, which had herbs mixed with the oil.

Nick did the same. It was subtly flavoured with rosemary. "Mmm. Nice," he said. "So you think Montalcini could be right?"

"Actually, no. It would be out of character. Angela and Claudia told me independently how committed Julian was to the dig. He could hardly bear to be away from it."

"That's exactly what Dawn said he'd be like. But what about this thing with Francesca? Wasn't that a straw in the wind?"

She shook her head. "I think Francesca was nothing more than a temporary distraction. It shouldn't have happened but I can't see that it makes all that much difference. Why should he up sticks and leave behind something he's so absorbed in?"

She took another piece of bread and stabbed it in the oil.

"I agree. And then there's what we found in his cabin. Did you notice anything missing?"

Lucia thought for a moment. "Nothing that I can think of."

"Precisely. If he'd taken off somewhere, would he leave all that stuff behind?"

"Very unlikely."

"I'll get forensic to go over the cabin but I don't think they're going to find anything. There weren't any signs of a struggle. It looked like he just got up during the night and went out. He couldn't have been planning to leave – he didn't even take his jacket and passport. And as for the stuff on the chest of drawers – well, maybe he was in such a hurry he left all of it behind, but I doubt it. You'd have to be in one hell of a hurry not to take your room key."

"Maybe he got up during the night to go to the loo."

"That's a possibility. So what would he do? He wouldn't get dressed. He'd slip the jacket on over his pajamas, put the key in a jacket pocket, and put on his shoes. Yet the jacket and the key and the shoes are still in the room."

"He might have been wearing a different pair of shoes when he went out."

"Possible. But did he really have three pairs of shoes? He was travelling light – that wasn't a large suitcase."

"So what's the alternative?"

"My guess is he did go out, maybe just as I described. And somebody came back to the room later with his jacket, keys, and shoes."

"Well, whoever did that must have killed him."

He nodded. "There's still an outside chance of kidnap, but we can more or less rule it out. They've had more than enough time to claim responsibility or make a ransom demand and we haven't heard a dicky bird. And why put that stuff back in his cabin? It doesn't make sense. No, I think he's been murdered all right."

"Where's the body, then?"

"If they'd found a body we wouldn't be here, would we? We'll have a damned good look for one tomorrow, though. Let's suppose we find it. What conceivable motive was there for killing him? What about Francesca? He led her up the garden path. She must be pretty pissed off with him."

"Francesca's a slip of a girl. She doesn't have the strength to kill a man as big as Julian Lockhart and then dispose of the body. There is Orkut, though – Orkut Mansur, the Turkish boy. He's absolutely besotted with her. He must know something about what's happened, and he's insanely jealous. He's not as tall as Julian but he's built like an ox. He's capable of doing something like that, physically at least."

"Have you talked to him?"

"I tried to. He doesn't speak Italian and his English is very limited. I'll have another go tomorrow."

They paused as the waiter came by and set down two large mixed salads.

Lucia added oil and vinegar to hers, and started to pick absently at it with her fork.

"What about this Justine girl?" Nick asked, when the waiter had gone.

"She's strongly built, too. And there's something bitter about her. But I don't really see her as a killer."

"And Claudia and the English girl – what's her name again?"

"Angela. Angela Johnston. They're both very sensible. In fact they're the only ones I've spoken to so far who actually seem to be getting something out of their experience here. Both of them say Lockhart was an inspiring teacher and they enjoyed working with him. It wouldn't make sense for them to kill him."

"That leaves the Italian boy."

"Pippo. I'll talk to him again tomorrow. I can't really make him out at the moment. He keeps himself to himself. Not a whole lot to go on, is it? I've left a card with each of them, so they can contact us in case they think of something else – standard procedure."

"Good."

"There is one thing, though. Both Angela and Claudia said the two professors were always at loggerheads. The students could hear them arguing in the office. The last occasion was shortly after the discovery of that gold ring with the intaglio. Julian and Claudia found it, apparently. He went up to the office later that morning. They heard raised voices, really angry. After that Julian didn't return to the dig. He just kept coming and going in the small 4 X 4..."

She tailed off, seeing the waiter on his way again. He set down the two steaming dishes, then gestured at the half-empty glasses.

"*Desiderate qualcos'altro da bere?*"

"Do you want anything else to drink, Nick?"

"Ah, no thanks. I'm driving. I'll make this one last."

Lucia gestured with a flat hand. *"Nient'altro, grazie,"* she said.

The waiter said, *"Va bene. Buon appetito, signori,"* and went away.

"I'm just about ready for this," Nick said. The risotto smelled wonderful.

"Go on, then. Don't let it get cold."

They ate in silence for a while. Out of the corner of his eye Nick watched the elegant way Lucia wound the spaghetti, holding the fork vertically and twisting it with thumb, forefinger and little finger. He was glad he'd ordered the risotto.

"You know," he said, returning to the subject between mouthfuls. "The rows don't really bother me. A bit of academic rivalry, a bit of professional jealousy, maybe. But normal people don't kill each other for that. This missing ring, though. That's something else."

"You raised it with Montalcini?"

"Oh sure. He said he hadn't seen it and there was no record of it." He set his fork down. "He showed me how the database works, Lucia. The way it's set up, the records are automatically numbered in sequence, and you can't alter them. And if you delete a whole record it leaves a gap. The finds on that day were in an unbroken sequence. It's like it never existed."

"But Julian saw it, and the students saw it!"

"I know. Julian was convinced it was stolen. He wanted to search everyone's quarters for it – even Montalcini's. That was what the row was about."

"Well there's your motive," she said. "Whoever stole it found out what he was planning to do and they panicked. They killed him rather than risk being discovered."

"What, for a stolen ring? How much could it be worth? Five hundred pounds? A thousand? Two thousand? I mean, is that enough to risk a life sentence for murder?"

"Maybe not on its own. But if being discovered also meant the loss of your reputation, your career...?"

"Jesus."

Nick took several more forkfuls of risotto, thinking furiously and eating too fast. "There's another dimension to this," he said finally, wiping his mouth on his napkin.

"What's that?"

"We don't yet have any idea what a prominent mafioso was doing at the lecture."

"Maybe Montalcini's passing stolen goods to the mafia."

"But it's so obvious! Why should someone like Carlo Rossi come there like that and sit through an academic lecture with a bodyguard on each side of him. It's almost as if he was there to intimidate. Maybe that was it. Maybe it was some kind of reminder."

"Nick?"

"Yes?"

"We're going to have to watch our step."

Chapter 26

The helicopter thrashed across the bay. It flew over the ships and cranes of the Castellamare docks, over the marinas with their serried ranks of yachts, and over the peeling shells of apartment buildings whose one denial of dereliction was washing, draped from the vacant windows. It banked and turned over the railway lines and the autostrada, then flew low over the shops, the hotels and the palm-line esplanade, before it landed, rotor still turning, on the helipad.

A door slid back. Nick ran across the concrete apron to the helicopter bent double, his hands covering his ears, and climbed into the empty front seat. Umberto was in the back, sitting behind the pilot.

"This is Maurizio," Umberto shouted, pointing at the pilot.

"Nick," he shouted, shaking hands.

He pulled the seat belt across and fastened it. Maurizio handed him a headset and Nick put it on. The noise of the helicopter was instantly muffled. Waves of sound intruded as he adjusted the earphones to sit more comfortably; then he pulled the microphone stalk close to his mouth. He ran his fingers down the lead and held up the plug; Maurizio pointed to a socket. As soon as he was connected, Umberto's voice came over the intercom.

"Okay, Nick? We are going straight there."

Nick gave a thumbs-up and the pilot increased the rotor speed. For a moment they dangled above the pad. Then the helicopter rose and tilted forward and the roofs of houses started to slide under them. Over the toes of his shoes Nick could see cars streaming along the autostrada, then vineyards, citrus orchards, and olive groves striping the slopes. A road peeped out from under a dense canopy of pine, beech, and chestnut, winding back and forth in a series of crazy hairpin bends. To their left, the thickly populated shore line curved all the way to Naples. From there a broad, flat plain extended inland and towards them, ending in the foothills of the Lattari mountains over which they were flying. The backdrop to the scene was Vesuvius, blue in the shimmering heat, its magnificent bulk possessing the entire landscape.

Fingers of habitation pushed out into the valleys below, then dwindled into isolated farms, cubes of pink and white amid the green. Maurizio tilted the helicopter and they began to ascend, following the profile of the hills to gain the benefit of ground effect.

Maurizio pointed to a notch in the line of mountains and said something to Nick in Italian. Umberto translated for him.

"If you go through there, eventually you get down to the Amalfi coast on the other side."

The trees thinned out and a few minutes later the dig came into view. Nick saw the open scar of the excavation first, then the L-shaped group of cabins and the brightly coloured tents. There were seven people working in the dig; some stood up and waved.

He knew Lucia wouldn't be among them. By the time they'd finished at the restaurant in Naples it was too late to return to the dig so he'd suggested she spend the night at his hotel in Castellamare. She was planning to do some shopping this morning, and he'd arranged to meet her after the helicopter search.

An hour later the helicopter turned back to Castellamare. They had seen only two areas of disturbance. One was the dig. As Nick said, it would be the last place you'd want to bury a body; the whole area was being systematically excavated, so anything there would be sure to be discovered. The other area was where the farmer had been lifting the rocks. Each rock had left behind a greyish depression.

"I think it'd be pretty obvious if anyone turned over the soil under one of those," Nick said to Umberto over the intercom, "but it needs to be checked out. I'll do it while your search party is going over the woodland. Did you manage to set it up for this afternoon?"

"No, I am very sorry," Umberto said over the intercom. "Maresciallo Valentinuzzi could not arrange for today or tomorrow. But he says we can do Thursday morning, for sure."

Nick was disappointed at the delay, but he could appreciate the difficulties. "Okay, Umberto. Could Maurizio drop me off in Castellamare again? I'll pick up Lucia and we'll drive up to Naples this afternoon. I'd like to have another word with the Commissario."

"I will tell him to expect you."

"Thanks. Actually there's something else you could do for me, Umberto, if you don't mind. When we went to Professor Montalcini's lecture I noticed that he included the National Archeological Museum of Naples in the credits. But he told me they didn't support this dig. I'd like Lucia to make a few enquiries there. It would be really helpful if you could phone the Museum and explain that we're working together. You know, ask them to give her their full cooperation. That sort of thing."

"Sure, I can do that. But I am not sure that the office you want is at the Museum. I will find out. I can arrange for one of our drivers to take her there, if you like."

"No need for that. If you can get me the address I'll find it. It shouldn't be too hard."

"Look out, Nick!" She put a hand to her chest. "God, I thought he was coming right into us."

Lucia was accustomed to the driving in northern Italian cities. Even so, the sheer speed and density of the Naples traffic had come as a shock to her.

"Take it easy, Lucia. I did do a police driving course, you know."

"What, in traffic like this?"

"Well, no. Not exactly."

Ahead of them a scooter shot out of a one-way street. She pointed.

"He's going the wrong way!"

"I know. They don't take much notice of traffic lights or pedestrian crossings either."

There was a brief squeal of tyres and the 4 X 4 dipped as they stopped, inches from the bumper of the car in front. He grinned at her.

"I think I'm getting the hang of this."

"Really? Do tell me when you've mastered it completely."

They turned off into a narrow road lined on either side with bookshops, then crossed two intersections and continued down a street not much wider than the car. It seemed like the whole population was down here. They passed a group of old men seated at a table, playing cards. Some youngsters occupied the middle of the roadway, sitting astride their scooters and motorbikes and talking to their friends. Nick tooted lightly as they approached; one manoeuvred out of the way, another mounted the pavement and roared past them in the opposite direction. Ahead of them people were walking into the road around a colourful display of fruit – peaches, nectarines, bananas, melons, grapes, oranges, lemons, prickly pears, and pomegranates.

Nick started to glance down the side streets. They were so narrow here that the ever-present washing had been strung between the buildings from one side to the other.

Lucia frowned. "Are you sure this is right? It looks like a very run-down area."

"I'm only going by what Umberto said. We're not that far from the National Museum actually. Whoops, this is the one."

It was a tight left turn and almost immediately he had to steer round a cluster of overflowing rubbish bins and cardboard boxes on which had been piled an enormous mound of refuse, some in plastic bags and some spilling over the roadway.

"That's appalling," she said, looking over her shoulder. "There must be a strike of rubbish collectors. And in this climate!"

"I don't know what the problem is. It was just as bad in Castellamare. Ah, here we are: Number 42."

He'd stopped outside the peeling walls of a building that looked no different to the decaying tenements on either side. She looked at it, then back to Nick.

"It can't be."

He pointed to a brass plate on the wall. It was tarnished and streaked and she had to get out to read it.

SOPRINTENDENZA ARCHEOLOGICA

DELLE PROVINCE DI

NAPOLI E CASERTA

UFFICIO ARCHEOLOGICO DI NAPOLI

She turned back and spoke to him through the open window. "You're right. You did fantastically well to find it."

He smiled and shrugged. "They should be expecting you. I'll leave you to it. If I come by again at three-thirty will that give you enough time?"

"Plenty, I should think. Take care in that awful traffic, Nick."

"Don't worry. You know, this is a crazy town but it kind of grows on you. *Arrivederci.*"

"A presto."

She watched him drive off and took a last dubious look up and down the street before entering a featureless courtyard. On the left there was a flight of plain concrete steps. She mounted them to the offices above.

Speaking in Italian, she identified herself to the secretary and showed her badge.

"Ah yes, Sergente. Capitano Gardi told us to expect you. Please take a seat. We will only keep you a moment."

She sat down, her document case on her knees. One of the things she liked about working with Nick, she decided, was that he gave her scope to use her initiative. He didn't say, "I want you to get a list of x and ask about y..." He said, "You know, Lucia, we could just be looking at part of a bigger scene. What we ought to do is check out the personnel on archaeological digs here in Italy. See if you can sniff anything out. Okay?"

It wasn't the only thing she liked about him, of course. When he'd suggested the previous night that she stay at his hotel she'd opened her mouth to protest, but before she could say anything he'd added, "Don't worry, kiddo. You can have your own room." Fending him off had become something of a reflex response with her and yet, when he'd said that, she'd felt not so much reassured as vaguely disappointed.

It had always been a kind of clever game, keeping Nick at arm's length. Now, examining her feelings more closely, it was beginning to dawn on her that it was a game she no longer wanted to play. The really clever thing, she thought ruefully, would be to know how to stop.

And then she had an idea that made her feel both gleeful and deeply ashamed of herself.

The Commissario welcomed him and indicated a chair.

"So Ispettore, how is your investigation going?"

Oh, it's "my" investigation now, is it? Nick thought. *We're supposed to be doing this together. Maybe that's the way he wants to play it. Then if we come up with nothing he can shift the blame onto us.*

"Well, sir, we now think it's unlikely that Professor Lockhart left of his own accord. He was heavily involved in the dig, and we don't think he would have abandoned it just like that. There's been no ransom demand, so that rules out kidnap. I'm afraid that leaves only one possibility: that he's been murdered."

The Commissario nodded. "I see."

"Of course we'll keep searching for the body. What bothers me right now is the motive. We do know that Professor Montalcini and Professor Lockhart had a lot of disagreements. It seems that, among other things, they argued about artifacts that had been recovered from the dig. What I was wondering was whether there was another party interested in those artifacts. Since you know the local scene better than I do, I thought I'd ask you."

"Who were you thinking about?"

"The mafia."

There was a stunned silence. Then the Commissario burst out laughing.

"Not you as well!" he said. "So in England they still believe in this curious idea of a worldwide criminal society?" He shook his head.

Nick found the man's condescension highly irritating. If the

178

Commissario really believed what he was saying, he was seriously out of touch. If he didn't, then maybe someone was paying him to look the other way. He couldn't resist a retort.

"Oh, sorry. So back in 1992 it wasn't the mafia who blew up your magistrates Falcone and Borsellino, then?"

The Commissario opened his hands wide.

"I do not say we have no gangsters in Italy. Especially here in Naples. It is well, no? Otherwise you and I do not have a job!"

He laughed again.

Nick smiled wanly.

"But this idea of a secret society," the Commissario continued, " – this is for books, for Hollywood, not for us."

Nick decided it was pointless to argue. Instead he said, "Commissario. Just now you said 'you as well'. Who else has been asking you about the mafia?"

"Who? Oh, it was Professore Lockharter."

Chapter 27

"Sergente Fabri?"

Lucia looked up to see a tall gentleman wearing a grey suit, with a striped shirt and plain tie.

"I am Vincenzo d'Antona. Please come this way."

She followed him to his office. He placed a chair for her, then sat down behind his desk.

"Now, Sergente."

"Signor, you know why we are here?"

"Yes. Capitano Gardi explained the circumstances. It is most unfortunate, but I am not sure how we can help you."

"Well, I don't know if you have the records to hand, but I wanted some details of excavations here in Italy over the last twenty years or so. Mainly the personnel: the people who led them, the people who took part, that sort of thing."

He pursed his lips.

"It is difficult to find such information all in one place. You know there have been many such excavations and the funding comes from many different sources, from governments, from charities, not just in Italy but in other countries, like the United States and The Netherlands."

"The Soprintendenza has been associated with many of these projects."

"Ah, this is true. But we can no longer provide funding on such a substantial scale. We do not have the resources."

He's trying to deflect me, Lucia thought. She decided to nail him.

"All right, but you've had an involvement with digs in the past. Would it be possible for me just to look at those?"

The Director raised his eyebrows, then nodded slowly.

"Yes, this is possible. It may take a little while. Much of the information will be in the Annual Reports; we have a set on this floor. I do not think you will find there the personnel on the digs, though. For that you will need the full records, which are kept with the archive material. I will ask my secretary to help you."

Nick was incredulous. "Professor Lockhart asked you about the mafia, and you didn't think to tell me?"

The Commissario stiffened, then waved it away. "It was not important. The Professore was very excited, a little..." he tapped the side of his forehead. "You cannot rely on information from people in this state."

Even if they get knocked off afterwards? Nick thought.

"So he asked you about the mafia, and you said such an organization doesn't exist, and he went away again?"

"No, he did not go immediately."

"Oh?"

"He asked me if he could have the use of a computer here."

"Did he say why?"

"No. I assumed he wanted to access the Internet."

I don't buy that, Nick thought.

"Commissario, do you think you could show me the computer he used?"

He shrugged. "Me? No. But we can ask someone. Come."

They walked down to the end of the corridor. A door there opened onto a large open plan office in which there were about thirty people, all sitting at computers.

While the Commissario went over to have a word with someone, Nick drifted behind him, looking at the work stations. It seemed to be a mixed network: most of the machines were PCs but one or two were Apple Macs. His hopes rose. *Please,* he thought. *Let the computer Lockhart used be a Mac.*

The Commissario returned with a policewoman.

"Appuntato Ferreira will help you," he said, and walked off.

"Thank you, Commissario," Nick called after him.

The woman led him over to an empty desk in the corner. "This is the computer the Professore used, Ispettore."

Nick looked at it. It was a Mac. "You're sure it was this one?"

"Yes, I am sure. He wanted an Apple Mac. He said he did not know to use PCs."

Interesting, Nick thought. *According to the guy in Oxford's Research Support Office it was just the other way around.*

"We do not use this machine very much," she added.

"You didn't ask him what he wanted it for?"

"No, of course not."

"Do you remember whether he used it more than once?" Nick was thinking of what Montalcini and the others had said about Lockhart going back and forth.

The Appuntato looked thoughtful. "I do not remember him being here for long, the first time. He came back a few days later and worked for several hours. I don't think I saw him again after that."

"Thank you very much. Do you mind if..." He pointed at the computer.

"Not at all." She leaned over and pushed a button to switch it on. "Help yourself, Ispettore. I'll be at my desk over there. Let me know if you need any help."

With the assistance of the secretary, Lucia worked backwards through the years, beginning with the annual reports and then going on to the archived records. She started to write down names but the secretary offered to take documents to the copier for her and that enabled her to progress more rapidly. The number of digs increased as she got back to the early 1990s. Then she pulled the record for a dig in 1989, ran her finger down the names of the personnel and stopped dead. She blinked, staring at the name in front of her.

Nick knew enough about Macs to go straight to the Applications folder. He looked at what was installed: Microsoft Office, Filemaker Pro, InDesign, Safari, Mail... It wasn't there.

He pushed the chair back and chewed his lip. He'd been so sure he'd find it.

There was a wastepaper bin under the desk. Out of sheer habit he picked it up and had a quick look inside. It had been emptied.

He started to replace it, then frowned and drew it out again. The bin was a cheap metal cylinder, folded inwards around the rim to make a smooth edge. Something had caught Nick's eye, something lodged under the fold. He carefully removed a scrap of paper and smoothed it out on the desk. It was only a fragment, probably part of a note that had been torn up after it was made. He'd seen some of Lockhart's handwriting in the files at the Research Support Office in Oxford – large and loopy, very similar to the writing in front of him. There was one complete word and part of a word, written in pencil: "Titus Sa..." or possibly "Titus So..."

Titus? He was a Roman Emperor. So was Lockhart sitting here just to do historical research? That seemed unlikely. Was it a meeting place? There was an Arch of Titus in Rome. "Arch of Titus, Saturday"? *Come on, that's only one; there must be dozens of places named after Titus.* Was it a person – Titus something? Did they still call people Titus?

He checked around the rim of the wastepaper bin in case it had trapped any other fragments but it hadn't. He put the torn slip of paper into his wallet. It might make more sense later; at the moment there just wasn't enough to go on.

He checked his watch. It was almost time to pick up Lucia.

Lucia had worked back to 1975. The same name had come up every year for ten years, but not any earlier.

What did it mean?

She glanced at her watch: three-fifteen. There wasn't much more she could do here, anyway.

She thanked the secretary, asked her to convey her thanks to Signor d'Antona, and went down to the lobby to wait for Nick.

Chapter 28

Nick drove slowly up the narrow street, looking for the address. Then Lucia stepped out from the courtyard ahead of him and waved. He stopped and opened the passenger door.

"All right?" he asked, as she climbed in.

"Yes, I'll tell you about it. Where to now?"

"Well, there's just about time to call on the Pliny Institute. I remembered seeing a Naples address on that grant application I looked at in Oxford. I found a telephone directory at the Questura and looked it up."

"Do they know we're coming?"

"No, but it's worth a shot. It's not that far."

The administrative offices of the Pliny Institute occupied part of a floor of a tall, grimy building in a street off the via Foria. The door was locked. Nick pressed a buzzer on the squawk box and waited, but there was no response. He pressed it again. This time a metallic voice emanated from the speaker. Nick caught the word *chiuso*.

Lucia spoke into the device in Italian, then straightened up.

"She's coming. She said they were closed but I convinced her otherwise."

The door was opened by a middle-aged secretary. Lucia held out a police badge and there was a prolonged exchange in Italian. Then the woman wagged her head, conducted them to a waiting area and went away again. Nick surveyed the freshly decorated room. This place looked a whole lot better inside than it did outside. Maybe it was culturally acceptable around here: so long as you had nice surroundings to live or work in, it didn't matter if the exterior went to hell. Through the open door of the secretary's office he noted a handbag, lipstick and compact on the desk. She'd obviously been making up prior to going home.

Lucia had spotted it, too.

"Seems they only have a small staff here, Nick. Apparently the office manager's already left, and she was about to go herself. I told her it would be enough for the moment if we could have copies of the Annual Reports. All of them. I hope that was okay."

Nick smiled. "That was very smart of you, young lady."

She blushed. "We aim to please," she said, in a low voice.

His voice was even lower. "Not nearly enough, though."

She shot him a practised glare but couldn't suppress a smile, which rather neutralized the effect.

The secretary returned, still looking flustered, and handed over about a dozen slim pamphlets with thick glossy covers. She accepted Lucia's thanks with a gracious nod and saw them out.

Lucia paused outside the door to tuck the reports into her already bulging document case.

"Do you want me to carry that?"

"No, I'm all right," she said, tucking the case under her arm.

"It's a bit too early to eat here. Let's drive back to Castellamare."

Cars were hurling along the autostrada and Nick had to concentrate on the driving. Lucia seemed to understand that, because she didn't try to engage him in conversation.

When they entered the hotel lobby he hesitated. They needed a quiet place where they could compare notes. The obvious thing would be to use his room – or hers – but the suggestion was bound to be misinterpreted. He had a look at the sitting area provided for guests. It was a large, comfortably shabby room, furnished with low coffee tables and soft armchairs. These were arranged in groups, separated by planters overflowing with ferns and ivy. It was deserted.

"This'll do," he said. "You get settled while I order up some coffee at reception."

When he came back she was sorting through some papers on one of the tables.

"Looks like you had a productive afternoon," he said.

"I reckon so. Sit down, Nick, I want to show you something."

He perched on an armchair opposite her and she selected a

stapled set of sheets.

"This was a dig funded by the Naples Museum in 1979." She turned a page and handed it to him. "This is the list of personnel. Anything hit you between the eyes?"

He ran a finger down the names. He didn't recognize any of them. "No..."

She pointed. "This one? Donatella Badalamenti?"

He shook his head. "Sorry, it still doesn't register."

"The Badalamentis are a well-known Sicilian family. And I mean 'family' in every sense."

He looked at her in astonishment. "Mafia?"

"So it's believed. That's not all. Over the next ten years her name appears every single year on a dig recorded by the Museum. The last time is in 1989. Could be another connection, Nick."

He studied the name, wanting to know more, and wondering where to find the information. His head jerked round as someone entered the room, then he relaxed. Lucia cleared a space on the table and the white-jacketed waiter placed the tray on it. He looked like he was about to set out the cups and saucers but Nick pressed a note into his hand and thanked him. The waiter bowed almost imperceptibly and withdrew. Nick waited until the door had swung closed and then turned back to the papers.

"According to the Commissario," he said thoughtfully, "the mafia is a common myth."

"What? He said that?"

"'Fraid so. I must say it worries me. It must have bothered Julian too. Apparently he mentioned some concerns about the mafia to him and got the same dusty answer."

"Julian was there, asking about the mafia?"

"Yes. The Commissario hadn't deemed it important enough to mention it to me before."

"That's outrageous! What's he playing at?"

"I don't know. Anyway it seems that Julian went there twice, and he spent some time on an Apple Mac. I had a good look at the machine. Now why should Julian, who preferred to use PCs anyway, want to sit at a Mac for several hours?"

"You think he transferred the files from that laptop? The one they use at the dig?"

"That has to be the reason. He wanted to go through all the records himself. And he did it in Naples because he didn't want anyone else to know. Chances were, he was looking for that ring. The thing is, to look through the records he'd need to use the database software – Archetype – and I couldn't find it installed on that machine. That's not to say he didn't use it, of course. He might have erased the data and the software after he'd finished."

"He probably did. The data's confidential."

She poured coffee for both of them. He took the cup and saucer she held out to him.

"Thanks." He sipped the strong coffee. "I just find it disturbing that he's in a police headquarters and he's being careful to cover his tracks and not saying a word to anyone about what he's doing."

"That means he couldn't trust anyone – not even the police."

"That's right. He just tested the water with the Commissario. Maybe he thought the man was high-ranking enough. He probably got the same reaction I did and regretted saying even that much. After that he didn't confide in anyone. So who can we trust, Lucia? The Commissario? I don't think so. What about Umberto Gardi? Dammit, we can't do this investigation all on our own. Umberto seems like a good guy, and I need his help."

"We'll just have to watch what we say, Nick."

She picked up a plate of slim biscuits from the tray and offered it to him. He took one and bit into it. It tasted of almonds.

"Amaretti," he said. "Didn't you bring a box of these to work once?"

She smiled. "Yes, after one of my annual trips."

"Nice." He popped the rest into his mouth. "Apart from this Badalamenti person, did you find anything else?"

"No. I'll go through them properly again, but nothing leaped out at me. We haven't looked at the stuff from the Pliny Institute yet, though."

She delved in her document case, brought out the glossy pamphlets, and checked the dates on the front covers, to make sure they were all there and in sequence. Then she looked at Nick and down at the documents again.

"That's curious."

"What is?"

"Badalamenti's name was associated with digs in every year from 1979 to 1989. After that, nothing. But the first Annual Report from the Pliny Institute is dated 1990."

It took Nick only a moment. "You take half and give me half. See if her name appears anywhere."

They spent the next forty minutes going through the Reports. Nick also looked at the annual accounts to see where the money was coming from. Finally he put them down and Lucia did the same.

"Drawn a blank?" she asked.

"Yes."

"Same here. Maybe it was just a coincidence."

"Maybe. Look, time's getting on. Did you want to get back to the dig tonight?"

"Not especially. There isn't a whole lot I can do there at the moment. I'd sooner stay here if that's all right."

"Yeah, no problem. I booked your room for a few days." He scratched the back of his neck. "You know, for a while I thought we were really getting somewhere with that mafia lead. Now I'm not so sure. If only we had a body…"

He put the cups and saucers and the empty plate back on the tray, although his mind was elsewhere.

"Nick, let me ask you something. When you're at the beginning of a case – a difficult case like this one – do you ever get the nasty feeling that you're never going to solve it?"

He shook his head.

"You can't afford to think that way – it would sap all your motivation. There are answers out there; it's your job to find them."

"But suppose you can't? Suppose it's the perfect murder?"

"No such thing. Some come close – I'll grant you that. But techniques are getting better all the time. We just have to stay one step ahead."

She sighed. "I don't know. Look at this case. What do we have? No body, a few shots in the dark about motive, a whiff of mafia involvement. It's not much to go on, is it? It's like a sealed box and there's no way of looking inside it."

"You have to keep turning it over in your hands. Sooner or later you'll find one little crack, and then another. Before you know it, the whole thing's blown wide open. Patience, Lucia. It's early days yet."

"I wish I had your confidence." She gave him a taut little smile. "I shouldn't be talking like this, should I?"

"It's natural to have doubts. The important thing is not to let them overwhelm you. Look at it as a challenge. The tougher the case the greater the achievement if you solve it."

"Don't you mean *when* you solve it?"

He grinned. "Yeah, that's right, *when* you solve it."

"Okay, so where do we go from here?"

"Umberto couldn't arrange the search earlier than Thursday morning. Tomorrow's Wednesday. Right now I don't have anything planned."

"Perhaps you need some thinking time."

"That's not a bad idea. I could do with a chance to digest what we've got."

"You did promise me a trip to Pompeii, you know."

His face lit up. "So I did! Sorry, I almost forgot. Let's do it tomorrow."

Lucia paused for a moment, her fingers on the switch of the bedside light. With sleep beckoning, her mind had turned away from the difficulties of the case, and was embracing the exciting prospect of a day spent in the remains of a two-thousand-year-old Roman city. She smiled to herself, and as she did so she again felt a pang of guilt about what was in her mind.

She switched off the light.

Chapter 29

"Look Nick, it's a bakery!"

Nick wasn't sure what he was enjoying most: the wonders of this lost city, or Lucia's child-like enthusiasm as she pulled him from one revelation to the next. The sun bore down relentlessly. It reflected up from the shiny grey slabs paving the streets and its stored heat radiated from every porous, jagged wall. At least he was dressed for it, this time. He was even wearing a floppy canvas hat which, despite his protests, Lucia had insisted on buying for him. He thought it made him look faintly ridiculous, but he was glad of the protection nonetheless. When he tried to do the same for her, Lucia assured him she didn't need a hat. He knew it was true. She seemed to revel in the heat.

"These are the millstones."

"Turned by slaves or mules," he said, scanning the entry in the guide book. "The square holes are where the poles went."

"Just look at that oven! You know, the Forum and the baths and the temples and the villas are all marvellous but I'm not sure I don't prefer places like this. It gives you such a feel for what ordinary, everyday life must have been like here. You can almost see them pulling out the freshly baked loaves."

He pointed at the guide book.

"Round loaves, like big hot cross buns, according to this picture."

They walked on. The streets of Pompeii were thronged with tourists and the air was filled with a babel of voices. They detoured around guided groups being addressed in Italian, English, French, German, Japanese, and languages Nick didn't even recognize.

"In some ways," Nick said, "it would be a lot nicer to have this place to ourselves. On the other hand, this must have been more like it was. I mean, it would have been buzzing; there were something like twenty thousand people living here at the time of the big eruption."

"They've only found two thousand bodies so far."

"A lot were encased in ash, weren't they? I guess there are plenty that were never discovered. Still, it does make you wonder how many got out in time. There may have been quite a few parties like the ones at our dig. Maybe some even survived."

"We'll probably never know. They'd have been travelling through open countryside in those days. Now there's hardly a square inch that hasn't been built on. The evidence has gone. That's why the site up in the mountains is so interesting."

A short distance ahead of them a guide came into the street holding up a numbered flag. She was followed by a large party of American tourists. The guide moved into a doorway and the group gathered around, blocking the street.

As Nick and Lucia approached they heard her talking about Pompeii's food shops. She spoke good English, enunciating, with typically Italian precision, the end of each word. Rather than trying to barge through, they lingered to catch the commentary.

"...some restaurants, like this one, are set on each side of the entrance to a grand villa. This was quite normal. The appearance of the villas outside did not matter to the rich citizens of Pompeii; it was what you saw when you went inside."

Things haven't changed, then, Nick thought.

"Through that entrance," the guide continued, "is another world, a world of great privilege and wealth. Out here you have the ordinary life of Pompeii. This is a counter from which someone sold food and drink to the passers-by or perhaps to the families that lived in the upper levels of the small houses. Remember, these people lived many to one room and they had no ovens up there to cook with. Here they could buy fish stews and hot or cold drinks, including wine."

"They could afford to drink wine?" one of the tourists asked.

"Oh yes. Wines like the *Pompeiana* were not expensive and they mixed them with water. Such wines were for drinking young.

But in his writings Pliny mentions that one of the local grapes, the *Vennuncula*, made a wine that was suitable for keeping."

She paused and someone else asked:

"What did it taste like?"

"Come on, Matt," another voice piped up, "how in hell's name would she know that?"

The guide smiled. "I do not think this type of grape is still in cultivation. But there is a grape – *Falanghina* – which is very ancient also. It may have been the grape they used to make *Falernum*. This wine was very popular with rich people. They drank it a lot in Pompeii, sometimes spiced or with other things added. *Falanghina* is grown still in Campania and you will find it in the restaurants and supermarkets. So maybe you should try. Now, follow me, please."

The group moved off. Nick winked at Lucia. "That was a better answer than he deserved."

"We should try some of that *Falanghina* while we're here."

"We'll look out for it. What do you want to do next?"

"Well, I wanted to see the Villa of Diomedes and also the Villa of the Mysteries – someone said it has wonderful frescoes. But it's a little way from here, outside the Herculaneum Gate." She shot him an anxious look. "Are we overdoing it, Nick? You look ever so hot."

"I'm all right." He pulled the floppy hat off and wiped the sweat from his face with a damp handkerchief. Then he replaced the hat, took a map from his shirt pocket, and studied it for a moment. "Yeah, let's do it. I wanted to see that water installation thing – what was it called? – the *Castellum Aquae*. We can go there on the way."

As they started walking, Lucia said, "It's funny, isn't it? All the years I've been coming back to Italy and this is the first time I've been here."

"Nothing unusual about that. We always ignore what's on our own doorstep."

"Well, we did have some Roman ruins in Brescia but to see a whole city like this, it's just fantastic. I was always interested in archaeology. I don't know why I didn't take it up."

"I suppose in some ways it's not that different from detective work."

"True. Either way, you have to study the evidence and make deductions."

"That's right."

She followed him as he crossed to the shadier side of the street, stepping between the high pavements on the same big blocks of stone that the Pompeiians would have used two thousand years before. He looked round at her, about to comment, but she seemed lost in thought.

At the next intersection she waited while he consulted the map again.

"Nick?" she said, as he folded it away. "How would it be if I volunteered to help with the dig for a bit? I always wanted to do something like that, and I can keep an eye on the team. Sometimes you learn a lot more by watching people's behaviour than by interviewing them. What do you think?"

"It's a good idea. We'll see how we can fit it in."

By the time they'd finished their meal, the light was beginning to fade. The waiter came with coffee and took away the empty wine carafe.

"I've got to hand it to you," Nick said, raising his cup to Lucia before taking a sip. "It was a great idea to come here for dinner. Kind of rounded off the day."

"Well, I'd never been to Sorrento, and you said you didn't mind the drive."

"No, it was good to sit in an air-conditioned car for a while. God, it was hot back in Pompeii."

He looked up at the bower of vines over their heads.

"Still, it's nice and cool here, even though it's in the open air. You know, considering you've never been to Sorrento, you chose a terrific place to eat. I've never had a better pizza. And that oven looked just like the one we saw in Pompeii!"

Lucia seemed a little flushed. He thought it was probably the wine or maybe the sun earlier in the day. Whatever it was, he'd never seen her look more beautiful.

They finished their coffee in silence.

"Nick... I want to thank you. This has been such a wonderful day."

Nick stirred. Normally she avoided direct eye contact, but now he found himself locked into her gaze. The commotion it created inside him was both exquisite and deeply unsettling.

He reached across the table and took her hands in his. She didn't pull away. He leaned forward and they kissed softly.

"Let's not go back to Castellamare tonight," he whispered. "I'm sure we can find a hotel here."

She nodded.

When he checked into the hotel he asked for a double room with a double bed. She didn't demur.

Chapter 30

Both of them were subdued during the drive back to Castellamare. Once again Nick appeared to be concentrating on the driving, and there were few outward signs of the self-recrimination eating away inside him. He and Lucia had been getting on so well. Would he ever be able to regain that sort of understanding with her again? Over dinner the atmosphere had seemed so right; it had been the most natural thing in the world to end the evening in bed together. And then somehow it was all too much. Until that evening he'd never had so much as a kiss from Lucia, and suddenly to feel her full, ripe body pressed against him overwhelmed all his senses. They made love quickly, too quickly. He remembered falling back, breathing hard, veins buzzing with warmth – and then realizing what a fool he'd been. He'd had the chance and he'd muffed it. He could have shown her the way he felt about her, proved to her that he could be a tender and loving partner – but no, he'd made it look like a cheap conquest, taking his gratification like an oversexed teenager. The experience should have bonded them; instead they were even further apart. He wanted to say something at the time but it was difficult to know what, and it had been a long day and the heat in Pompeii had been exhausting and he felt drowsy and... somehow he'd fallen asleep. The next thing he knew, he was looking at bright sunlight coming through the thin curtains. His first conscious thought was to make up for the previous night but when he slid his fingers across the sheet he found the bed was empty. She emerged from the bathroom shortly after that, fully dressed and made up. They had breakfast together and drove off, and neither one seemed to want to talk about it.

It was mid-morning by the time they were back at the dig and someone had arrived ahead of them. They saw the minibus first, then the group of a dozen or so people standing on the other side of it, chatting and smoking. Then Nick spotted Umberto Gardi. They walked over to him. Nick introduced Lucia, and the two started up a polite conversation.

Meanwhile Nick was surveying the motley crew Umberto had brought with him. He turned to the Capitano and waited for a suitable gap in the conversation.

"I take it this is the search party, Umberto."

"Yes. You see, I promise."

"Do these people know the score? Do they know what's required of them?"

"Oh yes, Nick. They have done many times before."

"All right, good. Lucia..." He faltered as he realized it was the first time he'd spoken to her directly since they'd left Sorrento. She met his eyes expectantly. Again he felt the turmoil in his chest, coupled this time with the pain of having lost something he'd so nearly gained. It was only a momentary lapse but he rebuked himself for it. A man was missing, presumed dead. He owed it to him – and above all to his family – to find out what had happened, why it had happened, and who was responsible. If he couldn't stay focused on that, whatever else was going on in his life, then he shouldn't be in this job. And if that was true for him, then it applied equally to his Detective Sergeant. His jaw set.

When he spoke again his voice was more crisp than he'd intended.

"Lucia, you go with them and show them the woodland. I need to check out those patches where the rocks were shifted – the ones I saw from the helicopter. I'll join you later."

The almost imperceptible widening of her eyes showed that she'd picked up his change in manner, but she didn't miss a beat.

"Very good. If we find anything I'll come and give you a shout."

"Thanks. Okay, everyone, let's get going."

Umberto clapped his hands to get the attention of the group, introduced Lucia to them, and started to deliver some sort of pep talk. Nick hesitated for a moment, then headed in the direction of the dig.

He found Torretta and the students there, hard at work. There was no sign of Montalcini. Torretta stood as he saw Nick approach.

"Antonino, I need to borrow a trowel. All right?" Torretta looked at him, his expression blank. Nick went over to a small heap of picks, brushes and other tools at the side of the dig, selected a trowel and said, with exaggerated gestures, "I take, I bring back. Okay?"

Torretta nodded. Nick didn't know whether he'd understood or not, but it didn't matter much. He started off down the hill.

The slopes here were strewn with large irregular boulders. Nick strained to remember the details of Montalcini's talk. Some of these would be the calcareous rocks that were torn off Vesuvius by the rising jet of magma and hurled through the air in long, parabolic trajectories. He could imagine them smashing down trees, rolling and bouncing down the mountain, trailing smoke, until they came to rest on these lower slopes. Others would be pumice that had fallen as great shards of hot lava – volcanic bombs, Montalcini had called them.

Further across the hillside he noticed a gentle incline that was strangely clear of boulders. He guessed that would be the area the farmer was preparing for his vineyards. He made off in that direction.

The distances were greater than they'd looked from the air. It was fifteen minutes before he reached the first of the grey-white patches. He squatted on his heels, ran his fingers over the material and rubbed it between his fingertips. According to Montalcini, this whole area had been coated in fine ash like this.

He raised his head and scanned slowly around, narrowing his eyes, trying to visualize the scene. It would have looked like a snowscape: rolling grassy slopes, all glowing white in the half-light. And trees – there many more trees then – ghostly stands of oak and beech, their branches drooping and snapping under the weight of their strange white burden. He returned his attention to the patch in front of him. The great clot of lava that had landed here was probably already half-solid, having been lofted high through the atmosphere.

Elsewhere, the ash had disappeared from the hillside, washed and eroded away by wind and rain; only here, underneath this rock, had that dreadful day been preserved. He tested the surface with the point of the trowel. It had a crusty consistency. He pushed harder; the blade broke through the surface and he felt the smoother resistance as it slid into the soil underneath. When he turned the trowel a brown stain appeared, subsoil mixing with the lumpy grey powder on the surface.

There's no way anyone could bury a body here and keep it secret, he thought. *It would show up instantly.*

There were a number of other patches close by. He investigated each one in turn; in every case the greyish-white material was a thin crust. And then he stopped at one patch, the hair prickling on the back of his neck. He bent to take a closer look. Surely that was the imprint of a child's foot? He walked around it, to see the effect of light falling on it from different angles. Maybe it was just his imagination running riot. Certainly that party came across this way, but small children wouldn't have been walking barefoot through hot ash, would they? They would have been riding on the wagon.

He walked thoughtfully back up the hill, still watching the ground, and he didn't notice Lucia until she started to shout. He looked up to see her a few hundred yards ahead, waving at him.

He broke into a run and she waited until he'd reached her.

"Found something?" he asked, pausing for breath.

"I think so."

"What? What is it?"

"We don't know yet." She turned and strode quickly uphill, talking over her shoulder. "One of the searchers found a small area of disturbance in the leaf litter. They just marked it in case there were any other signs nearby. They've had a good look around that area but there wasn't anything else, so they're ready to dig now. I asked them to wait for you."

They reached the woodland. Just a few yards into the trees, the group had gathered in a circle; they parted to let them in. Umberto was there with a young man, who was leaning on a spade. Between the two was a stake, which had been pushed into the ground.

Umberto looked up as Nick approached.

"What have you got, Umberto?" Nick asked.

"Nadia thought this patch had been disturbed. I don't think it's big enough for a body, but we should look."

"Okay, let's go."

The young man pulled the stake out of the ground and set it on one side. Then he scraped away at the leaf litter with the spade inverted. There did seem to be a change in the colour of the soil here. He began to dig, taking a shallow slice and emptying it into a sieve held by one of the other searchers. She shook the soil through and then waited for the next slice. They repeated the process. Minutes went by, with everyone craning to see what was happening. The only sounds were the spade chopping into the ground, followed by the shuffling of soil through the sieve. Then there was an loud click. The man with the spade stopped, and spoke rapidly in Italian.

Umberto said to Nick, "He says the spade hit something. It may just be a rock. We will see."

The young man was on his knees now, with a trowel, gently prizing away the earth, feeling with his other hand. And then he straightened up and there was something in his hand, something shiny. He passed it to Umberto, who dusted it off and held it out to Nick.

Nick turned the metal box over in his hands. "It's a portable hard drive for a computer," he said. He scraped away a little more soil with a fingernail. "Look, here's the USB socket."

It was small enough to fit in a jacket pocket. But it had been badly damaged: a deep indentation ran from corner to corner. The impact had partially folded the box into a shallow V. Nick pointed to it.

"This wasn't done just now, was it?"

There was a brief exchange with the young man. Nick didn't have to ask for a translation: his gestures and tone of voice said that it was quite impossible. The young man touched Nick on the arm to get his attention, pointed to the box and then to the ground, and then brought the spade crashing down, to demonstrate the kind of blow that would be needed to cause that kind of damage.

Nick nodded. He turned back to Umberto. "I take it you haven't found anything else this morning."

"No, nothing." He pointed to the place where the box had been found. "Even this we could have missed very easily."

"Who noticed it?"

Umberto indicated the young woman who'd been sieving the soil.

Nick shook her by the hand. "*Molto grazie*," he said. "Lucia, I can't say it. Could you tell this young lady this could be a really important piece of evidence and congratulate her on doing such a great job."

Lucia came forward and spoke warmly to the woman in Italian. This was greeted, unexpectedly, by an rattle of applause from the other searchers. The woman smiled and blushed and nodded at everyone. She murmured, "*Niente*."

Umberto said, "We will dig a little more here, in case there is anything else. Otherwise I think we have finished."

"Fine. Umberto, do you mind if I hold on to this for the moment?"

"No, if it helps, Nick you take it for now. In the end we must put in a bag for evidence, but it is not so useful in a bag, no?"

Nick returned the grin. "You're a man after my own heart, Umberto," he said. "Okay, thanks a lot. We'll be in touch." He looked around the group. "Thanks everyone," he said. "Thanks very much. Lucia?"

They walked out of the cool, dark woodland and back into blinding sunlight.

"You don't want to hang around here, then?" Lucia asked.

"No. We were looking for a body. If anyone had buried Julian in there it would have made a lot of disturbance. Any one of them would have spotted it – they wouldn't have had to be as alert as that young lady. She did well. This," he held up the distorted hard drive, "is quite a prize."

"You think it was Julian's?"

"I'm convinced of it, but we're going to find out for sure. It's time we did a little old-fashioned leg work."

Chapter 31

They returned to the 4 X 4.

"What's the plan, then?" she asked as she climbed in.

He felt much more comfortable with her now that they were back in professional mode. In some ways, it was hard to believe that last night had ever happened.

"Well, right now the key question is: did Julian get that hard drive in England or over here?"

He manoeuvred out of the parking space and they started off down the track.

"I don't see why he'd want to bring it all the way from England," she said. "He'd have no reason to, would he? All the backing up of data was done on site and over that satellite link."

"I agree. I think he purchased it over here. Castellamare is the nearest town so that's probably where he went for it. I'll cruise around the town while you look out for computer shops."

They found one soon enough. Nick took a quick look up and down the narrow street but both kerbs were crammed with cars and scooters in both directions. They left the 4 X 4 double-parked.

The man who came over to them looked to be in his early twenties. He spoke good English. Nick produced the hard drive.

"Do you stock these?" he asked.

He looked at it, then at Nick. "What happened?" he asked.

"It was in a car crash," Nick said. "I don't suppose we'd be able to get the data off it, would we?"

The young man sucked in his upper lip and shook his head. "No way. This has wrecked the hard disk for sure. Do you want to replace it?"

"No. Can you tell me if it was bought here? We're trying to identify the owner."

Nick showed his police badge. The assistant glanced at it

without much interest and went back to examining the hard drive. He rubbed at the serial number. "Moment," he said.

They followed him to the counter and watched him tapping at the keys of a computer and reading successive screens. Finally he turned to them.

"No. We do keep that model, but it wasn't one of ours."

"Right." Nick held up one of the photographs of Julian Lockhart. "You've never seen this chap, then?"

The man studied the picture, then shook his head.

"Okay. Well, thanks for your time. Are there any other computer shops round here you think we should try?"

"There are two or three that maybe sell hard drives like that one. I'll write them down for you."

Minutes later they emerged from the shop armed with a list and some directions. As Nick unlocked the 4 X 4, Lucia said:

"You sit in the car. I won't be a moment."

He watched her hurry over to a food counter a few shops up the street. She returned with a paper bag and two plastic cups with lids on them, all clamped precariously between her hands.

"I thought we could use some lunch."

"Good idea. What did you get?"

"Panini with mozzarella, tomato and basil, and a couple of coffees. Okay?" She held it out to him.

"Yeah, that'll be fine. I can't stop here, though. The esplanade is just a couple of streets down. We'll have it there."

They found a vacant bench in the shade of a palm tree where they could look out over the shimmering expanse of the bay. At the horizon the sea blended into a clear cobalt sky. Above their heads the motionless fronds of the palm gleamed in the sun like metal. As they munched the panini they monitored the stately progress of a huge tanker on its way to the docks.

A gentle surf unfurled onto the beach. A horse trotted briskly over the firm sand drawing a man in a two-wheeled carriage.

Nick pointed. "Looks like something out of Pompeii," he said.

"Yes. Maybe he's collecting shellfish. I don't know. They don't do things like that in the North."

Nick got up and dusted off his hands and trousers, and Lucia stuffed the bag and cups into a waste receptacle. They went back to the 4 X 4.

The assistant in the next shop spoke only Italian so Lucia did the talking, but the result was the same. In the third shop they struck lucky.

"Certainly, I remember the gentleman. English, very tall. He wanted to be sure it would work on both PCs and Apple Macs. A car crash, you say. That's too bad."

"How much would this thing have cost?"

"I can tell you that." He consulted some printed lists, then looked up. "At the moment that item is retailing at 159 euro."

Nick whistled. "That much?"

"That's the regular price." He rocked his hand quickly back and forth. "Maybe I sold it to him for a little less."

"Okay. Look, thanks very much, you've been very helpful. In case I have to get back to you, do you have a card or something?"

"Here, take a flyer for the shop. I'll write my name on it."

Nick looked at it. "Thanks again, Signor Gambetta."

They went back to the 4 X 4. Nick didn't start the engine. He stared out of the windscreen, chewing the inside of his cheek, lost in thought. Lucia looked at him.

"Okay, you were right, he did buy it here. And presumably he didn't buy an expensive device like that only to smash it and bury it. So he was murdered and the murderer must have done it. Why? What was on it?"

"Well," he said slowly. "Presumably Julian copied the data from the laptop computer at the dig so he could study it at his leisure in that computer suite at the Questura in Naples. And there must have been something incriminating in the data."

"Did he have to spend that much just to copy some data?"

"Well, I guess he needed something he could put in his pocket. He didn't want anyone at the Questura to know what he was doing."

"Yes, but he could have bought a flash memory. It would have been a lot cheaper."

"Perhaps he didn't know what sort of capacity he needed. I mean, would you?"

Lucia thought for a moment. "Well, the digital camera they're using on the dig is a heavy duty professional type. You know Sally in forensics? She's got one just like it. If they're using it at full resolution, and presumably they are, it's going to be something like twenty megabytes for every shot."

"Well, there you are. They must have taken two hundred photos, at minimum, so the database has got to be at least four gigabytes. We're already getting out of flash memory territory, aren't we?"

"I suppose so."

"And then you've got to add the software – he couldn't examine the data without the software. It was custom-designed, so Lord knows how big..." He stopped short, staring into space. Then he closed his eyes, hit the rim of the steering wheel with the heels of both hands, and shook his head. "Why the hell didn't I see it before?"

"What? Nick? What?"

"It wasn't the data he wanted at all. It was the software!"

"What, you mean Archetype?"

"Yes, Archetype, the software the Pliny Institute insisted on them using to record the finds. My God, they made sure of it, didn't they? Even gave them a laptop with the program installed!"

"Hang on a minute, you're not saying the Pliny Institute is involved? It's a charitable organization!"

"I don't care. It must be a front. They're in on it as well. It's something about the way that software is written. Lucia, we've got to find out who wrote it."

"How do we do that?"

"Do you think you could get hold of that laptop?"

"You want me to break into the office?"

"No, it's too risky. Look, you said you'd like to take part in the dig. That's exactly what you should do. I'll take you up there in time to join them at breakfast. Go on the dig with them. Whenever they have stuff to record, the laptop will be around, and Archetype will be booted up. Choose your moment. Maybe there'll be a bit of excitement over something and they'll leave it unattended. That'll be your chance. Do you think you can manage it?"

"Well yes, I think so. So long as the computer's at the dig, and so long as there's plenty going on."

"Great. I'd do it myself, but I think you have a much better chance of bringing it off without arousing suspicion. And the information will be in Italian. I might get thrown by that."

"It's okay, I said I'd do it. Well, since we'll be staying here tonight I'd like to go back to my room in the hotel to freshen up a bit. Is that all right?"

"Sure, I'll do the same. Then we can grab a bite to eat. There's a place around the corner from the hotel actually. It's not at all bad."

In a long cool shower Nick shed the sweat and dust of the day. What he was unable to shed was a feeling of apprehension about the evening ahead. He knew he couldn't have suggested anything different, of course; they could hardly stay in the same town at the same hotel and eat separately.

It started well enough. The menu sparked off a lively exchange; Nick wanted to know if there was any need for so many forms of pasta, and Lucia tried to explain how they were suited to different dishes. But after the first course an uneasy silence settled on them. Nick wondered if he should be up front about what had happened in Sorrento, but there was a threshold for raising the topic with her and somehow he couldn't bring himself to cross it. She seemed equally disinclined to talk about it, so the matter remained in suspension, the weight of its unacknowledged presence hanging between them.

The waiter had just brought the second course when Lucia's mobile phone sounded. For once, the distraction was not unwelcome. As she listened her eyes flicked to Nick.

"Yes, Angela. What's up? Okay... yes, what time? All right, we'll be there. Listen, Angela, you haven't mentioned this to anyone, have you? Good, well don't. Not a soul. Not till we've seen you. Okay, you take care now. 'Bye."

She put the mobile away. "That was Angela Johnston. She's found something. She couldn't say much, but she wants us to meet her at the dig after dark. I said we would. She said not to bring the car right up. She sounded frightened, Nick."

"I wonder what she's found. What time are we meeting her?"

"Eleven-thirty. The others should all be in bed by then."

By now Nick had become quite familiar with the path up to the camp. At one point it turned left along a rise that would shield the sound of the approaching car. He stopped the engine there and they got out. The sky was full of stars but the moon had not yet risen. Nick took a torch from the car and switched it on, keeping his fingers over the lens. It gave them just enough light to see by without advertising their presence. They began to walk, saying nothing, savouring the silence and the sweet, cool air.

When they reached the dig, it was quiet and clothed in darkness. Somewhere in the background they could hear the hum of the generator but the loudest sound was the soft crunching of their shoes on the loose, gravelly surface. Nick checked his watch. It was just after eleven-thirty; Angela should be there. Was she afraid of revealing herself without knowing first who was coming? There was only one way to find out. He shone the torch on the ground to find the slope they used to get in and out of the dig at this end and they went down cautiously until the ground flattened out. Now they would be surrounded by the steep banks that had been cut by the excavator; rising above that would be the ridge that blocked the view from the cabins and the tent area. None of it was visible, and it felt as if the sides were pressing in on them.

"Hold still," he said to Lucia, then shone the torch briefly on her face and then on his own.

A whisper pierced the darkness from what seemed like a long way off. "Over here."

They found Angela crouched at the far end of the dig.

"Thanks for coming," she hissed.

"Angela," Nick said gently. "Just speak in a low voice; it doesn't carry as far as a whisper. Now what is it you've brought us up here to see."

"I'm not sure, but I think I've found Julian."

Chapter 32

"What, you don't mean here? In the dig?"

"Yes. Pretty much where we are now," Angela replied. "Can you shine your torch over here? I marked the place with some pebbles."

Nick swept the beam around until Angela said, "There, that's it."

She placed her fingertips on the spot to hold it and reached around to the side with her left hand. Nick followed it with the torch, the pool of light moving over a small pile of tools. She picked out a brush, passed it to her right hand, and started to sweep the soil away, speaking quietly as she did so.

"Lucia, you remember what I said about being the only one on this dig up to now who hasn't turned up any human remains? And I'm the one who's thinking about doing forensic anthropology! It was really starting to get to me. Then this afternoon I was working over here and I uncovered some bones. I was just about to jump up and down and give the rest of them a shout and I very nearly did, too, only something stopped me. It was odd the way the soil was sticking to them, quite different to the bones the others found. And I could smell something too. So I carried on quietly and at the end of the day I didn't say anything, I just covered it over with loose soil. I waited, and later on when it was quiet I called you. Ah, here we are. Mind yourselves."

She was brushing the soil away from a large area now, and blackened outlines were appearing in the beam of the torch.

"Okay, it's lying on its left side. Here's the upper limb, see? These are ribs. And here's the lower limb, quite folded. Now look at the length of the long bones, the humerus here and the femur here. That's one of the things that caught my attention. If this man was contemporary with the others we've been finding he would have seemed like a giant. So I got to thinking, maybe he's not contemporary. And then look at the radius. It's fractured but the broken edge isn't charred. Most of the fragments we've found so far have been charred all over, broken edges as well. We were thinking these people had been hit by falling rocks – seriously big ones, big enough to break their bones – and then the bodies were burned by a fire that came afterwards. But this one doesn't fit that pattern; it was broken *after* it was burnt. Well, okay, he could have been a giant of his time, and the bones could have been broken after they were buried. But look at this."

She brushed more soil away above the upper limb, revealing the blade of a scapula, a line of vertebrae, and then what looked at first like a broken china saucer until they realized it was the skull.

"Okay, here's the cranium. It's pretty badly smashed. That's not unusual. The frontal bones are intact though. Prominent brow ridges, see? I haven't checked out the pelvis yet but you don't really have to with a skull like this; it's almost certainly a man. Here's the mandible, the lower jaw. It's smashed too. Now that *is* unusual – the mandible's very robust; usually you find it whole. The teeth are a puzzle as well. The front teeth are here all right, but where are the molars? I've sifted through this area and I haven't found a single one. And remember, when I was doing this it was broad daylight. Teeth would have shown up, for sure."

Up to now Nick had been listening in a high state of excitement but now his spirits had started to sag. There were a lot of skeletons in this dig. Was this one really different? What Angela was presenting to them was very circumstantial. Had her imagination been working overtime?

Lucia was evidently feeling the same way. She said, "Maybe they'd been extracted, Angela. We know the Romans practised medicine and surgery. Perhaps they had dentistry too."

"Yeah, they almost certainly did. But the incisors and canines are all present, and they're in good nick. From what I can see, the jaw bone is, too. So why are the molars missing? I got to thinking, see, the molars are the ones most likely to have fillings. If someone wanted these bones to look like they'd walked from Pompeii they'd have to take away any teeth that had fillings, wouldn't they?"

Nick murmured a grudging assent.

"All the same, Angela, I'm not convinced..."

"Hang on, I haven't finished yet. Look at this. Here, shine the torch where I'm holding this trowel."

She used the tool to prize up some of the skull fragments. She selected two, turned them towards Nick and Lucia and fitted them gently together. At the junction of the two fragments was a square hole, nearly a centimetre on a side. Nick felt, though he could not see, Lucia's eyes on him.

"This is the occipital bone – back of the head. This isn't like the fractured bones. See? It's charred inside. This was made *before* the body was burned."

"Would that have been a fatal blow?" Nick asked, anticipating already what the answer would be.

"Well, put it this way: the owner of this skull didn't survive the injury. If he had, the edges would be smooth and rounded due to osteogenesis."

"Due to what?"

"Bony outgrowth from the damaged surfaces – it's the body's way of trying to close the defect, you see it in skulls that have been trephined. There's no sign of it here. In theory actual death could have been caused by another injury, like a stab wound, but in my view this wound would have been fatal on its own. You know why? If the weapon that made that hole had any length at all, it would have penetrated the brain stem. Death would have been instantaneous. And I think it did have enough length."

"What do you mean? How can you tell?"

"Well, look at this."

Angela had moved her hands back into the darkness and Nick searched for them again with the beam of the torch. When he found them she was holding a hand pick, of the type they used in the excavation. She placed her fingers on either side of the sharp square shaft and ran them up to the pointed end.

"Are you saying...?"

"Not this one, maybe, but one just like it."

"Good grief."

For several minutes no one said anything. Nick turned off the torch and they crouched there, enveloped by the silence and a blackness that seemed like a solid wall in the sudden absence of illumination. He could hear Angela breathing through her mouth, in quick excited gasps. Gradually his eyes adapted, and the faces of the two girls emerged as pale patches from the gloom. When he spoke again it was in low, measured tones.

"This is, without doubt, the most ingenious murder I've come across in my entire career," he said.

"You think it is Julian, then?" Angela asked, her voice husky.

"I'm almost certain of it. Individually you might be able to explain away those findings. Even that skull injury could have been caused by a Roman weapon for all we know. But when you take all of them together – plus the fact that a man has gone missing – the coincidence is just too great. No, it's Julian, all right."

"Oh. You know, I don't know whether to be glad or sorry. Half of me was hoping it was him, and the other half was hoping desperately it wasn't. It's such a waste of a brilliant man. I don't understand what's going on. Why should anyone want to kill him?"

"I think we owe you some sort of explanation, Angela – it's only fair after all you've done. There are still details that we don't understand yet, but since you ask I'll tell you what happened, the way I see it."

Chapter 33

Nick didn't like to involve civilians in a murder investigation. But, like it or not, Angela's discovery had already involved her, and up to the hilt. She needed to know what they were up against. He took a deep breath.

"Julian discovered – or was close to discovering – some sort of racket, a way of spiriting valuable finds out of the world of scholarship and into the international market. So they decide to kill him. Someone calls on him during the night. We don't know what he tells him – maybe it has to do with that gold ring he's so upset about, the one with the intaglio. Whatever it is it's enough to get him to pull on some clothes over his pajamas, put on a pair of shoes and follow them down to the dig. He bends down to look at something and they kill him with a single blow from a pick just like the one Angela showed us.

"Now there's a problem. Julian's a big guy and it's going to take some effort to shift him any distance. Vehicles are out because they're parked right between the cabins and the tents and someone's bound to hear an engine start up. So they can't go far and wherever they bury him he's likely to be found, sooner or later. Then everyone will know he's been murdered and the finger will point to one of the people up here. But they've thought it all through. They do the one thing no one – certainly not me – would expect them to do: they burn the body and bury it where they're sure it will be found. First they empty his pockets of identifying objects that wouldn't be incinerated – keys, penknife, that sort of thing. They take his shoes, too, for the same reason. Then they set light to the body. They probably start it off by soaking it with some of that fuel they use in the tractor and the generator. Maybe that's what you could smell, Angela; that or the body fat."

"Just a minute, Nick," Lucia interrupted. "Are you saying they burned the body right here? How come no one noticed?"

"All this happened during the small hours. It would be out of sight inside the dig. In any case there's a ridge and a good stretch of ground between here and the cabins. The tents are even further away. And don't forget what Alex Cothill said: it had been a hot day and everyone was tired out. Also they'd had a lot of wine with dinner." He added, as an afterthought, "Maybe that part was managed, too."

"What about the smell?" asked Angela.

"On slopes like this any breeze would be downhill at night. Heard of katabatic winds?"

"Kata – what?"

"Katabatic. At night the higher ground radiates heat and the air in contact with it cools and sinks down the hill. The breeze would have carried the smoke and the smell away from the camp."

"I can't believe it. It's horrible."

"It gets worse. When the body's finished burning they smash the bones a bit, to make them look like the others, and they take the molars because, like you said, Angela, fillings would give the whole game away and the remains could be identified from dental records. Then they bury it at a depth that ensures it will be discovered when the team starts to dig to the next level, and they compact the soil over it as best as they can. All that's left is to return the shoes and the keys and things to his cabin. Job done. Now they can put about the story that he's gone walkies."

"I don't understand," Angela said. "Why deliberately bury it where it can be found?"

"That's the really clever part, Angela. The team's been uncovering skeletons all the time. It won't be any surprise to find another one. It'll get bagged up like the others, numbered and placed with the finds. Then they can do a disappearing act with the bones, just like they do with the valuable finds, finds like that gold ring. And once that's done they'll be disposed of, leaving not a single trace of what's happened here. Like I say, it was a very clever plan. They only made one mistake."

"What was that?"

He spoke slowly.

"They didn't reckon on those bones being dug up by a student of human biology, one who used her wits and her intelligence in a way that even a top class forensic anthropologist couldn't have bettered."

For a moment no one spoke. Nick knew he'd embarrassed Angela but the praise was well deserved. All the same, there was something else in that heavy silence. Nick couldn't see Angela's expression but he heard the girl's erratic breathing and picked up the tension. She'd been excited, yet perfectly detached, when she was describing the skeleton. He cursed inwardly. She was probably more vulnerable than she seemed.

"Angela? Are you all right?"

He heard her swallow. She answered, very quietly.

"Yes, sorry. It sort of came home to me in a rush. I was remembering how he was when he was alive, how much he had to offer, all the things he could pass on. And someone just goes and snuffs it all out with a hand pick. Who'd do a thing like that?"

"We don't know yet. But it would have to be someone who knows how bodies burn."

"Oh my God, the Professor..."

"Shhh. Let's not jump to conclusions. But you see how important it is not to say anything to anyone?"

They were silent again as the two girls absorbed the information. Then Lucia's voice came out of the darkness.

"Nick, I hate to say this, but I still don't think the evidence would stand up in a court of law."

"You're right, Lucia, but we're not finished yet. First of all, I'd like to get a DNA identification of this material. Angela, you must be up on this sort of thing. Do you think that would be possible?"

"I doubt it. The DNA would have been denatured by the heat. Wait a minute, though... I just remembered something we learned at Liverpool. If there's intact DNA anywhere it'll be in the petrous temporal bone. It has lots of cavities which could have insulated the inside. Hang on, if you shine the torch over here I'll see if I can find it. It shouldn't be too hard; the bits of skull haven't been spread around."

"Okay. If possible, Angela, can you try not to handle it? Lucia, could you take the torch for a moment?"

He rummaged around in his jacket pockets, brought out one of the evidence bags he invariably carried around, and held it open.

A few minutes later, Angela came up with a piece of bone on the end of the trowel. Lucia followed it with the torch until it dropped into the bag, which Nick sealed and replaced in his pocket.

"Thanks," he said. "I think I'll get a courier service to take this back to the U.K. We need to do the analysis over there because we'll have to take DNA samples from his wife and daughters for comparison. I'll set it all up by phone. After that there's just one minor matter left: we have to nail his killer."

"And how do you propose to do that?" Lucia demanded.

"Well, the finds, including the bones, have got to be transferred to the vaults in Montalcini's Department. Montalcini told me they were already overdue for a trip. That's the point at which Julian's bones have got to be removed and destroyed. When those finds leave here I'm planning to be with them, every inch of the way."

Angela's voice came out of the darkness.

"The soonest that can happen is this Saturday. That's the day after tomorrow."

"I know."

Again there was a silence.

"Nick," Lucia said slowly. "I'm not happy about this. Shouldn't we be...?"

She hesitated.

"Shouldn't we be reporting it to the Italian police? Is that what you're saying?"

"Well, yes..."

"You're right, of course. If there's a body this is a crime scene. It should be reported, taped off, photographed, fingertip-searched. That's proper police procedure. But think about it. This body burned fiercely. There's a fair chance the DNA in that sample's been cooked. If it has, what are we going to be left with?"

"The lab could still analyze the mineral and isotope content of the bone."

"Sure. They might be able to say that whoever these bones belonged to didn't come from here. They might even tell us he wasn't contemporary with the other remains. But none of that proves it was Julian, and it won't give us his killer. Play it by the book and report it as a crime scene and in no time flat this place will be swarming with cops. No one will make a move and we won't be any further ahead than we were when Angela called us over. Do it my way and there's a chance we'll end up with a positive I.D. on the bones and the killer in handcuffs."

"I suppose," Lucia said thoughtfully, "we could say we're not actually certain it's a body. After all, the evidence we have is only suggestive. And in a sense the scene was compromised the moment Angela uncovered the skeleton."

"Precisely. And that's what I'll tell Umberto. He'll see the point. He's a smart guy, and he wants the killer as much as we do."

"It's a heck of a gamble, though, Nick. Suppose they manage to slip the bones away from the rest of the finds without you seeing? We'll be left with nothing."

"Okay, I hear what you're saying. Do you have something in mind?"

"Yes, I do. At some stage after the bones have been recorded and numbered, we swap them with another set of bones, genuine Roman ones."

"Oh, now that is lovely! They try to disguise Julian's bones as Roman ones, and we play the same trick back on them – there's a real poetry to that! Unless... Angela, the bones aren't marked individually, are they?"

"Not at this stage. There just isn't time. Later on, when they're being analyzed I guess they will be. No, that could be done all right. The bag is a grip-seal type. It wouldn't be hard to swap the bones between two bags."

"Nick, we were talking earlier about me helping on the dig.

I'll tell you what: I'll stay up here tonight. When I see the others at breakfast I'll tell them I'm going to be around just to lend them a hand. I'll say I've always wanted to do something like this. Well, that's near enough the truth, isn't it? I'll elect to help Angela. It shouldn't take too long to get the whole skeleton out between us, should it, Angela?"

"No, a lot of it's loosened already. We could probably do it in the morning but we'll have to take a bit longer than that to make it look convincing."

"Okay. And then tomorrow night I'll slip the lock on that office, get in there and make the swap."

"That's far too dangerous," Nick said. "Montalcini's right in the next cabin. Those walls aren't thick. He's bound to hear something and then he'll come to investigate."

"It's better if I do it."

For the moment Nick and Lucia were too astonished to respond. Then Nick spluttered, "We can't possibly…"

Angela interrupted. "I wouldn't do it at night. Look, it's not suspicious for one of the team to be in the office, we're in and out of there all the time. I can always dream up a reason. Only I'll plan to do it when no one else is around. Probably tomorrow afternoon, later on."

"I don't know," Nick said. "I don't like it."

"It was my idea," Lucia added. "And now it's you taking the risk, Angela. That can't be right."

"Come on, it's no big deal."

"How would you get in?"

"They don't usually lock the office door during the day. Just in case they do, Lucia can show me how she would have opened it. It's not hard, is it?"

"Not with that lock. I could show you on my cabin door. It's the same."

"All right, then, that's settled. Now I'd better get back to my tent, in case Claudia wakes up and starts to wonder where I've gone."

"You share with Claudia?" Nick asked.

"Yes, why?"

"I just had a thought... How clued up is Claudia, would you say? I mean, could she interpret these bones the way you have?"

"No way. She's a mechanical engineer. She's smart all right, and she's probably learned a lot while she's been here, but she won't have encountered the kind of thing we've been talking about."

"Good, because what I'd like to suggest is that you get her to help you tomorrow, instead of Lucia. It would attract less attention that way."

Lucia added, "You're right, Nick, I should have thought of that myself."

"Okay," Angela said. "That won't be a problem. Since Julian disappeared we've been more or less assigning ourselves to the bits of the dig that needed doing. I'll ask her in the morning, and we'll get started straight after breakfast."

Chapter 34

Lucia spent the whole morning on the dig, helping first one member of the team and then another. It was hard to focus on what she was doing; she was also trying to keep an eye on Angela, and looking for an opportunity to access the laptop. Antonino was using it to log the finds, and so far there was no sign that he'd be relinquishing it to do a bit of digging.

Lucia hadn't been far away when Angela had told Claudia about her find. Claudia had been delighted.

"Human bones? You are sure? But that's wonderful, Angela! Finally you have your chance!"

"Would you like to help me with it, Claudia? It's quite a lot to do on my own."

"Sure, I was only working with Pippo. There isn't much happening over there."

Lucia cast frequent glances in the girls' direction. They were working in the deepest part of the dig. Claudia was tall, but when she stood up ground level seemed to start at twice her height. Now that she was viewing it in daylight, Lucia could see that the sides of the dig were not vertical but they were very steep. That was why everyone got in and out at the sloping end, the end closer to the path.

Montalcini made frequent appearances. That surprised Lucia, who'd never seen him on site before, but he toured around, offering words of encouragement. At one point he stood at the top, overlooking Angela and Claudia. Lucia found herself holding her breath.

"So, Angela. At last you have found some human bones. Congratulations."

Angela got to her feet and stretched her back.

"Thank you, Professor. Do take care – that edge is very

crumbly."

"Yes, I know."

Even so, Lucia noted, he stepped back a little.

"That skeleton looks fairly complete," he observed.

"Yes, I think it is. I'm not missing anything so far."

Except a petrous temporal bone, Lucia thought.

"Well, I would like to have a closer look, but I don't want to hold you up. We are working against the clock now. I will have my chance later when we examine these finds in the laboratory. Well done, anyway."

The morning went by quickly and they stopped for lunch. The conversation over the table was lively. Lucia didn't pick up any hostility towards Francesca, even from the girls. Perhaps they'd decided that she was an unfortunate victim after all, especially now that Julian had disappeared.

By the time they returned to the dig, Lucia had come to the conclusion that if she was going to get her hands on that computer at all she would have to make it happen. For a while she scraped away with a trowel, working alongside Pippo. Then, when things were fairly quiet, she straightened up conspicuously, one hand in her back, and strolled over to Antonino. She spoke to him in Italian.

"Phew, I'm not used to this. My knees and back are killing me."

He smiled.

"Would you mind taking over for a spell, Antonino? Perhaps I could record the finds instead."

He shrugged.

"If you like." He handed over the laptop.

Just like that, she thought.

"Er, what do I do?"

"If someone has a find, click on the new record icon, here. The number is assigned automatically; all you have to do is type the description next to it. We are not taking photographs at this moment, so the camera is in the office. If we do need to use it, the image is inserted into this column. I can show you how, or I will do it myself. Okay?"

"Yes, I think so. I'm not used to Apple Macs, I use PCs most of the time. Do I have to save anything?"

"No, it will save automatically each time you open a new record."

She watched as Antonino picked up a trowel and went over to work with Pippo. Then she glanced over her shoulder, but there was no sign of Montalcini. She turned her attention to the computer. She used the trackpad to navigate the cursor to the name of the software, "Archetype", and clicked on it. A list dropped down; the first item was "About Archetype". As easy as that! She moved the cursor to open the item, then jumped. Someone was calling her name.

She looked down to see Francesca.

"Bag, please, Lucia."

She looked around her in confusion. On the ground she saw a large plastic bag, inside which were more plastic bags in a variety of sizes and a marker pen.

"How big, Francesca?"

"Quite big. It's more pottery. I think we will put all the pieces together. They are clearly from the same article."

Lucia squatted at the edge of the dig and passed the bag and marker down. Francesca dropped some large, curved terra cotta fragments into the bag, sealed it, and waited with the marker poised.

"What's the number?"

Lucia cursed her own slowness. She clicked on the new record icon and a line appeared at the end of the list. She read off the number to Francesca: "*zero-tre-quattro-cinque*", "0345".

Francesca wrote on the bag and handed it back with the marker. Lucia was about to ask her how she should record the item when she saw that Francesca had added a brief description in the label area. She copied it into the database. Then she looked up but Francesca had already gone back to work. The others seemed occupied too. She moved the cursor back to "About Archetype" and clicked on it.

The small window that opened carried the logo of a Roman

head in profile and the word "Titus".

Underneath that, she read: "Archetype, a product of Titus Software Solutions: custom computer applications for accounting, inventories, sales contact management, databases, business models."

A list of names followed, and a Rome address. She closed her eyes, committing it to memory; she couldn't write it down now, it would be too obvious, especially as they weren't supposed to be making written records. She went to close the "About Archetype" window and felt a moment of panic: there were no symbols for doing it! If she couldn't get rid of it everyone would be able to see what she'd been up to! She placed the cursor on the window and clicked, and to her relief it disappeared.

Once again the screen displayed just the list of finds, with Francesca's fragments of pottery on the last line. She scanned the list briefly and noticed other terra cotta fragments recorded in Italian on the lines above, presumably by Antonino. Some of those fragments may have come from the same pot and at some stage somebody was going to have to piece all of it together. It was a painstaking business, this archaeology.

Nick answered his mobile. "Hi, Lucia. How's it going?"

"Okay. Where are you, Nick?"

"Rome, Fiumicino Airport. Where are you?"

"In my cabin. People are changing and cleaning themselves up before dinner. What on earth are you doing in Rome?"

"Oh, I've had a right runaround. There was a police courier service from Naples all right but it was only for destinations in Italy. To get a courier to the U.K. it had to go via Rome. I wasn't going to take any chances with it going astray. I've brought it here myself. I'm hoping I can catch the guy before he leaves."

"Okay, I'll be brief, then. I've got the people who wrote that software and you're in the right place: they're based in Rome."

"Great stuff! Hang on, let me get my notebook. Yes?"

"Titus Software Solutions."

"Titus...? Hang on a moment."

He dipped into a pocket and brought out his wallet. Inside was a torn piece of paper.

"Good Christ, so that's what it was."

"What?"

"I clean forgot I had this. When I was looking at that computer at the Questura in Naples I found a scrap of paper in the bin. It looked like Julian's handwriting. It said 'Titus something'."

"He must have been on to it as well."

"Yes, he must. Did you get an address?"

She gave him the address and he took it down.

"And was there a telephone number with that, Lucia?"

"No. If there was, I couldn't have memorized that as well. I thought I was doing pretty well to remember the address."

He sensed the irritation. "No, you did very well. Okay, I'll get this package to the courier and then look these people up. It'll probably be too late to see them today. I'll give them a ring and go there first thing in the morning. Has Angela had a chance to swap the bags yet?"

"Not yet. But Montalcini went off somewhere this afternoon so we're going to do it after dinner when the coast is clear."

"All right, I hope it goes well. I'll phone you later, shall I?"

"Make it tomorrow morning, Nick. It's been a hard day and I think I'm going to be pretty bushed by the end of it. I'm aiming to have an early night."

"Okay, I'll talk to you tomorrow. Good work, Lucia. Cheers."

Angela came out of the area behind the kitchen where the two chemical toilets were located. She saw Lucia sitting, as arranged, at one of the tables, ostensibly reading a paperback that Angela had given her earlier. With dinner over, the team had retired to their tents. As usual, everyone was drained by the heat and the day's exertions.

She raised her eyebrows to Lucia, who nodded in return. She moved quickly to the office and tried the door. It was locked. She took the credit card from her pocket and fumbled with it, trying to use it in the way Lucia had shown her. After a moment or two she felt something give; the bolt slid back, the door opened and she stepped into the office. Then, as Lucia had instructed her, she returned to the lock, rotated the handle to retract the bolt, and set the latch. The idea was to make it look as if the last one out had left it that way. There was only one problem: now anyone could walk straight in on her. She would have to depend on Lucia to give her adequate warning.

She crossed straight to the set of drawers where the finds were kept. The last few drawers hadn't been labelled yet. She opened one and shuffled the bags around, looking for the number "0349", which she'd noted carefully when the bag containing Julian's bones was recorded. The numbers ended at "0344" so she opened the drawer below it. "0347", "0348"... "0349". Her heart missed a beat. The bag was there, and it was labelled "0349" all right, but it didn't contain bones. It was full of pieces of terra cotta pottery.

Lucia pretended to read the book while using her peripheral vision to pick up the slightest hint of movement. If anyone appeared she would get up casually and stroll off in the direction of her cabin, her hand at her side, ready to rap on the door with her knuckles as she passed the office. Two knocks for Antonino; three for Montalcini. So far it had been quiet. And then her senses bristled. She could hear the sound of an approaching car.

Angela's initial reaction was one of indignation which quickly turned to anger. She had a strong sense of ownership of these bones. How dare anyone take them! She started to work backwards through the drawers, opening them rapidly, one after the other, ignoring the numbers, just looking for a bag with her special collection of blackened bones. She pounced on one large bag but closer inspection revealed that these were genuine Roman bones from the dig. All the same she noted the number – "0295" – before returning it. She opened the drawer above and immediately saw what she was looking for. The bag was labelled "0349", so what was it doing in a drawer marked "0292 – 0296"? She shook her head in annoyance, then opened the drawer below and retrieved the bones marked "0295".

Three knocks on the office door made her jump. Montalcini was back!

Hurriedly she emptied the two bags onto the desk and started to sweep each set of bones into the opposite bag.

A car door slammed.

She sealed the "0295" bag, which now contained Julian's bones, and replaced it in the open drawer.

A key rattled in the office door; it wouldn't turn because the lock had been latched.

She opened the drawer above, sealed the "0349" bag and put it in.

The key rattled in the door again.

She slammed the drawer shut, grabbed a chair, and sat down at the desk. As she did so she felt her scalp contract as she noticed that the bones had left behind a smudged line of dusty soil.

The door opened and Montalcini came in. He stopped dead when he saw her. She rose to her feet, casually brushing her forearm over the desk.

"Good evening, Professor," she said, trying to control her breathing.

His eyes narrowed.

"Angela. How did you get in?"

"How? Oh, it was open, on the latch."

"It is late, Angela." His mouth twitched slightly. "What are you doing here?"

"Waiting for you, sir. You are normally back around this time so I thought I'd wait for you in here. You don't mind, do you?"

Again he surveyed her carefully.

"What do you want?"

The words tumbled out.

"Well, I'm sorry I haven't had a chance to approach you about this before but there never seems to be a good moment. During the day we're working hard in the dig and at meal times there are other people around. Basically I'm finishing my degree this year and after my experience here I've decided I really do want to register for a Masters' course in forensic anthropology. So I was wondering if I could use your name as a referee."

"Certainly, I have no problem with that. You have worked with great commitment. I would be happy to support your application. Where are you applying?"

Angela was on her back foot now. She hadn't actually identified such a course. She swallowed hard.

"Well, in the U.K. these courses are usually heavily oversubscribed so I thought I would apply to several. But it would make a big difference, I'm sure, if I had your backing. I'd be very grateful. Well, that was all really. I hope I didn't disturb you or anything."

Montalcini was standing between her and the door. It didn't look like he was going to move.

Angela's mouth was dry and she hoped desperately that her face didn't look as hot as it felt. If she screamed Lucia would come but that would blow their little plot wide open.

"Good night, Professor," she said firmly, moving towards the door.

At the last moment he stood aside.

"Good night, Angela. Please drop the latch on that door as you go out."

Chapter 35

It was the phone call he dreaded having to make.

"Dawn. It's Nick Roberts here."

"Nick! I was wondering how you were getting on."

"I meant to phone you before but there's been a lot going on."
He hesitated. "I'm sorry. I'm afraid the news isn't good."

There was a heavy silence. When she spoke again her voice
was low and controlled.

"I was expecting that. Have you found him?"

"I'm not one hundred per cent sure. I'd like to do a DNA
analysis."

"My God, are you saying he was unrecognizable?"

He winced.

"No, well – look, I don't want to go into it on the phone. Can
we wait till I see you?"

"I'm coming out there."

"No, Dawn, please. Trust me on this one. The investigation's
at a critical stage. If you come out now it could blow the whole
thing."

There was another long silence and Nick started to wonder
whether she was still on the line. Then, huskily:

"All right."

"Good. Thank you. Look, I'm in Rome right now. I've sent a
tissue sample via the police courier service to our own forensic
lab. You'll be contacted by Dr. Sally Forrester. She's first-rate.
Thing is, we're going to need samples from your daughters. I
guess you can keep Sophie home from school for a day. Is Kendra
on long vacation?"

"Yes. But she's not at home; she's got a holiday job in
Bristol."

"Do you think you could get her up there as well? Then Sally can see all three of you at once."

"Yes, all right. I'll arrange a time and make sure they're here for her."

"Thanks." He paused. "They'll know why we're doing it. You'll have to break it to them gently."

"I think they're prepared for the worst but that's not the same as having it confirmed. It won't be easy."

"I'm sorry, Dawn, I really am. I wish I could have been the bearer of better news."

"It's not your fault, Nick. What are you going to do now?"

"Me? I'm going after his killer."

Angela was working in the same area as on the previous day, sifting through the soil to see if she'd missed anything. There was nothing special about that; it was normal practice at the dig whenever human remains were turned up because there could be associated items, such as rings, pins or brooches. In this instance, of course, she had other reasons for being thorough. Lucia was working alongside her. She'd been shocked by Angela's encounter with Professor Montalcini in the office and filled with admiration at the cool way the girl had carried it off. But from now on she wasn't taking any chances; she would be staying close to her.

Nick was impressed, too, when she related the incident to him over the phone. Then she told him how the bones had been in the wrong drawer and about the pieces of terra cotta pottery with the same record number.

"Nick? You still there?"

"So that's how they do it," he breathed.

"What? What are you saying?"

"It's so obvious now. See, any item they want to steal, they just duplicate the number. Then all they have to do is delete the record and the sequence is still unbroken. I suspected that much, that's why I'm calling on Titus Software later this morning – I want to find out how they managed something the software's supposed to prevent. But what Angela's discovered, that's the really neat part."

"You mean, putting the item in the wrong drawer was intentional?"

"Oh, yes. No wonder Julian couldn't find the ring! Think about it. He looks it up on the computer; it doesn't exist. He remembers the number so he looks in the drawer; it's not there. He could have searched the team's quarters for that ring until he was blue in the face; he wouldn't have found it because it was there all the time – it was just in a different drawer! It gets transported to the Department with all the other finds but it doesn't go into the vaults – oh, no. That's the point where it actually gets spirited away."

"But Nick, isn't that a bit risky? Julian could have found that ring, just as Angela found the bones, simply by looking in the other drawers."

"That's easy enough to do for bones; it's a longer job for things like that ring because it's small and it would be wrapped up in tissue paper. But the main thing is: it's less risky than trying to hide it. See, in the unlikely event that someone does discover the item in the wrong place with a duplicated number, it can be passed off as an oversight. You know the kind of thing, 'The finds were coming thick and fast, and somehow it got numbered without being entered into the computer and got stored out of sequence.' Human error. It's not even suspicious!"

"I get you. They'll lose that particular item from their haul but the operation can carry on as before, which is the important thing so far as they're concerned."

"Exactly. Thank Angela for me, would you, Lucia? That girl is a total ace. I just hope she hasn't put herself at risk, that's all. You'd better stick close to her."

"Don't worry, I already am."

"And take care yourself, you hear? That's an order, Sergeant."

She laughed. "Ay, ay, sir."

And now she was back in the dig, next to Angela, scraping down through the soil to the next level. It was a monotonous job and her mind kept wandering back to Nick. He'd been so warm and supportive on the phone and it made her feel all the worse for the way she'd set things up the night before last. She'd virtually pushed them into sleeping together. He'd dealt with it very sensibly, taking them straight back into professional mode again, and God knows there'd been plenty to keep them both occupied. But things shouldn't have been precipitated that way. She wanted to get closer to him, but a relationship like that takes time to mature; it should have been allowed to develop naturally. Instead she'd rushed him into it and probably ruined everything. She wondered what he thought of her now. She felt she'd cheapened herself in his eyes and that hurt, it hurt badly.

Preoccupied with these thoughts, she barely registered the little stream of soil that had started to trickle down the steeply sloping side of the dig, a few feet from her head. She heard the creak at the same moment as Pippo's voice rang out in alarm and just in time to look up and see the huge broad blade of the bulldozer plunging down on top of them.

Titus Software Associates was located in the Aventino Quarter, not far from the Circus Maximus.

The taxi dropped him at the address in Viale Aventino and he walked through a doorway to find himself looking up at what appeared to be a modern apartment block. The area in front of it was paved and planted with evergreen shrubs. It seemed like a pleasant working environment. He couldn't help comparing it to the Soprintendenza in Naples where he'd dropped Lucia three days before.

There was a squawk box at the side of the entrance; Nick ran a finger down the names and pressed the buzzer. He showed his badge to the young man who'd come to the door.

"I'm Detective Inspector Roberts. Was it you I spoke to on the phone?"

"Yes, it was. Paolo Schifani."

They shook hands.

"Come in, Inspector."

Titus Software Solutions occupied the ground floor. It was clearly a small, egalitarian affair. The office was open plan, with half a dozen staff all working at computers.

They sat down together at a vacant desk.

"First of all, thanks for seeing me at short notice, Signor Schifani."

"Paolo, Inspector. No problem. How can I help you?"

He spoke English rapidly, with a faint American accent. Nick thought he was probably in his mid to late twenties. The rest of the staff looked younger still.

"It's like I said on the phone: I wanted to know a bit more about a piece of software your people wrote here."

"Yep, which one?"

"The Archetype program you designed for the Pliny Institute."

Nick watched him carefully for a reaction, but his expression was neutral.

"Yes, I remember. What do you want to know? I can't give you design details, you know. If a client pays to have software developed the deal stays confidential, and we don't sell the software to anyone else, either. That'd be unethical."

"Yeah, I understand that. Look, we may not need to go into that much detail anyway. Could you just show me what it does – at the user level, I mean."

"Sure, I can do that. Actually I haven't used it myself for some time, but I think it's a reasonably straightforward database. Just a minute, I'll get a disk. We can put it on this machine here."

Paolo spent the next twenty minutes giving him a guided tour of Archetype. It was essentially as Montalcini had presented it to him a few days earlier, although the software engineer gave him a more comprehensive idea of its capabilities.

Finally Nick said:

"Okay, so the entries can't be altered, and you can't delete an entry without leaving a gap in the sequence."

"Correct. That's the most important feature of this kind of software. No one can fool around with it. The client knows they're getting a complete archaeological record."

"Well just suppose you had something to record and you didn't want to assign the next number in the sequence. Suppose you actually wanted to give it the same number as the previous record."

"Why are you asking me again? I just told you: it can't be done. It's a safeguard."

"Good." He nodded approvingly. Then:

"Tell me, has anyone else asked you that same question in the last few weeks?"

Lucia used every ounce of power in her legs to launch herself from her crouched position into Angela. The impact knocked all the breath out of Angela but it carried both of them to one side. There was a deafening crash as the blade of the bulldozer smashed into the ground inches from their feet. Lucia glimpsed the yellow cabin, teetering above them. Without a moment's pause she leaped to her feet and dragged the dazed Angela over the uneven ground. With a great moan of protesting metal the machine toppled sideways and came to rest where they had both been lying instants before.

Angela was on her back struggling to get her breath. Lucia straightened up and whirled round. The others were all on their feet. Justine, Orkut and Francesca stood motionless, open-mouthed. Pippo, Claudia and Antonino were hurrying towards them.

"Look after Angela," Lucia snapped, as she scrambled up the steep slope out of the dig.

The loose soil shifted under her feet and she slid backwards, clawed fingers trailing, seeking a hold. She got up again and ran at the slope, only to slide back once more.

At the third attempt she managed to get a fingerhold on the firm ground at the top. She hauled, fingers and arms shouting with pain, and slowly pulled herself up until she could get one foot over the edge and roll over.

She got to her feet, ran up the ridge, and scanned quickly in all directions, from the path to the cabins, to the woodland, and down the hill, looking for a running figure. There was no one in sight. She grimaced. In the time it had taken her to get out of the dig, whoever released the brakes on that tractor and pushed it over the edge could have made it to the woodland. She was tempted to go in there but it was far too dangerous; they could be waiting for her with a knife or a gun.

Then she saw Montalcini, hurrying towards them from the direction of the office. Her eyes narrowed. Had there been enough time for him to get back to the office and out again?

Paolo Schifani seemed surprised. He shook his head. "No."

"You're sure? No one phoned you about it?"

"Hell, no. I wouldn't discuss something like that on the phone, anyway."

Nick took one of the photographs of Julian Lockhart out of his pocket and showed it to him.

"Have you ever seen this man? Tall, English."

Paolo studied the photograph and handed it back.

"No, who is he?"

"An archaeologist. So he didn't come here to talk to you?"

"No, I just said, I've never seen him."

Nick decided the man was telling the truth. Evidently they got to Julian Lockhart before he had a chance to follow up the Titus lead. He put the photograph away.

"All right, let me ask you a hypothetical question, Paolo. Suppose someone came to your company with a piece of software, Archetype or something like it, with all the safeguards built in. And they said they'd pay well for a new feature, a feature that allowed them to bypass the safeguard."

The answer came without hesitation.

"I'd tell them go find somebody else."

"Why?"

"It's obvious, isn't it? The whole idea of incorporating the safeguards is to prevent fraud. Anyone wants to bypass them, they're doing it for all the wrong reasons. We wouldn't take on anything like that, and I don't know of any reputable software outfit that would."

"But it could be done?"

"Oh sure, it could be done."

"But no one ever asked you to include this feature in the software."

"No, they haven't, and if they had – well, you already know

232

my answer."

"Suppose someone did take it on, someone less ethical than you. How do you think they'd go about it?"

Paolo half-closed his eyes, immersed in thought.

Nick waited.

"They'd write something like a computer virus," Paolo said eventually. "They'd bury the routine quite deep in the system. And they'd make it so you could activate it with a key combination – three or four keys, to make it unlikely anyone would hit the right combination by chance."

"Would it be hard to do?"

"No, not really. A computer hacker would have no trouble at all. In fact he's just the sort of guy they'd go to."

"Thanks very much for your time, Paolo. You've told me everything I needed to know."

Montalcini looked alarmed. "I heard the shouting. What is the...?" He reached the edge and saw the tractor, lying on its side at the bottom of the dig. "Oh my God! Is anyone hurt?"

He looked round at Lucia, who was standing, hands on hips, breathing hard, her face, hands, and clothes covered in soil.

"Sergente, you are all right?"

She nodded brusquely.

He looked down into the dig, where Angela was getting to her feet, helped by Claudia. She was cradling the side of her chest.

"Angela?" Montalcini called. "Angela, you are all right?"

"Yes," she said weakly, "I'm okay, thanks to..." She looked up, squinting into the bright sky. Lucia realized she'd lost her glasses. "Is that Lucia?" she asked. "You saved my life, Lucia."

"I hope I didn't break a rib, Angela," Lucia said. "I hit you pretty hard."

Montalcini was clasping and unclasping his hands. "This is dreadful, dreadful," he was saying. "Sergente, I don't know how to thank you. How could such a thing happen..."

"I am responsible."

Torretta was standing at their side.

"It is my fault," he repeated in Italian. "The Sergente warned

233

me to move the tractor back from the edge in case there was another earthquake. It slipped my mind, and now look what has happened."

This was no earthquake, Lucia thought.

"Antonino," Montalcini said. "This is a very serious matter. Someone could have been killed."

"I know, Professore. I cannot say how sorry I am. It is very fortunate that we had Sergente Lucia with us. Thank you for what you have done, Sergente."

Lucia didn't like the way the conversation was going. She deflected it by pointing down at the tractor.

"You're going to have to get that thing out of there somehow," she observed.

"You are right, Sergente," Torretta said. "We will have to put it back on its wheels and then winch it out. Professore, may I suggest that I take the small 4 X 4 and drive over to the farmer? I am sure he will have suitable equipment."

"All right, then, off you go." Montalcini turned to address the team. "Everyone has had a great shock. Let us all go back to the kitchen and have some coffee. We will do no more work today."

He turned and led the way. Lucia hung back for a moment, casting an eye over the dig. Angela was making her way slowly towards the ramp, supported by Pippo on one side and Claudia on the other.

"Well, Angela," Lucia muttered under her breath. "You can say one thing about all this. If someone's trying to kill us, we must be getting mighty close."

Chapter 36

After they'd taken a short break, the students went their different ways. Angela was still trembling. Her chest was hurting and one hip was badly bruised where she'd landed on her side. Her glasses were somewhere under the tractor but she told Lucia she had a spare pair. Lucia took her to her own cabin and helped her onto the bed. She wanted to have a look at Angela's injuries but the girl jumped and protested at the slightest touch so she decided she'd let her rest for the moment and come back later. Antonino drove off in the small 4 X 4. Justine and Orkut returned to their respective tents, with mutual glances that suggested they might not stay confined to their respective tents for very long. Claudia stood up and said, "Well, I don't know about you but it does not suit me to do nothing. I prefer to go back to work." Montalcini remonstrated lightly, but he was clearly pleased. Francesca and Pippo said they'd join her and the three went down to the dig. Suddenly the place was deserted.

Lucia grabbed the opportunity to contact Nick. She tried several times, but his phone was switched off. He was probably on the flight back from Rome to Naples, She texted him instead.

"Phone me when u get in L"

When she returned to the cabin Angela was asleep. Lucia toyed with the idea of going down to the dig, but it wasn't sensible to leave the cabin unguarded. She picked up the book Angela had lent her earlier, went back to the long table outside the kitchen and settled down to read. It was warm and pleasant, and the big cedar scented the air. It would be all too easy to fall asleep. She forced herself to turn the pages but her concentration kept slipping.

He phoned from Naples airport at six o'clock. Her mind leaped into sharp focus. Although she wasn't close to the office she took the call further away still and kept her voice low.

"How did things go, Nick?"

"Good, very good. We were right. It wouldn't be difficult to bypass the safeguards in that program. The code for doing it is buried somewhere in that laptop computer. The person who operates it knows the key combination and they can duplicate the record number whenever there's something worth stealing. They could do it at the dig but it would be almost as easy to do it afterwards. So now we know why the Pliny Institute throws in a laptop whenever someone gets a grant. How are you getting on?"

"Er, well we had a bit of an incident here."

She gave him a brief account of what had happened.

"My God. Right, that's it. I'm on my way. I just have to pick up the 4 X 4 and then I'm coming to take you away from there."

"No, Nick."

"What do you mean 'No'? You're not safe!"

"Nick, I'm staying."

"That's crazy! Give me one good reason why I shouldn't come right now and get you out of there."

"I can do better than that, I'll give you two. Number One: Angela needs my protection more than ever now and if I leave here she won't have it. I've arranged for her to sleep in my cabin tonight. It'll be a little cramped in that bed but that's too bad. I won't risk her sleeping in the tent. We'll be perfectly safe in the cabin. I'll put the door on the latch and pile a chair and the case against it, just in case someone gets ideas. Tomorrow's Saturday. The team will be going down to the hostel in Castellamare. Angela can go with them. We can arrange for her to be checked over at the hospital. Depending on the outcome we can decide what's going to happen on Monday. All right? Are you listening?"

Nick rumbled, "Yes, I'm listening. What's Number Two?"

"Number Two is your plan; we're not going to abandon it now. They want to move the samples to the Department in Naples and tomorrow morning is easily the best time for them to do it. I've worked it all out. I'm told breakfast is at eight a.m. After that the students will leave for Castellamare; I'll go with them. I expect Pippo will be driving. I'll get him to stop as soon as we're out of the line of sight and I'll double back. I've found a good spot in a small stand of trees where I can watch the parking area without being seen. I'll phone you when I'm in position and again the moment they start to load. And you'll be standing by, somewhere on their route, ready to follow it to Naples. Now we can't do any of that if you come and take me away, can we?"

"I don't know, I'm still not happy about it."

"Now stop fussing. Have you spoken to Umberto yet?"

"Yes. I spoke to him again before my flight left Rome. He's just waiting for me to give the word. He went over to the Department and had a word with the security personnel. He says the vaults are very secure, for obvious reasons. The good news is: they've got closed-circuit TV cameras down there as well. Normally the control room isn't manned but it will be this time and he'll be in there with the security staff, monitoring what's going on."

"Just the two of you?"

"Yes. I trust Umberto, but he's the only one I do trust, so the fewer people who know about this operation the better. Look, are you sure you're going to be all right up there? I'm your senior officer, you know. I'm responsible for you."

"Is this a purely professional concern, then, Nick?" she asked lightly.

His voice was low. "You know it isn't."

Her tone changed. "Listen, Nick. What you're doing is risky, too. You will take care, won't you?"

"Is this a purely professional concern, Lucia?"

"You know it isn't."

With the call over, Lucia stood looking at her mobile for a moment, lips compressed. It was reassuring to talk to Nick and to know he was worried about her. Somehow that had made it easy for her to sound brave and confident. But now she was on her own again, left with the reality. And the reality was that there was a killer up here on the loose. She looked over her shoulder and a small shiver ran through her.

237

It would be best to return to her cabin. She lifted her chin and squared her shoulders. She mustn't allow her fears to be transmitted to Angela; the girl was distressed enough.

Life was often like that, she thought, as she walked back; appearances were everything. You felt one way but had to act in quite another. And she'd have to keep up the pretence. Later on she would barricade the door, like she'd said, because it would make them feel safer. Then she'd climb into bed and pretend to go to sleep. She wouldn't sleep – she knew that. She'd be listening to every sound, every creak, every leaf fall on the roof.

It was going to be a long night.

Chapter 37

He was in position at eight o'clock, concealed just inside the entrance to an orchard. He wound down both front windows to take advantage of the slight breeze coming in from the Gulf, and there was an immediate increase in the noise of morning traffic on the autostrada a few hundred metres below. Whoever was bringing the samples down would have to come this way.

Years of patient police work had taught Nick how to wait. First he listened consciously, adjusting himself to his surroundings, hearing at first only traffic sounds, then bird song, then the rustling of leaves in the orchard and the distant clanking of machinery in the Castellamare dockyards. Finally he let all of them slip into his subconscious and let his mind wander to other things.

He felt better about Lucia now. He'd been afraid that things were irretrievable, but the warmth of her voice on the phone last night said otherwise. And she was smart, too, the way she'd looked after Angela and organized things for today. He was praying she'd be all right. With a murder and an attempted double murder up at the dig already there was plenty for him to worry about.

A sound emerged over the intermittent swish of tyres along the highway; the steady drone of a car engine. A few minutes later, up the hill to his right, the people carrier came into view. It disappeared around a bend and then reappeared in glimpses between the orchard trees. He couldn't see who was in it. He checked his watch; nine-fifteen. It would take Lucia fifteen or twenty minutes to get into position, depending on where they'd dropped her and how circuitous she was going to be in her return.

Half an hour later he was looking at his watch and checking once again that his mobile was actually on. Why hadn't she made contact? He toyed with the idea of phoning her but dismissed it. Even if her mobile had been switched to silent mode, the sound of her voice when she answered him could give away her position.

Another half-hour passed. He was running his bottom lip through his teeth now, tense and anxious. How long would it take them to load the samples? Not that long surely? Had they decided not to go today? That was inconceivable. Now that Julian's charred skeleton had been excavated and bagged the murderer wouldn't keep it a minute longer than he had to. It was crucial evidence and he would know it; he had to get rid of it fast.

Where the hell's Lucia got to?

Nightmarish thoughts began to crowd his mind. Had something happened to her during the night? They were going to be quite safe, she said. She'd latch the door and wedge things up against it.

He shook his head. Those cabins were flimsy; they could easily break through from the one next door – it would only take a couple of big swings with an axe. For a moment he contemplated the unpleasant image of the partition wall splintering in on the two girls, then dismissed it. It would make too much noise. They were brutal but they could be subtle too – look how they lured Lockhart to his death!

She'd never fall for something like that! Stop worrying, she's a big girl. She can take care of herself. Can't she?

Twenty minutes later something new started to insinuate itself into his troubled thoughts: a low rumbling that was growing in volume. The car began to shake violently and continued to shake for a long time. *That's the third earthquake this morning, or is it the fourth? They're getting more and more frequent and they're lasting longer.* The rumbling died away and he straightened up abruptly; the tremor had been masking another sound: the sound of an approaching car. It appeared moments later: it was the 4 X 4.

Shit, what do I do now?

He had seconds to decide. If he let it go, he knew he could wave goodbye to his one and only chance of nailing Julian's killer. But...

Why hasn't she called?

The 4 X 4 rounded another bend. It was now or never.

She's in trouble – they must have got to her. All right, that's it. She comes first.

He reached for the ignition – just as his mobile vibrated. He answered it quickly.

"It's on the way!" Her voice was breathless.

"What happened?"

"Too far from the satellite link... reception... chance to get closer..."

The 4 X 4 passed the entrance to the orchard.

"All right, I've got them. I'm off."

The starter motor cranked the engine into life. By the time he'd reached the autostrada the 4 X 4 was several cars ahead. He aimed to keep it that way.

He phoned Umberto.

"Pronto."

"Umberto? Nick."

"Where are you, Nick?"

"On the autostrada. The target's heading for Naples. I'm on his tail. Are you at the Department?"

"Yes, everything's ready here. We have the security cameras trained on the vaults. Look, it's Saturday so officially the Department is closed. There's a railing that goes right up to the entrance. The gate will be locked but he can open it; there is a keypad. The gate shuts automatically; you will not be able to follow him in. But once he is in the vaults we can watch him."

"Okay, I'll stay and keep an eye on the entrance, in case he goes somewhere after that."

"Excellent. Remember, he may not come here first. He may try to get rid of the bones on the way."

"I know, I'm going to stick to him like glue."

"Don't move too soon, Nick. You know we can't arrest him for being in possession of the bones. We have to catch him actually trying to dispose of them."

"Yeah, I know that. Talk to you soon."

The 4 X 4 started to wind through the streets of Naples. Nick hung on grimly. It was hard to know if the driver was trying to shake him off or if he was simply taking short cuts through the city. He saw it turn left at an intersection and just then a pedestrian held up a hand and began to cross the road.

Nick braked sharply and a crowd of people took advantage of the gap and poured in front of him. He cursed, easing forward, hoping that someone would hesitate. Finally an elderly couple paused and he roared through.

As he turned the corner he expelled a breath: it was still there, six cars ahead of him, waiting at traffic lights. His fingers drummed on the steering wheel. The lights changed and he watched the 4 X 4 cross over a broad thoroughfare and plunge down a narrow street opposite. The cars in front of him turned right and left but there seemed to be some sort of obstruction because the car in front of him was barely moving. The lights started to change again. He didn't hesitate; he swerved around the car in front and charged across.

The street appeared to be empty. He was about to accelerate when he saw something that made him hit the brake instead.

On the left was a railing and beyond that was a large building with a dark grey stone façade. He had spotted the rear end of the 4 X 4, protruding from some sort of entrance. He waited but it didn't move. Then it started forward and disappeared from view.

Nick counted to ten, then drove slowly past.

The gate was shut. He could see the keypad, mounted on a post next to it. Beyond that was a glass-fronted security office, empty.

He continued to the end of the street, turned round, and parked on the pavement. Then he got out and walked the short distance back.

A large pile of uncollected refuse was stacked against the wall. It stank to high heaven but he could watch the entrance from here without being seen. He took up a position behind it and reached for his mobile.

"We seem to be at the Department, Umberto. I'm across the street from the entrance. Are you watching the vaults?"

"Yes. No one has come in yet. Stay on the line."

He waited, holding the mobile close to his ear.

Umberto's voice again:

"Okay, Nick, here is someone. Yes, he is carrying plastic boxes."

"The Professor?"

"Not the Professor. I don't think I saw this guy before."

Not the Professor? Who, then?

"What's he doing now, Umberto?"

"He has come back with more boxes. Each one has something written on it, numbers, I think, I can't see properly. Okay, now he is opening boxes and putting things into drawers. This may take a while."

Umberto maintained his commentary. Whoever was down there seemed to be transferring the contents of the plastic boxes systematically to drawers in the vault. Then:

"Something different, Nick. He is holding the bag and he is looking at a piece of paper in the other hand. Ah – now this one he did not put in the drawers, he put in another plastic box."

"Could you see what was in the bag?"

"No. There, he did it again. Now he is putting more things in drawers again. Ah, another bag went into the plastic box, a large one. And another one, not so large. Okay, I think he is finished. He is taking out the empty boxes."

Nick passed his tongue around his lips. Several minutes went by. Then Umberto said:

"He has come for the last boxes now."

"Okay, Umberto. Stay connected. I'll tell you where he goes after this."

He waited, watching the entrance intently. A slight movement in the corner of his eye distracted him. Something stirred in the rubbish pile. It stirred again. Some pieces of sodden cardboard parted and a large rat emerged with something in its mouth. Nick watched it scuttle across the street and disappear. Then his head jerked up. A shadow was moving along behind the railings. It paused, he heard the gate creak open, and a figure appeared carrying a plastic box. Nick craned forward to get a clearer view.

It was Antonino Torretta.

Chapter 38

What the hell is Torretta doing here? Okay, he and the Professor must be in it together. So which one of them killed Julian?

There was no time to dwell on it. Torretta was walking off quickly, still carrying the plastic box.

Nick followed at a distance, talking quietly into the mobile.

"He's crossed the road at the lights, Umberto, and he's turned right. Okay, now he's turning left. Ach, there's bloody rubbish all over one pavement and cars parked on the other. I'll have to let him get ahead because I've got to walk in the middle of the road. All right, he turned left at the top, I'm going to catch up a bit… There he is, he's crossing to the other side. He's going up the steps to an entrance. It's a large building with two wings. New or newly painted. Light grey blocks up to a sort of waistline and orange above that."

He heard a murmur of Italian at the other end of the line. Umberto must be talking to the security personnel.

Then: "They say it is the San Gregorio Animal Hospital."

"What, you mean like a veterinary hospital? For cats and dogs?"

"Not just cats and dogs. It is also the Centre for Disease Control for farm animals, like chickens, sheep and pigs. One of these guys has done the rounds there. He wants to know where the target is going."

"Right, I've just followed him up the stairs and into the foyer. There's a corridor at the back; he's going there. Okay, he turned left down that corridor. I'm letting him get ahead… All right, I'm in the corridor now. I just caught sight of him at the end. He's going down some stairs."

A prolonged exchange in Italian.

Umberto's voice: "Nick, he's going to the basement. The macerator is down there. He must be planning to get rid of the bones."

"What the hell's a macerator?"

"It's like a big sink disposal unit. They use it to grind up the dead animals. What is left just gets flushed into the sewage."

"I thought they used an incinerator for that."

"Not in the town. Too much pollution."

"Right. Look, Umberto, I can't talk any more now. I'm going to switch off."

"Okay, good luck."

Nick disconnected, holding the button to turn the phone off as well. He couldn't risk an incoming call.

He went down three flights of concrete steps, which turned around the stairwell. The open area at the bottom was flanked by just one door, a fire door. He looked through the wire-reinforced window into a long basement corridor. Torretta was just over half-way down, backing through a pair of swing doors with the plastic box held in front of him. Nick waited for a moment, then pushed open the door and walked quickly down the corridor.

There was a distinctly animal smell down here, a smell of straw and cow barns, mingling with disinfectant and something more: a rancid odour, like rotting meat. He reached the swing doors, pushed one open a crack and looked in. His view was obscured by a full-width curtain of overlapping plastic strips that was hanging vertically in front of him, a couple of metres away. He slipped inside the swing doors. The smell was stronger in here. He stepped up to the plastic curtain and parted two strips.

He was looking into a large space, like an underground garage, with a concrete floor and roughly painted walls. On the left was a large pile of straw bales and beyond that dozens of sacks of animal feed. On the right were two freestanding shelf units, stacked with large bottles and carboys. Torretta was over in the far left-hand corner, mounting a set of concrete steps. There was a sort of dais there, surrounded by a low rail. Nick saw a large sign and picked out the word *"periculoso"*. No prizes for guessing what that was.

He needed to get closer. If he used the shelves as cover... He tested a shoe against the floor; it made a gritty noise. He thought about taking his shoes off but decided against; he'd chance it.

He parted the plastic strips and stepped forward, crouching low.

And then the whole world exploded inside his head.

"I'm really sorry, Lucia. I know I'm a terrible drag."

"It's not your fault, Angela. If anyone's, it's mine. Hang on a minute, I can use this sheet to make a bandage."

"There's a First Aid Kit inside the kitchen."

"I know, I've got it here. But I need a long broad adhesive plaster and they've only got the usual little ones."

She took the end of the sheet in her teeth and then pulled with both hands, tearing it along its entire length.

"I'm not blaming you, Lucia. You had to hit me that hard. The thought of any part of me being crushed under that huge machine gives me the horrors. I was dreaming about it last night."

"I'm not surprised. Hold up your right arm, love. I'm going to fix the end with a strip of plaster here and then I'll start winding."

She felt Angela flinch.

"Sorry. That rib's bruised all right; it might be fractured. You're not out of breath, are you?"

"Not exactly. I just keep wanting to take a deep breath and if I try to it's agony."

Lucia passed the long end of the improvised bandage around Angela's back and drew it taut. Then she did it again.

"Keep the arm up. Really I'd like to get it X-rayed. Pippo would have taken you to the hospital, you know."

"I know. I just couldn't face that bumpy ride down. Not just yet."

"You'll have to face it sooner or later. Even if the hospital has a helicopter there's nowhere for it to land up here. They'd have to winch you up. I doubt you'd find that more comfortable."

"Ooh, don't."

The bandage was getting shorter and more manageable. Lucia added another turn.

"The best thing would be to fly you home, then you can get it attended to. The dig will be over in a few more weeks and you're not going to be in any shape to help before then."

"It's a shame. I hate letting people down."

"I think people would be quite understanding, seeing as you were damned near killed. Hold still, I'll just fix this with a safety pin. There! Does that feel any better?"

"Mmm. You really did that tight. I couldn't take a deep breath now if I tried."

"That's the general idea. When was the last time you took painkillers?"

"After breakfast. Nine o'clock or thereabouts."

"Okay. It's only three hours. Hang on for another hour and you can take some more."

"What's happening outside?"

"Nothing, it's quiet. Pippo and the others will be at the hostel by now. The small 4 x 4 went off about half an hour ago. After that I came straight back to you."

"Was Prof driving?"

"I couldn't see properly from where I was. He must have been. I don't know where Antonino is. In his tent, probably."

The first thing that swam into Nick's shifting vision was the face of Antonino Torretta. He was standing with his back to the dais, his hands in his pockets. The face drifted in and out, and then in again. The lips curled. Something came out in Italian.

"Antonino said you are very stupid, like all policemen."

The voice was coming from over his right shoulder, but he couldn't seem to turn towards it. Then he realized why. His arms were being held tightly by two men.

The voice was coming closer.

"As you see, Inspector, he has led you directly to us. It went rather well, didn't it?"

The owner of the voice was moving into the edge of his vision. Black suit, dark glasses, slicked back hair, matching tie and pocket handkerchief...

"Rossi!"

The man smiled, leaned forward and gave Nick's cheek a series of playful pats, a little too hard.

"*Signor* Rossi, Inspector. You should show a little respect. Yes, your *Sergente* did not deceive us with her little subterfuge. We knew she would not leave the girl Angela Johnston up there on her own."

The slaps had brought Nick's brain into focus. Even so, it felt like whoever had hit him when he came through that door had loosened every tooth in his head.

"What are you talking about? Angela went down to Castellamare with the students."

"No, Inspector. She did not feel well enough. It seems she is still suffering the after-effects of our little escapade yesterday."

"You bastard, you're the one who tried to kill the girls."

Rossi laughed. "Inspector, Inspector! I assure you, if I really wanted to kill those two they would be dead right now. Of course, some serious injuries would have made the whole thing even more entertaining, but that was not our primary goal. Do you remember, Inspector, where Antonino was when the accident occurred?"

"I understand he was in the dig, with the others."

"Precisely. And this is of course what everyone else will remember. You see, it was Vito and Cesare here who pushed the tractor over the edge. Antonino will not come under suspicion – either for this or the other, ah, unfortunate event which took place at the excavation. He will, of course, continue to work for us."

Things suddenly fell into place for Nick. "*You* murdered Lockhart!" he said to Torretta. "I should have twigged earlier. Montalcini would have taught his assistant everything he needed to know about how bodies burn."

Torretta said something in Italian and Rossi laughed. "Enough of this. What have you got for me, Antonino?"

Torretta stooped to open the plastic box which, Nick saw, was on the floor by his feet. He took out three plastic bags, passing each in turn to Rossi. Nick could just make out something silver in one of the bags and what looked like a remarkably complete pottery bowl in another. Rossi commented on the finds in Italian and transferred them to a nylon carryall. Then he said, half to Torretta and half to Nick, "Very nice. But of course you have saved the best to last."

Torretta dipped into the plastic box and came out with a large bag full of blackened bones. He jiggled it up and down, rattling the bones for Nick's benefit. At a signal from Rossi he bent down to the side of the dais. Some sort of emergency notice was pasted there, in the centre of which was a large, mushroom-shaped red button. Next to it was an industrial-style switchbox with a hinged transparent cover. Torretta lifted the cover and pressed the single green button inside.

There was a clonk followed immediately by a loud noise, like a cement mixer. He mounted the two steps.

Nick held his breath. Torretta had unsealed the bag and he was looking directly at the substituted Roman bones. He glanced up at Nick and gave him a crooked smile. With a brisk, theatrical flourish he turned the bag upside-down, emptying the bones into the macerator. There was a slight change in the note of the machinery, then it resumed as before. Nick breathed again.

Torretta descended the steps and hit the big red button with the side of his fist. The noise stopped.

"So." Rossi made a symbolic gesture of dusting off his hands. "That is the end of Professor Julian Lockhart. Your investigation has been a complete waste of time, Inspector. Without a body there is no murder, just a missing person – you know that, don't you?"

"You're an evil sonofabitch, Rossi," Nick said. "Killing a man like that just so you can continue with your nasty little racket. He was worth fifty of you, you lousy bag of shit."

Vito and Cesare tightened their grip on his arms, pinning them to his sides. Rossi moved up close and took off the dark glasses. As he did so Nick noticed for the first time that he was wearing a ring, a gold ring set with a deep orange stone. The fleeting moment of realization must have shown in his eyes because Rossi registered it. The corner of his mouth twitched.

"You like the ring, Inspector? It is rather nice, isn't it? Yes, it is the intaglio. Professor Lockhart was very taken with it. He was quite upset when it disappeared." His eyes glittered. "Lockhart got too close to our operation, Inspector – just as you have. But he has disappeared, leaving no trace, and now so will you. I was going to ask Vito or Cesare here to break your neck before we put you into the macerator, but I see you still need a lesson in manners."

He issued a series of commands in rapid Italian. Torretta laughed delightedly. Rossi returned to Nick. "I'm sorry, Inspector. You don't speak Italian, do you, and after all it's only fair that you should know. We are going to feed you into the macerator alive. Feet first."

Nick eyed that terrifying machine and panic rose in his chest.

He tried hard to steady his breathing. He needed to think, to dredge up something – anything – from his training that he could use. There was nothing. Each arm felt like it was trapped in a vice and his feet were barely touching the ground.

Rossi picked up the carryall.

"You will excuse me. I will not be staying – I must rejoin my family. I'm sure you agree that nothing is more important than family."

"Family, and *omertà*," Nick spat out. *Omertà*, the mafia oath of silence.

"Oh, so you do speak a little Italian? How nice! Antonino?"

Torretta lifted the switchbox cover and pressed the green button.

The machinery leaped into life.

Without apparent effort the two heavies lifted the struggling Nick forward and mounted the steps.

Chapter 39

It started with an insistent ringing. The sound was made by two glasses that had been placed on a shelf a little too close together.

Lucia stood motionless in the kitchen, suddenly alert. She'd come here to get some water for Angela to have with her tablets. The ringing became louder. Cups began to rattle on their hooks, saucepan lids agitated in the pans, the ceiling lights swung, something fell with a crash. The very ground was moving.

She put out a hand to the table to steady herself, waiting for the tremor to pass, but it didn't pass. The air was filled with it, a roar like continuous thunder. The flimsy wooden structure of the kitchen creaked and moaned; the door swung open. She ran outside and looked around her. Trees were shaking as if in a high wind, although the air was still. She hurried over to the corner of the line of cabins – and stared in disbelief.

The sky above Vesuvius was dominated by a column of dense black smoke, bulging and writhing like a living thing. From time to time flames flashed up inside it, adding more smoke and making it billow even higher. It towered, dwarfing the landscape.

She ran towards her cabin, missed her footing on the shifting ground and fell, picked herself up again. She went through the door as if someone had pushed her.

"What is it, Lucia? What's going on?"

"It's Vesuvius. It's erupting. In a big way."

Angela's eyes widened. Wincing and holding her ribs, she got off the bed and hurried outside. Her hand went to her mouth.

"Oh my God! Look at that!" She turned to Lucia, breathing fast. "What are we going to do?"

"We're going to move."

"But there aren't any vehicles up here."

"Sorry, love, you're going to have to walk."

"Where to?"

"I'm not sure. I just know we have to get away from here. Put your stuff together – I'll do the same. Take the bare minimum. You'll have to leave most of it behind."

They couldn't hear the rumbling over the noise of the macerator but they knew something was happening because the ground had begun to shake under their feet. The two men looked towards the door but their boss had already gone. The motion was greater now; the whole room seemed to be alive, the shelf units shimmying like crazed dancers. A bottle fell and smashed on the concrete. There was a violent jolt, the floor shifted and Vito, on Nick's right, staggered, slackening his grip. Nick didn't hesitate but kicked out hard, sending him back down the steps and into the nearest set of shelves. The shelves teetered backwards, then came forwards at an alarming angle, shedding a rain of heavy glass bottles onto Vito's head. Nick jabbed the heel of his free hand hard under Cesare's nose. The man barked with pain, releasing Nick's left arm. He staggered back; then his face twisted and his hand dipped inside his jacket. When it came up again he was holding a semi-automatic pistol.

Nick grabbed the rail of the safety barrier with his left hand and vaulted down the steps. Cesare rose up on his toes to get a better line on him. Nick's head was full of the sounds of machinery but he heard the shots all the same: two, in quick succession. He looked up. Cesare seemed to be suspended in the air. His pistol turned slowly towards Nick. There was another report and he dropped to his knees and fell forward.

Nick whirled to see Umberto at the door, crouched on one knee, his pistol held with both hands straight out in front of him. He lowered the weapon but before Nick could say anything three shots rang out from behind him. Splinters exploded from the door frame and Umberto dropped back with a cry. Vito was standing groggily, a semi-automatic in his left hand. A black fury surged up inside Nick and he hurled himself at Vito, grabbing the man's wrist and directing the pistol at the ceiling. They staggered backwards and forwards, then fell and rolled. Vito managed to end up on top of him. Still holding the wrist, Nick closed his other hand over Vito's, trying desperately to keep the arm out straight. It was hopeless: the big man was incredibly strong and he was leaning his weight into it. Their hands quivered with the effort but Nick's resistance was fading and Vito started to bring the pistol in. Out of the corner of his eye Nick could see the muzzle inching closer to his temple, the knuckle whitening as the finger tightened on the trigger. He took a deep breath, eased his thumb inside the trigger guard, and then in one lightning movement wrenched his head to one side, at the same time jerking Vito's wrist down and clamping hard.

The pistol plunged downward, the muzzle jamming into the floor by his head just as it went off. The backblast shot the slide of the automatic off and Vito's face disappeared.

Nick rolled out from under the heavy body, wiped a splash of blood off his cheek with his sleeve and started to get to his feet. Sensing movement, he looked up and saw Torretta charging at him, a knife flashing in his hand. Off-balance, Nick reacted instinctively. Blocking the knife hand with his left arm, he grabbed his assailant's shirt and rolled backwards in a stomach throw, straightening his leg hard to send Torretta in a high arc over his head. Too late he realized what he'd done.

He leaped up only to see Torretta's floundering arms on the other side of the safety rail. There was a long, gurgling scream and the macerator changed its note and recovered. For a few moments Nick stood rooted to the spot, his stomach lurching. Then his shoulders sagged.

It wasn't what he'd intended but he had no real regrets, not after what Torretta had done to Julian Lockhart. He expelled a deep breath, stepped forward and slammed the palm of his hand against the large red button. The rumbling of machinery stopped but he barely registered it; his ears were still ringing from the noise of the gunshot so close to his head. He turned unsteadily and made his way over to Umberto.

He lifted Umberto to a sitting position. The Capitano was pale and his teeth were chattering. The first two rounds had merely buried themselves in the woodwork behind him but the third had taken him in the left upper arm, and the shirt was soaked in blood.

"Christ, Umberto. For a moment there I thought you were a goner."

His voice was feeble. "You mean I'm not?"

"Not yet, you aren't. It's a good thing for you Vito had a few bottles land on his head – his aim was off. Come on, we're getting you to a hospital."

"You're crazy, Nick. Don't you know what's happening out there?"

"What, the earthquake you mean?"

"It's no earthquake. Vesuvius is erupting."

As if his words needed emphasis, the ground shuddered again and more glass crashed behind them.

"Shit." Nick blinked rapidly. "I know, we'll go for the helicopter. We'll fly you to Pozzuoli or Sorrento or somewhere."

"The helicopter has probably gone already."

"What do you mean? How do you know?"

"Maurizio – the pilot – told me how it was organized. If there was an eruption he would be paid to fly the Commissario and his family out and then he would return for the special guests."

"What, you mean government ministers?"

"Not government ministers. You know who his friends are, Nick. Carlo Rossi and his family."

"Rossi? I might have known. Where's your car, then?"

"I left it on the pavement at the bottom of the steps. When the tremor didn't stop we got out fast. I came straight here. I thought maybe you'd need my help."

"Well you were dead right about that."

"What happened, Nick? Were those Rossi's men?"

"Yeah, I'll tell you about it. First let's take a look at this arm."

Nick opened his pocket knife and cut away Umberto's shirt sleeve, exposing a dark hole from which blood was oozing.

"We need to get some pressure on this," he said. He folded his handkerchief into a pad and applied it to the wound, using the remains of the shirt sleeve to tie it tightly in place.

"Right, that'll do for now."

"Nick, forget about the hospital. I know what you really want to do."

Nick met his eyes.

"Do you think you'll be able to cope?"

"I'll be all right. The bleeding has almost stopped. You saw that."

"Okay, come on, let's get out of here. Put your good arm round my neck. Christ, you're a weight, Umberto. Why did you have to eat so much pasta?"

Angela was tucking things into a backpack. Then she frowned and straightened up.

"Lucia?"

"Yes, Angela?"

"Why has the sun gone in?"

Lucia looked around her, realizing suddenly how dark the cabin had become, even though they'd left the door wide open.

She went outside, followed by Angela, and gazed upwards, dumbfounded.

The column had grown enormously in size. It was as if someone had opened a great black umbrella into the sky, blotting it out.

Lucia swallowed hard. "It seems to be spreading in this direction," she said uneasily.

"There's not much wind."

"Could be much stronger at high altitude."

"Look at that!"

A wave of incandescent material rose from Vesuvius and disappeared into the base of the cloud. A few moments later it happened again.

"Ow!"

"What is it?"

"Something hit me on the cheek. A cinder, I think. It's all right, it just stung, that's all."

Lucia looked around and noticed for the first time the curls of grey smoke coming in several places from the grass. In the woodland, a short distance up the hill, something crashed through the trees.

"Come on. Back in the cabin. We have to take cover."

Inside the cabin, they stood by the small window, looking out and listening to the irregular pattering on the roof.

There was a louder thump and Lucia winced. "We won't be able to stay here much longer, Angela. These cabins are flimsy; they weren't designed to withstand this sort of thing. Look, there's one more thing I've got to do. You stay here."

"Where are you going?"

"To the office. I'm going to get the laptop."

"Do you have to? Can't we stay together? We could leave right now if you want."

"No, I have to get that laptop first. Nick's pretty sure it was tampered with, and there are people back home who can tell us exactly how. Then we've got the last bit of evidence we need: the motive for Julian's murder."

"All right. But take care, won't you?"

Lucia opened the door and ran down the side of the cabins, taking what shelter she could by staying close to them. She looked through the window of the office. No one was around. She ducked as a tremendous clang came from behind the cabins.

God, I hope those oil drums are good and strong, she thought. *I'd better get a move on.*

She tried the handle to the office door; it opened and she went in.

The laptop wasn't in its usual place on the desk. She started to open the desk drawers, first on one side, then on the other. She closed the last drawer, looked around her, and saw a small filing cabinet sitting in the corner furthest from the door. She hurried over to it.

The top drawer contained a row of suspension folders, most of them empty. She slammed it shut and opened the bottom drawer: inside was the laptop. She scooped it up, turned for the door, and suddenly there was a huge noise, the air was full of debris, she was flying and things were landing on top of her. The commotion continued for a few moments, then stopped. She lay there, stunned. Then she tried to get up and realized she couldn't.

A pattern of beams and laths and what seemed like yards of plasticized material had fallen over her chest and legs, pinning her down. She turned her head from side to side, trying to understand what had happened. There'd been some sort of explosion, that much was clear. It had blown in most of the wall separating the office from the kitchen, and the unsupported part of the roof above her had collapsed. Even as she was looking the roof sagged further, and a shower of small stones rattled onto the floor. On the other side of the room the door hung wide open, but curiously enough the window was intact. The pressure on her eardrums started to subside and she became aware of a roaring noise. Smoke started to drift through from the kitchen. She struggled desperately, trying to free herself.

What daylight had been coming through the doorway was suddenly eclipsed and she snapped her head round. A man was standing there. She narrowed her eyes, trying to make out who it was – and then she saw.

He moved towards her.

Lucia opened her mouth and screamed.

Chapter 40

Nick gunned the police 4 X 4, forcing his way out into the road, which was crammed with every sort of vehicle: small cars, big cars, vans, open-backed trucks, high-sided lorries. Drivers were sounding their horns and gesticulating wildly out of the windows. Nothing was moving except for a few bicycles, scooters, and motorbikes, which were weaving in and out of the lines of traffic and over the pavement. The air was full of the hum of engines and the noise of the horns.

Vesuvius wasn't visible from here but the cloud from the eruption had already covered half of the sky. The light that remained had a strange quality, like that during a partial eclipse of the sun.

Umberto was sitting in the back. Nick had found a first-aid kit in the car and fixed him up with a sling. He'd taken up his position on the right, a map spread out on the seat next to him, his left arm in the sling and his Beretta on his lap. Nick had pointed questioningly to the pistol and Umberto had simply responded:

"I can still use my right arm."

"You think you're going to need it?"

"We will see."

Nick managed to get out onto the road but there was a line of traffic that stretched as far as he could see.

"Use the siren, Nick."

"Where is it?"

"The switch on the left hand panel, top row."

Nick found it and the two-note siren started up.

The siren didn't extract much courtesy from other drivers but it gave Nick licence to drive like a madman. He steered an erratic course, cutting through lines of traffic, driving on the wrong side of the road and mounting the pavement, all at breakneck speed.

Umberto, completely unfazed by these antics, punctuated his progress with directions.

"Take the next right."

"Gotcha."

They turned up a narrow street. Ahead, half a dozen youths were bouncing on their toes as one threw a brick at a shop window. They were quickly in and out, carrying boxes. As he passed, Nick heard the clonk of something thrown at the car as a parting shot. Evidently there was little respect for the police down here.

The traffic came to a halt. Another gang materialized from nowhere and started to bang on the roof of a trapped car in front. Somehow they extracted the driver, threw him onto the pavement and climbed in themselves. Nick was ready to intervene but Umberto called out:

"No, Nick, no! Back off, and down the street on this side."

Reluctantly Nick slipped the car into reverse and turned down the side street. He was shaking his head.

"Sorry, Nick, we have no time for that. Turn right at the end."

He did, then hit the brakes.

"Uh-oh."

Montalcini bent over Lucia and she screamed even louder.

"Please try to compose yourself, Sergente," he said. "Are you badly hurt? Where is your injury?"

He dropped to one knee.

She opened her mouth to scream again but it bottled in her throat as she realized that Montalcini had started to clear away the debris that was pinning her down. He worked quickly, darting anxious glances in the direction of the kitchen. He threw aside a bundle of laths and noticed the laptop, which she was still clutching to her chest.

"What are you doing with that?" he asked.

"I was... saving it," she said.

"My dear, you should not have bothered. The data has been transferred. This can be replaced. Here, let me take it from you."

He reached forward and she shrank back, clutching it more tightly.

"No!"

She knew she'd said it too loudly.

There was a soft *whoomph* and a hot draught washed over her. Through the gaping hole in the dividing wall she could see into the kitchen. She swallowed hard. She still couldn't move, the kitchen was a mass of flames, and inside it there were several large bottles of compressed gas.

Bearing down on the police car, and filling the entire width of the road, was a silent procession. Heading it was a man in black vestments holding a simple wooden cross. Behind him were eight men carrying a platform on their shoulders. The platform supported a life-sized painted effigy, a man wearing a mitre, one arm raised, the open hand outstretched. Even hurrying passers-by stopped briefly to cross themselves.

"What in the hell..."

"San Gennaro," Umberto said. "They say his relics held back the eruption of 1631. Since then there have been many eruptions. The ashfall always went to the south and the east, not the north and the west, so none of them did any damage to Naples. They are invoking his help again."

For a moment Nick watched, fascinated, as the people walked slowly and implacably towards him. Nothing was going to get in their way. He had the feeling they'd be ready to walk into the mouth of the crater itself, such was the depth of their conviction.

Focused on the procession, he failed to notice the huge man until he appeared suddenly at his window. Nick didn't understand what he was yelling but the waving barrels of a sawn-off shotgun spoke volumes. He didn't hesitate. He swivelled in his seat and opened the door sharply, booting it at the same time so that it slammed hard against the man's shins and sent him sprawling onto the pavement.

As he pulled the door back and reversed with a squeal of tyres he felt cool air on his neck from Umberto's opened window. Out of the corner of his eye he saw the man, still on the pavement, scrabbling for the shotgun. Umberto shouted *"Non toccarla!"*, then he fired once, twice, three times and Nick heard a howl of pain as he accelerated away in the opposite direction.

"You didn't kill him, did you?"

"No, but he didn't pay any attention to my warning rounds so I left him counting his fingers. We were lucky he was on his own. Really you must keep moving all the time, Nick. Turn right here."

Nick turned and they raced up a narrow street.

"You're pretty handy with that Beretta, Umberto, even with one arm."

"I won a police Marksman-of-the-Year competition when I was a Sottotenente."

"Really? What was the prize?"

"I wanted to improve my English so I chose a six-month secondment to the British police."

"Whereabouts?"

"London."

"Six months with the Met and you still speak good English? That's quite an achievement."

Umberto laughed. "Turn right again at the end."

"You know Naples well."

"I used to patrol these streets. I remember it like yesterday. But now I must look outside the city."

Nick glanced in the rear-view mirror. He could see that Umberto was studying the map.

"So where are we going?"

"Most people will try to get away to the north and west. Some may go down to the docks – there is supposed to be an emergency evacuation by sea from there. I don't know if it is working but I am sure it will be chaos. I think we should head towards the north-east."

"Are we going to use the autostrada?"

"No, it will be very bad, both to the north and along the coast. I think our best chance is to make a big circle around the other side of Vesuvius, via Ottaviano and Terzigno."

They were approaching another intersection.

Nick said, "Where to now?"

"Straight over, then take the first left and the first right."

"Okay."

The siren wailed and Nick shot across the cars, to the accompaniment of screaming tyres and hooting horns.

He swung left into a tiny cobbled alley. The walls on either side were featureless apart from peeling stickers and graffiti. High above them, line after line of washing hung like gaily coloured bunting from side to side. Now it was lighter ahead: the end of the alley was coming up. A pile of refuse had spilled out over the corner. He crashed through it, skidding slightly, and they emerged onto a wider street, where Nick turned right. He kept the siren going and accelerated hard.

"That route sounds like a long way round, Umberto."

"It is a long way round, Nick, but I think we will make faster progress. And if we hit traffic there are many more opportunities to make detours than down on the coast."

"Where will we come out?"

"North of Pompei. From there we can drive south on small roads towards the Monti Lattari. We can get up to the dig that way, but the last part will be off-road."

"Okay, sounds good."

"There is one problem."

"Oh, what's that?"

"If Vesuvius is erupting to the south-east we will be directly under the fallout."

Montalcini threw a glance at the conflagration in the kitchen and started to work with renewed vigour. He used a short length of wood to lever a heavy beam out of the way and threw aside the roofing material. The oppressive weight on her body vanished.

"Can you move your legs?"

Lucia drew her legs up and began to roll onto her side.

"Quickly now, let me help you."

Again something blocked out the light from the doorway. It was Angela. She cried "Leave her alone! Let her go!", ran forward, grabbed Montalcini around the neck, and tried to haul him away.

"Angela!" Lucia yelled over the roar of the flames. "Angela! It's all right. He's helping me."

Angela faltered. Montalcini shrugged her off and gestured impatiently at the doorway.

"Outside, everyone! Hurry!"

They ran out of the office and across the grass. Seconds later a colossal blast came from behind them and sent them sprawling. A hundred yards further on, a line of dust arose along the ridge above the excavation as the shock wave spread and spent itself over the landscape. Lucia cast a fearful glance over her shoulder.

The kitchen was a tattered shell, its walls hanging open drunkenly. Above it, a cloud of smoke was mushrooming skywards and flaming timbers were raining down over the whole area. Montalcini scrambled to his feet.

"Come," he shouted, and they followed him, hunched low, over the open ground to the big cedar. There they straightened up under the relative shelter of its spreading branches, catching their breath.

Lucia brushed herself down, but she couldn't take her eyes off the cabins.

They were a complete inferno. Incandescent fragments billowed high and scattered across the darkened sky. The roar of the flames sent even the rumblings of Vesuvius into the background, although they could still feel the ground quaking under their feet.

She could hardly look at Montalcini.

"You saved my life," she said quietly.

"Yes, I suppose I did," he said. "But then, you saved Angela's yesterday. So it is even. What was all that shouting and screaming about?"

Lucia swallowed. "I thought you were going to..." She faltered.

"You thought I was going to what?"

"I thought you were going to Naples," she finished lamely.

"Naples? No. Antonino went to Naples. He wanted to go this time – he had other things to attend to there. He knows very well what to do with the finds. And you, Angela, why were you dragging me away from her?"

"I'm sorry, Prof. I've been a bit jumpy ever since that business with the tractor yesterday."

"My goodness, do you think I pushed the tractor?"

"Look, I made a mistake, that's all. I'm sorry." She gestured at the burning cabins. "What made this little lot go up?"

"I heard a terrific clang," Lucia said. "I think one of those rocks from the eruption must have damaged an oil drum."

"These pyroclasts come down very fast," Montalcini said, "They are also red-hot. If it was sitting in a puddle of leaking oil the whole lot was bound to go up. I did not see it happen. I was over at the dig."

"Really? What were you doing there?"

"Just looking." He gazed beyond the fire towards the horizon. "What a unique privilege it is – is it not? – to stand in the final resting place of fugitives from Pompeii, and see at first hand the very phenomenon that drove them from their homes and destroyed their lives."

Lucia glanced sideways at him. *The man is actually serious,* she thought.

Nick continued to weave through the streets. The sky was becoming blacker and the car rocked with the earth tremors as if caught in a gusty wind. He switched off the siren. Almost immediately he became aware of a new noise: a regular thwacking.

"What's that?"

"It's the helicopter. It must be coming back for Rossi."

"Aw shit, I wish I could do something about that. The bastard had Julian killed and he bloody near had me killed, and now here he is, about to make a nice safe exit."

"Forget about Rossi, Nick. You won't stop him now."

The sound faded.

They were on an overpass now, and below them they could see the section of autostrada that stretched to the north, towards Casalnuovo di Napoli. As Umberto had predicted, it was packed with stationary traffic. Nick sped on.

"I don't know what all the panic's about actually," he said. "There's been a lot of noise and smoke but there hasn't been anything else so far."

"That is what worries me."

Following Umberto's directions, Nick took a right turn onto a quieter road. The ground was rising now and they were starting to look down on the city.

There were many expensive villas here. He spotted another knot of youths, carrying computers, television sets, even vacuum cleaners. He moved to switch the siren on again.

"Don't bother, Nick. These are mainly summer houses. There is a law here. In times of disaster it allows homeless people to enter vacant properties."

"Are you kidding? These kids aren't homeless; they're just looting."

Umberto sighed. "I suppose the intention was good. It is people who abuse it."

Lightning forked through the black cloud over their heads. Mixed in with the thunder the noise of the helicopter rose again.

"At the end of this road you turn left."

"Okay. At least we're making some progress now. Jesus!"

Something dropped out of the sky right in front of them and exploded into glowing fragments all over the road.

Nick braked sharply and swerved to a halt. He glanced back at Umberto, who was straightening up painfully.

"Sorry, Umberto, it looks like things are getting lively after all. I'm not going through that lot. Those rocks are red-hot; if we get one caught in a tread it could give us a puncture or set the tyre alight. Hold on, I'm going to go off-road for a bit."

The car lurched and bumped slowly over rough ground.

Overhead, swarms of glowing projectiles were curving through the air and falling all over Naples.

The helicopter rose from the city below. Nick paused to watch it. In this strange half-light its form was barely visible but the beams of two powerful searchlights at the front were clearly outlined in the drifting smoke. It looked like footage Nick had seen of underwater robot vessels, searching for wrecks.

He didn't see the projectile that hit the rotor. There was just a shower of sparks and suddenly the whole craft was spinning like a crazed Catherine Wheel, the searchlights sweeping up and down and around. Still spinning, it plunged downwards. Moments later a brilliant ball of flame rose into the air and in every direction the landscape was etched in sharp relief. The flame dissolved into smoke and the light faded. The blackness that followed was impenetrable.

The whole sequence had taken a matter of seconds. They sat there in stunned silence, replaying it in their minds, reliving its fierce, balletic beauty.

Umberto murmured, "He's not a problem for you any more, Nick."

Nick grimaced and shook his head.

It wasn't Carlo Rossi he was thinking about. It was a gold ring with an intaglio, one that had been worn by a Roman General, which would never be seen again.

Angela followed Montalcini's gaze, studying the cloud over Vesuvius while rubbing unconsciously at her ribs.

A nearby explosion jerked their attention back to the cabins. Another ball of smoke was rising from the area of the kitchen. One wall of the office fell outwards in a shower of sparks.

Lucia looked at Montalcini.

"You had papers in there..."

"Nothing of any great importance."

"And your room is next door. Your possessions..."

"Possessions are not important. To survive; that is important. We must make decisions. The next phase of the eruption could be a lot worse. We have to get away from here. That volcano killed the people we have been uncovering in the dig. It could kill us, too."

"Couldn't we summon help?" Lucia asked.

"No, the fire has destroyed the satellite link." He shrugged. "It makes no difference: the emergency services will be much too busy for us. We will have to look after ourselves."

"I wish we had a vehicle," Angela said.

Montalcini picked it up. "I agree, in fact I think it is our only chance. The farmer who owns this land has several vehicles. I propose that we ask if he will lend one to us."

266

"I thought he lived at the bottom of the mountain."

"No, his vineyards and his winery are down there but his house is up here."

"How far is it?" Lucia asked.

"One kilometre – maybe two. But it is not an easy walk. I think it would be too painful for Angela. Either Lucia or I must go."

Angela looked darkly at Lucia. Clearly she still didn't trust Montalcini enough to be left with him. But Montalcini supplied the answer.

"It is obvious, no? I know where the farm is and I know the farmer, so I must go. You must wait here. I will be as quick as I can."

He strode away. Angela turned back to Lucia.

"Do you think we can trust him?"

"I don't know, Angela. I really don't know. But he did help me. And if he isn't genuine, he's a consummate liar."

"Suppose he doesn't come back for us?"

"Then we're stuffed."

"What about Nick?"

"Nick's in Naples. God knows what it's like over there; I just hope he can get away. He'd be nuts to come in this direction. Even if he did, he'd never get here in time."

Chapter 41

The police 4 X 4 rocked and trundled over the uneven terrain. Behind them a thick column continued to pour upwards from the volcano but the tremors had lessened. Umberto had holstered his pistol some time ago; he was hanging on to a strap with his right hand, trying to limit the movement.

Nick turned his head to take a quick look at his friend. The face in the rear view mirror was pale and set.

"How are we doing back there?"

The voice was weary. "I'm all right, Nick. You're driving very well."

"Actually this crate's not bad off-road. The traction's pretty good, in fact; what worries me is the ground clearance. If it gets much rougher than this we stand to leave our oil sump behind."

"Don't take any chances. A few minutes won't make such a lot of difference."

One wheel climbed over a rock and came off it with a jolt. Nick saw Umberto wince.

"Sorry, Umberto. I don't know, we ought to be somewhere near the dig by now, but I don't recognize a thing."

"You have not approached it from this direction before."

"True."

The car struggled over a ridge and, as they reached the top, Nick saw smoke rising from a point higher up the mountain. It was drifting away from them.

Nick shot an anxious look over his shoulder at Umberto; clearly he'd seen it, too. He changed course towards the smoke.

Twenty minutes later they were passing the grey-white scars in the ground where the farmer had lifted the boulders. The woodland appeared on the left and in front of them was all that remained of the line of cabins. Nick got out, Umberto followed.

A light wind was fanning the heaps of embers into white heat. Much of the structure had collapsed but some of the stouter uprights in the corners were still standing, burning steadily. Nick stood in front of it, stunned. Then he ran past the remains of the office to the tent area. The tents were still there but there was no sign of anyone. He returned to Umberto.

"She's alive, Umberto – I'm sure she is – she'd never have let herself get trapped inside. Where's she gone? There weren't any vehicles up here. Pippo took the people carrier and Torretta took the small 4 X 4."

"Maybe she decided to walk."

"Where to?"

"Castellamare?"

"It'll be pandemonium down there. She must have realized that, surely?"

"From up here it is difficult even to imagine what we have seen in Naples."

Nick's shoulders sagged. Then he looked up.

"Wait a bit. Angela was with her. She was hurt. That's why she didn't go to Castellamare with the others."

"In that case they may not have gone far."

Umberto walked towards the dig and the path that led down the hill to Castellamare. He stopped suddenly. "Nick?"

Nick hurried over.

"Look at this."

Umberto pointed to some tyre tracks in the dust. Nick squatted to get a better look.

"It's a heavy vehicle, from the tread," Nick said. "Can't be the earthmover. That's still in the dig – they hadn't pulled it out yet."

"It is not from an earthmover – the gaps are not wide enough. Some sort of truck, I think. And not so long ago – these tracks are still very clear. And what's this?"

He pointed to a black speck pressed into the dust. His finger wandered rapidly to others, some in the tracks, some lying on top.

"Cinders!" Nick exclaimed.

"Carried here by the breeze. *Allora*. The tracks are fresh; they were made after the fire started in the cabins."

"Where do they lead?"

They walked at the side of the tracks until they disappeared into the grass. Nick looked up, sighting along the twin lines of bruised grass.

"These aren't going down to Castellamare," he said. "What's up in that direction?"

Umberto shook his head slowly. Then he turned to Nick. "Is that maybe where the farmer lives, who owns this land?"

Nick eyes lit up. He pointed a finger at Umberto. "Good thinking. Stay here. I'll bring the car."

The tractor was so noisy that when the two-note police siren sounded behind them Lucia didn't hear it at first. When she did hear it she couldn't believe it. She stopped, turned the engine off and got down. Angela and Montalcini were riding in the open cart she was towing behind the tractor.

"Did you hear that?" she asked.

Montalcini got to his feet.

They saw it at the same time: a vehicle of the Polizia di Stato rolling and bucking up the slope behind them.

"Nick," Lucia breathed, and she started to run.

The car rocked to a halt, and she hesitated, a hand to her mouth. Then the door opened, Nick jumped out, and they ran into each other's arms. At that moment she was oblivious to everything except the joy of seeing him again. She held him tightly, feeling the warmth of his body, his hand at the nape of her neck, his breath in her hair. She tilted her head back and he kissed her with such intoxicating tenderness that she thought her heart would burst. Their lips parted – and she became aware of Umberto, Angela, and Montalcini standing there, grinning from ear to ear. Nick's eyes followed hers and they drew back self-consciously. Then Umberto started to laugh and they all joined in.

Montalcini shook hands with Nick and Umberto and expressed his concern at the Capitano's injured arm. Umberto said it had happened during the journey.

Lucia sighed. "Well," she said, kissing Nick quickly on the

cheek, "you're both safe now, thank God. What exactly went on back there in Naples?"

Nick's eyes flicked in Montalcini's direction. Umberto and he had agreed to say nothing at this stage.

"It's sorted. I'll tell you about it later." He pointed up the hill to the tractor. "I didn't know you could drive one of those things."

"I've never done it before, but the Professor hasn't either. He wasn't very confident so I said I'd give it a go. It's ever so heavy to steer and change gear. My arms are aching already."

"It's not exactly the height of luxury in the back, either," Angela added ruefully, rubbing her backside with both hands.

"Well I'm glad you could only go slowly. It was hard enough following you this far."

"I didn't think you'd even try to..."

An ominous rumble sounded across the landscape and the ground vibrated under their feet. Their heads all jerked towards Vesuvius.

A thick column of orange-red material was jetting up into the cloud. Montalcini narrowed his eyes, studying it.

"We are not out of danger," he announced. "This is a major lava eruption. Some fallout may come this way. That is bad enough but the real danger is when the column collapses."

Angela murmured, "Oh my God, a pyroclastic flow."

Montalcini nodded.

Lucia looked at Nick, then back at Montalcini. "It wouldn't come as far as this, surely?"

"It could – very easily," Montalcini replied. "When finally the magma is exhausted a tidal wave of superheated gas and ash will travel down that mountain and across the countryside. We cannot predict which way it will go, but if it comes in this direction it can be where we are standing in about..." He pursed his lips thoughtfully. "In about five or six minutes."

Nick blinked rapidly.

"Jesus!" he said. "We've got to get out of here."

"Yes, I think we should."

"How long do we have?"

"That is hard to say, it depends on a number of factors – "

271

"Roughly!"

"Eight hours, perhaps? Maybe a little more."

"That's long enough." Nick clapped his hands. "Come on, people. We're going to get moving. We'll leave the police vehicle here. I'll drive the tractor, Lucia, and you and Umberto can join the others in the trailer. All right?"

"Nick," Umberto said. "There is a blanket in the car and a fire extinguisher and the first-aid kit. Also we should be able to take out the back seat."

"Great idea, Umberto."

"Can we sit on it?" Angela asked hopefully.

"'Fraid not, Angela. We're going to strap it over the top of you. It's not much but it's better than nothing. There's a roof on the tractor itself, and that'll give me some protection, but you've got nothing over your heads if that stuff starts coming down."

The black cloud from Vesuvius spread overhead as the tractor laboured up the steep incline. Behind it, the four occupants of the trailer rocked from side to side under the makeshift roof Nick had rigged up for their protection. At Montalcini's suggestion Nick had also stripped the thick rubber lining out of the boot and removed the floor mats from the footwells, and they had laid first the blanket and then the matting over their outstretched legs.

Umberto sat on the extreme left so that no one would be thrown against his aching arm. Lucia sat next to him. She wanted to know more about their journey.

"I don't know how you managed it." She had to raise her voice over the burble of the tractor's engine. "It must be chaos on the roads."

"On the highways, yes. We took the scenic route, around the other side of Vesuvius."

"What about the eruption?" Montalcini asked.

"We knew we were taking a risk. It got bad at one point – somewhere near Ottaviano, I think. A lot of rocks were falling there. Did you notice the big dent in the roof? It made a very loud noise, that one! But I think we were lucky; everything went quiet after that. Then we came up the mountain and found the remains of the cabins, still burning."

"How did you know where we'd gone?" Lucia asked.

"We followed some tracks back to the farm. The farmer said that the Professore walked there and he came out in a truck to pick up you and Angela. He told us you had left not more than one hour before. He thought you were trying to get through the pass and down the other side to the Amalfi coast."

"That's right, we're heading for Positano. He was really kind, that man. He lent us a tractor. He said it was the only vehicle that could make a journey like that. He hitched a trailer to it so that one of us could drive and the others could ride behind."

"He should have gone with you," Umberto said.

"We tried hard to persuade him," Montalcini replied, "but he would not move. He said his family has lived there for generations and that mountain has never harmed them."

Lucia grimaced. "I hope he'll be all right."

She recoiled as a smoking cascade of rock and lava fell out of the sky and crashed down on the slopes just below them. More projectiles arched over their heads. Close by, a glowing lava bomb exploded into pieces.

They shrank back under their improvised shelter, painfully aware that the roof and the thick black mats offered scant protection from the molten masses that were landing like shells all around them. The lava ignited patches of dry grassland, which began to burn in ever-widening circles, consuming bushes and spreading to trees.

Blue smoke clung to the ground, pursuing them up the slopes and drifting into the trailer; Angela had to hold her ribs as she coughed, and Umberto was pale and tight-lipped. All conversation ceased.

Nick stopped the tractor, shouting to them to stay where they were, his words ending in a paroxysm of coughing. He got out a handkerchief and tied it over his nose and mouth. His eyes were streaming from the smoke and his chest felt raw. He engaged gear, let in the clutch, and they pitched forward again. He was going as fast as he could. The muscles in his arms were aching as he wrestled the heavy tractor up into the pass, peering ahead through the smoke and semi-darkness, trying to steer the quickest route while at the same time avoiding the rocky outcrops that threatened to turn them over and roll them for hundreds of feet down the mountainside...

Higher up the mountain the smoke thinned. The ground was rockier here, with few bushes and trees and only isolated patches of grass. They had left the fires behind.

The rubber mats over their legs were greyish-white from the fine ash that rained continuously out of the sky, but the big bombs had either stopped falling or were falling short. Angela shifted her position. For the first time in many hours the overwhelming focus on survival had receded and she could be a little more reflective. She felt badly about her behaviour towards Montalcini. She'd suspected him of murder – a man who'd risked his own life to save Lucia's. She glanced at him. His face was tranquil; he seemed to be lost in a world of his own. She gripped her ribs more tightly against the lurching of the trailer.

"Prof?"

He emerged from his reverie. "Yes, Angela?"

"I'm really sorry – you must be feeling pretty gutted about all this. I mean, we were trying to excavate the site before the farmer moved in and started to develop it. We hadn't nearly finished and now we never will."

"That is true. On the other hand, we have this." His sweeping gesture took in the trailer, the smouldering countryside below them, and the glowing column on the horizon. He looked at her. "At last I really know what was experienced by those people."

"You mean the ones we uncovered in the dig?"

He nodded.

Angela's eyes widened. It was as if a window had opened in her mind. "I know what you mean! I can feel it too – a kind of empathy. You know, when we were digging up skeletons I just thought it was an exciting thing to do – like detective work. It took all this to bring it home to me. Those were real people."

"Part of a great civilization. And here in Pompeii they lived and loved and had families, and maybe the more privileged ones had fine villas and servants and discussed politics and enjoyed the arts – "

" – and then suddenly they had to leave that whole wonderful world behind and flee for their lives." She shook her head. "They nearly made it, too."

The Professor smiled. "Any experience has to be worthwhile if it changes your thinking. You are fortunate to have achieved such insights at your age. It took me much longer. I know you and the others wondered why I did not take part in the actual excavation to any great extent. Perhaps you thought me idle."

"Well, no, I wouldn't say..."

"You see, to dig is one thing; to interpret is quite another. While you were unearthing the bones, I was examining them, and all the time I was trying to live their lives, trying to make sense of what they had done, what they were doing..."

There was a short silence.

Angela said quietly, "We haven't begun to discover the full story of what happened up here, have we, Professor?"

"We may never find out, Angela. But we have a duty to try."

PART 4

Oxford, England

Chapter 42

It's funny, Nick thought, as he drove to the outskirts of Oxford, *how quickly you can adapt.* England had been bathed in brilliant sunshine when he got back and he hadn't relished the prospect of having to wear a jacket and tie again, yet despite the continuing fine weather he now found it perfectly comfortable. And although his driving on the motorways and in the towns had been a little wild and erratic to start with, he'd quickly settled back into a more sedate style. *I've acclimatized,* he said to himself. *If I returned to Naples now, I bet I'd be shocked all over again by the heat and the chaos.*

With the thought came a stab of guilt. For the moment the comparative peace and calm of his present surroundings had numbed his mind to what he'd left behind.

Naples was still counting the cost of the eruption. As he now knew, only hours after he and Umberto had made their frenetic escape from the city the fall of lava had intensified, igniting fires that raged unchecked through the narrow streets and gutted whole neighbourhoods. Fire crews were powerless to help: the roads were paralyzed by abandoned vehicles and it was still too dangerous to attempt anything by air. While he and his party were struggling up to the mountain pass in the tractor and trailer, much of the population of Naples was trying to escape on foot. They converged on the Port, the streets flowing with people, mothers carrying babies, men, women and children struggling with whatever possessions they'd been able to salvage, all fleeing from the apartment blocks that were collapsing into smouldering heaps of rubble behind them.

Stricken as it was, the city had been spared a worse disaster. When the eruptive column finally collapsed, the ensuing pyroclastic flow raced not northwards towards Naples but southwards across the plain, destroying every living thing in its path and dissipating itself eventually on the slopes of the Lattari Mountains. By then, he and his party were approaching the Amalfi coast. They were bruised and exhausted, but at least they were safe.

Back in the U.K. it was headline news. The crisis had completely overwhelmed the local infrastructure and the Italian government had promptly declared a state of national emergency. Specialist teams had already flown in from Britain, France, Germany, and the U.S.A. to search the rubble and to provide front-line medical care. Trauma centres all over Europe had opened their doors to receive the seriously injured. As for the thousands of families who had survived but were now accommodated in tent cities, homeless and destitute, it looked like the aid agencies and local government would be struggling with that problem for a long time to come.

The big Georgian house came into view on his left, jerking Nick back to Oxford and his reason for being here.

He drew up to the kerb and switched off the engine. His watch showed five minutes to four; he was in good time. It would have been good to have Lucia with him, but this was one he had to do on his own.

As he locked the car, he glanced up at the sky. When he'd left his office it had begun to cloud over. Now a heavy stillness lay everywhere, threatening a stormy end to the current spell of fine weather. He straightened his tie and turned towards the gate.

The door was answered by a tall, bright-eyed girl with a pronounced cleft in her chin. He recognized her from the photograph.

"Hello, you must be Kendra. I'm Inspector Roberts."

"Oh, hi, Inspector. Come on in."

As he followed her into the wood-panelled hall she shouted out, "Mum? Inspector Roberts is here." She turned to him. "Come into the sitting room, Inspector."

She led the way to the comfortably furnished room that had so astonished him on his first visit.

"I'm sorry I couldn't make it to the funeral," Nick said. "I heard there was a wonderful turnout."

"Yes," Kendra answered. "I mean, it was awful, really, but it was so nice that his colleagues came – some even flew in from abroad. His former students are organizing a conference in his memory. They'll be publishing a festschrift."

"A what?"

"A festschrift. You know, a book where each person writes a chapter, showing how their work followed on from what they did with him." Her voice was beginning to catch. She hitched a breath and added softly, "We're going to miss him terribly, of course, but it's nice to know he was appreciated. Ah, here's Mum, I'll leave you two alone."

"Nick."

She crossed the room, took him by the elbows and kissed him on both cheeks. For a moment he was mesmerized by the silky brush of her skin and the perfume that wafted from her hair. She stepped back, brushed his suit collar swiftly with her hands and straightened his lapels. It was a wifely gesture and it caught him by surprise.

"You did so well, Nick. Are you all right?"

"Yes, I'm fine. I'm sorry I missed the funeral. Kendra was telling me it was quite a tribute."

"No more than he deserved, but it was nice that people made the effort, yes. The girls were wonderful. We're all supporting each other."

"That's good. And I gather you had a separate burial for the Jericho man?"

"It was high time. He deserved to have his bones laid to rest too."

"And unlike some of the other stuff around here, he had no commercial value."

She looked at him sharply and her voice hardened. "What on earth do you mean by that?"

"Perhaps you know already – Donatella."

For a moment her face was blank. Then she pursed her lips in the hint of a smile. "Nick Roberts, you've been doing your homework."

"Yes, I have. We looked at the personnel records for all the digs recorded in the last thirty years. From 1979 onwards, we noticed the name Donatella Badalamenti cropping up repeatedly. You were a volunteer on rather a lot of them."

"I enjoyed it. How did you know it was me?"

"Well, the last time you were listed was in May 1989, on a dig supported by the Soprintendenza Archeologica of Naples. Lucia went through their Annual Report for that year with a fine-toothed comb. She found a list of consultants whose fees and travel expenses had been paid. Among the names was one Dr. Julian Lockhart. He hadn't been mentioned specifically in connection with your dig but I had a hunch. I checked at the Family Records Centre in London. You were married a few months later. You'd changed your name to Dawn by then, but of course your father's name was on the certificate."

"It's true. We did meet on that dig. We fell in love. We got married. What's unusual about that?"

"Nothing. Nothing at all. But weren't the *families* unhappy about the loss of their prized operative?"

For a moment she was silent. Then she said, "Sit down, Nick. I'll get some tea."

He was sitting comfortably on a sofa when she returned. She put the tray on the low table, set out the silver service, and busied herself pouring the tea. Then she leaned back on the sofa and regarded him appraisingly, just as she had that first time she'd opened the door to him.

"You haven't cautioned me, Nick. Is this off the record?"

"Yes. I'm not taking notes. And I'm not wired."

"I know you're not. I checked that when you came in."

So much for the wifely gesture, he thought.

She looked over to the window, but her gaze went beyond anything out there. He waited.

"Donatella Badalamenti," she mused. Abruptly her focus shifted back to him. "Dawn Lockhart doesn't have quite the same ring to it, does it?"

"I always thought Donatella was one of the most beautiful names in the world. No wonder you speak good Italian: you were born in Italy."

"Sicily to be precise."

"Into the *cosca* Badalamenti."

"A branch of it. I was very fortunate. It was a loving family, and they had refined tastes. From childhood I was surrounded by wonderful things: paintings, sculptures, antiques... My father taught me about each and every one of them. Naturally, when it was time to go to university I read Fine Arts. At the Università di Roma. Then the family moved to the United States."

"Did you go with them?"

"No. Daddy wanted me to. The Corleonesi had become very powerful in Western Sicily and he thought all our lives were in danger. But I was enjoying my course and I didn't want to move. I felt safe enough in Rome. I never went back to Sicily; I spent the summers in the States."

"You graduated when... around 1978?"

"1979. I didn't know what I was going to do after that. I didn't have a job and I didn't have any experience. I was thinking about becoming apprenticed to one of the big art auction houses – a bit like Sotheby's or Christie's over here. But Daddy had other ideas. He'd always had a lot of off-island interests, archaeology being one of them. So we agreed that I'd enrol on digs, but only on the mainland. I had no trouble. I was already well qualified and after a couple of seasons I was an experienced hand."

"It surprised me that you always registered under your own name."

She bristled slightly. "Why not? I was proud of my family name."

"And your job was to route valuable finds back to your father?"

"It wasn't hard. If it was a difficult project, with the finds few and far between, I just did my work, like the others. That was all right, I loved it anyway. But if things were coming out thick and fast I could take advantage of the situation. The trick was to choose an object that wasn't too conspicuous, maybe something that came out at the same time as a really spectacular find – you know, like a gold necklace. Then all the attention would be on the necklace and I'd make sure the other object wasn't collected and numbered."

"And no one noticed?"

She laughed. "Well, no one said anything! No, I don't think anyone noticed. Normally these artifacts are only examined properly after they've been transferred to a museum or a university department for further study. The people on the dig don't see them again, so the chances that someone would remember something was missing are pretty slim."

"And you carried on like this for ten years."

"Yes, until I met Julian." There was a faraway look in her eyes. "We could hardly wait to be married."

"Your father disapproved, of course."

"He did at first. But he came round soon enough when I explained the advantages to him. You see, with Julian I had an entrée everywhere, not just to digs, but to conferences, major exhibitions, all that sort of thing. There was tremendous scope for making contacts with museum buyers and art dealers all over the world. The States is a big market; Daddy helped me find clients there. Some were legitimate; others less so."

"So you became a conduit for stolen goods."

"If you want to put it that way. Once I had Kendra it was more difficult to travel, but by then I had all the connections I needed. Now and then I'd receive a batch of stuff from Italy. There was no hurry to get rid of it, in fact it was prudent to allow a year or so to elapse. I enjoyed having them in the house. I even put some of them on display. It was perfectly natural for the wife of a famous archaeologist to have these things around. After a while I'd identify a buyer and something would be moved on. Something else would take its place. It was wonderful, like a constantly changing museum. You never had time to get tired of anything." She waved at the artifacts. "Of course, some of these are things Julian or I bought or had given to us. They're the permanent part of the display."

He nodded. "Who was sending you the stuff from Italy?"

"The flow dried up completely for a while, of course. Daddy and I had to rethink the whole operation. What I'd been doing had been very limited. One person, one dig at a time – some fruitful, others not. I felt it needed to be scaled up in some way. Then I had a brainwave. A legitimate organization that would cover everything we needed to do. I called it the Pliny Institute."

Chapter 43

"So it was *your* idea!"

"Yes. Rather ingenious, I thought. It appealed to my father, too. He put the wheels in motion straight away. Although he'd moved to the States he was still powerfully connected at home. Even so, he couldn't handle it all himself – he had to get some of the other *cosci* interested."

"That explains why Carlo Rossi was at Montalcini's lecture."

"Uncle Carlo was there? Keeping an eye on things, no doubt. It was a stupid thing to do. I never liked the man – or trusted him."

"And did you suggest pitching it to the J. Paul Getty as well?"

"Yes, of course. The money wasn't so important: having the support of a major international foundation would give the Institute credibility."

She met his eyes, and her voice softened.

"Nick, I wasn't blind to where the rest of the money was coming from. I know what some of the families are into: drugs, protection, money-laundering, arms smuggling, all that sort of thing. It's a way of life, and I was born into it, so I don't approve and I don't disapprove. But I did like the idea of channelling some of that money into archaeology. That way, everyone could benefit."

"Go on."

"It was simple enough. Funding for archaeology is limited. Lots of people would apply to the Institute for support, including the top people in the field. We set up a Grants Committee – eminent academics, directors of museums, and so on – all perfectly above board. Part of their job was to assess the likelihood of significant finds. Our people were represented on that Committee. We'd coached a small number of operatives in what was needed, and when a promising project got funded we made sure that one of them was appointed as a member of the team."

"How did you manage that?"

"We had to be included in the selection process – we'd built it into the regulations. Something about 'equal opportunities'."

"Of course. I remember now. And it all looked so innocent!" She smiled.

"What about the laptop and the software – 'Archetype'? Where did that fit in?"

"That came after Enrico Montalcini advertised for an assistant. Il Professore was very well thought of in archaeological circles. He was certain to be involved in some major projects. It was a chance to place one of our best operatives with him."

"Antonino Torretta."

"Yes. He'd been an enforcer for Rossi but he wasn't just muscle; he was smart. We faked a good CV and he got the job."

"Are you telling me the Professor never realized he wasn't properly qualified?"

"Apparently not. The coaching we'd given him got him through the interview. When it came to the work itself there were lots of new techniques to learn, ones not even a graduate would have come across. Torretta picked things up quickly. The one remaining problem was the Professore."

"He was incorruptible?"

"Absolutely. But it was worse than that. You see, Montalcini preferred not to take part in the actual digging; he would stand there, thinking and taking it all in. He kept a close eye on everything, though, and he was the one who labelled all the finds. Torretta couldn't do a thing. They asked me if I had any ideas. I thought up the special software. I couldn't write it, of course – I've never been much good with that sort of thing – but the Institute commissioned a small software company to write the program. Then our people had it doctored ever so slightly."

"How did you get Montalcini to use it?"

"Easy enough. First we added it to the regulations to make it a mandatory condition of holding one of our grants. Then we held a charity function and invited Montalcini. During the course of the evening, we made sure he was aware of the Pliny Institute as a potential source of funding. Soon after that he applied for his first grant from the Institute. And he got it."

"Complete with laptop computer?"

"Complete with laptop computer. Montalcini is computer-literate but only just; it took him a while to master the software. It must have been a relief when he saw how easily his assistant could handle it. After that it wasn't a problem. Torretta routinely recorded the finds. He just made sure the numbers were duplicated whenever they turned up something interesting."

"And in the meantime the Pliny Institute was awarding other grants...?"

"Yes, for a variety of digs. And now each one came with a laptop – and an operative who knew when and how to use it. Objects started to arrive here. The channels were open again."

"What did Julian think of all this? He must have known where these things were coming from."

"He had his suspicions, yes. You can imagine how much he hated the idea of valuable archaeological material going into private hands. If he was around when I put a new item out, he'd start to ask questions. I would say I'd bought it and then he'd demand to see the receipt. We had blazing rows about it. It was beginning to jeopardize our marriage and that was the last thing I wanted. There was no need for me to be doing this any more. My own career was flourishing – I was in constant demand as a critic and a consultant and it made no sense. I wanted out. So I flew to the U.S.A. Ostensibly I was there to attend a big art exhibition in Chicago. It was a cover. Actually, I went so that I could talk it over with my father. He told me what I already knew."

"Which was...?"

She closed her eyes.

"You have no idea, Nick, you just have no idea. We're talking here about an age-old code of conduct. These agreements between families – nothing is written down, but they're binding. It's a question of 'honour'. The worst thing you can do is to go back on your word – that's considered an act of betrayal. And there's only one penalty."

"They would have killed you."

"Not me – my father. The arrangement was with him, you see. He was expected to deliver his part of the deal and that included me. Do you know what they'd have done to him?"

He held up a hand. "I can imagine."

"I love my father, Nick. I couldn't bear the idea of that happening to him, and all because of me."

"So you carried on."

She sighed and nodded slowly.

"Yes, I carried on. I no longer displayed the artifacts in this room – I was desperate to hide all traces of the business from Julian. He was still suspicious though. At one point he actually threatened to expose me."

"But he never did."

"What could he do? He loved me, and he was devoted to the girls. He'd have lost me and deprived them of a mother. He didn't want that."

"And you, did you love him?"

She fixed him with her eyes, a hint of a smile playing on her lips. "At the very beginning, no – I admit it. Of course, he was physically attractive to me – that was strong with us right from the start. But I was in love with the possibilities – that was really why I married him. As time went on, something changed inside me and we grew closer. You mustn't think we had nothing but rows. We'd go for walks and have wonderful conversations about his work, and art, and history in general. We had the girls and he was so good with them. And we'd entertain visitors and sit around having fantastic discussions deep into the night. In the end I didn't just love him; I adored him." She sighed. "I was in the world of my dreams, and it was Julian who took me there."

Nick sipped his tea. "And then things backfired."

"You know, it had never entered my mind that Julian would have any first-hand involvement with the Pliny Institute. He'd worked in Italy before, of course, but you can only apply to the Institute for funding if you're an Italian citizen. What I hadn't anticipated was someone like Montalcini bringing Julian in as a co-investigator."

"Why did he do that, do you think?"

"Julian was an expert in Roman artifacts, so it was logical in a way. But it wasn't just his expertise they wanted. He could lend real stature to the expedition. Afterwards, when they'd be trying to publish the findings in reputable journals, having an English-speaking collaborator with an international reputation would be a real advantage. Of course, Julian was delighted to accept. The prospects were terrifically exciting and the funding had just dropped in his lap. Normally he had to work so hard to get a grant." She sighed again. "More tea?"

"Thanks." He placed his cup on the tray. She added a little hot water to the teapot, then poured tea for both of them.

"I knew there'd be trouble," she said, as she handed the cup back to him, "especially if there were a lot of valuable finds. Julian isn't an onlooker; he gets in there digging and he remembers what comes out as well. But what could I say?"

She bit her lip.

"When Julian told me a gold ring had gone missing, an important ring with an intaglio, I knew he'd never leave the matter there, not Julian. I think he found out how Torretta was using the computer."

"Yes, I believe he did."

"Poor Julian, he didn't know what he was walking into. I wish he'd never seen the damned ring. Maybe none of this would have happened."

"Just a minute. I saw that ring on Rossi's finger. It was part of your operation. Why didn't it come to you?"

"It should have, I was waiting for it. I had the vague idea I could go out to visit Julian on site, leave the ring where it could be discovered – anything to keep him away from what was going on. But very little of interest came here from that dig – certainly not the ring. At the time I couldn't understand it. It's clear to me now. Rossi had helped to set up the Institute but obviously he was doing a lot more than protecting his investment. He must have kept Torretta on his payroll. The better finds were going directly to him and he was keeping them for himself or using his own contacts to move them. When Julian started to figure out what was happening it wasn't the police Rossi was worried about: he didn't want the other *cosci* to find out he was cheating them. Julian had become a problem... he had to be stopped..."

Something about her manner made him sit up. Normally low and melodious, her voice was becoming thinner, tighter. She looked at him with a kind of desperate intensity, her mouth trembled, and tears flooded into her eyes.

"They killed him, Nick! They took my lovely man away from me!"

She buried her face in her hands.

Chapter 44

Muffled sobs shuddered through her body. He crossed to the other sofa and put his arm around her shoulders. He didn't know what to say, other than, "Dawn, Dawn..."

It took a long time for her to recover. She found a small lacy handkerchief in her handbag, blew her nose, and wiped angrily at her eyes with the back of her hand. Then, with an edge in her voice that sent a chill down his spine, she hissed:

"I wanted revenge!"

She blew her nose again and straightened up, in control of herself once more. He stayed on the sofa with her but withdrew to a proper distance.

"You told me you didn't want justice," he said gently.

"Justice? No, not justice. Blood! Their blood for his blood! I was prepared to blow the whistle on the whole organization. I knew they'd kill me but I didn't care. Then I thought about Kendra and Sophie, left alone, unsupported – I couldn't do that to them. And what would happen to my own poor father? I decided it was better to let the police do the job. I knew the Italians wouldn't act, especially if they got a whiff that the 'men of honour' were behind it. So I used my influence to get the English police onto it."

"You could have warned me what I was up against."

"No, I couldn't."

He got up slowly. "Of course." He resumed his seat on the sofa opposite her. "You were hoping we could solve the case without uncovering your involvement."

"That's right. It was a gamble. I lost. You and Lucia are good, even better than I thought."

He reached to the tray for his abandoned cup of tea and settled back with it.

"So now you're being open with me. Why?"

She shrugged.

"You had most of the pieces; I wanted you to have the whole picture. The way it escalated, how in the end it trapped me. The Pliny Institute seemed like a wonderful idea at the time but it became a living torment. For years I was torn between my duty to my father and my love for my husband. I stood it until Julian disappeared, and then something snapped. I knew the risk I was taking when I brought you into this. I set all that aside because more than anything else I wanted the *bastardi* who killed my Julian. Well you did it, Nick. You took them out. I'll always be grateful to you for that."

"I didn't mean to – I'd sooner have had all of them in handcuffs. Torretta's death was a miscalculation. Vesuvius took his own revenge on Rossi. I was pretty lucky to come through it myself."

"I'm very sorry it put your life in danger, I really am. But as for the others, they got what was coming to them. Rossi was way out of line; they're not supposed to act outside the island, let alone order a hit in someone else's territory. In one way, the volcano did us all a big favour; if the eruption hadn't killed Rossi, then the Sicilian *cosci* or the *Camorristi* would have done it. Either way it would have sparked a whole round of bloodshed."

Nick pondered what she'd said. The final death toll from the eruption hadn't yet emerged but it would run to many thousands; it was odd to think that Vesuvius may have saved lives too. His thoughts turned to Maurizio, the helicopter pilot, who'd died with Rossi and his family. He was an innocent victim. So, too, was the farmer whose discovery of the footprints had led to the dig and who – despite his scepticism – had helped them. Nick fervently wished they'd been able to persuade him to come with them. Now he'd never have a chance to plant his vineyards. Maybe Montalcini would get a second shot at the site, after all.

A heavy silence settled between them. Dawn blew her nose again.

Suddenly she said: "How's your friend, the Capitano?"

"Umberto? He's back at work – with his arm in a sling. You

know the Commissario's been suspended? The magistrates were hopping mad. Even if they can't prove the mafia connection they'll get him on dereliction of duty, misappropriation of police property, and maybe manslaughter too. Umberto's been appointed acting Commissario. It's temporary but we're hoping they'll make it permanent. We got the CC to send a special commendation."

"I spoke to the Chief Constable at the funeral. He told me they're putting you in for a promotion too, Nick. Detective Chief Inspector Roberts. I hope you get it. You deserve it."

Nick smiled. "Thanks. Lucia's been put forward, too – for Inspector. That would be good – we could do with the money. You know we're getting married?"

"Really?"

"'Fraid so. We'd have been just as happy to move in together, but her family's very traditional that way. They want the whole deal. Lovely people."

"Well, congratulations! You'll make a great team. Just don't plan on a honeymoon in Sicily."

"It wasn't top of my list."

"So what now, Nick? Are you going to hand over a large dossier on me?"

It was the question he'd been turning over in his mind ever since he'd discovered her true identity.

From a purely practical point of view the case was thin. Being born into a mafia family didn't automatically make her a criminal. The evidence she'd given him was off-the-record and unwitnessed – she could deny she'd ever had this conversation. Doubtless there were stolen items in this room but she could simply say they were part of her late husband's collection; Julian wasn't around to deny it, and without any record of them at source no one could prove they were removed illegally. The organization would have made very sure the money trail was well covered. One way and another, it would be a very tough job to make a prosecution stick.

If he did pursue it, the machinery of the judicial system would shred her reputation, whatever the outcome. As an arts critic and consultant, she'd be finished. Was that what he wanted?

From a nearby room came the sound of a door slamming, followed by the rapid thudding of someone running upstairs. Kendra? Sophie? His mouth tightened. The girls had lost their father. Dawn had lost her husband. If he turned her in, he'd make their grief and distress ten times worse. A voice inside him was saying: *You've solved the major crime, the perpetrators are dead; it's time to move on.* On the other hand, she was the expert coordinator of a trade in stolen antiquities. He couldn't simply look the other way.

"You're very quiet, Nick."

"I'm sorry. You're still waiting for an answer."

He put the cup and saucer back on the tray and pointed to the display shelves and their precious burden of artifacts.

"Look, it depends what you intend to do with this little lot. Are you going to carry on shifting it?"

"No. The National Museum in Naples is going to receive a large anonymous gift of valuable articles. It'll be up to the Soprintendenza to decide what to do with them."

"And the Pliny Institute?"

"I suggest you reveal your findings to the Illicit Trade Advisory Panel. Get them to take it up with the J. Paul Getty Museum. The Museum will withdraw funding at the first hint there was something illegal going on. They'll probably do it very quietly but I'm sure you could leak the information to a newspaper. As soon as it makes the headlines in Italy the Grants Committee will resign. The Antimafia Commission may start an investigation but they won't get far. By that time the damage will be done. The Pliny Institute will fold and with it all the trade in cultural property that it funded."

"What about the *cosci*?"

"By now they'll realize what Rossi and Torretta were up to. Those two were foolish enough to murder a British citizen and that's what led to the police investigation that uncovered the trade. There's no reason why the *cosci* should blame Daddy or me for that."

"And the racket stops?"

"Yes, thank God. The racket stops."

"All right, then. That's how we'll play it."

Her voice was almost inaudible.

"Thank you."

He got to his feet. He wasn't looking for gratitude. He knew he'd gone further than he should, but so what? He was damn near killed solving this case; he was entitled to a say in the way things came out.

She walked with him to the front door.

Outside it was like twilight, the air like jelly. He looked up at the darkened sky.

"Looks like we're in for the mother and father of a..."

The clouds were suddenly illuminated by lightning and almost simultaneously there was an enormous crack of thunder. Rain started to fall in big, fat drops.

"I'd better run for it. Goodbye, Dawn."

"Goodbye, Nick."

When he reached the gate he turned and looked back at the figure still standing in the doorway. She gave him a little wave and he lifted a hand in acknowledgement. Then he ran for the shelter of the car.

Safely in the driver's seat he turned back his soaking collar and brushed the surface water off his jacket.

Then he sat motionless, watching the rain battering and coursing down the windscreen in cascades silvered by more flashes of lightning. The car shuddered with the sound of thunder. Once again he relived the tremors, the darkened skies, the falling ash and red-hot lava as he and the others escaped across the mountains. And, in a moment of startling clarity, Nick Roberts projected himself back in time nearly two thousand years, and experienced the uncomprehending panic of the fleeing Pompeiians as the ground shook beneath their feet, their day turned into night, their heavens crackled with lightning, and their quiet, vine-clad mountain brought them death.

APPENDIX 1

SEQUENCE OF EVENTS DURING THE
ERUPTION OF VESUVIUS, A.D. 79

It has been estimated that the eruption of Vesuvius in A.D. 79 unleashed energy equivalent to 100,000 Hiroshima atomic bombs and ejected 2.6 cubic km of rock into the sky. This settled a blanket of pyroclastic material many metres thick over much of Campania, burying in the process Pompeii, Herculaneum and other cities and outlying villas. Unlike the Hiroshima bomb, however, this was not a single explosive event: it occurred in phases, mainly over the initial two days.

Modern geological analysis of the layers of material, together with data from well-documented eruptions such as that of Mount St Helens, enables a timeline to be constructed for the sequence of eruptive events. This correlates to a remarkable degree with the eye-witness accounts that Pliny the Younger sent to the historian, Cornelius Tacitus, twenty-seven years after the eruption.

The following summary is drawn from several sources, but I am particularly indebted to de Carolis and Patricelli for their scholarly account (see Bibliography).

9.00 – 10.00 a.m. August 24: Initial explosions, as the rising magma contacts water bearing layers of rock. Deposition of thin layer of grey ash and rocks east of Vesuvius in area of Terzigno.

1.00 p.m. August 24: Paroxysmal eruption of Vesuvius. Large projectiles follow ballistic trajectories. Some residents of Terzigno flee towards Pompeii and Oplontis.

1.30 p.m. August 24: Formation of cloud 15 km high, dispersing to the south-east and releasing a heavy rain of pumice, stones, and ash on Pompeii and the rest of the region to the south-east. The pumice, in pieces 40–50 cm across, begins to accumulate. Only minimal airfall in Herculaneum, to the west.

3 p.m. August 24: Some residents of Herculaneum flee to the north or to the beach, where they take refuge in barrel vaults. In Pompeii others flee towards Nuceria (east), Moregine (south). Yet others reach the port, only to find there is no escape by sea.

5.00 p.m. August 24: In Pompeii roofs begin to collapse under the weight of accumulated pumice. The eruptive cloud rises to 26 km. Heavy falls of pumice on Stabiae.

7.30 p.m. August 24: Pyroclastic material has deposited to a thickness of 1.4 m in Pompeii. Houses collapse in Terzigno and Oplontis.

8.00 p.m. August 24: Sudden transition from white to larger, denser grey pumice. Partial collapse of eruptive column generates the first pyroclastic flows (Sa, Sb) to the east of Vesuvius, in area of Terzigno.

8.00 p.m. August 24: Further fall of grey pumice. Roofs and colonnades collapse in Oplontis.

1.00 a.m. August 25: Surge S1, a turbulent cloud of gas and particles, closely followed by a denser pyroclastic flow, rolls to south and west, killing inhabitants of Boscoreale and Oplontis. It moves through Herculaneum, destroying all life and leaving 40-50 cm of ash, more at the shore.

2.00 a.m. August 25: Surge S2 travels more quickly. It causes deaths in Terzigno and on the northern flank. In Herculaneum it damages buildings and carries along masonry. The associated pyroclastic flow deposits 5 m at beach.

2.00-5.00 a.m. August 25: Further falls of pumice, but lessening. Strong earthquakes. The sea recedes.

5.17 a.m. August 25: Sunrise, but landscape remains in total darkness. Eruptive cloud is 32 km high. Pumice in Pompeii is now about 2.7 m thick. In Stabiae the depth is 2–2.5 m. Pumice enters upper windows and blocks doors.

6.30 a.m. August 25: Surge S3 reaches Pompeii, extinguishing life in Villas outside Herculaneum Gate, but stops along north side of city wall. Sweeps over Herculaneum, leaving it under 10 m of deposit.

7.30 – 8.00 a.m. August 25: Surges S4 and S5, minutes apart, bury Pompeii and areas south, including the river and sea ports, under 15-20 cm of ash; there are many deaths. S5 leaves Oplontis under more than a metre of ash (later flows will increase this to 5 m). Further deposits on Herculaneum.

8.00 a.m. August 25: Surge S6, the largest, most destructive, and most lethal surge of all. A tide of scorching ash and gas and rock, it sweeps without pause over the countryside, extinguishing in its path any life that remains, and hurls through Pompeii with explosive force; columns collapse, bodies and materials are carried along. It leaves behind it 1.2 m of ash. Surge continues out over entire region, to Misenum in north and Stabiae in south. Herculaneum now under 23 m.

Activity continues for days, at a reduced level.

APPENDIX 2

Readers may be puzzled by references, in the Pompeii story, to the port, and the possibility of escape by sea. It needs to be recognized that the coastline was different at that time. The Sarno was a substantial, navigable river, and represented an important waterway for imports and exports. It appears to have ended in a bay or lagoon, which is mentioned by Seneca. Ash and rocks from the eruption, together with the pyroclastic surges that went out to sea, raised the seabed, while water drained into the emptying magma chambers 5 km below the surface, lowering the sea level dramatically. These events occurred at the time of the eruption and have been extended by more gradual geological changes over the last two millennia. The original coastline is now further inland by, on average, about 1 km.

Bibliography

Philemon Holland, translator: C. Plinius Secundus *The Historie of the World. Book I* (1601)

John Bodstock and H.T. Riley, (translators): *The Natural History of Pliny, Vol. 1* (Henry G. Bohn: London, 1855)

Betty Radice, translator: *"The Letters of the Younger Pliny"* (Penguin Books: Harmondsworth, England, reprinted 1981)

Edward G. Bulwer-Lytton: *The Last Days of Pompeii* (Dent: London, edn of 1906, reprinted 1973).

Ernesto De Carolis and Giovanni Patricelli: *Vesuvius, A.D. 79: The Destruction of Pompeii and Herculaneum* (Getty Publications: Los Angeles, California, 2003)

Colin Amery and Brian Curran, Jr: *The Lost World of Pompeii* (Frances Lincoln: London, 2002)

Tom Holland: *Rubicon: The Triumph and Tragedy of the Roman Republic* (Abacus, Time Warner Book Group UK: London, 2004).

John Dickie: *Cosa Nostra: A History of the Sicilian Mafia* (Hodder & Stoughton: London, 2004)

Salvatore Nappo: *Pompeii: Guide to the Lost City* (Weidenfeld & Nicolson: London, 1998)

I have also found the following web sites helpful:

Vesuvius: the eruption, the towns

http://www2.pompeiisites.org/
http://www.archaeology.co.uk/cwa/issues/cwa4/pompeii/index.htm
http://www.fieldmuseum.org/pompeii/
http://www.vroma.org/~bmcmanus/baths.html
http://www.mnsu.edu/emuseum/archaeology/sites/europe/pompeii
.html

http://www.fieldmuseum.org/pompeii/
http://vulcan.fis.uniroma3.it/vesuvio/79_eruption.htm
http://en.chinabroadcast.cn/1641/2006/03/07/65@58902.htm

Roman clothes, language, weapons, roads, transport, food, history

http://www.crystalinks.com/romeclothing.html
http://www.24carat.co.uk/nervaframe.html
http://archives.nd.edu/latgramm.htm
http://www.romancoins.info/
http://www.vroma.org/~araia/litter.html
http://www.crystalinks.com/romeroads.html
http://www.cwu.edu/~robinsos/ppages/resources/Costume_History/roman.htm
http://www.vroma.org/~bmcmanus/clothing.html
http://www.vroma.org/~bmcmanus/clothing2.html
http://www.web40571.clarahost.co.uk/roman/calhis.htm
http://www.guernsey.net/~sgibbs/roman.html
http://www.roman-empire.net/society/soc-dress.html
http://www.class.uidaho.edu/luschnig/owl's/Recipes/8.htm
http://www.vroma.org/~plautus/foodweise.html
http://www.lowchensaustralia.com/names/romannames.htm
http://www.everything2.com/index.pl?node=Imperial%20Roman%20Legion
http://www.ancientedge.com/subcategory_40.html
http://www.romancoins.info/MilitaryEquipment-Attack.html
http://www.romancoins.info/MilitaryEquipment-Remake.html

Lightning Source UK Ltd.
Milton Keynes UK
28 March 2011

170013UK00001B/140/P